DORIS

A GAME OF SNAKES AND LADDERS

Doris Elizabeth Langley Moore (*née* Levy) was born on 23 July 1902 in Liverpool. She moved with her family to South Africa when she was eight. She received no formal education, but read widely, under the influence of her father.

Moore moved to London in the early 1920s, and wrote prolifically and diversely, including Greek translation, and an etiquette manual. In 1926 she married Robert Moore, and they had one daughter, Pandora, before divorcing in 1942.

She published six romantic novels between 1932 and 1959, in addition to several books on household management and an influential biography of E. Nesbit.

Moore was passionately interested in clothes, and her own clothes formed the basis of a collection of costumes, to which she added important historical pieces. Her fashion museum was opened in 1955, eventually finding a permanent home in Bath in 1963.

In addition to books, she also wrote a ballet, *The Quest*, first performed at Sadler's Wells in 1943. Moore also worked as a costume designer for the theatre and films, and designed Katharine Hepburn's dresses for *The African Queen* (1951).

Doris Langley Moore continued to write books, with a particular emphasis on Lord Byron. Her last novel, *My Caravaggio Style* (1959), about the forgery of the lost Byron memoirs, was followed by three scholarly works on the poet.

Doris Langley Moore was appointed OBE in 1971. She died in London in 1989.

TITLES BY DORIS LANGLEY MOORE

Fiction

A Winter's Passion (1932)

The Unknown Eros (1935)

A Game of Snakes and Ladders (1938, 1955)* **

Not at Home (1948)*

All Done by Kindness (1951)*

My Caravaggio Style (1959)*

* available from Dean Street Press and Furrowed Middlebrow

Selected Non-fiction

The Technique of the Love Affair (1928, reprinted 1999)

E. Nesbit: A Biography (1933, expanded edition 1966)

The Vulgar Heart: An Enquiry into the Sentimental Tendencies of Public Opinion (1945)

The Woman in Fashion (1949)

The Child in Fashion (1953)

Pleasure: A Discursive Guide Book (1953)

The Late Lord Byron: Posthumous Dramas (1961)

Marie & the Duke of H: The Daydream Love Affair of Marie Bashkirtseff (1966)

Fashion Through Fashion Plates, 1771-1970 (1971)

Lord Byron: Accounts Rendered (1974)

Ada, Countess of Lovelace: Byron's Legitimate Daughter (1977)

** Published in 1938 under the title *They Knew Her When: A Game of Snakes and Ladders*. Revised and reprinted in 1955 as *A Game of Snakes and Ladders*. Dean Street Press has used the text of the 1955 edition for its new edition.

DORIS LANGLEY MOORE

A GAME OF SNAKES AND LADDERS

With an introduction by

Sir Roy Strong

DEAN STREET PRESS

A Furrowed Middlebrow Book
FM39

Published by Dean Street Press 2020

First published in 1938 by Rich & Cowan, and (revised) in 1955 by Cassell & Co.

Cover by DSP

ISBN 978 1 913054 55 7

www.deanstreetpress.co.uk

To my Niece and Friend

CAMILLA HASSE

INTRODUCTION
By Sir Roy Strong

"I WAS the first writer to take the reader through the bedroom door". That announcement to me by Doris Langley Moore (1902-1989) has always stuck in my mind. I only came to know her late in her life, in the mid 1960s when I was involved in establishing The Costume Society. I already knew her work for I was early on fascinated by the history of dress and consumed her pioneer volumes *The Woman in Fashion* (1949) and *The Child in Fashion* (1953) while I was still at school. I had also travelled down to Eridge Castle in 1953 where Doris opened the first version of her Museum of Costume which was to find its resting place in Bath some ten years later in what is now called The Fashion Museum.

She later became a friend, a formidable one making me quickly grasp why she had gained a reputation for being difficult. She was. But any encounter with her tended to be memorable providing fragments of a larger mosaic of a life which had been for a period at the creative centre of things. Later encounters were remarkable like the one when she took me out to lunch at The Ivy so that I could sign her passport photograph as a true likeness when transparently it had been taken through a gauze! This was the occasion when she suddenly volunteered that she had been the handsome Director of the National Gallery Sir Philip Hendy's (1900-1980) mistress.

If the material existed Doris would be a good example of the new emancipated woman who burst on the scene in the 1920s flaunting convention. She, of course, rightly takes her place in the *New Oxford Dictionary of National Biography* but what we read there raises more questions than it answers. Here was the Liverpool born daughter of a newspaper editor who, having passed most of her childhood in South Africa, suddenly arrives on the scene with a translation from the Greek of *Anacreon: 29 Odes* (1926). Two years later came the even more startling *The Technique of the Love Affair* (1928) under a pseudonym 'a gentlewoman' of which Dorothy Parker wrote that her whole love life would have been different if she had had the good fortune to have read this first. It has apparently stood the test of time and was reprinted in 1999. Two years before

Doris had married and, although she did not divorce her husband until 1942, one would conclude that that marriage rapidly went on the rocks. Indeed I recall being told that her husband had gone off with the nanny of her only child, a daughter called Pandora. She never married again.

Doris was an extraordinarily multi-talented woman who moved with ease within the creative art set of the era. She was closely involved in those who were to become the Royal Ballet and, in 1943, wrote the scenario for a patriotic ballet *The Quest* to get the future Sir Frederick Ashton out of army. The music was by William Walton and the designs by John Piper, and Margot Fonteyn and Robert Helpmann dance in it. Again I recall her telling me that the members of what were to become our Royal Ballet at the opening of the war were all up in her house in Harrogate. And, after I married the designer Julia Trevelyan Oman, she took us out to dinner with William Chappell, the designer of Ashton's *Les Patineurs*. Then there were connexions with the Redgrave family who appear dressed in Regency and Victorian costume in her books. Vivien Leigh also figures in these books, again Doris remarking disparagingly of Olivier's part in the famous break up.

Between 1932 and 1959 she wrote six romantic novels, appreciated today by a readership which scours the Net for copies. All of this sat alongside a sharp academic mind which she applied in particular to a life long obsession with Lord Byron. Again I recall her opening a lecture on him describing how she had fended off a young man trying to kiss her at her first ball by drawing back and saying "Have you read *Childe Harold*?" Her first book *The Late Lord Byron* (1961) revolutionised Byron studies and two more of equal importance followed, *Lord Byron, Accounts Rendered* (1974) and *Ada, Countess of Lovelace* (1977).

But her greatest legacy must be The Museum of Fashion in Bath. Doris was obsessed by fashion and details of dress. I remember her noticing the way that I followed in town the correct gentleman's etiquette of wearing one glove on the hand which held the other. She herself followed fashion and indeed her hats were the subject of a Sotheby's sale. Why was her contribution in this area so important? Doris was the first person who moved the study of dress out of the antiquary's study into the land of the living. When it came to wheeler dealing with historic dress she had no equal. To her dress was vivid visual evidence of the attitudes and aspirations of a whole society. In that she ranks as an original enabling others to follow in the path that she blazed. She began collecting in 1928 and was to campaign for a museum for some twenty five years until at last it came to rest in the Assembly Rooms in Bath. And, typical of Doris, it embraced the new from the outset inaugurating the annual Dress of the Year Event which took off with a Mary Quant mini-dress. But then we can still see her in action for we can go on line and watch her in the first ever BBC colour television programmes from 1957 on the madness and marvel of clothes.

Roy Strong

From the Author to her Publisher:

Dear Sirs,

In answer to your enquiry, my book is about two girls who arrive in Egypt with a theatrical company at the end of the First World War—that period, just before the well-explored mid-Twenties, which seems to me a sort of Forgotten Epoch. Lucy is stranded, Daisy stays behind from choice, and against an exotic but by no means romantic background, they make the curious moves allotted to them by character or luck. If Lucy's is not quite a "sob story", Daisy's is certainly a "snob story". (There were snob stories in real life then; we pretend there are none now.) Daisy mounts several Ladders through her attractions for a rising financier; Lucy's course, on the other hand, is beset with Snakes.

Fanny Burney would not approve of some of my chapters, but it was my affection for the novels of her school, in which the heroine goes through all kinds of distresses but emerges in a sweeping triumph at the end, that made me long to try my hand at the same theme—treating it, however, in our down-to-earth twentieth-century way.

There is a much more varied assortment of characters than I usually attempt; and the scene which begins in Alexandria in 1919, ends in London in 1937, with a ball for the Coronation of George VI.

Yours faithfully,

Doris Langley Moore

The author wishes to make it clear that, in depicting characters not altogether pleasant belonging to the cosmopolitan community of Egypt after the First World War, she had not the smallest intention of casting any slur on race or creed.

All the dramatis personae *are meant to be individuals, and are certainly fictitious ones.*

CHAPTER 1

DURING the First World War, as during the Second, all the lighter kinds of theatrical business flourished. Great multitudes of people wanted distraction at almost any price, and money was circulating freely. Actors who had the good luck to be judged unfit for military service could afford to pick and choose the roles in which they would keep the home fires burning. Some very naturally preferred to 'carry on' in distant lands. They braved the dangers of mines and submarines to escape from food shortage and the nagging menace of air-raids small in scale but quite adequate to disturb the sleep of Londoners: or, to give it fairer terms, they took immense risks in order to convey the latest entertainments to Britons overseas.

In December of 1917—English midwinter, Australian summer—the S.S. *Lodore*, zig-zagging a good deal out of its pre-war route from London to Melbourne, carried among its passengers a group of players so numerous that the ship's concerts had quite a professional air and the whole voyage was considerably enlivened. This was the 'Prince of Palermo Company', taking its title from the chief item in its repertoire.

A musical comedy of the more ambitious sort—almost, in its grander moments, a comic opera—*The Prince of Palermo* contained all the ingredients which, in those days, could be relied upon to ensure a fine run. Its background was exotic, its songs were at once pretentious and easy to follow, and there was a chorus of picturesque brigands, male and female, who sang about the Sicilian view of drinking, freedom, and life in general. A double instance of mistaken identity at the end of the first act caused the heroine to disavow the hero in melodious grief and gave rise to humorous interchanges between a comical tourist and his newly married wife. To make the lovers' situation more and more difficult and the farcical elements more and more hilarious, so much counterplot was introduced that no one ever quite knew how it was all unravelled. It was enough that before the curtain came down, the persons of the drama were unanimous in seizing upon any pretext they could find for considering their troubles at an end.

Australia, like England, was delighted with it, and so, in due course, were various large cities in the Indian Empire and one or two in China. It ran so well that only one other piece in the repertoire was called into service, an economy by which the backers gained money and the company leisure. Cables sped between the advance manager and the London promoters, who agreed without hesitation to extend the tour. Their first endeavour was to come to terms with South Africa, but there were no theatres to be got, and they were obliged to fix their attention on a less coveted territory.

In Egypt the only cities of theatrical importance were Cairo and Alexandria, and even there the population was composed so largely of Italians, Greeks, Frenchmen, and natives, that it was doubtful whether a costly English production could draw houses worth playing to. On the other hand, some support might be expected from the British troops who were being detained there in large numbers to quell a serious political uprising; and travelling expenses would not be heavy since Port Said lay directly on the route home.

The Adelphi in Cairo had recently been taken over by an even more than usually enterprising Jew, who was also responsible for the building of the Lyrico, a new theatre in Alexandria. These and several much smaller houses scattered over Egypt he had placed under the control of one management, the Polyglot Amusement Co. Ltd. It was by this firm that *The Prince of Palermo* was eventually booked.

Twelve months were now gone by since the troupe had sailed from England, and there had been a few changes in the personnel. A soubrette had got married in Adelaide, and her place had been filled locally. The musical director had changed from a convivial drinker into a drunkard, and they had been compelled to leave him at Singapore. The understudy who led the chorus was homesick for England, and even the necessity of travelling in an overcrowded boat under conditions of the utmost discomfort could not prevent her immediate return from Hong Kong.

There was one more prominent member of the company who longed in vain to follow her example. Lucy Kendon, the second lead, would gladly have given all the fabled splendours of the Orient for the shabbiest square mile of London, but pride forbade her to make the exchange. She had come abroad partly because she wanted to see the world, partly because she could not get such good work in London, and chiefly as the consequence of a sharp and wilful quarrel with her lover which, somehow, had never been put right. And now, little more than a year after their parting, and just when she had become finally convinced by the process of trial-and-error that no substitute could possibly be found for him—just when she had begun to work out ways and means by which they might achieve reunion—she had seen, glancing through a copy of the *Illustrated London News*, the photograph of a wedding party, and in the midst of it was Lord Henry Felix with his bride leaning on his arm.

So there seemed nothing to do but stay with the company until it was at last disbanded, and perhaps by that time she would have reconciled herself to the idea of losing Henry definitely and for ever; would be placed beyond the temptation to ring him up, or even—worst of all!—to frequent the restaurants and places of amusement he patronized in the hope of a meeting that would seem accidental. It was the more necessary to remain absent from England until her pride had learned how to keep out of harm's way, because Henry was the second son of the Marquess of Redfarrow and a grandson of the Duke of Surrey, and the whole family received so much attention from the Press that one would never be left long without some reminder of one's disappointment.

Lucy realized now that she had been treasuring in her heart a quite irrational belief that he would want her back and grow willing to admit it. This increasing conviction, stored safely and quietly away from analysis, had given her patience, gaiety, and a sense of security. If she had been of that ruthless stuff of which sirens are made, she might have sought him out, marriage or no marriage, to win him again or confirm her loss; but she had been brought up, like so many actresses of her day, in a country parsonage, and was still under its influence in more ways than she suspected. Henry married became a remote and unfamiliar figure, another woman's belonging. His wife would have nothing to fear from his earlier attachment.

Therefore when *The Prince of Palermo* opened in Cairo towards the end of February 1919, Lucy's name was still in its accustomed place on the programme, and it was her voice, a strong and versatile mezzo-soprano, which rang out loudest and clearest in the famous sextet called 'Try a Little Dose of Love'. At that time she had just completed her twenty-seventh year. Her hair was a splendid ruddy gold and her complexion was of great natural beauty. Hair-dye and make-up were not then so widely and freely used as now, and consequently fine colouring was of more value to the possessor. Lucy was generally reckoned very handsome—she had begun her theatrical career in the chorus at Daly's—but her features would not have come out well from critical examination. She had a tall and statuesque figure, and that too was an asset worth more in 1919 than a few years later.

In disposition she was cheerful and tolerant, and she would have called herself a Bohemian—the word having not yet gone out of fashion. But though she had violently reacted against life at Market Rookestone, her late father's parish, its principles were nevertheless a solid framework to her present mode of existence. The careful housekeeping of the vicarage, the almost tiresomely scrupulous honesty, the high sense of duty, the contempt for those who 'gave way', the reticence in discussing emotional or closely personal matters—all these, whatever revolutionary sentiments she might profess, had left their traces on her character. She had little or nothing of what is known as the artistic temperament.

As for her talents, they were adequate but not outstanding. Reliability and a capacity for hard work, rather than dazzling brilliance, had raised her from the chorus. Her singing was, perhaps, better than the average; her acting carried about as much conviction as musical comedy demands. She had not struggled into the world of the theatre under the impetus of a need to express herself dramatically, but simply because she had her living to get and, since theatrical life stood for everything that excited Market Rookestone's disapproval, she had long been stage-struck.

Such was Lucy Kendon in the year that brought her to Egypt—twenty-seven, good-looking, amiable, more conventional at heart than she was willing to acknowledge, prudent and reserved in spite of herself, hard-working, determined to make the most of her gifts, and disappointed in love.

Chapter 2

'Who would have thought this damn show would have been a frost here too?' Daisy Joy exclaimed when she read on the call-board that they were to begin rehearsing tomorrow for *Oh, Aunty!* 'If *The Prince of Palermo* won't bring them in, what will?'

'Nothing,' said Lucy. 'We might just as well pack up and go home. It was crazy to let us come so soon after that other English company.'

'But they did good business, and it naturally looked as if we'd do even better. After all, they weren't nearly such a well-known company as ours.'

'They got in first, and that's all that mattered. Musical comedy's a dead letter now in Cairo and Alexandria. Even the troops don't want it.'

'The troops don't seem to want theatres at all out here,' Daisy admitted with disgust. 'What with rules and regulations and native rebellions, and moving pictures, not to speak of private entertainments—very private entertainments—a show like ours hardly gets a look-in.'

'Well, thank goodness our big flop comes at the end of the tour and not the beginning,' said Lucy. 'Personally, I don't care one way or the other. Egypt likes me just about as much as I like it.'

'Funny,' rejoined Daisy. 'I can't see why the place gets on your nerves so much. I must say that, outside the theatre, I've loved every moment of it.'

'No wonder, seeing you had the luck to get off with the man who's running the whole show. *You've* got nothing to grumble at.'

It was only Lucy's good nature which made her pretend to envy her friend the conquest of Mr. Siegfried Mosenthal, for the managing director of the Polyglot Amusement Company compared very badly with Lord Henry Felix. Indeed, even without that comparison, it seemed to her amazing that a charming girl like Daisy could be so very ready to place herself at his disposal. Certainly he had power within his little realm and money, and nobody whose life had been as full of struggle as Daisy's could be expected to ignore these assets, but his rude manners and inconsiderate behaviour should have placed a sensitive woman beyond his reach.

Lucy recalled how bad a loser he had proved when the company had failed to pay its way in Cairo, how insulting he had been to the advance manager, how contemptuously he had spoken to the actors, as if they had deliberately chosen to draw poor houses. And his attentions to Daisy were paid in the manner of one bestowing favours. He had made it clear that he thought it rather magnanimous of him to be seen about with anyone less important than a leading lady.

Daisy was the soubrette who had joined the cast at Adelaide on the marriage of her predecessor. Lucy herself had got her into the company, eagerly pleading her merits and her need to a producer who believed that she was too well known locally and would take the gloss off his impressive array of 'London artistes'. He had favoured the idea of giving a chance to someone in the chorus, but he was a kind-hearted man, and Daisy had an almost irresistible hard-luck story. And now she was doing so well and had so completely freed herself from the bondage of unhappy associations that this story had grown quite dim in the memory of everyone who had heard it, and dimmest of all, it sometimes seemed, in her own.

No trace of it hung about her as she passed with a sprightly step from the dust of the theatre into the clammy night air of Alexandria: and this was fortunate, for Mr. Siegfried Mosenthal was a difficult man to please, the most blasé member of a most blasé profession. His views on women might be described as Oriental of the old school. When they were not simply impersonal slaves—employees, one called them—they were either the half-despised playthings of one's leisure or the protected caretakers of one's home. A wife's or a mother's experiences were decently bounded by the family circle; as for women of the other sort, their function of light attractiveness was lost if they made themselves objects of pity by telling hard-luck stories.

Daisy had known Mr. Mosenthal's tastes instinctively from their first meeting, and had set out to gratify them without consciously accounting to herself for anything she did or said, admitted or concealed. Lucy knew them only from distant observation, but her judgment was shrewd, and, while she was surprised and sometimes dismayed at the ease with which Daisy had cut every thread that could jerk her back to a disagreeable memory, she acknowledged freely that this ruthlessness was the foundation of her friend's present success and well-being. She acknowledged it freely but in silence. It was obviously a tactless blunder nowadays to talk to Daisy on any topic that involved a reference to the distresses of the past.

They strolled along the nearly deserted street towards their respective hotels. Until their arrival in Alexandria, Daisy had invariably stayed at the same hotel as Lucy, and frequently they had even economized by sharing a room, but now that she had reached the dignity of being followed from Cairo by Mr. Mosenthal, she lived on a more expensive scale. It was only as a visitor that Lucy crossed the threshold of the luxurious Hôtel de Paris et New-York—a visitor to be hustled away as rapidly as compatible with charm of manner when the great man required to be amused. Today he had gone back to Cairo for a board meeting and, as they went along, Lucy was invited by her companion to take a cool drink on the veranda.

'Just what my soul and body are craving for,' said Lucy, for already, though March had still some days to run, the weather was hotter than English midsummer, and they had done a hard evening's work—all the harder for its having been offered to an unresponsive audience. 'Damn!' she cried a moment later. 'There's that awful man who calls himself Chappie Paulos. Do let's avoid him!'

She indicated a figure gazing into a still-lighted shop-window on the other side of the street.

'Oh, he's not so bad,' said Daisy with an indulgent laugh. 'I wouldn't mind having some of his beautiful silk stockings from Paris. All you've got to do is to rave about his collection of perfumes, and he gives you half a dozen pairs of stockings—haven't you heard?'

'No, that's a leading lady's allowance. It's three pairs for the likes of you and me, and one for the ladies of the chorus.'

'How do you know?'

'My dear, it's written in the annals of Alexandria. Shall we get round the corner before he sees us?'

Daisy laughed so loudly and gaily that one might almost think she wished to be heard. At any rate, the man heard her, for he turned round and began briskly yet with a non-committal air to cross the road. As soon as he was near enough to identify the ladies, his demeanour changed and became as purposeful as before it had been idle. Although there was no longer any chance of their escaping him, he quickened his pace to something absurdly like a run, and, breathless from haste and eagerness, started to address them while he was still several yards away.

'Good evening! Good evening! You girls are going home late from the theatre tonight, aren't you? Isn't no one looking after you?' He spoke English extremely fluently but with a displeasing accent and many lapses of grammar; yet since his speech was full of colloquialisms, he forfeited the indulgence usually accorded to foreigners. He was, in fact, an Alexandrian Greek and he knew three or four other languages, including his own, as well or as badly as he knew English.

'We have to get used to going about alone.' Daisy's smile blended sweetness and condescension in equal proportions. 'It wouldn't do if we all insisted on having a chaperon, would it?'

'It wouldn't do for me,' said Mr. Paulos in the sportive style which he kept ready for actresses not of the first eminence. And pressing on without loss of time towards the accomplishment of his end, he continued, 'Anyhow, you are chaperons to each other tonight, so it can't do no harm if I make you a little invitation, eh?'

'An invitation!' Daisy affected surprise. 'At this time of night?'

'We have a rehearsal quite early in the morning,' said Lucy.

'You'll be in your beds,' Mr. Paulos assured them urgently, 'in one hour from now. If I keep you more than half an hour, you can go all round Alexandria and say, "Chappie's a liar." Now I'll tell you what I want you to do—you've heard about my collection of perfumes?'

'Oh, yes, of course, everybody has,' said Daisy, and, with rather less enthusiasm, Lucy seconded her.

'Well, I got two new ones today and I want you to come and tell me what you think of them—my flat's right here at the corner—and if you're good girls and don't lead me astray, I give you both a little souvenir.'

Daisy needed only enough persuasion to appease gentility, and Lucy's distaste for Mr. Paulos succumbed to curiosity. He was, after all, a sort of absurd civic institution which one might try to regard impersonally. His perfumes, his gifts of silk stockings, and his peculiar snobberies, had become a legend in green-rooms much farther afield than Alexandria, and it would perhaps be regrettable to leave this city without learning at first-hand whether report exaggerated.

For it was said that Mr. Paulos felt such a fanatical respect for celebrities, or near-celebrities, or those who had the remotest chance of ever becoming celebrities, that he would go to the most prodigious expense and trouble to attain their acquaintance: and as theatrical people are on the whole more responsive than those who achieve distinction in other professions, it was towards them that his liveliest efforts were directed. So that now, after many years of assiduously pursuing them, he felt that his credit was in some way impaired if he could not vaunt his intimacy with every actor and actress—but more especially every actress—who came to Egypt.

It was common knowledge, however, that his standards of intimacy were not very exacting. To be called by his chosen nickname, to receive a photograph gaily or gratefully inscribed, to be able to refer to some occasion when the notable person had visited his flat—he took a childlike joy in such privileges as these, and seldom asked for more. His reputation for harmless toadyism was so firmly established that Daisy believed she could accept three, or preferably six, pairs of stockings from him without incurring the censure even of an implacably possessive lover.

An artiste's prestige could be gauged to a nicety from Chappie Paulos's manner towards her. The leading lady of *The Prince of Palermo*, with the leading man and the comedian, had been invited to a carefully prepared luncheon, and flowers had been sent on the opening night—but the bouquet was less costly than it would have been if the company had brought laurels from Cairo. Its failure in Alexandria was signified by this haphazard treatment of the two principals next in importance. They likewise would have had a luncheon, less elaborate but still well worth eating, if only their success had deserved the compliment. As it was, although it was proper that they should be numbered among those who had admired the perfumes and given signed photographs in return for presents, formal overtures could be dispensed with.

The young ladies might have received the impromptu invitation very coldly indeed if they had known that it conveyed a somewhat low opinion of their standing. Fortunately they were only vaguely aware of their host's methods, and so followed him with more amusement than resentment into what he pleasantly called his little grey home in the East.

It was, in fact, an unmistakably Eastern home, for that was one of the latest European fashions and Egypt had to follow it. European ideas about the Orient have always been hazy and romantic, and at that time they took the shape of wide divans, black-and-gold cushions adorned with numerous tassels, and some very striking styles in lampshades. Mr. Paulos's flat had just been decorated by the best French firm in Alexandria, and he displayed it with pride. Still more proudly did he show the numerous photographs of distinguished persons of every nationality adorning his sitting-room walls. (The minor celebrities were in the vestibule.) Most particularly he called attention to inscriptions that were flattering or familiar. His guests were duly enthusiastic, and if from time to time they felt obliged to exchange a glassy-eyed look, he was not allowed to notice it.

'But where are those perfumes we've heard so much about?' asked Lucy. 'I *am* looking forward to the perfumes, aren't you, Daisy?'

'Oh, yes, but I really have enjoyed seeing over this lovely flat,' Daisy replied with her usual charm.

'Well now, here it is, my little collection,' said Mr. Paulos, flinging back a heavy plush curtain. 'Here it is—what I may call my life-work almost.'

He had uncovered a wide recess, lighted by a brilliant lamp and lined with rows of shelves enclosed in glass. Upon them, against a background of blue velvet, were arranged with exceedingly good showmanship hundreds of small flasks and bottles, plain, ornate, business-like, fantastic; and each one bore round its neck a neat ivory label. It was a dazzling sight for feminine eyes. Daisy and Lucy hailed it with cries of unfeigned delight.

'Nice, aren't they?' Mr. Paulos savoured his understatement with relish.

'Oh, but they're marvellous!' Daisy clasped her hands together ecstatically. 'Wherever did they come from?'

'From all over the world they come—anyhow, from all the countries where perfume is made. See here, if you want to look at them, you just push back these glass fronts, so. Return each bottle where you take it from, won't you?'

'Oh, of course!' they agreed, and Lucy began to investigate, but Daisy paused to ask intelligent questions.

'I *would* like to know how you got them? I'm sure you can't buy half these in the shops.'

'Ah! When you've been collecting as long as I have, my dear, then I'll tell you.'

'Is it very difficult?'

He shrugged his shoulders to imply that the difficulties were immense but that he faced them unflinching.

'I suppose you have to know a good deal about scents to go in for them in a big way like this?' she went on with an interest that was almost all genuine. 'How long have you been at it?'

'Twelve or thirteen years maybe. They don't seem so much for all that time, do they?' he added as he saw their eyes measuring the extent of the display. 'But perfume's not like wine, you know. It doesn't get no better with keeping, and when it goes off I have to throw it away.'

'Throw it away!' Lucy's dismay was as vociferous as Daisy's and much more profound; all the thrifty principles of a well-ordered country house were behind it. 'Do you mean to say every bit of this beautiful, expensive perfume is just going to go down the sink?'

'No, my dear, not exactly every bit. Quite a lot is used up on ladies' handkerchiefs and all that while it's still fresh. If I'd known you was coming I would have told you to bring all your handkerchiefs with you so I could put different scents on them.'

The guests murmured appreciation of his generous thought.

'Last month,' he continued, 'we had Michaela here—the famous Spanish dancer who I showed you the photo of. "Now look here, Chappie," she said, "I want everything I have to be scented—dresses, nighties, undies, everything." The Spaniards are a bit like the Moors and the Arabs in that way; they love perfume, strong perfume—not what you English girls would care for at all. "Well," I said, "there's one thing I never do, my dear lady, and that is to give away something off these shelves. If I once begin that, where would be the end of it? In a couple of months I shouldn't have no collection left. But I'll tell you what I'll do," I said. "If you like to send me round some of your clothes, I'll see they smell nice when you get them back." "Very well, Chappie," she says, "it's a bargain. I'll send you everything I got."'

'And did she?' Daisy asked, polite and incredulous.

'I'll say she did,' replied Mr. Paulos, and delighted with the sound of this new and smart Americanism—it happened to be the first time he had used it—he repeated it slowly and with gusto. 'I'll say she did. She sent her dresser round with everything you can think of. I was hours choosing different scents for them. You saw what she wrote on the photo she gave me? *"A Chappie de Michaela avec ses sentiments reconnaissants."*'

'Is Chappie a Greek name?' Daisy inquired hastily, not caring to admit that she did not understand French.

Paulos laughed. 'Greek! Nothing could be less Greek! No, it's just a friendly nickname, my dear. You see, my real name is Jesus, and that seems to make my English pals laugh. One night a few years ago there was a big supper party—it was the opening of *The Merry Widow*—and a young fellow who had come put on some engineering job got so blotto he simply couldn't stand, and he kept saying: "Where's the perfume chappie? Where's the perfume chappie? Tell him to bring me some eau-de-Cologne. That's the way to put me right." So after that, people began to call me the Perfume Chappie, and soon it became plain Chappie.'

While Daisy stayed her hand to listen with sympathetic attention, Lucy was busy among the scent-bottles, and it surprised her slightly to see how many of them had never been opened, but still wore over their stoppers immaculate little hoods of white kid. Their virgin condition was a reminder.

'What about those two new ones you wanted our opinion of?' she demanded.

Paulos looked bewildered, but managing after a brief pause to recollect the reason he had given—the first that had come into his head—for pressing them at a late hour to visit him, he produced two splendid bottles, both from Italy, and began reluctantly to open one of them. The young ladies' opinion was actually a matter of very small concern to him, and it exasperated him to find his pretext taken seriously.

'It's been difficult to get stuff like this lately,' he said, trying to suppress his annoyance, 'and if that war had gone on much longer, we shouldn't have had no more of it at all. This is an essence of the most beautiful Florentine violets. How do you like it?'

Daisy smelt it first and pronounced it to be exquisite. Lucy was more critical.

'It's very nice,' she said, 'but is it supposed to be the real thing?'

'The real thing? What do you mean—the real thing?' he asked in astonishment.

'I mean is it genuine violets?'

'Certainly it's genuine violets.' Mr. Paulos was affronted. 'All my perfumes are genuine.'

'Well, you know much better than I do, of course, but I thought this smelt like a composition.'

'What are you talking about?' said Daisy, a little ashamed of her friend's presumptuousness.

'Real violet essence is so dear that it's generally adulterated with cheaper scents, like cassia and orris root. That's right, isn't it, Mr. Paulos?'

'Oh, quite right,' he said crossly.

'But what makes you think this one isn't real violets?' Daisy persisted.

'I used to have rather a nose for scent.' Lucy felt obliged to give a deprecating laugh. 'A great-uncle of mine was a chemist who worked for Rimmel's, and when I was in my 'teens I sometimes went to stay with him. He had all kinds of essences—not in lovely bottles like these, of course, just plain ones like chemists use. And he was always experimenting and producing the most heavenly concoctions, sometimes out of things that smell horrible by themselves. Then he used to show us how various scents could be imitated, and test our sense of smell by making us guess which was which.'

'You must be quite an expert,' said Paulos, and his tone was sarcastic, but nervous too, for he was suffering the acute mental discomfort of one who perceives that the hiding-place of his ignorance is in danger of being ruthlessly invaded. As an amateur of perfumes his only skill was the skill of the showman.

When Paulos, who was by profession a cotton-broker, had first become rich enough to devote himself freely to the sport of hunting lions and lion cubs, he had possessed no other equipment than his enthusiasm and his moderate affluence. It was plain that he would need something more—but what? He thought of wine, he thought of pictures, but there was so much to be learned about these luxuries, and numbers of people had what appeared to be a working knowledge of them, so that it might be difficult to sustain a bluff. To set up as a connoisseur was certainly a good idea, but the subject cultivated would have to be an obscure one.

Obscure, yet wide in its appeal—something pleasant and unhackneyed that everyone would be interested in. Was there no hobby that answered this description? The memory of a row of scent-bottles on a lady's dressing-table flashed upon him like an inspiration. Elegant and graceful, expensive, but not prohibitively so, compact, easily housed, glamorous from its associations, breathing of culture and refinement, alluring to women and, through them, agreeable to men, a collection of perfumes would undoubtedly be an asset of peculiar value. Moreover, not one person in a thousand was likely to have any technical understanding of the subject, and it would be quite superfluous for him to undergo the fatigue of studying it.

At first he concentrated entirely on handsome bottles, but later he realized that a row or two of plain flasks gave a business-like air which carried weight, and later still he hit upon the excellent device of ivory labels on which names or reference numbers were scrawled in the most impressive manner. By this time he had almost come to believe that he was an expert. In the course of making hundreds of purchases he had picked up little pieces of information which he could repeat convincingly, and he had become known to the trade as a client who would pay high prices for rarities, so that many really fine and curious items did find their way to his collection. He had established a reputation for himself, and the celebrities and semi-celebrities and demi-semi-celebrities to whom he displayed his richly filled shelves seldom seemed to question his authority.

But just occasionally someone came along who disturbed his complacency with questions he could only answer by guesswork, or—crueller still—turned out to know much more about it all than he did.

That was dreadful, worse even than when tactless fools requested him to open bottles which, as he alone was aware, were years and years old and kept only for show.

There was nothing to do but proffer some other attraction immediately. He looked at his watch. 'Now I mustn't get on the wrong side of you girls,' he said, laying his hand ingratiatingly on Daisy's shoulder. 'I haven't forgotten you've got to rehearse tomorrow morning, and I promised I was only going to keep you half an hour. We go through all the perfumes another time, eh? And I put away the other new bottle till you come again. You see, I want you to choose a little present for yourselves before you go.'

'A present! Oh, how lovely!' cried Daisy. 'But really, I don't think we ought to take anything.'

'Neither do I,' said Lucy with slightly more sincerity.

'No arguments, my dears. I won't listen to no arguments.' He brightened considerably as he managed to steer them out of the alcove with his credit, as he believed, still intact. 'All the ladies take a little souvenir from Chappie. You have a look what I got for you and don't argue.'

He opened a small cupboard fitted with sliding trays, which, with a rapid and effective gesture, he pulled out one after another. His guests were compelled anew to give voice to their admiration. Set out as carefully as goods in a shop was a superb assortment of silk stockings in all the colours then favoured—white, various shades of grey, shell pink, salmon pink, rose pink, leaf brown, mushroom, royal blue, saxe blue, champagne, banana, mauve, and *eau de nil*. Fine stockings still have their charm, but in 1919 they were much rarer than they have since become. Paulos's were especially beautiful, being silk to the last thread; and that was unusual in a day when even luxurious women were content to wear cotton 'tops' that sometimes reached nearly down to the calf. Well might the two friends vie with each other in exclamations of joyful wonder.

'Such dozens of pairs!' 'Such lovely colours!' 'Such exquisite quality!' It sounded like a litany.

'What can you *do* with so many pairs?' said Daisy.

'Surely they must perish in this climate?' the prudent Lucy suggested.

'Perish! They don't have no time to perish. They go like hot cakes. I got a new consignment coming every three months.' He spoke with not unjustifiable pride; the stockings were his master-stroke.

In the early days of establishing himself as a connoisseur he had made it a practice to deal out bottles of scent, but as he very soon perceived, to take one trifling article from such a collection was, or appeared to be, a casual act, and the collection itself seemed less precious being broken into thus easily. No one had regarded these tributes as a claim to intimacy.

But the stockings were a very different matter. There is something undeniably intimate about stockings, and yet they are so generally acceptable that, offered at once lightly and pressingly as Paulos offered them, there could be hardly any excuse for a refusal. He set himself up as a universal provider of stockings, a genial, eccentric, open-handed fellow who frankly enjoyed present-giving and would not be restrained. Nevertheless, the extravagance of the gift imposed a sense of indebtedness, and won him at least the smiling semblance of friendship.

Now, as he displayed his wares with a running commentary, intended to show how many eminent ladies in all walks of life had partaken of them, he was inwardly wondering what quantity he ought to assign to actresses of such doubtful status as his present guests. Surely they were not really worth more than one pair each? Normally, as Lucy had been informed, their quota would have been three, but their show was a failure and they were being very little sought after. Their stock was low, but the troublesome part of it was, they might go back to London and become famous—that sort of thing had happened to him before—and then it would be annoying to think he might have given them better reason to remember him.

'Well, let's see what we got in your size!' he said with increasing uncertainty. 'What shoes do you take?'

Daisy wore fours; Lucy was obliged to admit to sixes—a somewhat damaging confession in view of the prevailing mode for short feet.

'Never mind! Never mind!' he comforted her. 'I shan't tell no one. There are bigger feet than yours, my dear—yes, among English society ladies too. Some I get who take sevens.'

'Really?' Lucy felt a little sceptical about Chappie's society ladies.

'Yes, English and also Americans—they got the biggest feet, if you allow me to say so without offending you girls. Last October at my birthday party I had here a lord's wife, and she had feet big like this.' He illustrated somewhat recklessly with his hands. 'Yet she comes from one of your best families.'

'Which lord's wife?' Daisy asked, with a mild degree of interest.

'She was Lady Felix.'

'Do you mean Lady Henry Felix?' Lucy made the inquiry impulsively, then corrected herself. 'Of course not! He wasn't married until November.' She blushed scarlet as she heard the words for they sounded more revealing than she had intended. 'It must have been Lord *Geoffrey* Felix's wife,' she continued with nervous explicitness, 'the one who was nursing in Salonika.'

Whatever the words conveyed, Paulos was too observant to miss the blush and the sudden embarrassment of her tone. 'Yes, that's right,' he agreed. 'She came in with a hospital ship. You know this family then?'

'Oh, just slightly!' Her manner was so sincere in its attempt to dispose of the subject that she rose in his estimation. He was alive to the prestige of the English nobility, not yet undermined by the loss of wealth and privilege, and, conscious of his own weakness, admired anyone who could know a distinguished person without boasting of it. If Lucy Kendon was the sort of actress who was taken up by members of the aristocracy, then she was worthy to receive two pairs of stockings. And, of course, he would have to give the same number to the other girl, wasteful though it might be.

'Now then, what colours do you like?' he said. 'Look, all these are in your size. And you'—he turned to Daisy—'oh, we got plenty pairs for you to choose from.'

Daisy consulted her friend. 'Which do you think? The pale green would go with that dress of mine, wouldn't they?'

'What dress of yours?'

Daisy wished to reply, 'The one that Siegfried bought me,' but in front of their host she found it more delicate to say, 'The one Mr. Mosenthal liked so much.'

It was Paulos's turn to be on the alert. 'Mosenthal! Is that Siegfried Mosenthal from Cairo?'

'Yes, do you know him?'

'Sometimes we have come across each other. Do you find him nice to work for?'

Daisy rather resented the assumption that Mosenthal was no more than her employer. 'Oh, yes, he's awfully nice, both to work for and to know. At first I was a little bit put off by his manner—some people are—but he's perfectly sweet once you get to *know* him.'

The astute Greek now understood exactly what Daisy had wanted him to understand and perhaps a little more. At once she was honoured with an even larger share of his respect than her companion. Lords and ladies in England were all very well, but Siegfried Mosenthal in Egypt was even better. He was an important man with interests growing constantly more extensive, and if this silly little creature with the fluffy golden hair was good enough for him, she was certainly good enough for Chappie. Three pairs of stockings at least she deserved—maybe even four! That would sound handsome if she told the story.

'I think the mouse-grey ones are more useful after all,' Daisy was murmuring, unable decently to make her choice until she knew what quantity she was to take. 'Of course the *eau de nil* are absolutely lovely, too. I don't know what to say, Mr. Paulos.'

Chappie fixed his thoughts on Mosenthal and took the plunge. 'Say both—two pairs of each. And don't call me Mr. Paulos! I am Chappie to everybody for so many years, I don't answer to nothing else.'

It was a lavish gift, and the ladies went away more than satisfied, promising readily that they would let him have photographs to remember them by. He did not offer to see them home for he had learned that Lucy lived a good way beyond the Hôtel de Paris et New-York, and he felt that he had done enough for her.

'My dear,' cried Daisy as they regained the street, 'wasn't it interesting? I *am* glad I went, aren't you? That wonderful collection of perfumes! I wouldn't have missed it for anything.'

Lucy took the view that there were certain doubtful features about the collection of perfumes, but at the vicarage of Market Rookestone she had been told it was dishonourable to accept hospitality and then criticize the giver, and somehow she had never been able to shake off the trammels of that lesson. So she only said that she too was glad not to have missed the occasion.

'And really, he isn't at all a bad sort,' Daisy went on, clasping the tissue paper that contained her silk stockings. 'I thought I wasn't going to like him, but, honestly, I believe he's rather a dear, don't you?'

Lucy could not bring herself to answer. She was not disposed to question the genuineness of her friend's opinion, but she sometimes found it a little disturbing that, even in such small matters as this, Daisy unfailingly managed to make her sympathies coincide with her interests. And she was relieved to see they had reached the entrance of the big hotel.

Chapter 3

The following week, exhausted from incessant rehearsing, the company made its first appearance in *Oh, Aunty!* Until now there had been no need to call this extremely light musical farce into production, but it had been chosen as an emergency measure on the principle that, as Cairo had not enjoyed *The Prince of Palermo* or either of its successors, and as Alexandria seemed disposed to follow Cairo's example, it would be wise to provide something as different as possible.

Oh, Aunty! was received with moderate enthusiasm by a fair house. The next day there was another rehearsal to strengthen the thin places, and at four in the afternoon Daisy and Lucy adjourned for tea at the Hôtel de Paris et New-York.

'I feel like a wet rag,' said Daisy, stretching herself upon her bed and fighting a cigarette, 'but things are brightening up all the same. The audience was certainly better last night.'

'I hate the damned show and my damned part in it, and the damned audience too much to notice whether anything's getting better or worse.' Lucy spoke with weary vehemence. 'The only good thing about Egypt is that we shall soon be leaving it.'

'You know, you're just run down,' said Daisy severely. 'Egypt isn't as bad as you think.'

'Isn't it?'

Daisy could not tell whether this was an ironical retort or a sincere inquiry, for the tone was expressionless. She glanced curiously at the tall figure reclining, none too comfortably, in the room's one armchair. Lucy had so many reticences that she was quite capable of going through some serious emotional disturbance without confiding in anybody. Remembering that all last week she had simply walked through her part, and yesterday had given a feeble performance, Daisy cast vaguely about for the possible cause of such a falling-off. Certainly there was no love affair—at any rate there had been none likely to give rise to the least unhappiness since she had joined the tour, and that was nine months ago. It was true that Lucy had shown signs of being a little sentimental over that Lord Something-or-other whom she had known in England, but Daisy was not inclined to credit much importance to this attachment. She thought her friend made the most of it, very naturally, because the young man would have been such a catch if she'd got him. Obtuse in some respects as she was sharp in others, she allowed it to be rather obvious that she took this view, and Lucy had been effectually discouraged from explaining what Henry had really meant to her.

But it was not Henry or any other man who was responsible for Lucy's discontent as she shifted her weight from one limb to the other in a vain effort to find a restful position. She had been suffering increasingly for several days from what physicians call an ill-defined malaise: she felt heavy in body and aggrieved and querulous in mind, and as it seemed necessary to have a reason for these unusual sensations, she blamed them on Egypt and her homesickness.

'Alexandria's a very fine city in its way,' said Daisy. 'And Cairo was most interesting, I thought. I wouldn't mind a bit if I had to stay another six months.'

'Wouldn't you?' Again Lucy's tone was lifeless.

'I only wish Siegfried would ask me.'

'You'd find the summer here too hot to bear.' Lucy felt a painfully realistic premonition of how hot the summer would be. Already its heat seemed to lie on her lungs and tingle under her skin.

'Oh, I grew quite used to hot weather in Australia. That wouldn't worry me. I rather like it. Besides, if Siegfried was going to look after me, I'd be able to take things easy, wouldn't I? No rehearsals, no stuffy dressing-rooms, nothing to do but live like a lady! What a dream!'

'Do you think you could get on with him if you were together for months on end?' In Lucy's present irritable humour it was with difficulty that she checked herself from expressing her astonishment that any woman could tolerate Mr. Mosenthal's company even for a week.

'You bet I could,' said Daisy. 'Why, I'd be a fool if I didn't,' and for a moment Lucy thought she was referring frankly to the material advantages derived from Mosenthal's patronage, but the sentence ended, 'because really, you know, he's an absolutely brilliant man.'

'I suppose he must be.' Lucy made only a faint attempt to give conviction to her words.

'Well, it's self-evident, isn't it? Look at the position he occupies and the money he's making.'

Lucy's assent was lacking in enthusiasm. She had often noticed how the sort of cleverness that makes money may be dissociated from all other forms of cleverness whatsoever.

'He doesn't deny that he began with practically no education or anything,' Daisy went on, and Lucy found herself unkindly wondering who would believe him if he did deny it.

'He came to Egypt with two pounds in his pocket. I can't help admiring a man like that, can you?'

'Where did he come from,' Lucy inquired with a slight access of curiosity. The origin of people with German names still excited a special interest.

'From South Africa. He was born there.'

'He's a British subject then?'

'I should just think so!' Daisy exclaimed a little warmly, for she was inclined to be on the defensive about Mr. Mosenthal's nationality, and that was why Lucy had never referred to it before.

At this moment there was a knock on the door, and almost before Daisy had time to say, 'Come in!' it was opened far enough to admit a dark head and a thick-set shoulder.

'Oh, you're busy?' said Mr. Mosenthal with a brief nod of recognition for Lucy.

Daisy's face assumed a sweet and welcoming smile. 'Not busy, only resting. We've had a terrific rehearsal.'

'You needed it. Well, if you're resting I'll leave you to it. I just came to see if you'd had tea.'

'It must be on the way up,' said Daisy. 'We ordered it ten minutes ago. Do have some with us?'

'The room's too small for a tea-party,' He glanced round it with eyes that had a singular power of belittling almost everything they looked at. 'You'd better come to my sitting-room if you want to be comfortable.'

Daisy accepted the ungracious invitation with alacrity, and Lucy, who would gladly have removed her now unwanted presence, could not on the spur of the moment think of any excuse within the bounds of good manners. Staying only to alter their instructions to the waiter, they proceeded to Mr. Mosenthal's suite, which was on the same floor, but, for discretion's sake, separated from Daisy's room by the length of a passage.

'This isn't much of a place,' he remarked, striding in before them, 'but it's the best they could do.'

Lucy, who had never been in Mr. Mosenthal's drawing-room before, observed politely that it looked very nice indeed, to which he replied that she must be easily satisfied if she thought so.

Mr. Mosenthal was only about thirty-eight years old, but he gave the impression of having reached full maturity a long while ago. He was stocky and of middle height. His skin seemed very pale by contrast with eyes which were nearly black; silky black hair was brushed in thinning strands across his white forehead. His features were by no means ugly—fine eyebrows, a long narrow nose, sensitively modelled lips, and a round, Grecian-looking chin—but he wore a perpetual sneer which was far from engaging. Adopted originally to console him for the fact that other people invariably seemed to have some advantage over him, it had now become almost as fixed as his features themselves. He sneered incessantly not only with his lips and eyes. His voice was full of scorn. His dominant emotion was contempt: cold contempt, angry contempt, humorous contempt—he generated every variety.

There were a few unquestionable values which he had learned in his boyhood—values all founded on Jewish religion, customs, and codes of morality—but outside the range of these he desired to cheapen and disparage everything. Being a success he could even afford to disparage the things that were his, and this meant that he seldom appeared to be enjoying anything. In reality he took a good deal of pleasure merely from being able to indulge in detraction.

His five senses were very alert, and through them, too, he obtained numerous satisfactions which he rarely acknowledged. In particular he was uxorious, and he always kept a mistress, whom he treated with as little sentiment or affection as a sultan with his purchased concubine. To his surprise, however, he had found that ladies were sometimes unwilling to maintain relations with him on these terms, and, on more than one occasion, he had been subjected to the most trenchant mortifications. But his character was far from pliable, and these experiences did not serve to change his attitude, but rather confirmed him in it.

Still, he had no wish to court disaster, and lately—after an especially painful episode—he had chosen to steer a safe course by bestowing his favours only where they were likely to inspire a lively gratitude. Daisy, submissive, appreciative, passionately eager to please, was exactly the woman he required. In addition to all her other merits, she had delectable pink-and-gold colouring (blondes were rarer then than they became a few years afterwards). Altogether he regarded her as a find that did the greatest credit to his judgment; but having no inclination to flatter anything, even his own judgment, in plain words, he kept his feelings to himself, or at any rate confined their expression to the giving of presents. Daisy was too shrewd to ask for more.

'What do you think of these?' said Mr. Mosenthal when Daisy had poured out the tea and he had complained that it was almost undrinkable. He tossed into her lap a jeweller's box which, upon being eagerly opened, revealed two gold slave bangles on royal blue velvet.

'Oh, but they're lovely! Absolutely lovely!' cried Daisy, and Lucy obligingly echoed her.

'You like them?' He affected surprise. 'I don't think much of them myself, but the jeweller says women are wearing that sort of thing.'

'Not half!' said Daisy. 'When they can get them! What don't you like about them, Sieg?'

'I'd rather have something with more workmanship.' He flicked a disdainful finger at the bracelet Lucy was examining. 'What's this? Nothing but a hollow tube that any fool of a metal-worker could make.'

'Still, they go awfully well with these new Eastern-looking evening dresses. Of course, beautiful workmanship is better, but these are nice too.'

'All right, have them if they're any use to you. They just happened to catch my eye when I called in at the jeweller's for some cuff-links, and I thought they were the sort of thing you might take a fancy to.' His tone implied that he did not admire her taste.

'Oh, Sieg! Can I keep them? Thank you hundreds and hundreds of times. Aren't they beautiful, Lucy? This is certainly my lucky day!'

In this manner Daisy continued to applaud her lover's generosity until his restive demeanour showed her that he was bored. Then she put the bracelets aside and quickly launched another subject.

'Do you think business is going to pick up a bit? They seemed to like *Oh, Aunty!* better than *Palermo*, didn't they?'

'They couldn't have liked it worse,' he answered with a down-turning smile.

'We did wonderful business everywhere else. I don't know why Egypt should be so hard to please.'

'Nor me either.' He was equally ready to condemn the players or the audience. 'But there you are!—the more ignorant people are, the more difficult it is to satisfy them.'

'Daisy tells me you are a South African,' said Lucy, swerving hastily from an assent that sounded a little too emphatic.

'Well, I was born in Johannesburg,' he responded without enthusiasm; and being defensive about his nationality in a way that was braver than Daisy's, he went on: 'My parents had the sense to get naturalized twenty or thirty years ago. It saved me a lot of trouble.'

'But they weren't German, were they?' Daisy put the question for Lucy's benefit.

'They came from a village on the border between Germany and Poland. Technically they were Polish. Still, being a British subject is a good deal better than being a doubtful Pole.'

'It's rather romantic,' said Daisy, determined to stress the non-German character of her lover's origin, for it had been her duty during more than four years to detest all Germans, 'it's rather romantic to think that, in a way, Polish is your native language.'

'Not at all. My native language is Yiddish.' He fixed his scornful dark eyes upon her to enjoy her discomfiture. 'We always spoke Yiddish in our home. I can still write it better than English.'

'Can you really?' said Lucy with some interest; she had been trying to account for the slightly foreign quality of his diction.

Lucy's attitude towards Jews was typical of the well-bred English gentile. She held them in high respect as an ancient and indomitable race, and, until her Eastern travels had brought her into contact with some of the inferior types, she had supposed that they were all brilliantly artistic and intellectual. Daisy, on the other hand, sprang from those humbler orders where Jews are not regarded with admiration; and though she herself took a pride in tolerance and breadth of mind, she found it trying all the same that Siegfried would never let anyone forget his ancestry. He for his part was over-assertive about it because he believed his Jewishness was despised, and it seemed that if he only called attention to it often enough, he would show people what a mistake they were making.

'Are your parents still alive?' Lucy asked courteously.

'Yes, thank God.' He reserved a special tone for the mention of his parents, who affected him with a sentimentality the more intense in that a long separation had enabled him to forget completely their weak points.

'Do they live in Egypt now?'

'No, no, they'll never leave South Africa. They're too old to move from one country to another.'

'I suppose you visit them over there every now and then?'

Lucy's eagerness to know about Mr. Mosenthal's parents was less profound than it looked. She was, in fact, making the heavy effort to be polite which is intended to conceal a desperate wandering of the mind. She had discovered that her head felt most uncomfortable, the tea she was drinking produced a sudden sensation of nausea, and for the first time the alarming thought arose, 'Perhaps I am sickening for something.' She had to exercise the sternest self-control to listen to Mr. Mosenthal's explicit reply.

'I haven't seen them for fourteen years, I'm sorry to say. When I first came here, in 1908, I'd been wandering round the world for quite a while trying to find a place where I could earn enough to live on.' (Like most self-made men he was guiltless of any desire to pretend his fortune had been acquired easily.) 'I landed at Port Said with two pounds in my pocket, and until a few years ago I couldn't afford either the time or money for a journey to South Africa. Then the war began, and that made more difficulties.'

'I see.' Lucy fixed her eyes on the carpet in a prodigious effort to pay attention. 'Will you be visiting them now the war's over, Mr. Mosenthal?'

Tm always trying to manage a visit, but I have a lot of business affairs to look after and, believe me, it's not so simple to get away.'

He explained himself with more precision than he usually vouchsafed to females of Lucy's insignificance because he was pleased with her for taking an interest in his parents. He moved in a circle where such urbanities were not ordinary.

Daisy, who noticed Mr. Mosenthal's reactions almost without being aware that she was watching him, made haste to express views that would be congenial: 'How wonderful it'll be when you all get together again! They must be proud of you, I'm sure.'

'Well, I do what I can for them,' said Mr. Mosenthal with a deprecating gesture. It gave him immense pleasure to think that he was not only sending his parents a handsome allowance but contributing also to the support of uncles and aunts, cousins and nieces, some of whom he had never seen. To keep up his princely generosity to his family, he had driven harder bargains than any other financier in Egypt.

Lucy was troubled by a variety of different desires. She wanted to soothe the hot dryness of her throat with a long draught of icy water, but feared she was too sick to swallow anything; she wanted to be alone so that she might lie down to cry unobserved, and she wanted also to be cosseted like a child, and made to do what was good for her, and relieved of all responsibility for the wisdom or folly of her behaviour. It was clearly necessary for her to get away, but the others must be prevented from seeing her plight. Daisy, basking in the comparative radiance of Mr. Mosenthal's good humour, would begrudge the least disturbance; Mosenthal himself was hardly likely to feel anything but annoyance with a young woman inconsiderate enough to be taken ill when he had admitted her to tea in his private room.

She set down her cup, embarrassing her ear with the clatter of a falling teaspoon. Stooping to retrieve it, she felt a momentary darkness pass across her eyes, and when she stood upright she had to steady herself by leaning on the table. She meant to say, 'I have a bit of a headache,' and retire with facetious apologies; but instead she found herself swaying against the table murmuring in a voice over which she had no control: 'I seem to be ill.'

'Why, what's the matter?' cried Daisy, taking her by the elbow.

'Get her along to your room,' Mr. Mosenthal commanded briefly. He was not unsympathetic about illnesses—they had their place in those memories of home-life which were outside the regions of his cynicism—but he regarded them as matters for women to deal with.

Daisy obediently put her arm round Lucy's waist and led her away, and Mr. Mosenthal so far relaxed his rule of determined bad manners as to open the door for them.

A few minutes later Daisy returned with a troubled countenance.

'I think there must be something wrong with her,' she said. 'I mean, really wrong.'

'Of course there's something really wrong,' he protested irritably. 'She isn't a good enough actress even to sham sick.'

'She was probably off-colour last night,' Daisy ventured.

'She was *certainly* off-colour last night,' he retorted with finality.

'Well, I don't know what's come over her now. She seems to be almost in a state of collapse.'

'You'd better get a doctor for her. Maybe she's in trouble or something.'

'Oh, no, I'm sure it's not that!' Daisy was a little shocked on Lucy's behalf. 'I'm just wondering if it's flu. She seems so feverish.'

'Get a doctor and then you won't have to wonder any more.'

'Yes, but where, Sieg? Ought I to let her go back to her own hotel, or do you think I should 'phone the doctor to come round here right away?'

Mr. Mosenthal felt it was all a great nuisance. Doctors had a way of suggesting that the patient should not be moved, and it would be exceedingly awkward if Daisy were let in for the care of an influenza case. His Jewish compassion for the sufferer struggled with his strong distaste for inconvenience and was obliged to compromise.

'Get her into a cab,' he said, 'and take her along to her hotel yourself. Ring up the doctor from there, and don't leave till you've heard what's to be done with her.'

'All right, Sieg. That really seems the best plan,' Daisy prepared to depart. 'And what about the show,' she inquired from the doorway. 'Do you think she can play tonight.'

'How the hell do I know? That's the doctor's business, isn't it? You'll have to ask him.'

'Yes, but supposing she's not able to go on, we oughtn't to lose any time about letting Mr. Clifton know. He'll need to get the understudy ready.'

'Send him a message to prepare the understudy in any case. Then he'll be on the safe side.'

Daisy did not pause to ask why, since she quite obviously had her hands full, Mr. Mosenthal should not send the message himself. It was her character to be acquiescent and agreeable just as it was his to be dictatorial. He seldom originated ideas, but when someone else had suggested a line of action he could give orders in a clear incisive manner which carried authority. Daisy admired this capacity very much indeed; she looked upon it as a typically masculine trait.

Thus tacitly acknowledging her feminine frailty, she hurried to the telephone to get in touch with the producer, and having succeeded, not without delays and frustrations, made her way back to the bedroom, where Lucy, shivering, with her hands pressed against her head, sat huddled up in the armchair.

Lucy submitted readily enough to being led downstairs and taken home in a cab, only demurring against her friend's goodness in accompanying her; but her protest was not very vigorous for she knew she was unfit to be alone.

'It's awfully kind of you to be looking after me like this,' she gasped, dragging herself to her own door with curiously uncertain feet after a nightmarish drive through streets that seemed to be filled with shrieking noises. 'I'm being a dreadful burden, I'm afraid.'

'No, you're not,' said Daisy, steering her into the room. And moved by the sight of such wretchedness, she made a difficult admission. 'As for being kind, look what you did for me in Adelaide! If it hadn't been for you, my dear, I shouldn't be here now. Now listen, you've got to stay here and keep quiet while I go down and see about ringing up a doctor. Don't move, will you? Promise!'

Lucy, already recumbent, faintly attempted to smile. She felt neither the desire to move nor the ability. The walls had begun to shimmer darkly in a rather terrifying way, and when she closed her eyes she became confused as to whether she was lying on her bed or travelling endlessly down in an unsteady lift. At the back of her mind she was quite vividly aware of the theatre, and the new show, and the necessity for the curtain to rise at the usual hour, but, hard-working and reliable though she had always been, it now gave her an almost luxurious sensation to think that tonight it would all be going on without her.

The doctor's visit was a hazy dream. She was aware of the strange presence, the fingers on her wrist, the thermometer in her mouth, and even heard herself mistily answering questions, but there was nothing in any of this that resembled real experience. From some remote point of consciousness she looked upon herself, prone, helpless, and indifferent, and thought, 'Can this be me? Am I really as ill as that?' It seemed very strange, for like most healthy people she had half-supposed herself immune from the sort of illness to which one must simply give in.

While she lay yielding herself up almost gratefully to the fact of her helplessness, Daisy stood in the corridor talking to the doctor.

'She'd better be kept under observation,' he was saying. 'There's quite a considerable degree of fever, and in a tropical country like this one never knows. She'll certainly need looking after.'

Daisy, explaining that she herself was tied to the theatre, suggested sending for a nurse.

'I think possibly a better plan would be to have her moved to more suitable quarters. It's never very convenient being ill in an hotel, and if she happens to have picked up anything serious, it'll be tiresome here for her and for everybody else. I could get her into the hospital right away—or do you think she'd prefer a nursing-home?'

Daisy perceived a delicate inquiry into the state of Lucy's finances. The answer seemed obvious. Lucy's salary was fifteen pounds a week—three pounds more than Daisy's own—and nobody would choose to go to a public hospital who could afford the privacy and comfort of a nursing-home. She said as much.

The doctor went away promising to make all arrangements for the patient's departure within an hour, and Daisy returned to the bedroom to tell her friend what was proposed and gather together a few necessaries for her. Lucy roused herself for a last desperate effort to care about the situation.

'My dear, what a nuisance for the company after all that beastly rehearsing! This is the first performance I've ever missed.'

'Don't worry about the show, Lucy. Clifton will see to that; he knows you're ill.'

'Is he cross?'

'No, of course he's not,' said Daisy untruthfully. 'And think of the treat for the understudy, being able to go on for you at last! It's an ill wind that blows nobody any good.'

'I'll get better as quickly as I can,' Lucy murmured without much conviction. But when she would have permitted herself to sink back again into lethargy, a painfully revitalizing thought broke into the darkness of her mind. 'Daisy, we sail in a fortnight. I've jolly well *got* to get better!'

'Well, naturally,' Daisy returned as one talking to a child. 'Influenza won't last a fortnight. What *are* you thinking about?' Whatever Lucy may have been thinking about as she drifted once more into a state of mute passivity, she was fortunately spared from any true vision of the immediate future.

Chapter 4

Influenza might, as Daisy believed, have been done with in a fortnight, but typhoid fever lasted six weeks and even then was reluctant to depart. Lucy had a worse attack than her physician had ever seen in a patient destined to recover. No complication, he afterwards assured her, was missing; each little improvement was followed by a speedy relapse, and at one stage—though he did not tell her this—her room at the nursing-home was booked for another case, so certain did it appear that she would soon vacate it. But at last, without any apparent reason—for in all her lucid intervals she suffered from fears and discomforts that made her ask only for oblivion—the illness passed and left her still alive.

Still alive, but with health shattered and beauty gone. Compared with the lovely young woman who had arrived in Egypt three months before, the sallow wasted creature who was wheeled out in a chair to the veranda of the nursing-home was a sight to arouse dismay. Her red-gold hair had been cut off weeks ago and was growing again, sparse, lank, and dull. Her high, fine colour had given place to an unwholesome pallor. Her once statuesque figure was thin to emaciation, and the features which had so often been thought charming revealed themselves in all their imperfection—mouth too wide and straight, nose too sharp, nondescript eyes, neither green, grey nor brown. Her prettiness had always depended on ornament rather than structure, and no one seeing her now for the first time could have guessed what she had been.

Lucy herself was too generally miserable and nerve-racked to give full weight to this calamity. She would stare at her bony hands with a slightly incredulous interest but very little emotion, like one who watches an unpleasant conjuring trick. Her brain, exhausted by long delirium, refused to contemplate the future, and the present had thus only an inconsequential reality. For many days after she was first allowed to sit up in a chair she would not ask how long she had been ill or why no one came to see her.

But this surface of indifference overlying a deep apprehensiveness could not remain unbroken. One afternoon nearly seven weeks after her collapse, the nurse, with bustling cheerfulness, prepared her to receive a visitor. Her heart leapt and her hands began to tremble, and when she saw Daisy walking towards her down the length of the veranda her eyes filled with tears. She acknowledged in a spasm of mingled relief and anguish how lonely and neglected she had been. 'Oh, Daisy, why haven't you come before?' contended for utterance with, 'Oh, Daisy, how glad I am to see you!' and she said nothing.

Daisy had been warned by the nurse to expect a great change in her friend's appearance; nevertheless it cost her an effort to conceal her shock. As brightly pink and gold as ever in her frothy summer muslin, she stood twisting a little opal ring upon her finger and telling Lucy, with the more fervour the more distressed she felt, that she was delighted beyond words to find her getting on so well. The nurse placed a chair for her, and, after hovering about in a benevolent but embarrassing manner for several minutes, retired with a cautionary word against exciting the patient.

Lucy stayed silent, her head bent forward to hide her tears—which fell, however, in a visible rain. Murmuring inarticulate sympathy, Daisy drew an arm about her shoulders, and Lucy caught the suspended hand and clung to it.

'Has the company gone?' she sobbed.

'My dear, a month ago.'

'No one came to bid me good-bye.' She knew the complaint was unreasonable even as she spoke it.

'It wasn't allowed, Lucy. They were ringing up and sending inquiries the whole time, but you were delirious, you know, and visitors were forbidden.'

'Why didn't anyone tell me afterwards?'

'It would have been such a setback for you, my dear. Besides, you never asked, and the matron thought it was best not to talk about such things till you mentioned them first.'

'I didn't ask because I was afraid to get the answer.' Thus, briefly and finally, she disposed of her pretended unconcern. 'What happened to you, Daisy?'

'Siegfried wouldn't let me go. He asked me to stay behind.' She spoke gravely to disguise a vast happiness that might have seemed blatant in the face of Lucy's disaster. 'And so I went back to Cairo with him.'

'Ah, then you weren't here—you haven't been here since the company sailed?' How comforting it was to know that Daisy had this good excuse for her long absence!

'No. They let me come and see you for a few minutes before I left for Cairo, but you didn't recognize me. I stood at the end of the bed and tried to talk to you, but you didn't know me at all.'

'What a beastly shame! I'm so sorry. I wrote for news of you. I got a letter from the matron every week to say how you were getting on.'

'You didn't write to me,' said Lucy wonderingly.

'Well, there was so much to tell, and at first you weren't in a fit state to receive letters anyhow, so I thought I'd wait until I could have a chat with you. I knew Siegfried would soon have to come over to Alexandria on business and I asked him to bring me.'

'It's awfully good of you, Daisy. I'm sure I don't know how to thank you,' Lucy was still in that weak state where each, gust of emotion renewed her desire to weep.

'My dear, I was only too glad to come. Naturally I wanted to see you before you sail. There are lots of things to talk about.'

'Before I sail!' Her hands closed nervously on the arms of her chair. 'Is it all right about my passage, Daisy?'

'Oh, yes, that's quite in order, thanks to the good old management. Barrett transferred your berth to the *Lutetia* before he left. As soon as he heard you'd turned the corner, he said you'd better have a passage booked, otherwise you might be stranded here for weeks and weeks waiting for a chance to sail. Every ship is still crowded to bursting-point.'

'Lord, I'm glad he thought of that! Barrett always was a good sort.' She relaxed with a sigh almost of pleasure. 'When do I go, Daisy.'

'From Port Said in a fortnight, I think. He couldn't book you any earlier in case you weren't ready in time.'

'I shall be all right for that.'

'Well, that's one thing off our chests at any rate.' Daisy's manner became uneasy. 'There really are two or three other matters I suppose we ought to discuss while we're being so business-like.'

'Money, for one,' said Lucy with a return of her former apprehensiveness. 'Shall we get the money question done with?'

'Perhaps we'd better,' Daisy fidgeted with her opal ring.

'How do I stand about my hotel bill, and what on earth is this nursing-home going to cost?'

'You only owed a little bit at your hotel, and I settled up that out of what you had in hand from the week before. About the nursing-home, I've paid them every week. Siegfried advanced the money for you.'

'It's terribly kind of you both,' Lucy returned gloomily. 'How much do I owe him?'

'I'm afraid it comes to rather a lot because, you see, there were so many extras—a special night-nurse, and all that sort of thing. It's somewhere near eight thousand piastres.'

'Eight thousand piastres!' Lucy performed the miracle of turning paler than she was already. 'But, Daisy, I haven't got such a sum!'

'Haven't you?' Daisy looked more uneasy than ever. 'Not even counting your salary up to the end of your contract?'

'I had no right to any salary while I wasn't working.'

'Ah, but that's all fixed up. They decided to pay you just the same—as a mark of esteem or something. You know what I mean. It's waiting for you at the theatre.'

Lucy expressed her gratitude for this kindness on the part of the English management (Mr. Mosenthal, who provided theatres, had no concern with the payment of the company), but found it necessary to point out that the sum thus gained was only thirty pounds, her contract having expired two weeks after the beginning of her illness.

She had saved very little, for living expenses on the tour had been heavy, the constant changing of theatres and hotels involved a good deal of tipping, and it was a necessary part of her stock-in-trade to be well dressed. Indeed the small sum which she had invested in traveller's cheques was the fruit of many real and persistent economies. Now it would all be used up in paying for this hideous catastrophe, and still she would not be free from a great load of debt.

With growing discomfort Daisy heard her stricken friend review the situation. She knew that she was herself largely responsible for it, not only in having rejected the proffered hospital accommodation—it had never occurred to her that the illness could last more than a week or two—but more culpably in having allowed the doctor and the matron of the nursing-home to over-estimate Lucy's resources. Daisy herself had felt so rich with Siegfried's affluence at the back of her that everyone about her had basked in a golden reflection, and she had been optimistically extravagant on Lucy's behalf.

But it was not in Daisy's nature long to acknowledge herself guilty even in the privacy of her own mind. A lifetime of hard battling had made her marvellously agile in self-defence; and when she believed herself forced into a defending position she was inclined, not unnaturally, to be resentful. She became slightly resentful now, supposing Lucy's complaints to be obliquely directed against her. But she was mistaken. Lucy knew nothing of Daisy's stewardship, and if she blamed anyone for her plight, it was the doctor himself, who had so imprudently sent her to this expensive nursing-home.

'What am I to do?' she cried, knotting her hands together in an agony of perplexity. 'I've never owed so much money in my life. Mr. Mosenthal too! I have no claim upon him whatever. And the doctor's bill, and heaven knows what else! I can't leave the country with things in such a state.'

'Now, now, you heard what the nurse said! You mustn't get all worked up, you know, because I shall be blamed for it, and then I won't be allowed to come and see you tomorrow.'

'But how can I help it? I feel frantic.'

'Cheer up! Things can't be so bad as they seem, Lucy. I'll have a talk with Siegfried about you tonight and then we'll see what can be done. A man who came to Egypt with two pounds in his pocket ought certainly to be able to give you some good advice.'

'I shall be lucky if I leave Egypt with two pence in my pocket,' Lucy rejoined, smiling wanly.

'Haven't you any relations or friends in England who could cable you some chink?'

There came into Lucy's mind a wild idea of sending an appeal to Henry, but she rejected it. 'I have very few near relations, and none of them are well off. My sister teaches in a school. She only gets enough to live on. My cousins and my two aunts have disapproved of me violently ever since I went on the stage.'

'Oh, but they'll let bygones be bygones in a crisis like this.' Daisy's tone was the facile one outsiders so often adopt for disposing of family difficulties about which they understand nothing. 'You ought to cable them straight away.'

'No, I couldn't—I really couldn't. In any case they wouldn't be able to help because I believe the war has hit them badly. They were pretty hard-up at the best of times.'

'Oh, dear! Is there no one else?'

'I can't think of anyone. I never went in for rich friends very much.'

'What about that Lord Thingummy you used to make such a song about?'

Lucy winced. 'He'—she could not bring herself to name him—'he came of a rich family but he never had much ready money. Besides, I lost touch with him a long time ago.'

'Well, we must think out some other way. The company would have helped, I know, but they'll all be disbanded by now.'

'Yes,' said Lucy, 'weeks ago.'

'Anyhow, old thing, you're not to worry, do you hear? I'm sure to have some suggestion tomorrow. Siegfried's got a wonderful head for money matters!'

At this point the nurse returned, bringing them a tray of tea, and the conversation took a lighter turn, but Lucy did not join in it. Her mind was entirely occupied with misery.

Daisy went back to the Hôtel de Paris et New-York, and over the dinner-table that evening she very apologetically explained Lucy's situation to her lover. The reason for her diffidence was that she was by no means sure of her own status with Mr. Mosenthal, and it seemed a dreadful risk to bother him so often with the troubles of a friend. The intense joy she felt at having attained her ambition to remain with him was sometimes shaken by the fear that such a triumph was too good to last. Her life had been desperately hard, and he, by virtue of his money, had given her the best she had ever known of ease, idleness, and luxury. And she loved him!

Daisy was one of those plastic and adaptable persons who are able to produce whatever sentiments expedience may demand of them. She had the happy faculty of adjusting herself, without either effort or knowledge on her own part, to people, circumstances, and surroundings. She held, upon almost every topic, exactly such opinions as it seemed advantageous to hold, and, if the paradox is tolerable, being quite without intellectual honesty, she honestly believed in those opinions.

Her mind, like an animal in the process of evolution, blindly shaped and moulded itself to the conditions of her life; but the conscious surface of it was full of vague aspirations. It was necessary for her self-esteem that she should credit herself with more exalted motives than simply the desire to live comfortably and get on in the world, and as quickly as they were required she produced them. From the moment she had discovered her power to attract the opulent Mosenthal, she had discovered also that he was 'a very interesting man'. Yielding, as if she found him irresistible, to his churlish wooing (he had stated explicitly that once rejected he would make no second attempt), she told herself that he was brilliantly clever, a remarkable personality, a conquest others must envy. And this conviction, reflected so artlessly in her behaviour towards him, was something he found much more gratifying than he was ever likely to admit.

Most of his women had been provoked by his habit of disparagement into some sort of retaliation in kind. Daisy's humility was her victory. He was not afraid of her. She combined the exotic allurements of a mistress with the submissiveness he would have demanded in a wife. She deferred to his judgment, flattered his taste, adopted his views—and all without a trace of insincerity. Fear banished, he settled down to emotional ease, and acknowledged, rather in his attitude than in set terms, the existence of a function for Daisy more comprehensive than that he had first chosen her for. She was his *companion*. No woman had ever filled that role before. If sneering had not become second nature with him, he would, for her, have ceased to sneer.

But Daisy's instincts, though good, were not unerring, and she did not realize her own security.

He felt only a slight annoyance at being called upon to solve the problem of Lucy. It was true his general demeanour towards hard-luck stories was sceptical, but here was one he had actually seen taking shape in reality. As a Jew, moreover, he thought it highly proper that Daisy should wish to aid an unfortunate friend of her own race.

He was not aware that to Lucy's kindness, directly or indirectly, she owed all she possessed in the world, for she had as yet given him only a sketchy version of the past. It was receding into a deceptive mist, and she neither spoke of it nor thought of it quite accurately. It was much easier and pleasanter to appear as Lucy's spontaneous benefactor than to explain that she was under obligations—and, in fact, her sense of beneficence was much stronger than her sense of obligation.

'Well, it doesn't look as if I've much hope of getting my money back,' said Mr. Mosenthal with a shrug and a grimace as the recital of difficulties came to an end. 'Good-bye, eight thousand piastres!'

Now if Daisy had only known it, this was his ungracious way of forgiving Lucy the whole debt, for though grasping in business he was capable of generosity in private life; but Daisy was so nervous of his displeasure that she took the words for a complaint, and hastened with undue eagerness to reassure him.

'Oh, no, Sieg! Lucy will pay you back, you can be absolutely certain. She's quite on the level, she is really, about things like that.'

'I dare say, but eight thousand piastres is eight thousand piastres.' He meant simply that he considered the sum too large for Lucy to repay, but Daisy again misunderstood.

'Honestly, Sieg,' she protested. 'You don't know Lucy if you think she wants to get out of paying what she owes you. She's the most independent person you ever met.' Then as a cynical smile moved his lips she added extravagantly, 'She'd rather die than owe money without paying it back.'

'Did she say so?'

'Well, not in those exact words, but she made it quite clear what she felt. You don't know her as well as I do.'

'I don't know her at all,' said Mr. Mosenthal with another shrug, 'but if she wants to pay me back, nobody's stopping her.'

His good intentions were much blunted by the defensiveness with which they had been met. He seemed to see himself charitably attempting to rescue the foolish young woman from her plight while she haughtily repudiated his help. It ruffled his pride; like many people who are careless of the feelings of others, he was himself quick to take umbrage.

'The question is how's she going to raise the money?' Daisy inquired, never dreaming what injury she had done her cause. 'Have you got a pencil on you, Sieg? I just want to work out how she stands.'

With the detached air of one who idly watches some process too trivial to engross all his attention, he followed the calculations she jotted down upon the back of the menu card.

'Remember,' he reminded her in a spirit of academic interest, 'she'll need something in hand for the journey to England.'

The journey to England! Those words set Daisy's mind off on an entirely new journey of its own. Suddenly she realized that in a fortnight, except for Siegfried himself, she would be entirely alone in this foreign country. She had had a taste of loneliness during the past few weeks in Cairo, and even though she was buoyed up by the sense of victory and disposed to enjoy the novelty of leisure to the utmost, there had been days when she was hard put to it to while away the time. They lived in a pair of service flats, so she had no domestic tasks but those she made for herself. Siegfried was often absent on business from morning till night, and there was no one to talk to and nothing to do but embroider silk underwear and read magazines. Perhaps in the course of time, if she was lucky enough to keep his favour, she would somehow get to know people and be able to pay visits and be visited, but just at present an intimate of her own sex would be a godsend.

Why not Lucy?

The idea was good enough to make her wonder for a moment why she had not thought of it before; but then Lucy's heart was so clearly set on London that it had been natural to picture her going back there at the first opportunity, and it was not until today that the financial difficulties had appeared in their full seriousness. Disbursing money on her friend's behalf with the officious freedom of one unaccustomed to such a trust, it had come as a slight shock to her to discover the completeness of Lucy's insolvency. But now, rapidly assembling the various parts of a new plan which would give her a companion in Egypt, she already saw herself as the unlucky girl's redeemer.

'Do you know,' she asked after a long pause, 'whether it would be possible for Lucy to get back the money that's been paid for her fare? It would come to well over two thousand piastres.'

'Very likely. And then what does she do? Walk over the ocean?'

'No; I mean, suppose she decided to stay in this country. You see, I was thinking—of course it's just a kind of vague idea—they might let her have the money as a special favour, and perhaps it would cover the doctor's bill if someone explained things to him. Then all the cash she's got in hand could go towards paying you back.'

'Really? And after that she puts on a few dirty old rags and goes round begging in the street?'

Daisy was too engrossed in her plan even to reward this pleasantry with a laugh.

'No, Sieg,' she explained timorously. 'What I'm suggesting is this—you might give her a chance of earning something, so that little by little she could settle up everything she owes you and save her fare to England as well.'

Mosenthal perceived a certain meanness in this scheme, and it was not the sort of meanness that tempted him, but he assumed that Lucy's friend was aware of Lucy's views, and had perhaps already discussed various projects with her. For all he knew to the contrary, she was actually desirous of prolonging her stay in Egypt as Daisy herself had been. His own favourite country was the one where he could acquire most money, and as he surmised that Lucy had been earning a higher salary on the tour than she could ever have had in England, it seemed very natural to him that she might be in no hurry to get home.

'Did she tell you she wanted to arrange it that way?' he asked.

He intended only to verify his theory, but Daisy, being in a particularly sensitive frame of mind, imagined some doubt or criticism behind the words. Her reaction was automatic. 'Now do you think,' she protested in a gentle voice, with a wistfully reproving smile, 'do you really think, Siegfried, I'd try to fix up a thing like that against Lucy's will?'

Mosenthal disliked being reproved even wistfully and gently, and he too was affected by an automatic reaction. It took the form of a sudden spasm of irritation in which Lucy's affairs began to appear as a burden to be summarily disposed of.

'Well, well,' he said with restrained impatience, 'if she wants work I'm quite willing to do what I can, though God knows she couldn't have chosen a worse time of the year for it. I suppose, in the circumstances, there won't be much difficulty about getting her passage-money converted into cash. She may regret it when she finds out what the Egyptian summer is like, but that's her look-out.'

'Thanks ever so! You are an absolute brick!' rejoined Daisy.

'The question is what can I do with her exactly?' He drummed softly on his lips with his plump yet delicate white fingers. 'You say she's lost her looks?'

'Yes, but with make-up and something done to her hair she'd be all right from the front.'

'There isn't a show to put her into, and that's that. Could she do an act on her own?'

'Singing, you mean? Oh, yes, I'm sure she could. She has a very fine voice, you must admit, and it wouldn't be any trouble to get some songs together. Then you could give her some concert work, couldn't you? She's just cut out for a concert artiste if you come to think of it. Don't you agree, Sieg?'

Ignoring her, he began to rub the knuckle of his forefinger slowly along the edges of his teeth, an indication that he had come to grips with his subject.

'There seems to be any amount of concert work going round these days,' she went on, 'much more than there used to be before the war. In Cairo there's no limit to it. Of course, it's on account of still having all these troops about.'

He interrupted his train of thought and hers to exclaim bitterly, 'There are too many damned amateurs at large! My God, as if the troops haven't had enough to put up with but they must be entertained by amateurs. And, mind you, I'm expected to lend them my theatres for nothing! Think of it, lend them my theatres for nothing when they're making themselves a nuisance to the army and doing me out of money. And if I refuse I'm anti-British. My God!'

Daisy shook her head several times with a solemn expression on her face to show that she felt for him, as in truth she did. Being anxious, however, to get her affair settled, she did not encourage him to dilate upon his grievance, but pressed on: 'Still, there's a lot of concert work all the same, isn't there? That is, if you count all this cabaret and *café chantant* business that's been so popular lately.'

'I don't call that concert work.'

'No? Well, it isn't really. But Lucy could do it and she could do the concert stuff as well.'

'Could she?' He turned his black eyes upon her with a mixture of admiration and good-natured mockery. 'I like to see one woman being loyal to another, Daisy, even if she has to lie like a cheap watch to manage it. Lucy can do everything, can she? Anyhow she's got a loyal friend, and I hope she appreciates it.'

Coming from such a source the compliment was inexpressibly gratifying. Blushing a little from sheer pleasure, Daisy felt that she was indeed a loyal friend and that perhaps Lucy did not quite appreciate her.

* * * * *

But the next day when she went to the nursing-home to unfold her now securely laid plans for Lucy's welfare, she was seized with a mysterious nervousness which made her reluctant to explain exactly how she had conceived them. It seemed good, in fact, to let it appear that they had originated with Siegfried. (Her motive occurred to her even as she spoke. Siegfried, who was going to so much trouble to be of service to Lucy, deserved the full credit of the benevolent scheme: for herself she wanted none.)

Lucy heard their proposals with impotent agony. Her hands were tied. If Mosenthal, to whom she had unwittingly contracted so vast a debt, required to be paid back by this method there was nothing to do but obey him. To attempt to evade her obligations was beyond the boundaries of her most rebellious thoughts. She might deplore the irresponsible way in which these obligations had apparently been thrust upon her, but in the face of Daisy's perfect satisfaction with all she had done on her friend's behalf it was difficult to express resentment.

The situation was rendered more delicate by Daisy's relations with Mosenthal. Enamoured as she was, it was quite certain she would take offence at any hint of a complaint against him, and Lucy was too weak and helpless to risk a quarrel.

It appeared to her that, for a rich man, Mosenthal was behaving anything but handsomely. She did not expect him to make her a present of a large sum of money, but his hurry to have it repaid before she left the country seemed altogether unnecessary. If she had been dealing with him alone she might have found courage to plead her cause, for she regarded him as a business man who had made his offer in a business-like spirit, but here was Daisy expecting her to be glad and grateful—Daisy, who now clearly looked upon herself as Lucy's indefatigable guardian angel.

At no time would she have found it easy to prick the bubble of such complacency, and in her present enfeebled state it was out of the question to attempt it. She had no strength for resistance. It cost her as much effort as she could summon to blurt out tremulously as Daisy prepared to take her leave:

'He could have trusted me to pay him back from England. It would have taken longer but I shouldn't have tried to get out of it.'

'My dear, it isn't only what you owe Siegfried: he's not in the least worried about that.'

'The doctor would have waited, if that's what you're thinking of.' Daisy was exasperated. She had forgotten completely and for ever that her own convenience had played a major part in these charitable designs—it seemed the merest side-issue—and the lukewarm reception they had been given was most disappointing. It was amazing to her that Lucy should not know which side her bread was buttered on. Why! with such a ruined appearance what chance was there for her in the English theatre? Until she had regained her looks, which might be a very long process, she was going to cut a pretty sorry figure in agents' offices! If it were not for her own influence upon Siegfried, Lucy might go back to London and starve. Now, how, without appearing disagreeable, could she convey this aspect of the case?

'Ah, but you can be sure,' she said with something more than her customary sweetness, 'you wouldn't really enjoy getting back home if you knew you'd left a pile of debts behind you. Besides, you'd much better wait till you're feeling up to the mark and looking your best again before you tackle work in England. Just think, my dear old thing, in a few months you'll be right back at the top of your form, ready for anything, and then you can sail with an easy mind.'

Lucy remaining silent, Daisy improvised further shrewd argument.

'Of course, you've been much too ill to work out what would be likely to happen when you arrive in London, but unless you've got relations who can afford to keep you, how *do* you expect to manage, darling? Everyone says the cost of living over there now is beyond belief, and you'd return with almost nothing. You might be practically stranded.'

'I should get through somehow in my own country.' The words were a reflection rather than a protest. Lucy knew now that Daisy could never enter into the emotion which made the lengthening of her exile so intolerable. It was not patriotism—Daisy had felt far more strongly on the subject of British victory and German defeat than Lucy did—but just plain homesickness. England was lovable not so much for superiority over other lands as because it was home, the place where one settled down, the place where one made oneself comfortable. Foreign countries were like other people's houses, perhaps richer and more splendid than one's own, perhaps more romantically ancient or conveniently up to date, yet never so snugly ordered, never so responsive to one's happiness, so sympathetic in one's afflictions.

But Daisy, having been brought up in rackety theatrical boarding-houses, could adapt herself easily to a homeless existence. A home to her was a possession by which one signified one's status in the world: a country was a place where one 'made good' or failed. Lucy realized it was useless to appeal to her to open the door of the trap.

CHAPTER 5

THE INTIMACY between Daisy and Lucy was of the shallow kind produced by force of circumstances rather than true affinity. In their normal surroundings each might have known the other ten years without attempting to form any closer bond than one of superficial politeness, but they had been thrown together under special conditions. The resulting friendship was not without sentiment, but its texture was somewhat variable.

They had known each other first when Lucy was a singer and the other a dancer in the chorus at Daly's. (It was not necessary at that time for a chorus girl to be able to sing, dance, and act as well: Lucy had seldom been required to express herself in any movements more exacting than the waving about of kid-gloved arms.) That was seven years ago, but their attachment, which dated only from an unexpected reunion in Australia, was less than a year old.

At Daly's they had found nothing in common. Lucy was twenty then and newly escaped from the vicarage, absurdly callow, naïve as a child; Daisy, just turned eighteen, was by comparison a woman of the world. Already she could look back upon a decade of theatrical experience, for she had made her debut at the age of eight as a pantomime elf, and before her fifteenth birthday she had travelled far and wide as one of the Ten Merry Midgets, Renowned Juvenile Singing and Dancing Act. In those days it was possible for children of the theatre to earn a regular living, and Daisy's little salary was important to her family.

Accustomed to scrambling against time through life as through work, she had passed from precocious childhood to a semblance of mature womanhood almost without a transition stage. The semblance was deceptive; but to Lucy, still struggling with her country gaucherie, she had appeared humiliatingly well poised. It had been astonishing indeed when, for all her shrewdness and sophistication, she had been captivated by a wastrel and had let him persuade her to run away to Australia.

Lucy knew a good deal about that elopement from the gossip of the dressing-room. But material for discussion soon wore thin; after a single confirmation of the news that she was married and had sailed, nothing was heard of her again, and the sequel of disaster could only be conjectured.

Lucy's slight curiosity had long ago evaporated when, in Adelaide, some chance had led her to go and see an ancient melodrama performed by a pathetically inadequate stock company, and the comedienne had turned out to be Daisy Spender, who had become Daisy MacLowrie on her marriage, and was now ironically passing under the briefer and brighter stage-name of Daisy Joy.

Acquaintances who meet by hazard in a strange country are likely to discover a congeniality as warm as it is sudden. The many barriers of taste, opinion, and character, which it had never been worth while to overturn in London, now at once became intangible, and into Lucy's ear Daisy could pour without reserve her tale of disillusion and defeat. How the good-looking husband (she still believed him good-looking) had revealed himself as the crudest of adventurers who had only married her because a pretty and pliable wife still in her 'teens might be turned into an asset of commercial value, how she had struggled against his vices and his treacheries, how cruelty and squalor had dispelled the last traces of her infatuation, and how, as the result of a crisis in her miseries, she had borne a dead child—all this Lucy heard with painful sympathy.

Gaining from this misfortune at least the spirit to break free, Daisy had gone back to the theatre for her livelihood, and had drifted for years from one kind of job to another, hoping against all the odds that she might one day earn a passage back to England. She was not a victim of nostalgia, like Lucy, who regarded getting home as an end in itself, but it was becoming a matter of necessity for her to escape. Australia wanted only what had recently been hallmarked with the approval of London or some other great capital. Moreover, the theatre-going public, being small, demanded a constant supply of fresh faces, and the actor who had been seen very frequently, so far from becoming a cherished favourite, after the English fashion, lost his prestige entirely. To be taken into a company that ranked as first-rate was certainly an uncommon stroke of luck for an artiste who had achieved such damaging familiarity as Daisy.

Lucy's kindness had not stopped at using every exertion to get her engaged; she had helped her with clothes and money, and traded on her own popularity to assure her of a welcome. And Daisy did her credit. The prospect of being able really to make a new beginning inspired her with a wonder-working joy. Her features, faded and sharpened when Lucy first encountered her, took on a most charming vitality. Her thin and wiry body gained just enough weight to give her back the softer outlines lost in her perpetual battle. The quality of her voice improved.

Besides growing more attractive as a person, she worked hard and gave excellent performances. The producer who had accepted her so doubtfully under the stress of Lucy's eloquence was bewildered by the swiftness of the change. The audience forgave her for having been seen a great many times before, and on her departure for England via the Far East, the Press flatteringly saluted her as an Australian girl who had made good.

It happened that, although on good terms with everyone, Lucy had not, before reaching Adelaide, formed any particular alliance, so Daisy and she were naturally paired off together. The company regarded them, and they almost regarded themselves, as old friends providentially reunited. Daisy always found it easy to feel affectionate towards people who were being actively useful to her, and Lucy could not help liking one for whom she had done so much: and the fact of their having been chorus girls in London together was glorified in recollection until it assumed the importance of a bond.

As the tour proceeded through India and China, there were days when each became alive to a certain radical incompatibility in the other. Daisy's little hypocrisies, her startling capacity for self-deception, a deep-grained coarseness in her, overlaid with a veneer of affected gentility—these sometimes made heavy demands on Lucy's forbearance, while Lucy's reserve and independence were occasionally, in some nameless way, exasperating to Daisy. But for the sake of a companionship which had many advantages they both suppressed a tendency to be critical and managed to remain, on the whole, pleased with each other.

Fortunately for their mutual approval, Lucy soon forgot how much her friend was indebted to her, and Daisy, having once cleared off her financial obligations, was able to thrust the rest into some back-cupboard of her memory where they were not likely to be troublesome. She could thus proceed without hindrance to the very essential business of enveloping the past in a rosy glow.

For many people today's enjoyments are actually heightened by contrast with yesterday's distresses: rich, they like to remember the hardships of poverty, and sought after, they take a special pleasure in recalling the days when they were neglected and alone. Not such was Daisy's reaction to good fortune. To maintain that surface of assurance on which blossomed success, it was necessary that she should let her humiliations and mistakes dissolve from her mind.

Lucy was puzzled the first time she heard her refer, apparently without a trace of irony, to the 'good old days' in Australia. But little by little she grew accustomed to Daisy's ingenuity in concealing from herself the unpleasant features of her landscape, and, being kind-hearted, she abstained from reminding her of them. It was only with extreme caution now that she even touched upon subjects which might be expected to have disagreeable associations. Happily Daisy carried about with her an air of well-being radiant enough to eclipse their remembrance. Her brightness made a mere dim shadow of the pallid and despairing young woman who had been rescued from the Antipodes.

Chapter 6

Mr. Jesus Paulos, seeking the shelter of his flat on a broiling forenoon at the end of May, was accosted in the street by a thin, white-faced, sickly-looking woman—of all types of women the one least attractive to him. Although he had an excellent memory for faces, it took him several seconds to recognize in this unlovely person one of the musical comedy artistes whom he had entertained, so much too lavishly, a couple of months ago.

'Mr. Paulos!' she cried in a tone as startlingly unlike what he remembered of her as her appearance—an agitated, uncertain, apologetic tone, contrasting strangely with her former self-possession. 'Mr. Paulos! Please! I wonder if you could spare me a few minutes.'

He felt perturbed. She was going to tell him a woeful tale and borrow money from him. That was the penalty of cutting a figure in the world, getting a name for being lavish: actresses borrowed money which they never, by any chance, paid back. At least, the small fry did. It was about time, he often told himself, that he confined his attentions to the eminent and affluent ones.

Lucy Kendon, judging by her look and manner at this moment, was not likely to become one of those. He was tempted to plead some immediate engagement, but realizing that this might be merely to postpone the awkward interview, he chose instead to look ostentatiously at his watch and murmur something about being able to manage a quarter of an hour if she would care to go along to his flat with him.

Lucy hesitated as if she had already thought better of her appeal, but deciding, apparently, that it was too late to retract, she thanked him nervously and fell into step beside him.

'I believe you had a serious illness,' said Mr. Paulos, decidedly uneasy.

'Yes, typhoid fever. I only left the nursing-home last week,'

'That's rotten luck, I must say. I met your little friend, Miss Joy, a day or two after you got ill. She said how things weren't too good with you, but I had no idea you would take so long getting better.' He was about to explain that he had offered at the time to send flowers, but had been told that she was too delirious to enjoy them, when it occurred to him that, having once admitted such a flattering intention, it might be harder to refuse a loan. Still, he had no wish to appear churlish, so he compromised by saying: 'I would have inquired how you were getting on, but I forgot to ask which nursing-home you'd gone to.'

'That doesn't matter. It's an awful nuisance having to ring up nursing-homes just to find out how people are. It isn't as if it does them any good.'

'Exactly what I think myself,' he agreed quite gratefully. 'Anyhow, I'm glad to see you about again.'

Once more Lucy expressed her thanks, much in the same tone one might use for exchanging courtesies with a dentist about to perform some excruciating operation.

'All the same, it isn't very sensible to go walking round the streets when the temperature is a hundred and ten in the shade. Nobody but an English lady would be foolish enough to do it, if you don't mind me saying so. Even the Arabs don't do such a silly thing if they can help it.'

'The Greeks are different, I suppose,' she plucked up courage to retort with a faint smile.

Mr. Paulos, although a Greek, had no taste for satirical humour, especially from young women who were almost certainly about to ask him for money. 'I was kept late at a business meeting,' he returned curtly.

Discouraged, she followed him into the welcome coolness of his flat. An Egyptian servant in a dirty white tunic scuttled out of the drawing-room at their approach, leaving a visible disorder of cushions and ornaments behind him. Everything looked much duller and less splendid than Lucy had pictured it—the familiar result of taking a first impression by artificial light.

'I'm sorry it's all turvy-topsy like this,' said Mr. Paulos, with real annoyance, for he was exceedingly house-proud. 'Shall I get that fellow back to finish up? No, I leave it because you are in a hurry.' Thus, with half-conscious skill, he doubly assured himself of a swift and easy termination to her visit.

Lucy, feeling too untranquil to sit down, notwithstanding that she was weak and exhausted from the heat, stood against the piano, and irritated her host intensely by pressing her hands upon the lid. Wherever they rested a clammy outline of finger-tips marred for a moment the exquisite polish of the wood.

'Mr. Paulos,' she began desperately, 'I am stranded. Unless someone will lend me my fare to England I don't know what I shall do.'

'Your fare to England! By Jove, that's a big order, isn't it?' Paulos was relieved: the more exorbitant the demand, the less difficult it would be to refuse. But first he must appease curiosity. 'What's the trouble exactly, Miss Kendon?'

'That's what I want to tell you.' She took a long breath, after the method she had learned for dealing with stage-fright, and continued with unnatural smoothness, 'My illness cost a great deal of money, and Mr. Mosenthal advanced it to me. I mean he gave it to Miss Joy to pay my nursing-home bills and all that.'

'Very good of him,' said Paulos, respectful even from the distance to the great man.

'Yes, very good indeed. But I had no choice about accepting because I was too ill to be consulted, and if I'd known I would have been moved to a free hospital. Anyhow, it's too late to talk of that now. I owe him the money and it's got to be paid back.'

'Mosenthal has plenty to go on with,' he remarked unctuously. 'Believe me, he can afford to wait. My word, I only wish I had half his money.'

'Yes, but it isn't as you think, Mr. Paulos. Let me explain.'

He leaned back in his armchair and, closing his eyes tightly so that he should not see her hands fidgeting upon the piano-lid, composed himself to listen to her story. Briefly, but with a painstaking clearness, she gave the outline of her finances—how she had three thousand piastres saved and another three thousand owing to her for salary, and how she had reckoned to use part of this money for the expenses that must arise before she could leave Egypt and the rest for paying something on account to Mosenthal and her doctor. She had never doubted that Mosenthal would readily grant a delay, and the doctor, she knew, would be generous on hearing of her difficulties.

'How did you expect to pay them off in the end?' Paulos inquired with a sceptical smile.

'I would have sent them so much a month out of my earnings when I got back to England.'

'Ah, England's a long way away, you know.'

'So Mr. Mosenthal appears to think,' she replied dismally, and proceeded to give him her honest but mistaken version of the alternative he had offered.

Paulos was bewildered and knew not what comment to make. It certainly seemed beneath the financier's dignity to bother himself to this extent for the sake of getting back a sum which must, to him, be almost trivial; yet to express this opinion would be an indiscretion. For one thing, it might get back to Mosenthal, for another an admission of sympathy might unduly raise her hopes. It was best to remain non-committal. But while he sat with sagely pursed lips, nodding and shaking his head in a manner which Lucy found even more baffling than he intended, the thought running through his mind was, 'Surely he can't be wanting her to stay because he has some personal interest in her? No, of course not! He's living with Daisy Joy. Besides . . .' His eye fell critically on his visitor's sunken cheeks and bony shoulders.

'Well,' she was saying in a voice that strove, not vainly but with increasing effort, to sound temperate and reasonable, 'the idea was that I should get up a lot of songs—music-hall stuff that I could work for cabaret shows and picture theatres, and a few popular ballads for concerts—you know the type. And Mr. Mosenthal arranged for Polyglot Amusements to give me a three months' contract at twelve hundred piastres a week.'

'That don't sound too bad to me.'

'No, if I'd wanted to stay in Egypt I would have been frightfully pleased,' she acknowledged conscientiously. 'Even as it was, when I thought it over I had to admit the experience was going to be valuable, and I could have just saved enough to get straight. But all that time here—oh! it seemed endless!'

'It sounds like you must be in love with somebody in England.'

'No, no, it's not that, Mr. Paulos.'

'For heaven's sake what then?' He was growing impatient. 'You must have had *some* reason for refusing!'

'I didn't refuse.' She approached the denouement slowly, not for dramatic effect, but because she was struggling to avoid the breakdown into hysteria which she felt must coincide with it. 'I was in a position where there was nothing to do but agree, so Miss Joy arranged the whole business while I was still in the nursing-home. She gathered my money together, and settled pretty well everything for me—all except half what I owed Mr. Mosenthal. When she'd finished I only had twelve hundred piastres. However, I was to begin working again quite soon, so that wasn't very serious.'

'Then what *was* serious?' he demanded with an air of long-suffering.

'This.' She caught her fingers together, and by focusing all her attention on the pressure of one hand over the other managed to say quite calmly, 'I can't work. I've lost my voice.'

'Lost your voice!' Paulos remembered that Lucy had a good voice, and was shocked enough to feel annoyed with her for having lost it.

This was a much greater trouble than he had expected, and it would be proportionately more difficult to get rid of the wretched girl without being thought heartless. 'How do you mean? How do you know?' he asked testily.

Turning away so that he should not observe her fumbling for a handkerchief, she stared fixedly through a window which, veiled in splendid silk by night, exposed by day a sordid dingy courtyard: it seemed as she stood there trying not to cry that that courtyard and window together were the whole of Egypt.

'When I came out of the nursing-home,' she answered with resolute composure, 'I wasn't quite fit for the journey to Cairo, and one of the nurses recommended me a boarding-house where I could live cheaply for a week while I got used to being at large again. It's queer, you know, at the beginning. There was a piano there to practise with, and Daisy sent me some new songs to try over. For the first two or three days I didn't feel strong enough somehow to sing, and I just hummed a few numbers over to myself, but even that sounded peculiar. I can't describe it properly. It was—sort of blurred and muzzy.'

She paused to steady herself, for it was very hard to speak without crying. 'Yesterday I realized that time was running on and I simply must get down to practising in earnest, so I began to—well, to let my voice go . . . and it just sounded ghastly. You can't imagine . . . dreadful cracked notes and no power at all behind them. Oh, it was horrible!'

'Now then, now then, keep your hair on!' said Paulos in sheer embarrassment. 'It's only to be expected you won't sing so good the first time after your illness. Tomorrow, I bet you, or the next day, you have your voice back again.'

Lucy shook her head, unable for the moment to utter a word; but when he would have amplified these reassurances, she went on carefully, 'I don't think I can count on that for a long time. Yesterday evening I went to my doctor, and he arranged for me to see a throat specialist at the hospital. I'd just come from there when I met you. He says'—she moved away from the depressing window and began to drift aimlessly about the room, hardly noticing what she touched or looked at—'he says very serious illnesses do sometimes affect the voice this way, even when there hasn't been anything wrong with the throat. Of course, all singers know they need good health to be in good voice, and this is the opposite extreme, I suppose. He couldn't do very much for me. It'll probably come right by itself, he says, but not all of a sudden—certainly not while I'm so run down and anxious.'

'I see, I see, I see.' Chappie compressed his lips to the utmost degree possible and nodded portentously several times to show that he was occupied with hard thinking. And so in fact he was, but the problem which exercised his mind was not so much how to be of service to Lucy—that looked more of a loser's game than ever now—as to how to get her off his hands with the least possible injury to his reputation as a 'good fellow'.

At last he inquired in a business-like tone, 'Have you told Mosenthal yet?'

'No, I shall do that today. Of course it means the end of my Polyglot contract, and I still owe him four thousand piastres.'

'I should leave worrying about that till later if I was you.'

'Yes. I've just got to concentrate now on getting to England.'

'But what are you going to do in England?'

'I don't know exactly. I shall find work of some kind even if I can't get on the stage again. At home there are plenty of jobs for women, and one knows how to live cheaply in one's own country. Even on a very small salary I could save if I had to.'

Her reply was thus explicit because she assumed from his manner that he was trying to find out what prospect he had of getting back such money as he might lend her. It had not entered her head that he could have listened closely and questioningly to her whole story merely to satisfy inquisitiveness.

Not that she had taken his aid for granted. She was only too well aware of her lack of any claim upon him, too sharply conscious of her guilt in asking so great a favour from one whom she could not esteem; and indeed it had been plain at first that he regarded her as a nuisance to be speedily shaken off. But she thought his attitude had changed as he followed her tale. He had been irritable, it was true, but yet so attentive, so searching, it was impossible he meant all the while to disappoint her.

She had taken Chappie, not at his own valuation, but at the valuation most generally accepted. His snobbery was transparent, a joke among the people he courted, but he was regarded nevertheless as a kind-hearted and generous man. It was hard to think otherwise of him when one only saw him squandering money to give his acquaintances pleasure. One realized, of course, that his gifts and hospitality were not exactly disinterested; still, it was natural to suppose that their original source must lie in some instinct for benevolence. Though he had aroused a certain distaste in her from their first meeting, she had been sufficiently impressed by his legendary character to believe he might come to her rescue.

The idea had been an impulsive one translated into action an instant after it was conceived. She had seen him in the street at a moment when fear and misery were stronger than pride. Here was a rich man who, whatever his faults, enjoyed being bountiful. Let her tell him her calamity, and perhaps this chance meeting would prove to be the turning-point of her ill fortune.

But Chappie was bountiful only by policy and his former experiences had made him consider all loans to young actresses as money one need not hope to see again—money, therefore, for which one must be sure of getting something else in return.

Lucy had nothing for him; he did not desire her as a woman, and it was now strikingly improbable that she would ever reflect glory upon him as a celebrity. Besides, he felt no liking for her. She had set him right about his perfumes—he had not forgotten that: her manner had always been aloof and unencouraging. So although he was sorry for her plight, he was less sorry than he would have been if he had found her more congenial.

Rising from his chair to signify, quite gently, that the interview had reached its closing stages, he began setting to rights the untidy heap of cushions on the divan, puffing them up one by one, grouping and regrouping them with meticulous care. 'It's a bit surprising to me, if you allow me to say so,' he remarked, 'that you didn't think first to see what your little friend, Miss Joy, can do for you. She's one of your best pals, isn't she?'

'But she has nothing, no money at all. Her salary was less than mine.'

'She has Mosenthal.'

Lucy shook her head, not to deny the relations between Mosenthal and Daisy—that would have been futile—but to express the impossibility of seeking further assistance in that quarter.

'Don't be foolish!' cried Chappie, frowning at her over a cushion. 'It isn't sense to turn up your nose to Mosenthal. The little lady only must ask him nicely, and he sends you home in a first-class state-room.'

'You're mistaken. He was keeping me here to work off the debt I owed him. Do you think that was the behaviour of a man one would borrow from a second time? Oh, it may have been very kind,' she added wearily. 'I know he was giving me good work and all that sort of thing, but it wasn't quite the same as letting me get back to my own country.'

Paulos, though an ignorant man was a shrewd one, whose reason was frequently illumined by vivid flashes of intuition. Such a flash broke upon him now, evoked by his eagerness to get Lucy off his own hands into the hands of the man whom he regarded as her natural protector; and he saw a likelihood that she had missed.

'Maybe,' he said, 'it wasn't because he was so keen to get paid back that he stops you from sailing. He might want some company for the little lady. He's a busy man and she must feel lonely being so much in the background after working on the stage. Mosenthal likes her to stay in the background, I can tell you that. He doesn't introduce her to anybody.'

Lucy reflected. 'But he must have heard from Daisy herself that I was longing to go, simply counting the days till I could get home.' A bitter doubt assailed her, and took strength from Chappie's answer:

'Perhaps he did hear it and perhaps it didn't matter to him so much as it matters to you, eh? And perhaps also he did *not* hear it.' He shrugged his shoulders as if to imply that between wise and tolerant people a little guileful concealment need hardly meet with very severe censure. 'Miss Joy too—she most likely wanted you to stay even much more than he did.'

'Surely she wouldn't deliberately keep me here when she knows I hate it!' cried Lucy, but the words did not ring true. She recalled, not for the first time, with what indifference to her shattered hopes Daisy had announced the scheme which deprived her of her fare to England. Now she had been given the clue, it was easy, only too easy, to believe that, partly through selfishness, partly through a lack of understanding, Daisy had fostered a stratagem for detaining her. And in this new light she saw how absurd it had been to suppose that Mosenthal had really created a job for her merely to be sure of getting his money back. It had taken the wily mind of the Greek to search out a more credible reason, but once awakened to it, she was not slow to piece confirmatory evidence together.

'Oh, you mustn't look upon it that way,' said Chappie, good-humoured because he saw his theory had impressed her. 'If it's true, it's a nice compliment for you. Besides—' he broke off, wondering, as Daisy herself had wondered a few days before, how one could call attention to an aspect of the matter which Lucy seemed hardly to appreciate. 'Besides, my dear, she thinks certainly she is doing the best thing for you, to get you a good job here just at this particular time. You're not looking so well, you know, after all your long illness. Even quite apart from losing your voice, it won't do you no harm to wait a bit before you try to get work in England.'

Lucy discovered she had no case which could be stated to an outsider. It would be futile to explain the hundred and one unreasonable reasons which had supported her belief that, once returned to her native soil, she would find means to cope with every difficulty. She saw with clarity that all the plausible arguments belonged to Daisy. Having come so far, she was even able to imagine the mental processes by which Daisy had already furnished herself with motives relating solely to her friend's welfare.

'Well, they may have thought they were doing me a favour,' she replied tonelessly, 'but that makes me all the more anxious not to ask for anything else. I just want *to go*, Mr. Paulos—to sail home in any boat that'll give me a berth. With three thousand piastres I could manage the whole journey, and I give you my word of honour I'll pay you back, bit by bit, as soon as I've settled with Mr. Mosenthal.'

He hesitated only to put one question to himself before disposing conclusively of her appeal—how much damage was it in her power to do him among those whose regard he so assiduously cultivated? If it were given out that he had turned a deaf ear to a pathetic entreaty people might criticize him; might say, for instance, that all his charity was reserved for pretty faces. Well, that wouldn't be so serious, and on the whole he was inclined to think she would refrain from discussing the incident. It wouldn't do *her* much good, going round describing her attempt to get money from a man who was almost a stranger.

'Now, look here, Miss Kendon,' he said, adjusting his last cushion and then taking a firm stand at the back of an armchair, 'you've come to the wrong person.' The slow shake of his head conveyed absolute finality. 'Mosenthal and your little pal, Miss Joy—with all the best intentions in the world, no doubt, they got you into the soup, and it's up to them to get you out of it. Isn't it so? Three thousand piastres to me would be a lot of money, but to Mosenthal it's a flea-bite. And he *must* help you, seeing he made you stay here and you've lost your voice.'

'How can I take anything more from him?' The protest was automatic. She had no hope now that Paulos would befriend her.

'Nonsense!' he admonished her briskly. 'You put your pride inside your pocket, and be a sensible girl. Go immediately home and write to Mosenthal or Miss Joy—no, wait a minute! Wait a minute!' A plan had that instant occurred to him for getting rid of his visitor with the minimum of embarrassment and the maximum of benefaction possible at a low cost, and he paused, snapping his fingers to hasten thought. 'It's better you see them. Much better you go and tell them all about it yourself. If you leave tomorrow morning, you can be in Cairo nearly as soon as a letter, and I pay your train-fare. I promise you, if you take my tip and do it that way, in a couple of days you'll be booking your passage.'

Lucy thanked him with as much enthusiasm as she could muster and declined his offer. She had no intention of throwing herself on Daisy's mercy while there remained a single expedient still to be tried.

Explaining politely that to travel to Cairo unless she were positively sure of the issue would be merely to put further distance between herself and England, she made her way to the door.

Paulos deigned to argue with her a little in favour of his proposal, for he had thought it excellent and was rather disappointed at her rejection of it. He would have liked it to reach the ears of Mosenthal how the good-natured, open-handed Chappie, hearing of this girl's unfortunate case, had dispatched her forthwith to her friends in Cairo at his own expense.

He suppressed an impulse to offer her a couple of hundred piastres to spend on rent or food, because it seemed certain that if he once began with loans of that kind, there would be no end to them, since she was going to allow herself to be stranded in the city where he lived; on his very doorstep, so to speak. That prospect—when his charity might have transported her safely to Cairo and Mosenthal within twenty-four hours—vexed him to a degree which made his parting words somewhat querulous.

But as he saw her hurrying away from him down the corridor, not pausing to ring the bell for the lift but moving blindly towards the stairs, he was seized with some obscure feeling of compassion which made him wish he had at least spoken more sympathetically.

He ran after her and called as he ran, 'Miss Kendon, Miss Kendon, I forgot to ask you something!' Then as she turned round with her hand on the stair rail, 'How did you like the stockings? Were they all right?'

'The stockings?' She stared at him bewildered. 'Ah, yes! They were very nice. I still have them.'

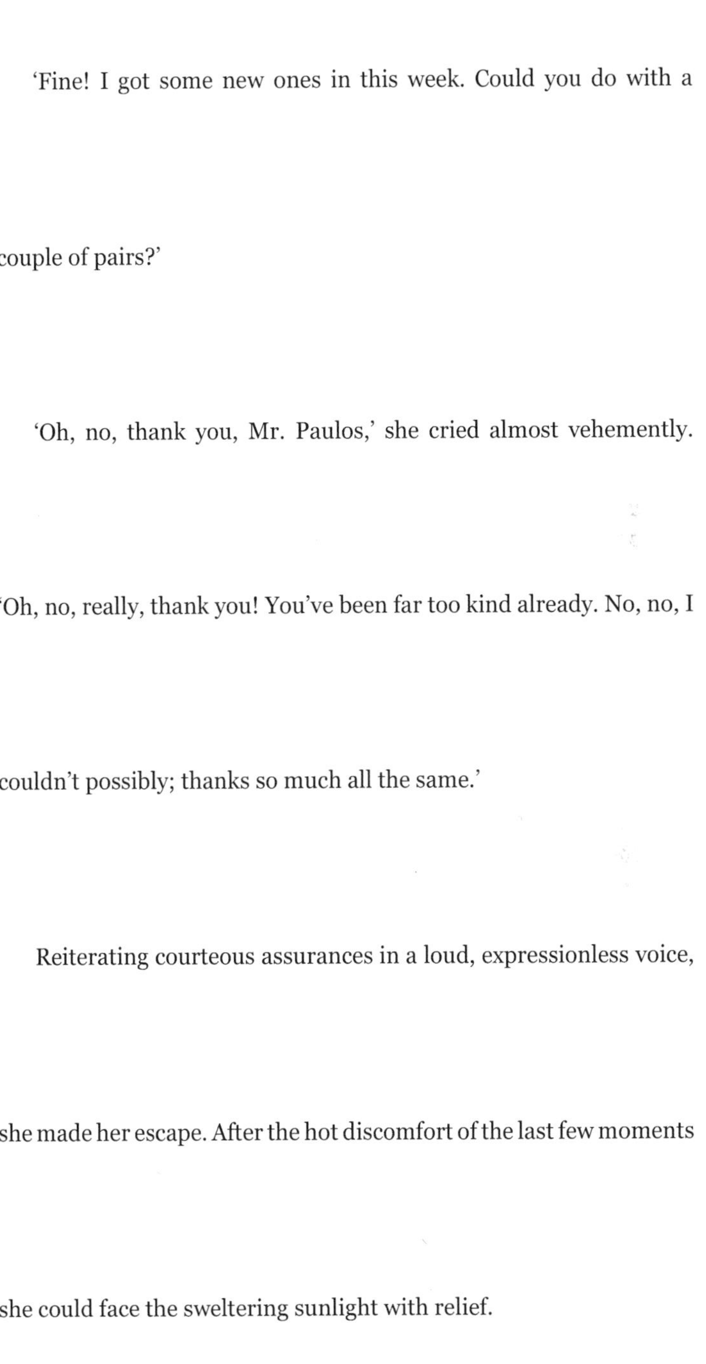

'Fine! I got some new ones in this week. Could you do with a couple of pairs?'

'Oh, no, thank you, Mr. Paulos,' she cried almost vehemently. 'Oh, no, really, thank you! You've been far too kind already. No, no, I couldn't possibly; thanks so much all the same.'

Reiterating courteous assurances in a loud, expressionless voice, she made her escape. After the hot discomfort of the last few moments she could face the sweltering sunlight with relief.

CHAPTER 7

DAISY HAD that strong sense of ownership, both as to things and people, which is dominant in those whose possessions have seldom been numerous or secure; and Lucy guessed she would not like her to hold any direct correspondence with her lover. So, although she would have preferred to report her calamity in business-like terms to Mosenthal, she was obliged to address herself to Daisy. Aggrieved as she felt, yet perceiving clearly that Daisy would never recognize her right to feel aggrieved, she had some difficulty in fixing the tone of her letter. Open resentfulness was out of the question, for Chappie's conjecture, though all the probabilities supported it, could not in the nature of things be verified. Equally, she found it impossible to commit herself to expressions of affection and gratitude.

She took refuge at last in pretended haste and scrawled her news abruptly across half a sheet of note-paper as if she had no time for courtesies. 'I'm just off,' she ended, 'to find out if the Consul can do anything about getting me back to England right away. I couldn't bear to trouble Mr. Mosenthal again. Sorry I shall have to leave the rest of my debt to him outstanding, but I'll do what I can as soon as I get home. Yours in a violent rush, Lucy.'

Daisy's first emotions on reading the letter were annoyance and incredulity. She had been looking forward greatly to her friend's arrival in Cairo, planning all sorts of amusements they would enjoy together, and her sense of frustration was acute. The loss of a voice was an inconceivable sort of disaster; one really couldn't quite believe in it. Lucy, so maddeningly blind to her own welfare, had hated the idea of staying in Egypt; and her hurried phrases referring to imminent departure seemed to have a ring of triumph. Well, she had certainly become unable to sing at a very convenient juncture.

In her heart Daisy knew such a deception was incompatible with all she had ever seen of Lucy's character, but her exasperation made her ready for the moment to think anything that was unkind. Without a single acquaintance of her own sex in Cairo, she had absolutely begun to depend on Lucy's companionship to round off her happiness. Now the future opened out before her in a long dull vista of days spent in the solitude of her flat with nothing to do but count the hours till Siegfried returned from his business engagements. And it was just her luck, of course, to have a lover who worked in the grilling afternoons when everyone else was idle.

As it happened, today she had not long to wait. He had been kept up late the night before, and came home to take a brief rest before attending a board meeting, so she was able to show him the letter while her dismay was at its most poignant.

'Well, poor girl, she seems to go from one catastrophe to another,' Mosenthal gave a shrug and a gesture of the hands, partly commiserative, partly to express his impotence in the face of so much misfortune. 'I tried to give her a chance, but her voice was the only asset she had, and if that's gone—' He shook his head significantly.

Daisy was about to make some remark on the ingenious manner in which Lucy had got rid of her one asset, when she suddenly remembered that Siegfried knew nothing of their protégée's longing for home. She did not say to herself: 'I led him to believe it was her wish to stay out here, and I mustn't show him that I lied.' Such an admission could never be made, even in the silence of thought. The purity of her motives must always remain unquestioned, and she checked herself, therefore, with reasoning which, if its vague outline could be captured in words, would appear thus: 'He took so much trouble to arrange that contract with Polyglot Amusements when she couldn't possibly have got work anywhere else, and it would hurt his feelings to tell him she wasn't grateful. Besides, she *is* my friend, and, after all, she has been through a frightful time lately, so I'll be very forbearing and not say a word against her.'

But though Daisy's mental faculties were remarkably agile and usually enabled her to take command of every trying or delicate situation, they were hardly equal to such a confusion of feelings as she was now experiencing. Disappointment, anger against Lucy as the begetter of her disappointment, pity for Lucy, who really had been having the rottenest luck, and wonder at her own magnanimity—all these fermenting together were merged suddenly in a great wave of pity for herself. With an abandon so complete that she did not even pause to consider its effect, she burst into tears.

Mosenthal was surprised and a little moved, for he had never seen her cry before, and there was something pathetic in the way the contours of her face broke up all at once into ugliness. Picturesque weeping would merely have irritated him—he had seen a good deal of it—but this recalled the abject griefs of childhood.

'No use going on like that,' he protested awkwardly. 'You did your best for her. She'll be all right, I dare say, when she gets back to her own people and has a few months' convalescence.'

Daisy's sobs became vehement, and he cast about for further sources of woe. 'I suppose you feel pretty foolish,' he went on, 'using up all her money to pay bills that could have waited. Of course we must do something about that. I don't think there's a snowball's hope that the Consul will help her. Heavens alive!—if they had to repatriate every British subject who gets stranded, the Government would be bankrupt. Naturally, I shall let her have her fare home, whether she likes it or not, so don't go working yourself up about that. The boats are packed, but I think I'll be able to wangle a berth for her if she travels first class.'

'What about me?' wailed Daisy, now reckless with self-pity. 'What about me? When Lucy goes I'll have no one—not a single solitary friend in the whole country except you, and sometimes I don't see you from morning till night. You never think what it's like for me, cooped up here day after day, day after day, with no one to say a word to!' Tears streamed down her cheeks faster than her moist handkerchief could gather them.

Mosenthal was nonplussed. This was the first time he had ever had so much as a hint of her loneliness, for in her intense anxiety to please, she had greeted him on his arrival each evening with just such sunny smiles, such gay chatter about her own doings, such intelligent questions about his, as would have befitted a heroine in one of the magazine stories she read to while away the hours of his absence. It was true she had recently suggested that it would be nice if she could go to Shepheard's or the Continental sometimes for lunch or tea, 'to have a look at the people', but when he had answered sharply that a pretty woman was asking for trouble if she wandered about alone in a city like Cairo, she had yielded with that instant submissiveness he had agreeably learned to take for granted.

It had seemed that, except for a little hankering after the bustle of hotel life, her contentment was almost perfect, and, jealous and selfish though he was, much of his satisfaction had consisted in observing hers. It mortified him more than he would have cared to admit to find that he had been mistaken.

'I'm sorry I've made a martyr of you,' he retorted. 'I didn't know you were having such a miserable existence, otherwise I wouldn't have forced you to put up with it.'

Daisy made a gallant struggle to pull herself together. 'Oh, no, Sieg, no! You mustn't put things into my mouth that I never said. You know I've been happier with you than I ever was in my life before.'

'You don't sound like it.'

'You're misunderstanding me, Sieg, you really are!' She paused to stifle weak sobs, apologetic now rather than reproachful. 'You see, I seem to be leading a sort of double life these days. When I'm with you, it's simply heavenly and I'm wishing all the time it would go on for ever; but in the daytime when you're working, and there's no one for me to talk to, and nothing to do and nowhere to go, I sometimes—you'll laugh at me, I suppose, but sometimes I take two or three baths a day just to help the time to pass.'

At this dismal picture she could not restrain fresh tears, but she saw now that he was mollified and even listening with an attention disposed to be sympathetic.

'I thought when we began,' she continued forlornly, 'that by degrees I should get to know your friends' wives and all that, but so far I've scarcely so much as shaken hands with a living soul. I suppose it's because I'm not respectable or something.'

'Oh, rubbish!' said Mosenthal not unkindly. 'You ought to know by now I have no friends—I don't get time to have friends—so how can you expect to meet their wives?'

'The men you mix with in business then.'

'Good heavens, do you think I can have you taking up with people like that? The riff-raff of about five nations!'

'Oh, Sieg, they're not all common. It's the artistic ones I mean, not the financial ones. The new conductor at the Adelphi is married to a very refined woman, and look at Mr. What's-his-name, that architect who designed the Lyrico for you—no one could say his wife's common.'

'Well, well,' returned Mosenthal, somewhat discomfited, for he hated any reminder that there were limitations to his power, 'I dare say when you've been here a bit longer, there'll be plenty of women ready to make a fuss of you, but just at present what can I do? You don't imagine I can go round telling the wives of men who work for me, "The girl I live with is lonely, so please come along and cheer her up!"'

'But, Sieg, you won't even let me go out for lunch or tea, and it would make such a break in the day.'

'Very likely, but I've explained to you before this is not a place where a decent woman should go around by herself. It's never been too nice at the best of times, and with all these troops about, there's precious little to choose between Cairo and Port Said. Now you've heard what I think, please don't bring up the matter again.'

'I didn't mean to bring it up, honestly. I was only trying to show you why I was so upset about Lucy not coming. We could have gone about together, couldn't we?'

'I suppose so, within reason, but she'd have had her work to do. You didn't think, because I gave her the job as a favour, that I was going to let her play about with it? My God, I wonder what would become of my theatres if I once started that sort of thing!'

'Of course,' Daisy agreed, vague but enthusiastic, 'we both realized that! Still, we could have spent a certain amount of time together, and it would have made a difference, just knowing there was someone in the background.'

Mosenthal began pensively to bite the tips of his fingers, one after another. This outburst of Daisy's, now that she had explained away its unflattering aspects, impressed him forcibly by its reasonableness. Indeed, it was so reasonable that it filled him with apprehensions. Bitter experiences had rendered him acutely sensitive to the possibilities of losing a mistress, and Daisy's brief hysteria had awakened ominous echoes of scenes that were preludes to desertion and defeat.

In its externals the situation was by no means new. An Oriental habit of mind in amatory affairs made him suspect that any woman who was not carefully guarded would surely be seduced into unfaithfulness. The complaint of boredom and of being 'cooped up' thus rang in his ears familiarly enough. What was unfamiliar was his reaction to it. Never before had he made the slightest effort to put himself in the other's place, to test by imagination whether the grievance might be a just one. On the contrary, it had seemed to him that if a woman—a kept woman—were well housed, well fed, luxuriously dressed, and regaled with numerous presents of jewellery, she could not legitimately grumble at anything. But Daisy, with her frank adulation, her hundred and one spontaneous ways of making him pleased with himself, inspired a sentiment nearer to affection than any he had known since he had left his family. With the enlarged vision of friendship he was able to see that much of her life was dull and empty, and with the foreboding of a natural pessimism deepened by all his pride had suffered at the hands of women, he told himself that unless he could supply her with some distraction she would go the way of the others.

But what distractions were there? To let her go about alone was inconceivable. He had no means of providing her with desirable associates, and he could never give countenance to the undesirables who would lead her into temptation. Yet these were the only friends it would be easy for a woman in her position to make. Lucy Kendon, he now perceived, would have been the ideal person to fulfil a very useful function. Those characteristics of hers which had caused him to set her down at their first meeting as 'stodgy and ladylike' were exactly what he approved in the companion of an attractive and idle young woman who was to be kept out of mischief.

'It's a hell of a nuisance about that girl having to go back to England,' he said plaintively. 'It would certainly have been nice for her to be with you here just while you're getting settled down. If only we were living in a house, you could invite her to stay with you for a few weeks, but as we are at present I'm afraid it wouldn't be practical.'

'In any case, I'm sure she'd never accept,' Daisy rejoined wistfully. She was thinking of Lucy's dislike of Egypt, but he supposed she meant to give him a reminder of that haughty independence of spirit which had been mentioned to him once before, and he answered harshly, 'Beggars can't be choosers.'

Daisy, not knowing what line to take about this, merely continued to look wistful, and after a pause which he filled out by examining his finger-nails minutely with a most contemptuous gaze, he inquired:

'How does she intend to earn her living when she gets home?'

'I don't know, Sieg. She doesn't say.'

'Can she do anything apart from singing?'

'She can act.'

'Act! Don't talk through the back of your neck! Without her voice, Lucy Kendon's acting is about as much use as a sick headache. Tell me something she's good at!'

Daisy tried again. 'Well, she can sew.'

'Do you mean she understands dressmaking?'

'She—she's sort of handy at dressmaking, but I don't think she could earn her living at it.'

'Haven't you any idea of something she *could* earn her living at?'

'Perhaps some kind of educational work, Sieg. She's had an awfully good education, you know, and her sister's a teacher.'

'Good education, eh?' He seemed to receive this information with more respect than Daisy had anticipated. 'Can she speak French?'

'Oh, yes, Sieg, she can—good French, too. I heard a Frenchman say so.'

'Was he trying to get off with her?'

'No, honestly, he said it behind her back. Besides, I've heard her myself lots of times, here and in China.'

'Are you supposed to be a judge?'

'No, but anyone could tell at once it was different from ordinary Englishified French. I believe they had a native teacher or something, and of course Lucy's got a wonderful ear.'

'Does she know anything about the theatre?'

Daisy could not follow such a bewildering train of thought. 'How do you mean, Sieg—'

'Does she know anything about the theatre?'

'She's been on the stage seven or eight years.'

'But does she *know* anything about it? Does she understand how anything works, or does she just do her own job without noticing that anybody else is doing a job at all?'

'Oh, Lucy's frightfully observant, if that's what you're getting at,' said Daisy, and although she was telling no more than she believed to be truth, she was warmed by a lively sense of generosity.

'Well, that's not much, but it's better than nothing.' With an unconscious suggestion of his manner in the board-room, he placed himself behind a table and, flicking his fingers lightly against the edge of it, addressed her in the incisive yet cautious strain which had always given confidence to his shareholders. 'Now I'm not making any promises—perhaps the thing can be fixed up and perhaps it can't—but I shall see Arthur Prince-Carter this afternoon and I shall bring the question up at my meeting; and it *may* be that I'll be able to provide some sort of work for your friend at the Adelphi.'

'Oh, thank you, Sieg, thank you ever so much,' Daisy returned somewhat doubtfully. 'But—but—I wonder—'

He brushed her words aside. 'It seems to me that with a little rearrangement there, we could really find a use for her. There are always dozens of odd jobs both at the back of the house and in front, and with a cosmopolitan crowd like we get here, French is distinctly an advantage. As a matter of fact, I've often thought of getting a Frenchman to assist Prince-Carter in the manager's office, but a girl might be better in some ways. Girls are more adaptable, and one who's been on the stage herself ought to be able to pick up the business side of it fairly easily if she isn't quite a fool.'

'It's terribly good of you even to think of it,' said Daisy, forcing a note of enthusiasm, 'but would there truly be enough for her to do? I'd hate you to go to all that trouble just out of kindness.'

'Listen!' Mosenthal raised an imperious finger. 'Whatever I may be in this private room, as far as the theatre's concerned I'm a business man, pure and simple. I may give Lucy Kendon a job for one reason or another reason—that's my own affair—but once she starts drawing a salary from Polyglot Amusements, believe me she'll earn it; so you can leave kindness out of the question.'

'Still, it does seem as if she's being an awful bother to you,' Daisy persisted feebly. She was wondering how she could break it to him that, kindness or no kindness, Lucy would find his scheme exceedingly unwelcome.

'The time to speak about bother is when and if she can't do the work. To give her a trial will be no bother to me. That's Prince-Carter's worry.'

'But how long will a job like that go on?'

'If she's satisfactory it can go on indefinitely.'

'You know,' said Daisy, assuming an air of casual yet intelligent conjecture, 'I've got a feeling that Lucy would prefer to get home if she can manage it.'

'You told me she was anxious to stay.'

'That was before she lost her voice, Sieg. I can't help thinking that if she has to leave the stage, she'll want to return to London.'

'Good God, where in London will she get a job like I'm prepared to give her?'

'Oh, I know she'd be frightfully silly to go, but after having had such bad luck here, I believe she will, all the same, if she can raise the fare.'

'Well, you can take it as certain that without me she can't raise the fare,' said Mosenthal bluntly. 'Not out here, at any rate, unless she's got friends you don't know about. Would you like her to stay or not? Give me a plain answer and the matter's settled.'

'But I've said I'd like her to stay, Sieg. Only, you see, I don't want her to think I'm being—sort of selfish about it. The first thing to bear in mind is—what's going to be best for Lucy herself? We mustn't consider *me* at all.'

Although she knew perfectly what his answer would be, she was so deeply touched by her own altruism that her voice trembled, and Mosenthal relaxed his board-meeting attitude to pat her on the shoulder. 'The one good thing you can do for her,' he responded with conviction, 'is to give her a way of earning a decent living till all these troubles blow over, and if that happens to be killing two birds with one stone, so much the better. You'll find a way of explaining to her; you can blame it on me if she makes any awkwardness. Now I must be off to see Prince-Carter and decide exactly what we can give her to do and how much we can pay her. Naturally she can't expect twelve hundred piastres a week in an assistant's job, because he doesn't get much more than that himself, and you couldn't ask him to stand for it. But I'll do the utmost I can for her.' With many expressions of gratitude on Lucy's behalf and her own—but chiefly Lucy's—Daisy flung her arms round his neck and kissed his cheek; a fond, domesticated kiss which reminded him of his sisters and that lost home-life cherished, in his sentimental Jewish dreams, scarcely less than his hope of attaining unbounded wealth and power.

Mosenthal went off pleased with having found so easy a solution to a problem that had for a moment looked serious; Daisy was as happy as a child whose tantrums, instead of meeting expected punishment, have secured it the fulfilment of its desire. Neither was distressed by any idea of having conspired against a defenceless victim, for it was obvious that they were, in fact, conferring a benefit which Lucy herself would ultimately acknowledge.

Not that Mosenthal was inclined to take much account of Lucy's feelings one way or another. He would rather do her a good turn than a bad one; but in the pursuit of his own convenience he was capable of an opportunism that was almost frankly ruthless. And even if her nostalgia for London had been fully and truthfully represented to him instead of only hinted at, it would hardly have seemed real to one who had never suffered from that sickness. To long for home, a house filled with one's nearest relations, that was comprehensible, but to long for a country would have seemed mere affectedness.

As for Daisy, she was sustained by a particularly enjoyable sense of well-doing. The more she considered the matter, the more apparent it became that for Lucy to be initiated into a new profession at this crucial time might prove her salvation. It was true she felt a qualm when she thought of having to compose the letter in which her protégée's good fortune was to be announced, but she was heartened by remembering that for the present she could lay the whole responsibility on Siegfried's shoulders. And later, when Lucy had come to appreciate what had been done for her, she would be able to describe how she, Daisy herself, had brought her soft persuasions to bear upon him. Whichever way the wind might blow, Daisy could always truthfully say that she had pleaded her friend's cause.

CHAPTER 8

LUCY STAYED, for she had no alternative. The Consul offered various kinds of assistance, but did not see his way clear to provide the amount required for her journey home and all its incidental expenses. Her application could scarcely have been made at a more difficult and discouraging time: post-war activity was at its height and every boat that sailed carried its full complement of passengers, most of them booked months in advance. To take a steerage berth, even if one had been available, would have been a desperate measure for a girl alone and in poor health; and the amenities of the 'Tourist Class' had not then come into existence.

Passing the cable office, she was tempted to entreat financial help from her sister, but that would have been a species of 'giving way' worse even than her shameful appeal to Chappie Paulos. Dora's whole income was her hard-earned school-teacher's wage, and to raise the large sum needed would mean a sacrifice greater than it was fair to ask. As for the other members of her family, who had always prophesied ruin from her going on the stage, Lucy took it for granted that their reluctance to come to her aid would only be exceeded by their impotence.

She had had friends in abundance, but not rich ones, and in the eighteen months of her travels she had lost touch with most of them, for she was a poor letter-writer, and the last desperate year of the War had drawn everyone into a fantastic game of General Post: one could never be sure where people were or what they would be doing.

Lord Henry Felix would, of course, be easy enough to trace, and she was driven to consider how she could approach him; but it was soon apparent that as a sequel to their angry parting and his marriage, the ignominy of making up to him with a sordid request for money would be more unbearable than even the misery of exile. No move seemed to be open to her but a petition to Daisy, and the thought of composing it momentarily paralysed her will-power.

All afternoon she lay on her bed reading a novelette. One part of her brain followed the words and felt amusement, and the other surveyed the scene of her ruined life with calm despair. It was like having some bodily pain not violent enough to prevent other sensations, yet too insistent to allow a moment of complete freedom.

By the evening post Daisy's letter arrived to tell her how Siegfried, with her best interests at heart, was proposing that she should stay in Egypt till she had recovered her voice, and was willing to make her the manager's assistant at the Adelphi in Cairo. Everything was painted in bright colours, and it was explained with evident truth that the salary of eight hundred piastres, while very much less than Lucy had been accustomed to, was considerably more than would be paid to any other beginner for the same work. She would still be able to save her fare to England, though not in such large instalments as they had originally reckoned.

Daisy was most affectionate and sympathetic, yet there were undertones in her letter from which it might be gathered that she considered it Lucy's manifest duty as well as her best policy to accept the offer. To refuse would be to answer, in effect: 'I ignore my debt to your lover, I ignore all your efforts on my behalf from the beginning of my illness till now. I place my unreasonable distaste for Egypt before every obligation. I am an ingrate.' Lucy, for whom the motive of the whole plan had become rather clearer than it was to Daisy herself, had reached a stage where she would not have minded much about appearing an ingrate if that had been the only price exacted for escape; but it was so much more difficult to acquire hard cash than moral courage.

She did not throw up the sponge without one further struggle. Gathering together her watch, her fur stole, her silver mesh bag, and even the trinkets that Henry had given her—insubstantial things, for he had never been able to afford, and she had not hankered after, presents of jewellery in the more important sense of the word—she spent a dreadful hour the next morning arguing the merits of her possessions with men who seemed, if that were possible, more compact of scorn than Siegfried Mosenthal. She had agreed within herself to accept any sum that would buy a passage home, however incompatible with the real value of the treasures now so humbled and dishonoured, but the best offers she could get were miserably inadequate, and feeling both defeated and degraded, she returned with her goods unsold.

England was lost: she must make the best of Egypt. She was essentially a reasonable young woman, and while she could not be grateful to Daisy for having disastrously mismanaged her affairs, she was able to suppress a tendency to blame her for everything that was amiss. Typhoid fever and its aftermath of lost looks and lost voice were scourges from a hostile Providence, and fairness compelled the admission that, without Daisy and Mosenthal to help her, she might have been in even worse case than now, indeed completely destitute. It was a very difficult admission because of the temptation to believe that, if Daisy had not taken things in hand, some other member of the company might have made a better job of it.

An earnest wish to act and think justly blended in Lucy with a frank recognition of what expedience demanded. Indebted to Daisy's lover, both for work and for money, she saw that it would be foolish and harmful to begin her new employment with the air of one who has been injured. Having accepted Mosenthal's proposition, she was determined to look pleased about it and to do her best. Only thus could she preserve what was left to her of independence.

CHAPTER 9

YIELDING with a good grace for the sake of appearances, Lucy found that a genuine resignation followed little by little upon that which was assumed. As her body began to gain strength, her mind recovered something of its normal brightness, and the nostalgia which had been almost a morbid obsession gradually lost its sharp edge. It did not vanish, it was never long forgotten, but its acute phase passed and she grew free to take an interest in other matters.

Daisy was tactful and disarmingly kind. Fruit and flowers welcomed Lucy in the hotel bedroom which had been booked for the first days of her return to Cairo, and when she set out on the dreary and fatiguing hunt for a convenient bed-sitting-room, Daisy accompanied her, and helped with enthusiasm to add improving touches to the lodging chosen.

It is never easy to maintain a grudge against anyone who places a flatteringly high value on our own society, and Lucy, deeply as she had suffered, was not implacable. Nor could she, even if implacability had been a merit, have found the firmness needed to keep at arm's length the one companion Egypt offered her. Propinquity had thrown them together with still stronger compulsion than in their Australian reunion a year earlier.

At first there was some lack of responsiveness on Lucy's side and a subtle defensiveness on Daisy's, and each felt a little unsafe and uncertain with the other, but by degrees as Lucy's situation came to be taken for granted, these doubts were thrust farther and farther back into the recesses of thought, and within a few weeks their manner had resumed its old gay or grumbling naturalness.

Meanwhile Lucy mapped out for herself a sensible course of conduct—to live on so much, save so much, and learn everything possible about her new work, not only because she would have been ashamed of inefficiency, but also for the sake of her dubious future. She could not but agree with Daisy that, if her career as a singer were ended—though they both pretended to regard this as quite absurdly improbable—it would be useful to have experience in another field.

But when she had had time to investigate the nature of her occupation, she found with a mingling of disappointment and relief that she was to be Jack of all theatrical trades and master of none. The post of 'manager's assistant' was not, as she had thought, synonymous with that of assistant manager. Her job was indeed to do 'odd jobs', and they were countless.

It was Mosenthal's peculiar habit to create positions of this type in all the organizations which came under his control—anomalous, ambiguous, experimental positions of which nothing was to be known in advance except that the person employed might be expected to turn his hand to anything. If the employee, being under some personal obligation, attempted to show gratitude by taking upon his shoulders labours that could not reasonably have been asked of him, then, according to his ability, his zeal would be his making or his undoing: he might find himself promoted to a much loftier place than he had ever aspired to, or degraded to the daily repetition of some dull toil originally undertaken out of good nature. By giving his subordinates vague and debatable functions to perform, Mosenthal widened his scope for studying their capacities; and although Lucy had been required to fulfil a private need, once she was involved in his business, automatically he regarded her as so much business material to be used to the utmost advantage.

In the quest for wealth and professional aggrandizement he was entirely single-minded, selfish, and inexorable. Those elements in him which were generous had never been reached except upon the neutral ground of social or domestic life. No indulgence could be looked for by anyone who, whether from choice or necessity, had once become a part of his machine for making money.

Lucy had known enough of her employer beforehand to be sure that her place would be no sinecure, but she had not suspected with what indifference to her feelings he would allow her to sink to the obscurest kind of factotum's office in a theatre where, a few months ago, she had been applauded as an artiste. Sometimes at first, try as she might to take a rational view, her pride was lacerated and tears would spring to her eyes as she contrasted the tasks now falling to her lot with the fortunes which were gone, but by a firm insistence on the temporary nature of the whole scene, she was usually able to argue herself into a more cheerful attitude.

She worked in the mornings and at night. Generally the afternoons were her own, and these were passed with Daisy. At the small but luxurious service flat in Lotus Buildings they would rest and chat and sew behind closed shutters; then, when the torrid daylight began to soften, they would venture out to eat ice-cream on the crowded veranda of some café or hotel; or to make the most of a little shopping. Towards seven o'clock they parted. Daisy dined with Mosenthal, and always took pains to make herself look elegant for him. Lucy went alone to a cheap French restaurant, and from there to the theatre, where she might spend the evening tediously running errands and checking up figures, or, with a competence astonishing to herself, stepping into some breach behind the scenes.

In normal times the theatre would have been closed during the hottest months of the off-season, but the city was still full of troops whose demobilization had been held up by political unrest, and there was also an influx of foreign travellers so eager to resume prewar freedom of movement that even Egyptian midsummer had no terrors for them. It was therefore worth while to provide amusement, though not on the scale customary during the season. From May to October, with the interruption of only a few weeks, the house was given over to a makeshift series of programmes—vaudeville on somewhat inexpensive lines, a French company recruited entirely from local talent, recitals by not very eminent performers. The staff was reduced to a minimum, and Lucy was expected to fill any gap created by illness, accident, or economy.

Within the first three months she had served at short notice in the exacting capacity of stage manager, had played understudy to the property master and the wardrobe mistress, had helped with the aptitude born of long experience to pacify irate artistes, and had held the prompt-book for the French company, whose system of prompting was different from anything ever seen in an English theatre.

These were tasks which she found interesting and often enjoyable. Unfortunately she had also to do a great deal for 'the front of the house', and this was almost invariably a source of boredom or discomfort. She particularly hated having to visit the newspaper offices with publicity material and, still more, being sent out to collect advertisements for the programme, for this entailed a favour-seeking attitude which she could never assume without reluctance. To avoid such distasteful errands she would pretend to something like enthusiasm for the services that demanded only impersonal contacts. Dull as it might be to sit behind the little window of the box office, to write out copy for the printers, or carry sums of money to the bank, it was pleasure itself compared with the sheer embarrassment of putting on a spurious geniality.

Losing her looks, she had lost as well the confidence that is so often a source of charm. At best her manner had been gay and kindly rather than graceful or persuasive, and her strong tendency to reserve had always been evident beneath her acquired Bohemianism. Now this reserve, among strangers, unconsciously grew a little arrogant, as if she were saying, 'I'm quite aware that you're not likely to want *me*, and you needn't imagine I am going to want *you*.' It was only when she was doing work in which she could be forgetful of personality that her natural good humour made itself felt.

Perhaps if Lucy had not regarded Egypt and all it contained as the scene of a transition period, she could have done more to repair the ravages of her illness. As it was, she accepted her lank and straggling hair, her hollow cheeks, her flaccid figure, as so many aspects of adversity that must simply be endured until she could get back to the surroundings where life would become real again. For Egypt was not real. Whether she enjoyed herself there or suffered, whether she was bored or interested, resigned or rebellious, Egypt was always a painted backcloth which would presently be furled and never concern her again.

To change this queer, incongruous setting it was necessary to save money, and this she assiduously did, counting every piastre she spent or put by, reckoning every pleasure and every necessity in terms of its price, until she became dismayed at her own preoccupation. She had decided not to return to England without something over and above the expenses of the journey; to arrive penniless in London was too great a risk. But it turned out to be far less easy to amass a substantial sum than she had anticipated, and after three months she was still a long way from the desired goal.

Saving up had become like a game, partly of skill, partly of chance, with innumerable hazards which one tried, with varying degrees of success, to foresee and circumvent. The cost of living was higher than it had ever been, and Daisy too set obstacles in the way of thrift, for she indulged in many little luxuries which Lucy for her own part would gladly have abstained from. Yet it was impossible to be in her company every day without bearing a share of their expenses.

Daisy never had much ready money (it was Mosenthal's conviction that a full purse would soon encourage any woman to dangerous freedom), but knowing her small supply could be renewed at pleasure, she saw no reason to be parsimonious. On the other hand, anxious always to appear to advantage, she liked to make her allowance of fifty or a hundred piastres last a little longer than the giver expected, and she was therefore gratified to find Lucy willing—so she put it—to keep her end up. It would have been tiresome if she, Daisy, had been expected to do all the paying, and very demoralizing for Lucy as well.

With the traditions of the Market Rookestone parsonage to support her, Lucy was never likely to become demoralized into trading upon the bounty of a not very generous friend, and this being palpable it seemed unfair that Daisy should habitually prefer cabs to trams and Shepheard's Hotel or the Semiramis to the modest cafés Lucy frequented when alone. Still, both tact and policy disposed her not to make it too plain that she was preoccupied with saving money to buy her escape.

Daisy's circle of acquaintances remained as small and unpromising as ever, and it was unlikely that she would let her boon companion go without some effort to dissuade her. Lucy feared such an effort, not because it could succeed, but because it would make her preparations for departure uncomfortable. It was obvious that she was considered to have forfeited her right to independent action. Reminders of her obligation were subtle and gentle (on the lines of 'How lucky, my dear, that Siegfried was able to help you!'), but their import was not to be mistaken by a sensitive ear.

Lucy could not argue for there was nothing tangible to catch hold of. The one reasonable course open to her was to keep steadily and quietly to her purpose, and to defer as long as possible the inevitable day of reckoning with Daisy. She would not lie, but she would lay no needless emphasis on the truth. There would be time enough for arguments when she could afford to book her passage.

Daisy, who was too shrewd to suppose that Lucy regarded Egypt as anything better than a makeshift world, was also of the opinion that there would be time enough for arguments, and so they continued to get on very pleasantly.

Chapter 10

Lucy's bed-sitting-room was on the ground floor of a new brick-and-concrete building a fairly long tram-ride's distance from the theatre. It was still unfinished when she went in; buckets and trestles stood about in the passages, the plaster and paintwork had a pervasive air of dampness, and there were electric wires without lamps and taps which could produce no water. In choosing this dwelling she had placed cleanliness before accessibility, before homeliness, and even before economy. Since she had lived in the Orient, cleanliness had come to mean chiefly the absence of vermin. Only where all was fresh and immaculate might one hope to avoid perpetual reminders that insect life in tropical climates achieves a nightmarish luxuriance.

By dint of unremitting precautions Lucy's apartment in Karnak House remained as immune as anywhere in Cairo. Fine net tacked over the window-frames kept out mosquitoes and the thick, blundering bodies of moths and flying beetles, while the absence of edibles and the liberal use of disinfectants made the room as unattractive as possible to domestic insects.

Her hardest battle was waged against the loathsome *blatta orientalis*, that gigantic and noxious cockroach which seems to have been gifted with as many attributes for self-preservation as if it had been the most precious creation of nature. Equipped with horny wings and wiry legs, strong in flight, incredibly swift in running, long and large yet able to accommodate itself in the smallest crevice, a ravenous eater extracting nourishment from the most unlikely substances, a fecund breeder flourishing in heat but hardy enough to support cold—Lucy soon came to regard this pest as a sentient enemy, an embodied evil against which she must be ceaselessly vigilant. Every tiny crack in wood or plaster was stopped up as soon as it appeared, the narrow gap under the door was closed with a felt roller, and the interior parts of the furniture were constantly examined.

Sometimes, in the daylight, as she placed saucers of sugar and borax in tempting spots under the water pipes or sprinkled a pungent sanitary fluid into the drawers and cupboards, her occupation would seem ludicrous enough to bring a smile to her lips; but late at night when she flung open the door with one hand and hastily turned on the light with the other, her eyes swept the room in the most dismal apprehension; and if, as occasionally happened in spite of all her care, the sudden illumination sent two inches of glossy darkness hurtling across the floor, she would stand for a moment almost paralysed, and only the certain knowledge that she had nowhere else to go could spur her to the courage needed for crossing the threshold.

One night in July when the weather was so hot that it was only possible to sleep lying coverless under the synthetic breeze of an electric fan, she came home from the theatre tired and overwrought after a day of altogether disagreeable work and turned her key in the lock with an even more than usually fervent prayer that she might be spared from encountering her foes.

No insect form sullied the purity of the walls and ceiling, nothing stirred among the rigid flowers and foliage of the linoleum. She shook the curtains—a nightly routine—and peered into all the shadowy places she knew to be dangerous; a curl of black wool was the most alarming object her search produced.

With a sigh of gratitude she undressed and washed, and was yawningly adjusting the electric fan to direct its current of air towards her bed when she remembered a small matter which, if not attended to tonight, might be forgotten in the morning. The French company was rehearsing a new play in which one of the actresses was to wear a black velvet hat. Lucy had exactly the right sort of hat among the possessions that would not be needed till she got back to England, and she had promised to lend it. She would unpack it at once, and put it where she could not fail to see it on going out tomorrow.

Her canvas hat-box was under the bed. She pulled it out, opened it, and gently laid upon the floor two or three extravagances useless now but still dear for their power to evoke a happy past. Smart, gay, sophisticated creations, the last of their kind for perhaps many a day to come, how charming they were! How agreeable the occasions when they were acquired—the long, luxurious tryings-on, the flattering saleswomen with their wily tributes to madam's hair and complexion, the pleasing difficulty of making a choice, the temptations defeated, and, still better, the temptations victorious! Hats had always been her favourite article of dress and the only one upon which she had sometimes been induced to spend rather more than she could afford, and these winter shapes of satin, fur, and velvet had now become so many cherished symbols of London. They enshrined the very spirit of the London shops whence they had come, the London streets and restaurants and theatres where she had first worn them, the London weather which had made them seasonable.

To think that in a few months she would be wearing them again! Yes, a good hat discreetly chosen did not go out of fashion for at least two years. These would still serve their turn in kinder circumstances. She picked up her favourite, a floppy-brimmed beaver dyed royal blue, and spun it round her outstretched finger, picturing how it would lie on thick coils of burnished copper hair next winter.

With an acute pang she remembered that her hair was now a lifeless brown and was only just reaching the length of an untidy 'bob'. The hat would no longer suit, no longer even fit her. It would look as inappropriate with her thin cheeks and sallow colouring as the frivolous summer models she was wearing out in Cairo.

'Still, I ought to have improved by then,' she strove to reassure herself. 'I shall gain weight when I'm out of this wretched climate, and if my hair doesn't get its colour back, why shouldn't I have it touched up a bit with henna.'

She could not refrain from putting on the hat and studying herself in the wardrobe mirror. Her pale and tired reflection gazed at her doubtfully. Perhaps if she were to use make-up—really bold makeup, not just the stealthy dab of rouge on lips and cheeks and the light dusting of powder which were all the artifices then sanctioned by respectability—the effect would be worth the risk of being mistaken for the sort of person she was not. 'When I get back to England,' she resolved, 'I'm going to experiment. I shall consult one of these face specialists.'

A little consoled, she picked up another of the hats and was about to admire it at arm's length when her attention was arrested by the astonishingly dilapidated condition of the lining. It had certainly been sound enough a few weeks ago, the last time she had this box open; but now the white silk hung in shreds scarcely holding together. Most silks perished quickly in hot countries, but here was a more remarkable example of swift decay than anything she had come across in all her travels. Annoyed and discomfited, she glanced into the box vaguely seeking the portent of destruction.

And there in the shadow of a ribbon on her velvet hat, quite still except for the waving of its horrible antennae, was the largest cockroach she had ever seen. She lost her head, and, springing up with a convulsive movement, flung away from her the hat she had been examining. It struck the open lid of the box and dropped inside with a rustle of disturbed tissue paper, and instantly three streaks of black lightning darted about her feet.

Lucy scarcely knew afterwards how she covered the space between the hat-box and the door. In one fraction of a second her eyes were following the headlong scurry of small but frightful bodies, in the next she was standing outside her room with a pounding heart and a skin that winced and tingled all over as if a thousand insect legs were creeping on it.

This was the worst visitation she had been called upon to deal with, and it had come, as evil visitations so often will, when she felt least equal to facing it. On other occasions, quivering but determined, she had contended with the invaders and had routed them, but tonight she could not—no, she *could* not nerve herself up to the squalid search, the inglorious battle. It would be preferable to roam the streets. At length, becoming more collected, she was able to recall that natives, either homeless or engrossed with some purpose of their own, were frequently to be seen squatting against the walls of the building at a very late hour. She would go out and ask one of them to come to her assistance. It would be a risky thing to do—at any rate the average white inhabitant of Cairo would think so—but Lucy feared her cunning enemy far more than any of the crimes supposed to prove so irresistible to low-class Egyptians.

Fortunately, despite the extreme heaviness of the atmosphere, she was adequately covered. Unless one wanted to look like a picture in *La Vie Parisienne*, one could not stand naked while one tried on hats, so it happened that she had slipped on a dressing-gown. Grasping it about her, she walked rapidly to the entrance hall. The passages were empty, as might be expected more than an hour after midnight, but against one of the pillars which separated the hall itself from the porch stood a man with a girl in his arms. Lucy politely averted her eyes: she had identified the head and shoulders of a good-looking young Italian who occupied a room in her own corridor.

She opened the door and stared out first to one side of the building, then the other, then along the dimly lighted street, but there was no one in sight except an old and very filthy-looking man lying asleep in the angle of the wall and the porch steps. Even from where she stood she could catch the nauseous reek of his voluminous stained and tattered garments, and as he drew deep rattling breaths, his limbs twitched. She turned away; it was out of the question to seek a rescuer in him.

Lingeringly she closed the door and went back, asking herself whether it could be reckoned an unforgivable offence, a social crime of the quite irremediable kind, to interrupt a young lover's wooing with a request that he would destroy a few cockroaches for her. The couple had broken apart when she saw them again and were standing alert and detached, watching her with evident curiosity. The man's bearing was a little sheepish, the girl's anxious, but the prevailing expression on both faces was hardly concealed bewilderment. They were eyeing her, thought Lucy, as if she were a madwoman. What could be in their minds?

She proceeded across the stone flags of the hall with a hesitant step, paused, half-turned, and proceeded again. Her brain was busy framing words to explain herself. At all costs to her dignity she would have to appeal for help, and so strong a dread of insects as hers was likely, she knew, to sound affected. Everyone here seemed to take such things for granted. She had been told repeatedly that she must just try to get used to them.

'I say, are you all right?' It was the girl's voice that spoke, a youthful voice, bold but with a latent uncertainty. Lucy looked round into a face which, at a full glance, turned out to be that of an adolescent.

A gaze at once direct and diffident was fixed on her eagerly, revealing only a shade of the embarrassment one would expect in a young woman who had been caught exchanging surreptitious kisses.

Lucy found it easy to answer simply: 'I'm afraid I've got an attack of nerves. My hat-box has turned out to be a nest of cockroaches.'

The girl, apparently as puzzled as before, translated the statement into good and rapid French for the benefit of her companion. He received it with humorously raised eyebrows.

Lucy thought their surprise a little exaggerated. She even got a displeasing impression that the young man was trying to stifle laughter, but since her only hope was to enlist his sympathy, she continued in a rational and apologetic tone to describe what had happened.

To be understood by both she spoke in French, and it was clear at once that either her fluency or her reasonableness had wrought a change in the listeners. The girl ceased to look as if she were witnessing some extraordinary phenomenon: the man's smile became frank and kindly.

'There's no cause to be frightened,' he said as if he were talking to a child. 'They are quite harmless. They don't sting, you know, and they're much more afraid of you than you are of them.'

The same old argument! She had heard it so often—she had heard it in Australia, in India, in China, and now she was expected to listen civilly while it was offered to her for the twentieth time in Egypt. Despite the obvious need to be ingratiating she could feel her brow contract to a frown. But the irritable retort she knew she must suppress was lifted, as it were, from the tip of her tongue.

'How stupid!' cried the girl. 'A skeleton is harmless, it doesn't sting or bite, but nobody wants to sleep with one. Really, men do say such ridiculous things!'

Lucy laughed gratefully. 'I'm afraid women often talk in the same way. Sometimes I think I must be the only person in the East who can't get used to insects.'

'Well, you're not, because I hate them too. Don't I, Vittorio? He had to come last night and kill one for me.'

The young man made a gesture of sardonic courtliness. 'Oh, yes, I'm quite accustomed to disposing of cockroaches for ladies. May I have the pleasure of coming to your aid?'

Lucy thanked him earnestly, and after a little further discussion—comfortable now because the Italian was openly facetious—it was agreed that she should wait in the hall while he made a drastic onslaught in her bedroom. He went off with a debonair wave of the hand, promising not to emerge until he could produce at least three of the enemy dead. Her sordid little catastrophe had become a gay and enlivening adventure, and she turned with a changed aspect to speak to the girl.

'What a nuisance I am! I must say it's tremendously good of your friend to do a favour like this for me.'

'Not at all. He's only too pleased.' Then, with that curious mixture of shyness and assurance which Lucy had noted in her first words, she hurried on: 'Look here, I do hope you didn't mind the way we stared at you. It must have seemed rude. We thought you were walking in your sleep.'

'Was my expression so glassy?'

'Yes, it was a bit glassy, to tell you the truth. But the hat was really what made us think you weren't quite—not quite—sort of . . .'

'The hat!' Lucy put her hand to her head and discovered with laughter and dismay that she was still wearing her royal-blue beaver. 'Oh, dear, what a sight I must have been!' The last remnant of her dignity was gone beyond recapture. 'A fur hat and a cretonne dressing-gown! Oh, dear! No wonder you both seemed to imagine I was crazy!'

'No, no! We honestly believed you were walking in your sleep.'

'I'd been trying the wretched thing on when the cockroaches appeared and, of course, I forgot all about it. What must I have looked like?'

'If it comes to that,' said the girl with a kind of dashing courtesy, 'what must *we* have looked like?' As Lucy's only answer was an awkward silence, she proceeded in a tone that was half-conciliatory, half-inquisitive, 'I dare say you were shocked at us?'

'I didn't expect you'd be so young,' said Lucy judicially.

'Why, how old do you think I am?'

Lucy submitted her to a candid inspection. She saw a plump comely face whose well-made features were perhaps destined to fine down to beauty, and a head of brown bobbed hair, untidy not only because it was ruffled but because it was badly cut and needed trimming. She saw a figure which, like the face, was of good proportions but wanting in the final mouldings of elegance. It was clad in a skirt and jumper, strangely set off by some ill-chosen accessories—ear-rings of pearl drops, a long glass necklace, and a fancy embroidered girdle.

Fictitious signs of maturity in the shape of rouge and powder, embellishments not then compatible with youth, could not deceive Lucy while she had before her so much evidence of aspiring yet callow and uncertain taste. 'You're sixteen,' she ventured, 'seventeen at the very outside.'

Disappointment was visible for a moment in the girl's clear, watchful eyes, but she responded airily enough: 'Jolly clever of you to guess, I must say. I'm seventeen all but two months. Everyone takes me for about twenty.'

'Well, you mustn't let them.'

'Why not?'

'Because later on, when you *don't* want to be taken for older than you are, people will say, "Oh, my dear, I knew her ten years ago and she was quite twenty then, so she must be every bit of thirty now."'

'Yes, I suppose that would be annoying—if one cared what people thought. I can't say I do.'

'Is that truthfully true?' Lucy asked, smiling.

There was a doubtful glance: then she gave back the smile. 'Well, I mean I don't care what they think about my age, and I can't see why I ever should. Nobody can help growing old. It seems awfully silly to me when women pretend to be younger than they are.'

'We might see what you have to say about that in another fourteen years or so.'

'All right, I'll tell you if we meet then, shall I?' They laughed, and she went on after a pause, 'If we're going to meet in fourteen years, we might as well know each other's names. What's yours?'

'Lucy Kendon. What's yours?' The sound of the question recalled so many schoolgirl overtures that, what with this and her display of childish fear and her absurd hat, she began to have the sensation of being herself very young and pleasantly ridiculous.

'Oh, mine's simply frightful. I can't bear it. Can you imagine anyone with the name of Conway calling their daughter Constance?'

'Constance Conway. It is a little unreal.'

'It's like the heroine of a school story, isn't it? Just the kind of person I'm not.'

'What kind of person are you?'

'I suppose you think I'm rather a shocking one?'

'I think you'd like to be.'

'Why should you say that?'

'Because it's a stage lots of us go through. I had it pretty badly myself a few years ago.'

'Don't talk about going through stages!' the girl protested with a fretful sigh. 'If you're young, everybody says that everything you do or feel is a stage and you're going to grow out of it. It's perfectly maddening, honestly it is. Yesterday I told my father I liked Byron, and he said, "Oh, you'll grow out of that. It's just a stage." *I* said, "Well, if everybody's bound to grow out of Byron, there can't be any grown-up people who like him at all, but as it happens, there *are*, and how do you know I won't be one of them?"'

'That's a fair argument,' said Lucy, considering. 'I do realize it's exasperating to be told you're going through stages, and often the people who say so are wrong, and the thing you feel is a thing you'll always feel—like my feelings about cockroaches. But all the same, you do change most of your opinions while you're in your 'teens, and you behave in a way that's so absolutely astonishing to look back on, sometimes the onlooker can't help remarking on it.'

'It's only waste of breath if the onlooker does remark on it. We've got to find things out for ourselves.'

'Yes, but you see, if the onlooker's always got to camouflage what he thinks about you, he's treating you as if you were still a child who mustn't have its feelings hurt. He's talking down to you. Do you want that?'

The girl kicked at the wainscot with the toe of her pointed shoe. 'Being sixteen is hell,' she said mildly.

Lucy was given no time to reply. There was a rattle of keys at the outer door of the building, and a tall figure in dress clothes appeared behind the glass of the porch.

'My father!' said Lucy's new friend in a low voice. 'Good lord, I thought he'd got home and gone to bed hours ago.'

Judged by his features the man who began to cross the hall could be hardly more than forty years of age, but there seemed little elasticity left in his well-fed body, and upon his face the remains of boyish attractiveness struggled in vain against an expression of discontented self-absorption. He went forward looking to neither right nor left, and might have passed out of sight unconscious of his daughter's presence if she had not brought herself to his notice with a nervous greeting.

'Hallo, Father!'

He turned and stared at her with displeasure, pulling out his watch. 'What are you doing up at this time of night? Are you aware it's half-past one?'

'As late as that? Heavens, I could have sworn it was only about twelve!'

'Only about twelve indeed! A nice hour for a young girl to be wandering about! Go to your room immediately, if you please, and don't let me find you up at such a time again.'

He retired on these words with stately dignity, not deigning to bestow on Lucy more than a moment's brief, incurious regard. He had been angry, yet much less so than she would have expected. It occurred to her that the necessity for making a show of anger had annoyed him more than the offence, but his reprimand was nevertheless effectual.

'Gosh!' said Constance, all her pretensions to adulthood falling away from her. 'That was a narrow squeak, wasn't it? I was positively sure he'd gone to bed. If you hadn't come along he would have caught me with Vittorio. Look here, I'd better skid off now because he may barge into my room to make sure I'm obeying him. You'll tell Vittorio what's happened, won't you? I'll see you again. I'll be on the look-out for you.'

She hurried away, leaving behind her an unreasonable but not distasteful impression that they were fellows in conspiracy.

Lucy went back to her bedroom, and sought information by putting her ear to the door. Slight movements could be heard behind it, but they told her little except that, if the war were still in progress, it was not a violent one.

Even the most innocent kind of eavesdropping produces a semblance of guilt in persons who do not take naturally to it, and Lucy gave a most uncomfortable start as her defender burst forth with an impetus that hardly left her time to draw aside. The start became a shudder as she saw that she had nearly overturned what he held in his hand—a tin lid strewn with small black shapes.

'Voilà!' said Vittorio proudly, waving it towards her. 'Behold your cockroaches! Four of them!'

She shrank away and, to her relief, he did not persist in showing her his trophies but flung them gaily through the nearest window. 'I thought you would be reassured to see the bodies,' he explained in French that was fluent and accurate, but heavy with slow Italian consonants and sonorous vowels. 'Every pest is completely exterminated. There will not be so much as a fly to alarm you.'

She drew him back into her room to press her thanks upon him and deliver Constance's message, which he received with no other emotion than slightly uneasy amusement. But while she began to set her disordered belongings to rights, he lingered near the door as if he were anxious to make some communication, and it needed no artifice to give him the lead he wanted.

'How strange that I never saw your friend until tonight, though she lives in the same building! Has she been here all the time—I mean, as long as you and I?'

'*We* came here before the paint was dry,' he said in a tone which made it seem as if there had been a silent intimacy between them from the beginning. 'No, Constance only arrived about a fortnight ago, and, really, it's not very strange that you have missed her, for she lives on the second floor, and besides, I think you are out nearly all day.'

Lucy retorted gently, 'Yes, but then she appears to stay up very late at night.'

He took the opening with a quickness that showed he had been watching for it. 'You are blaming me, perhaps, because of what you have seen this evening? Well, I tell you beforehand that I am entirely of your opinion.'

'It isn't my business to blame you for anything. I know nothing about the matter.'

'All the same, you are just a little shocked, eh? You think it is not quite right that a young English lady should embrace a foreigner late at night in the entrance hall of a building? You may say it. I am not offended. On the contrary, I agree with you.'

'You are both determined I shall be shocked,' said Lucy, deciding, by a contrary impulse, to be immovable. 'If you thought what you were doing was wrong, why did you do it?'

'Ah, mademoiselle, I am a man, a human being, not a block of wood.'

'Are you going to say "The woman tempted me" about this girl of sixteen?'

'That would hardly be gallant!' His raffish smile was undeniably seductive. 'But, you know, it's difficult . . .' His voice dropped and became confidential, a thing which Lucy guessed it might do often and easily. 'I do wish I could be good; but if I am, someone else will only be naughty. This poor girl, you understand, is absolutely alone, absolutely neglected. She lives the most unsuitable life; you couldn't help pitying her.'

'But she has a father,' said Lucy, rather as an inquiry than an argument.

'A father! *Mon Dieu*, you wouldn't say so if you knew him. He's a monster of selfishness, a man with a heart like marble. Give him three good meals a day and a bottle of champagne and he won't ask whether she's alive or dead.'

'What about her mother.'

'The mother is divorced and married to someone else. The father's an architect. He has come out here on some commission from a big firm in England. Constance was at school in France and he called for her on the way out and brought her with him. She wanted to come. Heaven knows why! During the whole six weeks they have spent in Cairo she has not had a single companion or a single occupation except to read or walk about the streets. He's busy all day and passes nearly every evening with his friends who hardly realize he has a daughter. Imagine such an existence for a girl of that age! Imagine the temptations!'

Lucy's private thought was, 'Yes, and you seem to be contributing to them pretty freely.' Aloud she said, 'Did she tell you all this herself?'

'Yes, mademoiselle, and it's true. I have plenty of reason to know that. Ask yourself whether a young lady who was properly cared for would become so friendly with a stranger in two weeks!'

'Oh, but certainly, in England,' Lucy rejoined, exasperated. 'Our ideas are different over there.'

'Even in England,' he protested with an apologetic smile, 'I think she would not be left alone all day and every night.'

Lucy was obliged to concede the point. 'I thought she might be exaggerating. Young girls naturally tend to be dramatic.'

'No, no, I have seen with my own eyes.'

'Then it's a great shame. I'm very sorry.'

'I was glad,' he told her naïvely, 'when you had occasion to speak to us this evening. You are the only other English lady in this building, and I have been living in the hope that you two would meet each other, and that she would then have a friend.'

Lucy knew the idea had never occurred to him until he uttered it (she met a number of Italians in the course of her employment at the Adelphi and was accustomed to their expansiveness), but she was none the less disposed to receive it favourably.

'If I had time to be the sort of friend she needs, you would regret perhaps that you had asked me.'

He took her meaning slowly. 'No, truly, no! I should be very happy to be prevented from misbehaving. I don't really want to do anything not *comme il faut*, you know, but there she is! Quite attractive in her way, and so young—she allows every feeling to show itself.'

'So young that her feelings are certainly extremely silly,' she would have liked to retort, but realizing that there was nothing to be gained and possibly something to lose by scoring off a young man who had obliged her, she only said, 'You are right in thinking she shouldn't be so much alone. I wish I weren't so busy, but, you know, I'm occupied at the theatre until late every night.'

'At the theatre!'

His astonishment sent a fresh wave of depression over her. 'Oh, I'm not on the stage,' she informed him with a perverse satisfaction in augmenting her own discomfiture. 'I'm the manager's assistant.'

'You Englishwomen, you are marvellous! You go everywhere and do everything.' He tried to infuse admiration into his voice, but could not conceal his distaste. 'Never, never, would one find an Italian lady, *sérieuse*, as you are, that's evident—living alone in such a city as Cairo, working in the theatre, coming home late every night without an escort. Really, it's extraordinary!'

'What danger am I in?'

'Oh, you are in no danger at all,' he admitted amiably.

'Not like our young friend who is exposed to many temptations?'

He perceived irony, and perceived also that he had been tactless. 'Ah, mademoiselle, I don't mean—I don't mean men would not—not—' He floundered helplessly. 'A pretty appearance isn't everything,' he stammered. 'Anyone can see at once, mademoiselle, your character is absolutely all that could be desired.'

Lucy found herself emitting a laugh that was almost wholly genuine: the blunder was now too abject to be painful except to the person who had made it. 'Well,' she resumed, yawning rather deliberately, for she was very tired and Vittorio seemed disposed to prolong their talk, 'I'll try to find some opportunities of getting to know Mademoiselle Constance a little better, and if I can help her I will. In the meantime you had better be good, hadn't you?'

'I shall do my best,' he replied, with a teasing, mischievous look which she supposed some women might find engaging, 'but remember, signorina, my blood is warm! I am not an Englishman.' Since he clearly had no serious intention of altering his conduct, she was left feeling a little puzzled as to his motives for so gratuitously broaching the subject.

CHAPTER 11

VITTORIO GUGLIELMI was not, as Lucy soon discovered, a person whose motives were easy to classify. An aimless and vacillating young man, he was liable to do or say anything that might be transiently suggested by his vanity, his good nature, or his need of company. He too, though nothing would have induced him to admit it, was lonely, and to increase his resources for conversation, even so unalluring a specimen of womanhood as Lucy had seemed worth cultivating.

He had been sent over from Italy a few months ago to fill a humble position in the Cairene branch of the Banco di Roma e Napoli, where, through family connections, there would probably be hopes of promotion for him later. His parents provided an allowance which enabled him to live in better circumstances than the average junior clerk, but they were not rich, and there was very little margin for pleasure. When he had taken his evening meal in a café and prolonged his stay to the last reasonable limit—his eye roaming round, sometimes not vainly, in search of companionship for an hour or a night—the only entertainment left to him was to make such friends as he could in the building where he lodged.

Lucy was not nearly so gregarious, but even for her Karnak House became a more cheerful home now that she was on sociable terms with two of her neighbours. New acquaintances, detached from the theatre yet easily accessible, turned out to be exactly what she needed to divert her thoughts from herself, her troubles, and her often uncongenial toils. The girl's youthful absorption in self-discovery, the man's natural egoism which made it a charitable exercise on his part to listen to any voice but his own, were rather an advantage than otherwise. She was politely allowed to tell her story, but not encouraged to dilate on it; they could not bring imagination to bear upon misfortunes so far outside their own experience. Genuine pity might have tempted her to dwell upon the bitterness of her lot. As it was, she kept her grievances in the background, and was the happier for it.

To Constance, at least, in this new friendship she gave much more than she got, and that in itself was pleasant and refreshing after having so long been compelled to accept obligations at the hands of others. Vehemently by the hour Constance would talk about her own opinions, prospects, moods, adventures, affections, and ambitions. She assumed unquestioningly that it must all be as engrossing to the onlooker as it was to her, and Lucy did not disillusion her. Little by little, she managed so far to project herself into the other's state of mind that she could follow the unfolding of her longings and perceptions with an interest there was no need to feign: but it was an occupation that required energy.

Vittorio made fewer demands upon the intelligence. Idle questions and random comments satisfied him perfectly; he only wished to chatter. Constance was a sincere and vital character who might be helped by kindness to find her level without too harsh a struggle: the intensity of her feelings drew one to survey her future with much hope and a little fear. Vittorio had already become all he was likely to be, a shallow, raffish, amiable, and complacent fellow.

With more regret than surprise Lucy saw that Constance was in love with him. It was normal, of course, for an impressionable young girl who was very much at a loose end to translate her awakening emotions towards manhood in general into an ardent sentiment for one man in particular. What was distressing was to watch her building up, with all the headstrong credulity of ignorance, a totally false picture of Vittorio and an absurdly idealized conception of their trivial relations.

The flirtation pursued by him in the lightest and most cynical spirit seemed to her a love affair of magnitude. The casualness of his behaviour afflicted her, but she was always ready to accept and believe his not less casual excuses. His airy good humour she took for evidence of the most brilliant wit. His typically Italian black eyes, glossy hair, and olive skin, she regarded as unique attributes.

This infatuation, new-fledged when Lucy first met her, grew by degrees obsessive. She could not long discuss anything without making some reference to Vittorio. No subject was too remote for him to be brought into it: as an example or criterion he carried unrivalled authority. Lucy could not always quench the temptation to laugh at her, but she refrained from the kind of mockery which might alienate. For the girl's own sake, she wanted not to discourage confidence.

Little trust could be placed in Vittorio: he was too fond of saying, 'I am a man of honour.' His principles were absurdly high-flown, but he could always condone his own lapses by admitting that, although honourable, he was after all 'only human'. It was pitiable, Lucy thought, for Constance, earnest, foolish, and generous as she was, to throw herself at this exasperating philanderer, who was quite capable of seducing her tonight and holding forth tomorrow on the necessity for chastity in women.

Lucy's working day did not allow her much chance of acting as duenna. At the times when Vittorio was at large in Karnak House—supposing he did not choose to seek his company elsewhere—she was in bondage at the theatre. When she returned home, Constance, who kept late hours in spite of all remonstrances, generally came to her bedroom for a talk, but in the meanwhile there had been abundant scope for indiscretions which, as his not wholly make-believe compunction waned, were likely to become progressively more serious.

She would have tried to exert the direct influence over Vittorio that he had seemed willing to allow, but he was seldom to be seen except in the presence of Constance. He was usually gone before she was about in the morning and in bed when she came home at night; for, having a great deal of prudence where his own health and comfort were concerned, he did not often stay up as late as on the occasion when Lucy had first spoken to him.

Sometimes in the beginning she had wondered whether she should find some method of suggesting to Mr. Conway that his daughter ought to be better cared for; but as she came to know something of him, she was glad that she had not endangered friendship by any measure so clearly destined to be futile.

Conway was an incarnate paradox—a bon-vivant with only the smallest capacity for enjoying life. He concentrated all his pleasures into the pleasures of the table, and beyond these and the careful accomplishment of professional tasks, he found scarcely anything that was not a burden and a bore. Even his meals, the supreme of his delights, he approached rather as a solemn ritual than a source of warmth and gaiety. He would study a menu or a wine-list as intently, as critically, as if it were a blue-print, and be equally disgusted when it fell below the standard of his requirements. He would seek out restaurants where something interesting might be drunk or eaten with as little regard for time, money, or convenience as a scientist investigating phenomena of the first importance. A real and painful indignation shook him when he saw fine food wasted on coarse appetites or cardinal rules of gastronomy flouted.

As an officer in France he had risked gun-fire to save a few bins of rare brandy, and something of that fanaticism still inspired his conduct. His bearing was ascetic rather than convivial: he despised people who took wine negligently as an accompaniment to light talking.

Yet for all his austerity he was sought after. A good-looking unattached man of forty is useful to hostesses, and when there was something to be hoped from the chef or the cellar he was capable of making himself agreeable. He was not a stranger in Egypt, and besides a fairly large circle of acquaintances made through ordinary social channels, he met a number of people of high official status, brought into contact with him through his being employed on work for the Government. He was thus engaged for at least three or four evenings a week, and he took care not to be encumbered with a daughter whom he still regarded as a schoolgirl.

Even on the nights when he had nothing in particular to do, Constance did not see much of him. He liked to dine at leisure in some restaurant of distinction. There could surely be no worse companion than a restless and untidy young female with a taste for fizzy lemonade, who bolted her food and was quite unsuccessful at concealing her impatience as he lingered over the dessert, the precious brandy, and the cigar he had looked forward to all day. It was more convenient and very much more economical to let her have her meals at a family restaurant run by the proprietor of Karnak House.

Economy must be a serious consideration to a man of moderate income who finds it necessary for his well-being to gratify the tastes of a connoisseur. When hunger had been appeased and he had returned such hospitality as it was expedient to return, Mr. Conway did not find himself in a position to supply his daughter with many of the luxuries which—as he dimly recognized—might be expected for her by those who did not understand his difficulties. Companionship, amusement, good clothes—these, as he had several times had occasion to explain to Constance, were amenities an intelligent girl ought to be able to provide for herself. A clever needlewoman could run up dresses out of almost nothing, and that in itself was an amusement, to say nothing of reading, walking, swimming, and sightseeing. He had never made any objection to her going about alone. Indeed, he thought and did not hesitate to say she would live to look back on him with gratitude for having allowed her so unusual a measure of independence.

At first—before she had become enamoured of Vittorio—not knowing how to use her empty freedom, she had begged to be given something definite to do; her father, grudgingly producing a little extra pocket-money, would tell her to *find* something to do like a sensible creature and kindly to refrain from making a nuisance of herself.

If he had foreseen his divorced wife's intention of marrying a man in Buenos Aires and leaving him irrevocably with the custody of the child, he would have taken care to arrange the legal proceedings on a very different basis. Constance was seven at the time of the rupture, a child with rat's-tail hair and an incomplete set of second teeth which appeared much too large for her mouth. There was nothing for it but to place her in a good boarding-school and count on friends and relatives to take charge of her for the holidays.

But the holidays, to his surprise and dismay, seemed to follow on each other's heels in endless succession. Constance had no sooner been bundled away for Christmas than lo! Easter was to be prepared for. Easter was hardly done with before the long implacable stretches of the summer loomed ahead. School trains to be met, mortifying inquiries to be pursued among those who might be able to give the child house-room, dreadful complexities when vacations had to be divided among two or three different families, incomprehensible inventories of clothing to be studied, letters from matrons and head-mistresses seeking to enforce upon him parental duties he considered beyond his power . . . for years the tenor of his life had been perpetually shaken by such annoyances as these. Good schools in England demanded a great deal from parents. The higher the fees, the more, it seemed, the parent was expected to do.

And then, just before the war, on a gourmet's holiday in the Perigord district, a solution of the problem had been vouchsafed to him. Why, he asked himself, had he wasted all this time and money on orthodox English schooling? An inexpensive French convent near Bordeaux, highly recommended by a wine-growing acquaintance, would take the now eleven-year-old child off his hands as completely and continuously as he could wish. Departure for the holidays was, in those days, optional; for a moderate sum clothing could be provided; and all the tiresome written and unwritten laws British preceptors make for parents might be relaxed. Foreignness alone gave a *cachet.* 'In a French convent' was a phrase to silence disapproving relations very neatly.

Constance was fetched and deposited with the nuns. Her father, a cold but not an actively cruel man, explained to her that she was being given a superb opportunity of learning French and acquiring the polish which only French methods of instruction can impart. The convent doors closed on her, not to be opened again for five years.

The war supplied him with irrefutable reasons for leaving his daughter immured. He took part in it, after a year or so of indecision, because on the whole it was a more tolerable fate to be an officer at the front than an objector of no particular conscientiousness at home, and from first to last, apart from his revulsion against dirt and ugliness, the strongest emotion he felt was on the subject of Rhine and Mosel wines, which naturally grew scarcer and dearer. His sang-froid made him a bold man and he ended with a very impressive record, such as, at that time, disposed certain influential persons to look kindly upon his merits as an architect. It was thus that, soon after resuming his ordinary activities, he succeeded in obtaining the Egyptian commission—good fortune only marred by the tiresome behaviour of Constance.

She had no sooner been told of his impending journey than he was beleaguered with a series of dismal—even agonized—letters, imploring him to remember that she was now getting on for seventeen and could not be expected to languish in the convent for ever. Her pleadings were soon reinforced by a blunt communication from the Mother Superior. Constance, she said, had been unsettled and unhappy for some time and was infecting other pupils with her own discontentment; now that Mr. Conway had returned to civilian life they would be glad to be relieved of a troublesome charge. Going to Egypt by way of Marseilles he had no choice but to pick up his vexatious and superfluous daughter *en route*.

For the first few weeks they lived in an hotel, and Constance had made an immense, excited effort to be an acceptable companion. She succeeded only in getting on his nerves even more than he let her discern. Her exuberance, her lack of poise, were most distasteful to him; her clothes appalled him, though he had never given her either means or training to be better dressed; her total ignorance of gastronomy came almost as a shock.

Discouraged, she relapsed into silent hostility. The sweets of liberty lost their savour. She looked back upon her miserable little life with despair. Cairo, that city she had longed to escape to, soon showed itself as dreary, squalid, and cruel. The heat was insupportable, and sightseeing by oneself proved to be at best only a truncated sort of pleasure. As for her hotel bedroom and her father's sitting-room, she could not imagine that the world contained any other apartments so depressing.

All this was changed by moving to Karnak House and falling in love with Vittorio. Living in the building, he imparted charm to it. Any place he had frequented or merely spoken of took on a special quality, and to wander about alone in Cairo was an occupation which might now create wistful yearning but never boredom. With new and rapturous emotions to light up her mind, all things seen were clear and memorable, all things felt were significant. The future was roseate.

This ecstasy only lasted until Vittorio had lightly forgotten one or two appointments with her (he had said something equivalent to: 'Well, see you tomorrow, I suppose!' and she had waited all evening for him, beginning tense with joyful expectation and ending abject with tears), but even after she had realized that she could not go on in the blissful spirit of first discovery, there were still occasions for elation. The shattering, unendurable truth, that Vittorio neither loved her nor wanted her to love him, remained as yet outside the regions of her understanding.

And while his presence shed enchantment over Egypt, Lucy helped her to make some practical use of the long slack hours which, before, had stretched across the day so heavily that time himself scarcely seemed able to move them.

The most profitable and by far the most interesting of the pastimes Lucy found for her was dressmaking. In the convent she had learned mending and embroidery, but the cutting and putting together of clothes was a process she had never so much as seen, far less attempted. Lucy helped her to choose a remnant and together they made a jumper. When it turned out to be wearable, her ambition leapt high and she pictured herself appearing before Vittorio in new and dazzling creations. Her pocket-money, instead of being spent on ice-creams, cinemas, and worthless trinkets, was now carefully hoarded for materials, and her father, not displeased to find her thus absorbed, added five hundred piastres to her savings.

In August the theatre was at last closed down, and Lucy, having no right to a holiday after so short a term of service, was commanded to revise an inventory of costumes belonging to the Polyglot Amusement Company. This involved a long spell of work in the rooms where the wardrobe was stored and new garments occasionally made; and the place being deserted, she took Constance with her each day and taught her how to use one of the sewing-machines. The dressmaking advanced by great strides then, and Lucy traded upon the influence she had gained to curb her pupil's unsophisticated taste and win it over from a childish love of ornament to a respect for careful grooming.

She had hoped that, while her duties in the theatre were suspended, she might have had the evenings to herself, but few of them were granted to her. Mosenthal, who in the pursuit of riches became impervious to heat and cold, had gone to Palestine to lay plans for an extension of his business there, and Daisy was even more in need of company than usual. Now that Lucy had new friends and new interests outside the theatre she sometimes found it not a little irksome to devote so much time to Daisy, but she looked upon herself nevertheless as one bound by an unwritten bargain which, if she kept it, would leave her free without obligation at the end. However greatly she might prefer to be with Constance, whose mind for all its immaturity was radically much nearer to her own, Daisy was always allowed the prior claim.

Yet, in spite of obstacles, she was able to see Constance at least for a little while every day and had the happiness of knowing that the girl's rapidly improving appearance and far more satisfactory mode of life were largely the product of her own good feeling. It remained now to prevent her from committing some irretrievable folly with or through Vittorio, and Lucy feared that task might need more skilful handling than could lie within her power.

One thing was clear. Constance was pouring out upon this vapid, trifling young Italian, not only all the quick and prodigal affection natural to adolescence, but also the unspent store of love that had been so long rejected by her father and mother. It would be a difficult and delicate matter to stem the tide of such a passion.

CHAPTER 12

ONE MONDAY night towards the end of September, Lucy, who happened for once to be free, invited Constance to go with her to a restaurant where there was an orchestra. Constance, by now desperately puzzled and miserable over Vittorio's caprices, was accustomed to spend her evenings hanging about Karnak House so as not to miss the slightest chance of being in his company; and he, secretly bored by her naïve devotion, had taken to whiling away as much time as possible elsewhere. Lucy tried in vain to represent how bad a policy it was to be always, unasked for, at his beck and call, but she was seldom able to cajole her protégée into risking the loss of even the briefest and most unsatisfactory meeting. Occasionally, however, he was considerate enough to let her know beforehand that he would be otherwise engaged, and then Lucy would take her to the theatre and give her a seat in one of the empty boxes. Tonight brought one of their very rare opportunities of an outing together.

Her mind fixed tenaciously on the problem of Vittorio's conduct, Constance was not in the liveliest of humours. But Lucy had been working at her accounts that afternoon, and had decided that she might safely hope to be in England for Christmas: careful saving for another five or six weeks should see her through, and the knowledge that she might now set a definite term to her exile made her feel happy enough to conquer unhappiness in others. She was resolved to have a heartening talk with her companion before the evening was over.

As Lucy chose a table at a suitable distance from the music, Constance's eyes were eagerly scanning the whole room.

'Vittorio sometimes comes here, I think,' she murmured nonchalantly when they had settled down and given their order.

'Well, he won't tonight, my pet, because he distinctly said he'd been asked to dinner at the bank manager's.'

'Yes, I just thought they might look in for some music afterwards. You never know.'

'My dear child, the bank manager has a comfortable home and a comfortable family. Why should he bring his guest to hear a café orchestra? Please get it into your head that there isn't anything more unlikely. Otherwise I shall have a thoroughly boring time watching you watching the door.'

'I suppose I *am* tiresome and silly,' Lucy always found her sudden generous candour rather touching. 'Oh, lord, I'm so *awfully* in love with him!'

'Con, you could get over it if you took yourself in hand.'

'No, I couldn't, never, never! Not as long as I live! He's the only man who could ever matter to me, Lucy. It's the real thing this time.'

'This time! Anyone would think you'd been having a long succession of love affairs.'

'I've been in love before in a sort of fashion. Of course it was nothing at all compared with this.'

'Do you mean the good-looking elocution teacher?'

'Yes, we were all mad about him for weeks and weeks, and the others were terribly jealous when he gave me two recitations to do at our concert. And he wasn't the only one. There was a man in the boat coming over—the second officer.'

'You've told me about him too.'

'I thought he was simply glorious. But, you see, I forgot about him in a few days.'

'What makes you so sure you won't forget Vittorio?'

'Oh, but it's different, positively, absolutely, utterly different. Do you imagine I could ever kiss another man after kissing him?'

'Certainly you could, and you will. Now don't look so outraged, Constance. I know more about such matters than you'd believe.'

'Oh, Lucy, you wouldn't speak like that if you'd been in love—really in love. You just couldn't!'

'My dear, I've been in love, real love and false love, quite as much as it's good for anyone to be.'

'Real love *must* last for ever. That's the whole point of it.'

'Some of my love will last for ever, Con dear, and some is as dead as a whole barrel of doornails. The trouble is that, at the time, one can't possibly tell the one kind from the other, so it behoves one to go rather carefully. Do you know what I think is the difference between the real thing and the false thing?'

'Well, what?' said Constance defensively.

'The false thing is what you think about a person who happens to come your way when you're lonely, and needing to love somebody, as everyone does most of the time, and you're so glad to have an object for all the emotion you've got pent up inside you that you deliberately *let* yourself be carried away. You want to love so much that you insist on believing the person is everything you'd like him to be, and afterwards, when you begin to find out he isn't, you can't bring yourself to admit it and you love him more than ever out of defiance; but, in a way you hate him too and want to punish him. Real love isn't defiant at all. It only comes when you meet a person who'd always be congenial, always attract you and please you even if there were fifty others to choose from—a person you'd like and get on with wherever you came across him. That's the difference . . . only it takes so long to tell which is which.'

At the sight of their waiter approaching with a tray, Lucy paused. The picture of Vittorio was gone from her mind, and in its place she saw Henry, her charming friend, her impetuous darling, lost for ever but always to be loved. She gazed about her at the marble-topped tables and the shoddy-looking crowd. How queer to have travelled so far from Henry's compact and graceful little world, softly lighted, full of sweet smells and things pleasant to see and touch, and leisure to enjoy them. Henry himself, trudging along the sodden roads of Flanders, had scarcely travelled farther. And he had been able to go back; all had been kept in readiness for him. Against herself, with every claim to a passport gone, the door was now fast closed and likely to remain so.

The waiter had set down their refreshments and hurried away, and Constance, with a not very convincing attempt to sound sweetly reasonable, was venturing upon her reply:

'Vittorio would always be congenial, and I should have fallen in love with him no matter how many there'd been to choose from.

Honestly I should. You only see the—sort of—ordinary, unromantic side of him. You don't know how fascinating he is when we're alone together.'

'At the risk of making you very cross, Con, I'm going to say, it isn't so much Vittorio who's fascinating as what he stands for.'

'What *does* he stand for?'

'For "love and kisses", my child. Very useful and important things, and if we can't get them from the right people we generally try the wrong ones. I don't say that isn't better than nothing, but we ought to be cautious.'

'Lucy, Lucy! How can you speak in such a horrible, cynical, beastly way!' The natural vehemence of her tone could no longer be suppressed. 'I don't agree with one single word you've said, not one word. One knows about love by instinct. You've got to believe your instincts, haven't you?'

'Yours tell you that no other man in the world is ever going to do for you—only Vittorio. I wonder how they've found out?'

'Don't you believe in God, Lucy?'

'For heaven's sake, child! You're not going to tell me God has ordained that you should have a crush on Vittorio?'

Constance, looking injured but patient, was about to give an answer when the orchestra produced some admonitory chords, and they both glanced up to see what was happening on the platform. A young man of extraordinary plainness had made his way to the front and was timidly clearing his throat and twisting a sheet of music in restless fingers. His lack of every kind of attraction combined with his harassed and amateurish bearing made it astonishing to Lucy that he had succeeded in obtaining a professional engagement even in so humble a sphere as this: but when the ordeal of a twice-played introduction was over and he released his voice, his whole manner underwent a change, and his very appearance seemed improved. At any rate, he squared his drooping shoulders and threw back his head so that the light glowed kindly on his ill-made features.

His song was not good music but he sang it with enough energy and earnestness to numb the critical faculties both of himself and most of the audience. It was a rousing, masculine ballad of the type which had enjoyed a great vogue during the War. The first verses were full of the specious vigour which can only be rendered in a loud voice; then came a pathetic stanza to be delivered nearly *sotto voce* and with lingering slowness, and then a swift return to virile cheerfulness. A vast, ringing, protracted note to end with brought a very fair measure of applause.

He relapsed for a moment into a sheepish attitude, but when the orchestra was launched upon a new introduction, he once more gathered courage from some inward source, and in soft, mellifluous tones, with a good deal too much 'expression' conveyed at a deplorably slow tempo, he began:

> 'Dusk and the shadows falling
> O'er land and sea . . .'

Then his voice swelled to a great gust of triumph:

> 'Somewhere a voice is calling,
> Calling to me.'

There was a reprise; softer than ever and this time with almost embarrassing wistfulness he repeated the whole statement.

Lucy knew the song well, but tonight it sounded quite unfamiliar, and suddenly she felt an intense, distressing pity for the singer. He had become the symbol of yearning loneliness, the visible representative of all the unbeautiful, unwanted members of the human race. Here he was, vainly, absurdly, endeavouring to console himself, to hide the bitter wounds that would never, never be healed. There was no voice calling to him. No eyes tried to hold the image of his face. The lover, full of passion and tenderness, whose shape he struggled, by honeyed cadences, to evoke, was a figment of his frustrated dreams.

'Oh, dear!' she thought, all her good spirits evaporating. 'Suppose I should remain as I am now? Suppose I should have to compensate myself with imaginary voices calling? Could anything be worse than becoming a woman with yearnings!'

The song was over, and the young man, bowing clumsily in response to a mild and sporadic demonstration of enthusiasm, retreated from the platform. The little orchestra rearranged itself to play without a soloist.

'Good heavens!' cried Lucy, seeing the pianist rise to hand some sheets of music to one of the other performers. *'Good heavens! Can I believe my eyes?'

'Why, what is it?'

'My dear, that's Eugene Pryor! He used to be our conductor.'

'Which do you mean? The fat one—the pianist?'

Lucy nodded and then gave a sigh of fervent compassion. 'What an awful come-down for a man of his gifts!'

Constance leaned round their table as far as she could to get another glimpse of him, for sitting down he was concealed from their view by the piano.

'Didn't he leave Egypt with the rest of your company then?'

'He wasn't with the company at all when we came here. He stayed behind in Singapore. Well, to tell you the truth, we had to come away without him. He was always getting tight, and once or twice he let down the show pretty badly. Poor old Eugene! When he was sober he was the most cultured, most charming person you could wish to meet, but when he started on a bout of drinking, he became simply a different creature.'

'He looks sober enough tonight.'

'Yes, but that's one of the oddest things about Eugene—you can't tell from his manner, only from what he does. His speech doesn't alter at all, except when he's absolutely at the passing-out stage, and he never staggers about or anything like that. The only change is in his character. When he's himself he's a thoroughly nice man; when he drinks he just goes bad.'

'How?'

"Oh, all sorts of ways. Money matters chiefly. He did down every member of the company at one time or another.'

'Are you going to talk to him?'

'I'd like to. Do you mind?'

'Of course I don't. I was only thinking that if he did down every member of the company, he probably did you down too.'

'I've forgiven him,' said Lucy with a smile, and for the sake of renewing a contact made in happier days, she resolved to forget how gladly, at this moment, she would receive back the fifty rupees lent to him on their Indian tour—ostensibly to be cabled to a mother in distress, in reality, as she afterwards learned, to purchase a new hat for a barmaid who was treating him with favour.

As soon as there was an interval, she sent a waiter to him with a note. He hurried eagerly to their table, and, although for a painful second or two he was completely silenced to see her so much changed, he managed to find words for a cordial greeting. She told her story summarily, but he was sensitive enough to deduce much of what she left undescribed, and his sympathy was quick and convincing.

'And what of you?' she demanded, when she had rounded off her swift précis. 'Tell me about yourself.'

'Just what you'd expect, my dear. I've been travelling steadily downwards until I am where you see me. Is there anything more to say?'

She had not intended to call forth such frankness, and thinking it might be unfair to encourage him to speak intimately in the presence of a stranger, she countered with a non-committal inquiry: 'Is it long since you arrived?'

'Three weeks. Our Indian Empire was growing a little too hot to hold me, and I managed to raise a ticket to Port Said.'

Seeing he was in no mood for reticence, but was rather disposed to castigate himself by giving publicity to his weaknesses, she said mildly, 'Then you still persist in doing things you hate, Eugene?'

'An hereditary curse, my dear. I get it from my father.' With a quick gesture he raised an imaginary glass to his lips.

'But Eugene, *must* you behave like your father?'

'So I ask myself, and sometimes for weeks on end I manage to believe I needn't, but after a while back I slip into the old rut.' He glanced at them both with a quick, ironically beaming smile. 'I know it's very weak of me, but if you only realized what an effort it costs not to be in that rut all the time!'

While he revealed himself thus, Constance sat gazing at him with an interest which actually banished Vittorio from her mind for several minutes together. For one thing she had never met a self-confessed drunkard, or indeed any sort of drunkard, before, and it made one feel very adult indeed to be admitted to such a conversation as this; for another, Eugene Pryor was an impressive and curious person even without his claim to attention as a profligate.

It was odd, for instance, for a young man, or at any rate a youngish man, to be so decidedly fat, and still more odd for a decidedly fat man to look neither ungainly nor heavy. It was as if he were a mere façade of *embonpoint* without real substance; he reminded her almost ludicrously of one of those vast inflated figures made of rubber which appeared in French carnival processions. Again, it was odd that such small features should inhabit so large a face. The eyes, it was true, were enormous—great, shiny dark eyes with an expression of stillness and sadness that suddenly changed to luminous vivacity: but the fine, pointed nose and the delicate mouth with its little sharp-looking teeth, seemed to have been made for a thin person. And one expected fleshy faces to be ruddy or perhaps unwholesomely pallid, but his was brown, a deep sailor-like brown, and his hands were the same.

He talked, as one would expect from the shape of his mouth, delicately. The words came clear and rounded from his lips: his voice was beautiful, smooth, compelling. Altogether, considering his disabilities as a fat man and an addict of vice, he created a singularly attractive effect. She was quite sorry when he rose and prepared to go back to the reassembling orchestra.

'Shall I be able to find you here again?' asked Lucy, who had prudently decided not to remind him that she was accessible at the theatre.

'Oh, yes, indeed, but I must see more of you tonight. We've only just begun to talk.'

'What time do you finish?'

'At midnight generally; at ten on Mondays. Can't we do something afterwards? I'm told I ought to see the Sphinx by moonlight. Youve done that lots of times, I suppose?'

'Not even once. I saw it by daylight when the company was here, and never since that time.'

'Let's go then!'

'Can we get back? Do the trains run so late?'

'Oh, come, we can materialize a taxi between us,' he answered airily; and without waiting for her reply he hurried to the platform.

Lucy turned to her companion. 'How do you feel about it, Con? Have *you* seen the Sphinx by moonlight?'

'No, but I think I ought to be getting home.'

'Why, pray?'

'Well, I—my father—I sort of—'

'My good child, we told your father you were going out with me, and he doesn't care a button. And don't say you're tired and want to go to bed, because you've never yet been known to get tired.' As Constance was silent and looked sulky, Lucy pressed on with a warmth which sprang from her sympathy not less than her conviction: 'Oh, darling, you must—you honestly must get it into your head that it simply puts Vittorio off to know that every single night you're going to be there, waiting for him. Do try and have a little faith in me! I only speak like this because I'm fond of you. If I didn't care for you, what would it matter to me how foolishly you behave?'

Constance's face gave evidence of a struggle which brought her to the verge of tears. Then she said dismally: 'I know it's foolish, but I can't help it. I can't stop. Every morning I say to myself, "Today I'm going to keep out of his way. I won't go near him—I'll just wait and see if he comes to me." But somehow or other, when he doesn't come, I've just *got* to see him. I can't live unless I see him.' Lucy stretched out her hand, and in an affectionate gesture turned the girl's averted head towards her: 'Tonight you're going to see the Sphinx instead and let Vittorio get to bed in peace for once. Remember, he has his work to do every day, and all this kissing business at night is more of a strain than you probably realize.'

'I understand what you mean.' Constance stared at the tablecloth, frowning intently. 'Lucy, if I were to ask your advice about something would you give it me *properly*? I mean as if I were really a friend of yours? Or would you treat me as a dear little girl in her 'teens who mustn't be led astray?'

'I should certainly be honest with you. Why not?'

'Most people think it's wrong, somehow, to tell you about things frankly until you're so old that you've had heaps of experience and don't want telling anyway.' She picked up a lump of sugar in the tongs and dropped it back into the bowl from a height which made its arrival a little precarious. 'What I want to know is this. Does it make a man care more for you to let him be really and truly your lover, or does it make him care less? Of course, we're always told that once two people have gone that far together, it's all finished from the woman's point of view, and the man will simply look down on her and have no further use for her at all. But even a convent girl of seventeen may know enough to make her wonder if that isn't just a feeble story invented to keep us out of mischief. What do you think, seriously?'

The portentous nature of the question held Lucy speechless for a moment, and Constance, giving her a quick sideways glance, dropped another lump of sugar and missed the basin.

'I think'—Lucy took the tongs firmly out of her fingers—'that it depends entirely on the individuals concerned, and on their moral outlook, and the kind of upbringing they've had, and a hundred other things.'

'Oh, Lucy, you're going to be vague! I wish you wouldn't.'

'Do you suppose your question can be answered with a downright yes or no? On the whole—though I dare say I should be considered a dangerous person for saying this—it seems to me that most men do care more about a woman when they've really been lovers, but then there has to be a fair degree of love to begin with.'

'Do you mean love on his side, Lucy? Wouldn't it do if she loved *him*—enough to give him everything?'

The stagy words, so earnestly spoken, gave Lucy a most uncomfortable twinge. 'Is Vittorio asking you to give him everything?' she inquired gently.

'No, not in so many words, but he says things which make me so afraid I'll lose him if I don't. Last week he was out every night, as you know, and when I spoke to him about it this afternoon—I couldn't help crying because he seemed so horribly unkind!—he explained that it was impossible to go on for ever making love without anything happening except kisses. He said it was childish. He said it was like a pendulum swinging without a clock.'

Lucy smiled. 'But he didn't ask you to provide a clock?'

'Not exactly. Still, I know he would ask me if I managed things differently.'

'Perhaps he would. I hope you won't be so silly as to put any more temptation in his way. Vittorio is not at all the sort of person who'd love you more afterwards.'

'Why do you say that?'

Lucy could not bear to tell her the unadulterated truth, that she was forcing herself upon a man who was already restive under the burden of her blind and hungry emotion. She compromised by replying: 'He was bred in the Latin tradition that a woman who is no longer pure is unfit to marry and as good as ruined. Given sufficient encouragement, I've no doubt he could quite easily get rid of all his scruples, but in a few hours you may be sure they'd come trooping back, and then he'd feel guilty towards you, dreadfully guilty . . . and that's the worst method of making anyone love you that you can possibly imagine.'

'There might be some way of getting him not to feel guilty.' Beneath Constance's meek tone there was an undercurrent of strong resistance.

'It would be better not to take the risk. Believe me, Con, it is a risk, even in the year 1919.'

'But, Lucy, I love Vittorio! Risks don't count when you love someone.'

'Why ask my advice if you've made up your mind? Most people would have talked sanctimonious drivel to you because you're young and need looking after; but I spoke exactly as I would have done to any friend of my own age. And all I find is that you haven't the slightest intention of listening to a single word.'

She stopped short, surprised at her own irritability. Ever since her illness she had been afflicted with a tendency to give way suddenly to fits of bad temper with no very tangible provocation. She must take herself in hand: there had been one or two occasions at the theatre lately which had left a certain residue of ill-feeling.

'I'm sorry,' she said, laying her arm across Constance's shoulder. 'That's a ridiculous exaggeration. Don't take any notice of it!'

Tm sorry also,' Constance returned in a puzzled and humble voice. 'I talk too much about Vittorio and it gets on your nerves. It would get on anybody's. Now, Lucy, if I say another word about him until we've seen the Sphinx, you must throw something heavy at me.'

Lucy pleasantly agreed to do so.

Chapter 13

Eugene discovered, or decided, that it would only be a little more expensive to hire a car for their whole excursion than to go to Giza by train and return by taxi; and although Lucy would have been glad to husband her money, she felt she could not quibble on such an occasion as this. A bargain was struck, and they set off with the luxurious sensation, rare to all of them, of being idle tourists for whose entertainment had been preserved the wonders and beauties of the world.

The conversation was of England. Lucy's homesickness had infected Eugene, and he professed himself almost as eager to get back as she was. It was his one chance of permanent reform: from one's native soil, he said, one drew a certain self-respect never vouchsafed to the uprooted. It was much easier to 'go to pieces' in exotic surroundings and among strangers. He spoke of his temptations with unaffected candour.

He was in a less pessimistic frame of mind now than when they had met in the café. Lucy's firmness in tackling misfortune had put new heart into him, and he was inspired to emulation. If he could maintain his present sobriety, why should not he too save his travelling expenses within a few months? Once home he would be prepared to defy even the laws of heredity. After all, he had never drunk recklessly until he had become a wanderer.

They both urged him to make England his goal and not to weaken, Constance adding her persuasions to Lucy's, since he seemed to treat her likewise as a sympathetic friend rather than a stranger. He had an amiable way of reposing trust in the kindness and understanding of almost everyone he met who was not absolutely unfriendly, but Constance supposed he had recognized her as a particularly tolerant and enlightened person and was flattered.

A queer discussion ensued which again ousted Vittorio from her thoughts. Eugene told them the method by which, sometimes for weeks on end, he managed to remain temperate. He was safe, he explained, so long as he drank no spirits. Total abstinence was too irksome to persist in for more than a day or so together, but by taking only pure, unfortified wine he could enjoy the pleasures of drinking without the penalties of drunkenness. Danger began for him with wines that contained brandy, and he was therefore obliged to close his mind rigidly against the attractions of sherry, port, or champagne. As for brandy itself and all other frankly spirituous liquors, they exercised nothing less than an evil magic over him. Invariably at the first sip some control within him snapped, and he was not only under a compulsion to continue drinking until forcibly restrained, but became, he admitted, perfectly numb to ethical considerations which normally would mean as much to him as to anyone.

Moonlight and the rays of street-lamps shining into their taxi revealed his eyes, still and sombre, as he described with a kind of detached regretfulness, like one surveying the doings of some other person nearly related to him but beyond his influence, a few of the nefarious acts he had committed during his lapses. But he brightened again as Lucy reminded him that he could and must return to his own country where, being only thirty-three, he might still contrive to re-knit the broken threads of his career.

As they drew up at the edge of the desert a swarm of native guides, vendors, and beggars sprang from the sand like so many dirty jack-in-the-boxes and obscured their view of the pyramids. It cost them several minutes of united and strenuous effort to make it clear that they had no intention of hiring donkeys or dragomans, or of purchasing stamps, postcards, beads, carpets, or pseudo-Oriental curios; and even after they had induced the frustrated horde to let them pass, they had repeatedly to turn round and implore two or three who were more tenacious than the rest to desist from following them.

'Do these fellows never go to bed?' cried Eugene when they had moved off as quickly as their feet, impeded by the soft, deep sand, could carry them. 'Are they in waiting here at any hour of the night or day to spoil it for everyone who comes? I think they must belong to the underworld—the ghosts of the slaves who built these things by forced labour, and now they haunt the scene for ever and destroy half its grandeur. That would be poetic justice.'

'Wouldn't it be poetic justice of a much better kind,' said Lucy, 'if they were the ghosts of the kings and rulers who compelled the wretched slaves to build for them?'

They all looked towards the Pyramid of Cheops, its vast outline, so familiar, yet so strange, looming up against a sky resplendent with stars and moon.

'However often one came here,' she went on after a silence, 'I believe the pyramids would always be bigger than one had remembered. Don't you find there's something rather terrifying about them?'

'I find there's everything terrifying about them—their size, their age, their history as far as we can guess it, and even their purpose. After all, they're tombs, and this whole place is a stupendous cemetery.'

'Do stop talking about ghosts and tombs and cemeteries!' Constance pleaded with a half-genuine shudder. 'I feel quite creepy enough as it is!' An instant later she caught her breath in wholly unfeigned alarm. An evil-looking beggar who had been hobbling after them had plucked her by the sleeve. Lucy commanded him in Arabic to cease from molesting them, but Eugene found it more efficacious to warn him off with a few piastres, and they made their way without further disturbance towards the hollow where the great stone beast of the desert lay crouching, a broken temple between its paws.

'When one reads Marmaduke Pickthall,' Eugene remarked with a backward glance, 'one gets quite a lovable impression of cadging Orientals. To us they seem the lowest dregs of humanity, considerably viler than savages, but after a little course of Pickthall, one is prepared to admit that, judged by their own standards, they may not be so loathsome. He even makes us see, in a dim sort of fashion, how reasonably they might dislike *us*.'

Neither Lucy nor Constance had ever heard of Marmaduke Pickthall, nor could they, at that moment, imagine any virtue in books which represented Egyptian extortioners in a favourable light. Eugene passed pliantly on to the subject of Herodotus, and what he had written twenty-three centuries ago of the marvels that now surrounded them, already more than two thousand years old at the time of his coming. They listened to this respectfully and with pleasure, for Eugene had an agreeable and unpretentious way of imparting information.

At last, after a short but fatiguing walk, they reached a point of vantage, and sat down to shake the sand out of their shoes. The moon was brilliant, but the face and breast of the Sphinx were in the shadow. It seemed to carry its own darkness and to throw darkness about it. The rigid yet easy poise of its head, the restful attitude of its body, gave it an air of superb indifference to the motions of men and nature alike. A party of white-clad guides and tourists standing beneath one of its shoulders looked as evanescent as snowflakes.

'I think,' said Lucy, 'the Sphinx is more impressive than the pyramids—than even the Great Pyramid—although it doesn't begin to compare in size. It's odd, isn't it, that it should be so awfully impressive when it's dwarfed by another monument quite close by.'

'No,' returned Eugene, 'I don't see it as odd. The Great Pyramid is a mathematical construction—I nearly said a mathematical abstraction, for it hardly seems like a real object—but the Sphinx has a sort of inhuman "human interest" which excites the imagination. Whose brain conceived it? What man or what mood does it represent? What is written on its face? Contempt for mankind? Or pride in mankind? Or nothing?' Lucy and Constance, deferentially mute, encouraged him to proceed. 'The pyramids are very magnificent, but they have no features, no posture. The human attributes of the Sphinx give us at least an illusion of personality, and since it is so immense and so old, the personality seems immense too and full of the wisdom of antiquity. We can't believe we're looking at mere lifeless rock without opinion or feeling of any kind. We think, "Surely there is a spirit there that sees and knows and could answer our riddles!" It becomes a symbol of all spirit—in fact, of all mysterious power, of Fate itself. And one goes on questioning: "Is it friendly? Is it hostile? Is it ruthless? Is it benevolent? *What* is it essentially?"'

'It is sphinkies,' said an unctuous voice immediately behind him. 'Sphinkies five t'ousand years old.'

They wheeled round, angry and a little frightened. A group of Arabs had performed the customary desert miracle of rising, to all appearances, out of the ground. The foremost of them was a guide, who immediately, without waiting for any evidence that his services were desired, began to regale them with disjointed fragments of information in a feverishly cajoling manner. 'Sphinkies buildy by Chephren. Him come after Cheops. Chephren buildy also Second Pyramid—him there where you look. Cheops buildy Great Pyramid, biggest pyramid everywhere in world, and many other tomb what I go show you.'

Eugene interrupted him with numerous injunctions to begone, and Lucy, whose vocabulary of Arabic was small but useful, assured him vigorously that they would neither listen to him nor pay him. Lucy's intervention made the native bystanders laugh, partly because her speech contained some amusing mistakes, partly because by using this particular species of Arabic at all, she showed that she was a resident and that their friend, the guide, had drawn a blank.

But the guide, only a shade daunted, turned the whole battery of his wheedling supplications upon Constance. 'Missy, you want I should make sphinkies to smile? Yes, please! Only ten piastre. Please, missy, you tell me make sphinkies to smile!'

His companions, hearing what he was about, took up the cry, and Eugene's indignant requests that they should go away were quite lost among the tumult of voices.

Lucy found the required number of piastres in her bag, and nodded her consent to the guide. She had just realized what he wanted to do, and as the din subsided she turned to the others with an explanation. 'He has a strip of magnesium wire, and he's going to light up the Sphinx's face. It seems a bit sacrilegious, but I've heard it's something to remember.'

They stepped forward, away from their Egyptian cohort. A light flared up, effulgent but with no warmth of tone; a light fantastically, dazzlingly silver which rose in a great beam across the Sphinx's bosom, neck, and chin. It travelled upward swiftly, but yet, as it seemed, pausing to awaken life in each feature separately. As the darkness ebbed from the cheeks, there was an effect of movement. A cold and fleeting smile played upon the scarred lips; the eyes appeared to give forth rather than reflect a glow of silver fire. The mutilated nose which, in daylight, was an ugly reproach to the destructiveness of men and time now took on a kind of integrity with the whole face. The cruel gashes, veiled by moving shadows, could no longer mock the beauty of the mouth and brow. A king, an artist, and some labourers had triumphed over five thousand years, and one saw only what they had meant to show.

The frosty radiance died. For a few wildly unnatural seconds it had shamed the moon, and the night seemed black by contrast. The natives, who had been politely silent during the spectacle, broke into noisy chatter. Encouraged by Lucy's weakening, they suggested other diversions—fortune-telling, a visit by candlelight to the interior of the Great Pyramid. The English party, stoutly refusing, endeavoured to depart, but it turned out that more than ten piastres must change hands before they could be allowed to do so. *Baksheesh* must be paid to the boy who had provided matches to light the magnesium wire, *baksheesh* again to the boy who had actually struck the effective match, and yet a little extra *baksheesh* to the young man who had interposed his form between the flame and the breeze. With no very good grace they distributed some small coins to equally dissatisfied recipients and made their escape.

'I am more than ever convinced,' said Eugene, 'that those are evil spirits. I should be far from sorry if they all returned to hell. What say you?'

Lucy did not answer, and he turned at once to Constance and began to talk to her of what they had seen. Lucy did not answer because it had occurred to her as a very curious and fearful thing that, day upon day, night upon night, year after year, and age upon age of time, that massive face, that brooding monster, stared over the desert with sightless eyes, unchanging, unwearying, and immovable. There it was in the scorching sunlight, there it was in the drenching rains. It had been there for thousands of years before she was born: it would remain there no doubt thousands of years after she was dead. When she lay in her bed at night she would think of it crouching between the city and the desert untroubled by hot winds laden with sand, impassive beneath skies filled with thunder. When she was rejoicing, when she was sorrowing, in all moments when her emotions made her believe herself important, she would think of it—such was her transient but painful impression—as it had looked in that bath of pallid light, when she and her companions had seemed like little insects not worth the trouble of brushing away.

CHAPTER 14

DAISY WAS anything but pleased to hear that Eugene had turned up in Cairo as the pianist of a café orchestra. On the contrary, she speedily acknowledged her determination to avoid him, and begged Lucy not to be so foolish as to become mixed up with him in any way. She pooh-poohed the idea of his reformation, cited various instances of his abortive attempts in the past, and recalled how everyone who had come into contact with him had sooner or later been cheated. Lucy listened doubtfully and ended by saying that she saw and fully appreciated Daisy's point of view—for Mosenthal would certainly frown upon her association with a character so disreputable—but that she herself had better behave as kindness seemed to demand. She had no time and no wish to see Eugene very frequently, but an occasional meeting for talk and sightseeing would be enjoyable for her and perhaps encouraging to him.

Secretly Daisy looked upon her friend's behaviour as not only imprudent but inconsiderate. She could not forget that she and Siegfried had a proprietary right over Lucy, who was surely not entitled to consort with persons they disapproved of. More unquestioningly even than Siegfried himself, she regarded his employees as being virtually his possessions, and in Lucy's case ownership was strengthened by great personal obligations. It was most improper of her to insist upon going about with an acquaintance whom Daisy, on his behalf, found so undesirable. But she did not represent this aspect of the matter to Lucy, because she wanted to remain agreeable and there were more important things to talk about.

Siegfried had thrown her into a state of glorious confusion. Suddenly, of his own initiative, without even furtive promptings, he had expressed the opinion that she ought to divorce her husband, and on being reminded that she was hampered by ignorance of his whereabouts, he had brusquely commanded her to interview a certain solicitor, who would instruct a brother solicitor in Australia to set on foot the necessary investigations. It would be costly, but it was worth doing. He had thought out the whole procedure and had already taken legal advice.

What could this portend except a leaning towards matrimony? She did not ask the question of Siegfried himself, for she knew that the smallest suspicion of an attempt to make him commit himself would bring about immediate resistance, but she engaged Lucy in discussion of the topic down to its least detail day after day for hours on end. Never had her confidante proved such a useful safety-valve.

The problem of where and how Hugh MacLowrie would be traced and in what manner the negotiations for divorce were to be conducted was as nothing compared with the ever-present mystery of Siegfried's intentions. Sometimes he referred to the future as if he clearly expected to have her at his side, no matter how distant the date, and this she took to be a very good augury for marriage: but he never made any sort of proposal and never gave any reason why she should be divorced except that it was a nuisance to be tied up by law to a bounder whom, with luck, she would never see again. There was one unutterably depressing evening when he spoke at length about the sacred integrity of the Jewish people and roundly stated that it was wrong for Jews to marry Gentiles. But a few days later he wrote his lawyer a substantial cheque for the expenses of private inquiry agents in Australia; and it seemed out of the question that this could be sheer disinterested kindness. Her spirits rose: they reflected her imagined prospects like a barometer.

Strange as it might seem to Lucy, Daisy passionately longed to become the wife of Mosenthal. The reasons were manifold. For one, she was in love with him, for another, he was rich and strongly determined to be a great deal richer, and his money would reflect its splendour on her more brilliantly if they were married. But above all, he could open the way to a mode of living she had never known in anything like security, and which now she found time to hanker after constantly. He could give her respectability, set her up in a fine house with servants to manage, and guests to be impressed, and they would have children.

Yes, they would have children. He would never consider married love proper or complete without them, and neither, for the matter of that, would she. An exceedingly maternal woman, she could scarcely see even the least attractive baby without exclaiming on its sweetness, and it was certain that she would find any offspring of her own adorable. But even if sentiment had been lacking, she would still have desired to produce children. They conferred solidity upon a household. Where the financial position was sound, they could be a great social asset. She looked down a vista of years and saw her highly eligible family in demand among the best circles of Cairo, those circles which, at present, ignored not only her existence, but what was very much more remarkable, Siegfried's.

Of course, this was taking a long view, but when the present is monotonous, the future grows wonderfully vivid. Daisy, though still sensible of her good fortune, was undeniably bored. The novelty had nearly worn off those luxuries which had afforded her active pleasure six months ago—the clothes, the expensive scents and trinkets, the absence of any need for plans and contrivances to make ends meet: and it had been a painful disappointment that the range of her acquaintance was hardly wider now than at the beginning. There was a dinner from time to time with visiting artistes or some financier whom Siegfried had a reason for entertaining; there were occasional concerts which she attended because they were a means of seeing and being seen by the *élite*; and there were the various social functions to which one could obtain an entry by buying tickets, though Siegfried was not very often persuaded to escort her to these. But when she had enjoyed every amusement within her reach, the weeks as a whole slipped by colourless and, but for Lucy, sequestered.

And as, earlier on, she had imagined that nothing could be lacking for happiness if only her lover would desire her enough to keep her with him in Egypt, so now she felt assured that the dignity of marriage was the one solvent for all discontentments. If they were married, Siegfried, with his patriarchal training, would unquestionably wish to become domesticated, and she knew him well enough by this time to be quite sure that he would establish his home on a grand scale or not at all. In spite of the many months which, at the most optimistic reckoning, were bound to elapse before she could obtain a divorce, already her heart was fixed upon a magnificent house where she would preside as the accomplished and admired châtelaine. She never doubted that once in possession of marriage lines she would be found an acceptable member of any society she might desire to enter.

Siegfried did not yet occupy that station in the world to which as a potential captain of industry he was entitled. She would change all that. When—and, naturally, if—they were married, she would cajole him, for the sake of their children, into taking such steps as might be requisite to win favour with the higher notabilities of Egypt. And life would become full of glittering activities.

This was the ultimate end of her ambition, her rosy dream, the vision which lighted up her obscure existence. But though her conversations with Lucy were now largely composed of speculations about the outlook for marriage, she never gave any very precise description of the shape it had assumed in her mind, because it is not easy to admit, even to one's best friend, even to oneself, that one proposes to embark upon a career of social climbing.

CHAPTER 15

NEITHER Lucy nor Eugene had caught more than a superficial glimpse of the Arab quarter, that network of ancient and decaying byways which were highways until, with the street known as the Mousky, Napoleonic methods of expansion pierced them through and thrust them into the background.

Lucy, with two or three other members of the company, had been taken round by a guide on her first arrival in the city. They had admired various mosques, and rested in a delightful courtyard where there appeared to be an open-air school for religious youths, had listened with rambling attention to such names, dates, and historical details as the guide chose to give them, and had made the usual comments among themselves on picturesque squalor, Oriental indifference to progress, and the fact that it was all very, very interesting and quite a wonderful experience. On other occasions they had paid visits to the bazaars behind the mosque of El Ghury, coming away laden with presents for their friends and families. But having travelled much in India and China, they were in truth a little glutted with the marvels of the East, and felt no temptation to penetrate farther into the medieval town.

It would, in any case, have been highly dangerous to do so at that period, for the disquiet among the natives had been great enough to keep some thousands of British troops on the *qui vive*, and tactful Europeans confined their footsteps to the beaten track.

As for Eugene, he had not seen even as much as Lucy. He had landed at Port Said drunk, had spent his first two or three days painfully achieving sobriety, and had then been compelled to devote his whole attention to the very pressing business of earning his living. Luckily, his personality and talents had made his search a brief one, but the job he found kept him occupied either rehearsing or performing the greater part of every day, and he was seldom free except during those hot hours when even the Egyptians try to stay indoors.

But within three weeks after their unlooked-for meeting they found an opportunity of making another excursion. By a coincidence they were both free from the early evening onwards. Not only was there nothing to do at the theatre, but a part of Eugene's café had been taken over for the annual dinner of a club, and the chairman wanted no music to disturb the proceedings.

They decided to ramble without a guide through old Cairo, and soon after dusk strolled away together down one of those long drab streets, seamed with tramlines, in which the city abounds—a straggling, apathetic street with no particular character either of Orient or Occident, but blending the ugliest features of both.

'You thought best to leave your young friend at home this time?' said Eugene, taking her arm with a gesture that managed to be at once intimate and neutral. 'You were probably wise. They say there are parts of the Arab quarter which are "calculated to bring a blush to the cheek of the young person".'

'I couldn't have got her to come anyhow. She's had an awful blow—poor Constance! Actually it's the best thing that could possibly happen, but at present it looks like the crowning misfortune of her life.'

'Her first affair gone wrong, I presume?'

'It's been doing that ever since it started, but now, I think, it's reached its death-throes. The young man I told you of, the Italian, is leaving for Assuan tomorrow. He's been transferred to another branch of the bank, and although he's known about it for a fortnight, he only broke it to her yesterday.'

'That seems rather brutal, doesn't it?'

'I believe he meant it to be kind—and of course he wanted to spare himself a series of emotional farewells. Oh, dear, I do feel so sorry for poor Con. She's heart-broken. And the last straw is, he's going out with somebody else this evening.'

'He really sounds a bit of a blackguard.'

'I suppose he is, in a negative sort of way. To do him justice, he didn't know what he was bargaining for when he began a little idle flirtation with Constance. I can't help wondering if the transfer to Assuan was made at his own request. He's not had much peace in the last few weeks.'

'It'll turn out best in the long run, as you say. At that age one's feelings are dreadfully intense but, fortunately, they burn themselves out.'

'One gets very much singed in the process,' said Lucy with a sigh.

'Beneficially so. I wouldn't give tuppence for any adult who hadn't learned how to love in the hard school of trial and error.'

'I agree in theory; but in practice when I see any nice person suffering, I just want to smooth things out for them, don't you? I would have stayed with Con tonight or brought her with us, only she so obviously didn't want me. Vittorio let fall that he was coming home early to get his packing finished, and she's waiting about for him. Silly, silly creature! My heart aches for her.'

'Never mind. She'll be all the better for it.'

Lucy made a murmur of reluctant acquiescence and tried to cheer herself up with the silent reflection that, at any rate, when she departed from Cairo she would not leave Vittorio behind her. She flattered herself that her presence had caused him to assume his best behaviour, and it had troubled her a good deal to think that, after she was gone, his virtue in the face of temptation might quickly slacken. That danger was happily averted.

The idea of her voyage, looming so near that she might count the weeks and soon reasonably begin to count the days, had an instantaneous effect upon her spirits. 'I chose my berth yesterday morning,' she informed Eugene triumphantly. 'At least I saw it on a plan; the boat is so booked up already that to talk of "choosing" is a polite fiction. Half the population of Australia and India, not to mention Egypt, seems determined to be in England for Christmas.'

'Lucky Lucy! When do you go?'

'December the third. The best day in the whole calendar! I've paid a deposit on my ticket. You have to nowadays to make sure of a passage.'

'And Daisy? Have you broken it to her?' He had been told something of the situation that existed between them.

'Well, I've thrown out every possible kind of hint. At the moment she's so utterly wrapped up in one theme that she doesn't pay much attention to anything else.'

She was glad to be able to say this because it was a way, if only a feeble one, of accounting for Daisy's refusal to see him. She did not like to tell him that he was looked upon as unfit to know, so she laid as much stress as she could on Daisy's intense absorption in Mosenthal and her future prospects.

'I shan't say anything definite to Daisy,' she went on, 'until I've got all that I need—every penny. Then I shall feel safe.'

'How soon will that be?'

It was his habit at all times to be interested in the most prosaic details of his friends' circumstances, and Lucy had thus been encouraged for the first time in months to talk about her own affairs. After the various preoccupations of Daisy and Constance his kindly inquisitiveness made him a very agreeable companion.

She answered with relish: 'I have three thousand five hundred piastres now, all hoarded up in four months—don't you think that's good? And before I go I shall want a thousand more. I can save that in about four weeks. That'll give me a good ten pounds in hand when I get to London. If only they'd let me keep my job at the theatre right up to the end, I'd be in clover.'

'Will they?'

'Yes, I think so, if Daisy stays in a good humour. They'll need someone. There's plenty to do—more and more as the season draws nearer.'

Eugene was silent for a moment, then he said earnestly: 'Lucy, your character fills me with profound respect. The way you've tackled all these difficulties of yours is marvellous. I don't want to be sentimental, but I must tell you you're going to be a guiding star to me, no less. You've set an example that I intend to try and live up to.'

'Oh, it *is* nice of you to say that!' Lucy turned to smile into his still, sad face. 'You're so clever and talented that, if I thought I could help you to get back to where you belong, it would almost seem worth while to have gone through these last six months.'

'Sweet kind Lucy, you make me see that I *must* pull myself together. You're the nearest contact I've had with decency and sanity for God knows how long.'

'You *have* pulled yourself together,' Lucy returned cheerfully. 'You did that before I appeared on the scene. Now you must stay pulled together so that we can meet again in England. Won't it be lovely when we can talk about all our miserable adventures abroad as if we were quite proud of them?'

'You'll have your voice back, and I shall be a happy connoisseur of tea.'

They had turned, without interrupting their conversation, into a side-street leading to a back-street. Now the remarkably changed character of their surroundings forced them to take notice of the fact that they had reached the Arab quarter.

They were walking in a narrow lane of shops most of which were still open—for, where the heat lays waste several hours every day, business activities must be prolonged until late in the evening. The small square shop-fronts, uncovered by glass, looked like tiny lighted stages on each of which some scene was being played for the entertainment of the passers-by. People rather than goods seemed to fill the windows. Here a garrulous barber was shaving the head of an obviously bored client in full view of all who cared to look. Here a tailor with his apprentices sat cross-legged on cushions, stitching imperturbably. The maker of tarbooshes arranged his crimson felt in moulds and paused occasionally to converse with customers and promenading acquaintances. In numerous *boutiques* thirsty Mussulmans, forbidden wine, were being refreshed from great glass jars of liquids coloured as if to attract the eye of a child. (Lucy remembered with affection the enormous decanters of water mystically dyed green, blue, or purple which were the insignia of chemists' shops in England.) The baker piled up flat round cakes of bread still smoking from the oven; they exhaled a savoury and tempting odour, but the sight of a well-grown rat creeping along a shelf in the background effectually broke that appetizing spell for the English sightseers.

They began to tread gingerly then, for their eyes, in spite of themselves, grew keen for further evidences of the filth which then made the quarter so notorious, and they saw much they would have preferred to ignore. Huge rats moved along the gutters, so bold by virtue of their numbers that when they were compelled to emerge into the open they scarcely changed their pace. An immense population of flies clustered on the walls of the confectioner's shop; others, deceived by the light, feverishly infested the sweets and pastry. The shopman regarded these and indeed every variety of insect with the utmost indifference; and neither were his customers more concerned.

But what was strangest of all—so strange that it carried the whole scene into the realm of fantasy and made its squalors unreal and therefore endurable—was the throng of bats, gigantically larger than the European species, which swooped with a diagonal motion up and down between the congested roofs, like swallows in a nightmare.

Lucy and Eugene walked on, never pausing for a moment in case they should be molested by beggars, itinerant vendors, or the shopkeepers themselves. Their cautiousness turned out to be not so necessary, however, as in the neighbourhoods more consistently frequented by tourists. By pressing steadily forward, as if to some known destination, they were able to pass through several thoroughfares of the same kind, without either buying unwanted goods or giving *baksheesh* for unneeded services.

Soon it was apparent that they had reached the end of the shopping district. The streets were now mere dark alleys, sometimes consisting only of a flight of stone steps between two rows of houses. The shadows were thick and sinister, and among them were gathered lounging figures, some solitary, some in little groups. There was no traffic and no other noise than vagrant murmurs of conversation with here and there a jangling laugh, a snatch of tuneless singing, or the music of unfamiliar instruments behind barred shutters.

Everything gave the impression of being enclosed, secret, and in some fashion, malevolent.

From time to time a startlingly painted face materialized out of the darkness, and they would be accosted with a brief, hardly articulate query. They shook their heads and passed on, and no one attempted to detain them. Still, Lucy could not feel comfortable. The streets were so narrow, so silent, so exotic. Trams and taxis, polyglot crowds, theatres, cafés and offices, respectable suburbs, might have been a hundred miles away. Egyptian women with painted, naked faces looked queerer to her now than those who went through the main streets so heavily veiled that the only human feature they exposed was one eye.

'Shall we go back to what passes for civilization?' she asked casually. 'I think we can say we've done the Arab quarter now. The mosques you must see by daylight.'

'Well, the Arab quarter can't say it's done us.' Eugene laughed. 'I've never had a cheaper expedition in my life. I put money in my purse, too, thinking it might be an expensive evening.'

'Expensive evenings, Eugene, are not for people who're saving up. You'd better get that into your head once and for all.'

'Oh, come, my dear Lucy, don't be extreme! A man who works God knows how many hours a day banging at a café piano is entitled to have his fun once in a while. He'd go mad otherwise—or get drunk. And that comes to the same thing with me.'

'But what fun could you have here?'

He paused to give a courteous refusal to a pair of oddly bedizened street-walkers before replying: 'There must surely be some entertainment apart from what these ladies stand for. You're prepared to put up with a *little* impropriety, aren't you? I'm told they make a speciality of the *danse du ventre* in this part of the world. Would you be too shocked to see it?'

'Not at all,' said Lucy sincerely, remembering the innocuous wickedness of the performance as it had been presented in a Parisian music-hall. 'But I believe the authorities have forbidden it. They had a lot of trouble with the troops, and had to place the quarter out of bounds and forbid everything meant to entice soldiers here. That's why it's so dull and quiet, I suppose.'

'I have a feeling that the *danseuses du ventre*, if I may call them so, don't take that prohibition very seriously. You may not have noticed it, but several of the girls who've approached were offering to dance.'

'Oh, is that what they wanted?' exclaimed Lucy, who had been too shy and too surprised at the seemingly indiscriminate nature of their advances to look or listen very closely. 'Well, where do they do it? Not in the public thoroughfares, surely?'

'No, I should think there must be premises of some kind.'

'How much would it cost, I wonder?' said Lucy doubtfully. She was anxious that Eugene should not consider his evening entirely wasted, and for her own part was willing to admit to some curiosity, but the question of economy was paramount. She could not accept hospitality from a friend even poorer than herself.

They had arrived at the end of an alley which turned out to be a cul-de-sac, save for a passage through which they could see the gleam of water; and as they paused, debating whether to go through and explore or return by the road they had left, a girl came up and touched Eugene on the shoulder. Like all the others they had seen she was made-up as heavily as an actress about to face the footlights: the rims of her eyes were black with kohl, her cheeks and lips were rouged with the most vivid carmine, and her hair was frizzed out to a crinkled cloud against each cheekbone; but beneath these frankly artificial embellishments, one saw contours so round and simple that one could not suppose her to be more than seventeen years old. Taking into account the swift maturity that burdens the women of her race, she was probably nearer fifteen.

Her youth inspired pity and regret, but it also allayed fear. No danger could be suspected from a child who looked into one's face with an ingenuous smiling gaze. Instead of hastening her steps, as she had done almost unconsciously at other approaches, Lucy stood still and allowed Eugene to open negotiations.

'Dance?' the girl inquired in a light, confiding voice.

'How much?'

'Fifty piastre.'

'Both of us?'

She looked blank, and Lucy repeated the question in Arabic. 'No, fifty piastre you and fifty piastre you.' The girl insisted on airing her tiny stock of English. 'Good dance. You like.'

'It's much too dear,' said Lucy in a quick aside. 'Why, I should want to see Pavlova for that price. Come along, let's go, Eugene!'

'Oh, we can beat her down. She quite expects it.' He began gaily to barter, and Lucy could see he was too eager now to be readily deterred. She allowed him to close the bargain at thirty piastres each, which he paid there and then, and consoled herself with the reflection that, during the ensuing week, she could wash and iron her own linen.

Lucy had formed no very clear idea of the conditions under which the dance was to be performed, nor did she even understand who was to give the performance. Her anticipations were confused between what she imagined of the Arab quarter and what she remembered of the music-hall in Paris; and if she had any picture in her mind at all of the scene she was about to behold, it was of some dirty yet highly coloured Oriental saloon where massive women in spangled costumes (a recollection of Paris) would practise movements more laughable than provocative, to the sound of pipes and tabors. It did not seem likely that this slender child was to devote her own person to such inappropriate contortions, and Lucy assumed she was seeking an audience on someone else's behalf.

It was disconcerting to find that, instead of leading them to the sort of dance-hall or concert-room she hazily expected, their guide's footsteps went no farther than one of the narrow, shuttered houses in the cul-de-sac. Not a chink of light could be seen behind the heavy jalousies. No building in Cairo could have looked less promising as a place of amusement. Yet someone there was evidently on the alert; the girl's movements had been observed from within, for the door swung back before Lucy had time to express her misgivings, and by a process too rapid and astonishing to be resisted they were drawn inside and coaxed and pulled and pushed up two flights of dimly lighted stairs. Lucy made a visible effort to retreat as the room which was opened for them on the landing turned out to be a bedroom, but the staircase was blocked by three unpleasant-looking Egyptians, including an old woman whose vicious face, rendered still uglier by what was evidently intended to be a winning smile, was more intimidating than the burly forms of her male supporters.

Eugene looked a trifle crestfallen, but he endeavoured to keep his companion's spirits up. 'I think we'd better stay since we're here,

Lucy.' He took her arm in his most reassuring manner. 'It will be an experience for you—perhaps not a very nice one, but interesting to look back on from respectable cities in England when you're touring the provinces. I'm sorry: I honestly didn't know it would be like this, but we might as well stick it out, my dear, and see what we shall see.'

By this time they had penetrated the sordid bedroom, lit by an oil-lamp hanging from the ceiling. It was a small apartment at least half-filled by a vast curtainless four-poster on which lay a feather mattress with neither sheets nor blankets. A rickety washstand, as old in fashion as the bed, stood in the corner; grey, soapy water filled the basin, and a soiled towel dangled to the floor. Near the windows was a little bare space of linoleum, and around this were arranged half a dozen chairs. One of them was dusted for Lucy, and she sat down, requesting earnestly in Arabic that a window might be opened, for the smell of the lamp and the Egyptians together was overpowering.

The window led on to a balcony, and Lucy drew her chair near it, grateful both for the fresh air and the illusive sense of freedom that it gave. From the moment of entering the room, the young girl had been busy undressing herself and flinging her discarded clothes upon the bed, where the old woman gathered them up with encouraging sniggers. Lucy tried to be interested and not shocked, but in spite of all her painstaking efforts she was very shocked indeed.

If the same spectacle had been staged with professional bravura in cleaner and more showy surroundings, she might have been beguiled into enjoying the thrill of its strangeness and scandalousness, but it was all so amateurishly done. There was something quite pathetic in the sight of the girl's crumpled cotton underwear, trimmed with cheap embroidery, and shaped after a style so out of date that at home it would have been regarded as comical. The ridiculous stays and buttoned drawers made her seem more childish than ever, and reminded one dismally how wrong it was to countenance such behaviour in a young person who needed protection.

There was neither music nor costume for her dance; she performed in artless nakedness to a rhythmic clapping of hands by the Egyptians. She had little skill, and Lucy was soon tired of seeing her breathing in and out and swaying her hips from side to side in an absurd effort to convince them and herself that she was displaying a masterly control over her stomach muscles. Even Eugene, who had been in the mood for appreciation, began to show signs of restiveness.

At last with a cry meant to convey her excitement and abandon she threw herself into his arms, and he was compelled to harbour her there for a moment. Patting her in a kindly but abstracted manner, not without a half-humorous, half-apologetic glance towards Lucy, he managed to release himself.

'This is a ludicrous affair,' he declared, rising. 'And now what do we do? Trundle off home, I suppose, wishing we'd kept our money in our pocket.'

Lucy rose, too, with alacrity, but the people of the house immediately gathered before the door, all speaking together at the top of their voices in a mixture of their own language and a few rags and tatters of English from which only one intelligible sound emerged, the peculiar word: 'Exhibish'.

'Are they referring to the exhibition we've just seen or some exhibition still to come?' asked Eugene. 'I rather think they're going to show us something more to make up our money's worth.'

'I have already been bored enough,' said Lucy. She did not care to make the admission, so humiliating in 1919, that she had also been shocked.

'If the "exhibish" still to come is what I think it's going to be,' he muttered, pursing his small mouth, 'you won't be bored, only horrified. To me it doesn't matter one way or another; such sights aren't quite new to me. What shall we do—go or stay? After all, it's an adventure—of a sort.'

'The wrong sort for me.' Lucy made a movement towards the door. 'Do let's get out of this depressing house!'

At once the gibbering of the natives began again, and this time there was a note of indignation in it. Lucy concluded that to go without seeing the rest of the entertainment was regarded as an insult to its quality. Perhaps the poor little dancer would get into trouble afterwards for having failed to amuse them. She stood hesitant, and in that instant a tall Egyptian young man, only half clad, a dingy white tunic tucked about his waist, was admitted to the room. The girl flung herself towards him with gestures of feigned rapture, and Lucy, realizing in clear terms at last what was to be the nature of the exhibition, cast away her pretence of being unshockable. The cumulative effect of all the disgust she had felt since coming to the quarter swept over her in a sickening flood, and she hardly knew what she was doing or intending. Her way to the door was barred by leering Egyptians, and she ran out upon the balcony, almost inclined, for one desperate moment, to escape by leaping over it. Below she saw the black water of a sluggish river. The houses on either side were smooth-walled and closed in, like the one in which she was constrained. Behind her was a room filled with vileness. She had a sensation of panic. She was a prisoner who dared not raise her eyes from contemplation of the unwholesome water.

But in less time than she believed had passed, Eugene was at her elbow, kind and consoling. 'Lucy, you were right to turn your back. Shall we go?'

'Have they finished in there?'

He glanced in through the window. 'Yes, they're stopping now. They realize the whole audience has walked out on them. Come along! We're off now, my dear.'

He was mistaken. They were not to be allowed to take their departure so easily. The girl, the old woman, and the men, whose number was now increased to three, drew together as before in a resentful knot, shouting and gesticulating. An incomprehensible assortment of noisy protests was their only response to Eugene's demand, first suave, then openly irate, that they would let him pass.

'What is it? What do you want?' cried Lucy in her rough Arabic. 'We have seen the dance. We have paid. Why do you stop us from going?'

A babel of voices informed her hotly that they must produce more money. They had paid for the dance only, not the exhibition. A white rage surged up in her; her few words of Arabic tumbled over each other, hardly a syllable right, in her effort to convey what she thought of such rapacity. But it was in vain for her to point out that they had refused to look at the exhibition, that they regarded it with loathing. Her vehemence and frustrated eloquence only aroused mirth, and she perceived, almost weeping with dismay, that they were caught in a particularly undignified trap.

'I'm afraid I've brought you into a den of thieves,' Eugene lamented. 'What are we to do? Pay up? Or shall we make a dash for it?'

Lucy had already considered the futility of attempting to slip through the fingers of five watchful plunderers; to try and fight a passage out would be equally absurd. Nor did there seem to be any point in calling for help. They were on the second floor of a solidly built house overlooking a deserted waterway: who could tell what might happen to them before their cries were answered? She was thoroughly frightened, and Eugene seemed scarcely the man to lean upon in such an emergency. She decided, shaking with vexation, to take the line of least resistance.

'How much do you want?'

There was a shrill parley, then the oldest of the men rejoined: 'How much can you pay?'

'Oh, this makes my blood boil,' Eugene groaned as she translated. 'I feel so helpless. I don't even know the blasted language to tell them what I think of them!' He turned impulsively to the Egyptians and, drawing forth his pocket-book, commanded in a blaze of wrath: 'Tell me what you want, and let us pass.'

After that everything became confusion. Lucy could not, even as soon as ten minutes later, have sorted out clearly any single detail in the violently swift succession of noises and movements which led to their escape. All was comprised in a kind of whirling picture of which the principal features were hands—hands grabbing, clutching, striking, and pushing; and this picture spun before her eyes to the accompaniment of a most horrible cacophony of voices. Someone, it seemed, had snatched at the pocket-book, and someone else had grasped it away from the snatcher, and Eugene had tried to get it back again, and then everyone except the bewildered and paralysed Lucy herself had begun scrambling and clawing. To any ear which could distinguish them, the furious chatterings would doubtless have resolved themselves into claims and protests: Lucy heard only a din that might have come from the throats of animals.

Before she could consciously ask herself how it was going to end, she found that Eugene had her by the wrist and was pulling her through the doorway and down the stairs, and after a heart-quelling moment while he fumbled in the darkness with the great bolts of the front door, they were in the street. They walked off swiftly and in silence, Lucy breathing tremulously, Eugene panting from his exertions and his anger.

Neither uttered a word until they came to the next alley and were out of sight of the odious house; then she asked limply: 'Did you get back your pocket-book?'

'No, indeed I did not.'

'Oh, dear! What an appalling business! We'd better go to the police.'

'Police! My child, are you really willing to face a police-court with a story like this? It won't sound too well, you know, described in cold blood. People who go into bawdy houses to be amused are expected to take what they get.'

'We didn't know it was that sort of place.'

'We ought to have known. It was breaking the law anyhow if the *danse du ventre* has been forbidden.'

'Still, we can't let those robbers go scot-free just because we're ashamed to own up to our own foolishness. We *must* do something about it. I shall tell the first policeman I see.'

'Don't be silly, Lucy! Your job may be safe enough, but I'll certainly lose mine if I start getting publicity for an escapade of this kind. Besides, I doubt whether the police would help us, and even if they did we'd have an awful business getting our money back. For my part, I'm glad to have shaken the dust of that house off my feet at any price.'

Lucy was torn for a moment between her passionate desire that justice should be vindicated and her immense revulsion at the idea of being brought into contact again with those beings whom she would always remember as the living symbols of wickedness beyond redemption. She capitulated.

'Well, it depends how much they've taken. I shall pay my half, of course.'

'You will not do anything of the sort, my dear. The whole business has been my fault from start to finish. I wouldn't accept a penny from you.'

'Now, that's just rot!' she protested quite sharply. 'You know I intended to pay my own share, the same as I did when we went to see the Sphinx. That was clearly understood.'

'All right. You may pay your share, if you like. It comes to exactly thirty piastres; the price of admission we agreed upon before going into that wretched den. But if you think that, after letting you in for a dismal ordeal like that, I'm going to make you stand half the losses, you're very much mistaken.'

'You didn't let me in for it, Eugene. I went as willingly as you did.'

'I don't think so. And, anyhow, I ought to have foreseen what we were in for. *You* couldn't.'

Lucy was inclined to admit the validity of this reasoning, but it was not in her character to let the whole burden rest on shoulders that could ill afford to carry it. Waving his arguments aside, she put the downright question:

'How much was in your pocket-book?'

'An amount which is no concern of yours, my dear.'

'I wish you'd tell me. It only makes me miserable to go home knowing you're dreadfully out of pocket and won't let me pay my half.'

'I'm not so dreadfully out of pocket as all that—nothing to lose any sleep about.'

'I happen to remember what you said earlier on about having put money in your purse.'

'So I did, but not enough to ruin me. Let's forget it. If you feel as uncomfortable about my lost cash as I do about your rotten experience, we're quits.'

Lucy laid friendly fingers on the plump brown hand which clasped her arm. 'You're too generous, Eugene. You'll never get to England at this rate. Come, don't be foolish! I intend to square things up, whatever you may say.'

Thus mildly wrangling, with only those interruptions from street vendors and mendicants which they were in the mood to dispose of very briefly, they found their way back through the vermin-ridden lanes and under the long archways of darting bats' wings until they were restored again to the trams, the electric lights, the hoardings, and sophisticated shop-fronts of modern Cairo.

'Well, here we are back in our world,' said Eugene. 'A drab world but comparatively a safe one! Let's go and take a drink to wash the taste of the Arab quarter out of our mouths.'

'A drink!' She could not repress a note of apprehension.

'A glass of wine, my child, a harmless glass of wine. Not a danger to me, Lucy; a safeguard. Besides, we haven't had dinner yet.'

'Personally I shall have coffee and a sandwich. I feel anything but hungry.'

'*Burgundy* and a sandwich would do you more good. Will your resources run to burgundy and sandwiches for two?'

They selected an unpretentious restaurant, and so that she might seem companionable, Lucy took a glass of burgundy instead of the coffee she would have much preferred. He drank the remainder of the bottle with deep uncriticizing relish and, true to what he had led her to expect, rose from the table sober and satisfied.

The odours of the dark alley and its terrible inhabitants had grown fainter in her nostrils, and she resolved to defer the question of the stolen money until her next pay-day. Eugene's whole earnings were hardly likely to be more than six or seven hundred piastres a week at the most generous calculation, so the sum could not be large enough to embarrass her seriously.

Chapter 16

Constance's bedroom overlooked the street, and, glancing up at its windows when she returned to Karnak House, Lucy saw that they were lighted and that a shadow moved against the blind. She remembered with a qualm that the girl was in the depths of misery and, regarding the fight as an ominous sign, hastened at once to the second floor.

Constance must be alone: Vittorio never went near her room for fear of encountering her father who lived in the same corridor. It was eleven o'clock, just the hour when Lucy expected them to be engaged in preludes to farewell. Evidently the unkind young man had abandoned his intention of coming home early and was remaining out with his friends, and in that case it was certain that Constance would be in a state bordering upon despair. Lucy hurried to take her what comfort affection could give. Perhaps the story of the evening's misadventure would serve for a distraction. A slightly bowdlerized version. It would not be right to tell a girl of seventeen about the 'exhibish'. (And yet—already certain aspects of the 'exhibish' were beginning to seem a little funny. She would have liked, at any rate, to talk about it to Daisy. But Daisy had grown so respectable lately: she was sure to disapprove of the whole excursion, especially in the company of such an outcast as Eugene.)

The response to her rap on the door—a friendly, signalling rap, so that Constance should immediately know her visitor's identity—was hesitant. There was a sound of rapid steps and movements and when a disconcerted voice invited her to 'Come in!' the door at first turned out to be locked.

'She must have locked herself in to cry,' thought Lucy sorrowfully. 'What in the world can I say or do to console her?'

But there was no sign of weeping on the face that appeared in the doorway. Instead Lucy recognized the frowning smile of unsuccessfully disguised annoyance, and she could not but acknowledge a painful impression that she was admitted grudgingly.

'I'm sorry! I forgot I'd locked it,' said Constance, 'I must have done it without thinking.'

Her constraint was so marked that Lucy looked round nervously, half-expecting to discover Vittorio; but that embarrassment was spared her.

'What, are you going to bed already!' she exclaimed, for Constance's clothes were scattered over the room, and she was wearing her shabby, faded wrapper, long outgrown.

'Yes, I—well, I just undressed.'

'Didn't Vittorio come in?' Lucy could not but ask. It was odd if Constance had given up waiting for him at this comparatively early hour; on less important occasions she had kept vigil till far later.

'Oh, yes, he came in at ten o'clock.' The tone was at once casual and a little defiant. 'We had quite a long talk while he did his packing.'

'Really?' Lucy commented lamely, recalling the outburst of passionate grief she had witnessed only a few hours ago. 'It seems to have made you feel happier.'

'Yes, it did.' With that she began to talk glibly, unconvincingly, and as her listener perceived, at random. 'I'm not going to see him off tomorrow. He hates being seen off at the station. I quite understand that, don't you? Those last few minutes before the train goes out are frightful. One can't say anything except "Take care of yourself!" and "Write to me!" Vittorio must have been awfully popular at the bank. They all subscribed to give him a parting gift—a pair of hairbrushes. He showed them to me. By the way, I've forgiven him for not telling us before about leaving Cairo. It was very considerate in a way. He didn't want to upset me, and he imagined if he told *you*, you'd be certain to pass it on to me. Don't be cross with him. He doesn't know how good you are at keeping secrets.'

Lucy made appropriate murmurs, but her eyes were wandering and her thoughts with them.

The nightdress which showed itself under the short, childish dressing-gown was made of silk. It was the only silk nightdress Constance had ever had; Lucy had given her the length of stuff for her seventeenth birthday because she had grumbled so bitterly—and, Lucy felt, so justifiably—about still being obliged to wear the shapeless garments of calico favoured at the convent. But once acquired and made up, the precious *crêpe de Chine*, emblem of sophisticated maturity, had seemed too fine to use and had remained, folded reverently away in tissue paper, in the drawer assigned to treasures.

That was the first thing Lucy noticed. The second was that, although the girl was wearing her old wrapper, a kimono made recently of cheap but pretty Japanese crêpe was lying on the bed. And last, it was evident that she had been interrupted in the midst of doing her hair—not brushing it for the night, but arranging the front pieces in what were known as kiss-curls. The tongs, which had apparently fallen on the floor at Lucy's knock, were still hot when she stooped to pick them up.

This was not a night when Lucy could sympathize with the longings and the follies of adolescence. Perhaps because her nerves had already been strained to a high tension, her suspicions seemed frightening. The round, ingenuous face before her with its absurd embellishment of kiss-curls called up another image—another round face, younger and still more unsuitably bedizened, a face that lurked in shadows where rats crept.

'Con!' she said, cutting suddenly across the stream of chatter. 'You were not really going to bed.'

'I don't think I said I was.'

'What are you getting ready for?'

'To say good night to Vittorio.' The words were jauntily spoken, and as if she were relieved to cast deception aside she flung off her shabby dressing-gown and slipped into the new one.

'Con, you don't mean to say he's coming here? Your father's in. There's a light showing under his door.'

'No, I promised to go down. Oh, don't look so outraged, Lucy! What's the use of pretending to be a prude? This is his last night. I've *got* to go.'

'But won't your nightdress rather surprise him, my dear?' Lucy tried quite vainly to sound playful.

'What I wear,' said Constance coldly and slowly, 'is surely my own business.' She leaned towards the mirror of her dressing-table and carefully applied powder to her face. Then, impulsively remorseful, she went on addressing Lucy's reflection. 'You've been tremendously good to me, I know that. You've been the very kindest friend I ever had. But you treat me sometimes as if I were a child, Lucy, and I won't be treated as a child. In big things like this I know my own mind. It's no use lecturing me and it's no use giving me advice. This is Vittorio's last night and I am going to do what I like.'

'Big things like this! Then you do understand what you're doing?'

'Of course I know what I'm doing.' Angry bravado now supplanted the attempt at friendly candour. 'Vittorio's waiting for me. He's going tomorrow. It's the last chance I'll have of being all in all to him, and if you think I'm going to miss it, that just proves how little you know about love.'

She strode with a fierce step towards the door, but Lucy caught her by the wrist and held her in a tremulous grip. 'All in all to him, you little fool!' She spoke harshly, even mockingly, in spite of herself. 'Do you suppose a couple of hours' amusement in bed with you is going to make you all in all to that trumpery young Italian? You must be as innocent as an unborn child!'

'What do I care for the names you call him, or for your horrible dirty-mindedness?' Constance's eyes and cheeks and utterance burned with proud fury. 'I love him! Do you understand? I love him and I'll always love him.'

Lucy was moved from anger to compassion. 'Does he love you?' She let her grasp end as an embrace. 'Oh, Con, don't deceive yourself! Don't bolster yourself up with romantic nonsense! Does he love you?'

Constance was under a pressure of opposing emotions too intense for any one of them to remain long in ascendancy over the others. With a childish gesture she leaned her head upon a chest-of-drawers and burst into tears.

'He might love me,' she sobbed, 'after tonight. I know what you said about Italian traditions and him not respecting me afterwards and all that; but it isn't true. I asked him about it and he said it wasn't true. He's not an ordinary Italian; he's different. Oh, I shall never meet anyone like him again.' She opened the drawer beneath her hand and in a blind movement brought forth a handkerchief.

'But what good can it do?' Lucy tried to remember some passion of her own youth from which she might draw skill to deal with this. 'If you could keep him here by taking such a step, there might be a little sense in it—not much but some. As it is, the thing seems crazy. You may be absolutely ruined, and he'll go away and forget you.'

'Oh, Lucy, you're so frightfully old-fashioned.' Constance jabbed at the chest-of-drawers with an impatient foot. 'No one would ever think you'd been on the stage. People don't get ruined nowadays: that's just pre-war stuff. Besides, after tonight Vittorio may not forget me as quickly as you think. He doesn't know anyone in Assuan, and he may miss me once he gets there.'

'He makes friends easily; we both know that. And in any case, even if he does miss you, what's the use of it? You won't be there to see.'

'I shall go to him,' she answered solemnly.

Lucy felt almost inclined to laugh. 'Go to him! How? Why? What on earth are you talking about? You don't seriously mean you want to run away, and throw in your lot with Vittorio? My dear idiotic child, what can you imagine a junior bank clerk is going to do in a foreign country with a girl of sixteen on his hands?'

'Seventeen now. People marry at seventeen. Being in a foreign country doesn't make any difference.'

'Marriage! Oh, the idea's madness, pure madness.'

'I don't see why.'

'If I were to begin to tell you I'd be talking till tomorrow morning.'

'Well, don't, because I've been here too long already.'

Lucy's words had sounded more derisive, less benevolently reasoning, than she had intended, and Constance seized on them swiftly as an excuse for a brusque rejoinder by which she could end the conversation. 'Vittorio will wonder what's become of me,' she muttered, gathering herself together for departure.

Lucy leaned against the door. 'Vittorio will know what's become of you because I shall go down and tell him. I'll explain to him quite truthfully exactly what we've said and give him any message you like. And, darling,' she hurried on desperately in the face of Constance's rage, 'he'll be relieved, honestly he will. He doesn't want this to happen, I swear to God he doesn't, whatever he feels like tonight.'

'Please let me get out!' Constance dared not shout for fear of being heard by her father, but her voice, subdued with difficulty, conveyed her disgust quite as effectively. 'Let me get out of this room at once! What right have you got to come interfering in my affairs? If that's why you were kind to me—just because you wanted to go round interfering—then I wish to goodness you'd left me alone!' Lucy stood her ground, and after a moment of glowering silence, Constance continued: 'It won't be very dignified for you if I have to push you out of the way.'

'It won't be very dignified for *you*,' said Lucy.

'If you force me to it, I'm not to blame. After all, this is my room.'

'I shall go the minute you promise to keep away from Vittorio till morning. If you don't, I'll'—she had meant to say, 'I'll tell your father,' but realizing in time that this threat was not going to ring true, she changed it to: 'I shall tackle our friend downstairs.'

'You mean you'll go sneaking and preaching to Vittorio? Ah, but you can't, for I shall get there first! If you want to make a scene, you can jolly well make it outside the door.'

'All right, I will. It'll be very unpleasant for me, and very unpleasant for everyone concerned, but that won't stop me. You'd better get it into your head, Con, that I'm determined not to let you make a fool of yourself.'

Constance began to sob again, dramatically now, walking up and down the room with hands pressed to her temples. 'Oh, you're hateful,' she cried, 'spoiling everything like this! To think I regarded you as a friend—the person who's ruined my last night with Vittorio! Why, you're the biggest enemy I've got in the world! You're a nasty, meddling schoolma'am. I wish I'd never seen you. All the same,' she burst out afresh as Lucy remained immovable, 'you needn't think you've beaten me. I *will* go down to Vittorio, and you can make what scenes you like. A fine way of protecting me, to turn me into a laughing-stock for everyone in the building!'

Bending urgently towards the mirror of the dressing-table, she began to set her disordered hair and tear-stained face to rights.

Lucy argued no more, for she perceived she was dealing not with a rational creature, but with a child in a fever; and she had just closed her hand upon a weapon to supersede argument. From her position at the door it had been easy for her to extract the key from the lock. Now she had only to decide whether the moment for using it had come. She felt mean and treacherous, she scarcely believed it was herself who had planned so underhand a trick, but she was wrought up tonight to a pitch where, to save Constance from a folly which might have lifelong repercussions, she was willing to appear what the ridiculous girl had called her. Later, when the subject of infatuation was well removed, she would be forgiven. Constance would see then that she had acted in pure disinterested affection.

To lock her in was the only safe solution. Otherwise she could not be prevented from getting to Vittorio's bedroom (Lucy pictured the ludicrous chase down two flights of stairs and several passages), and it was out of the question really to remonstrate from the outer side of a closed door. She would gain her point—Vittorio at least was sure to surrender—but there would be gossip in the building and much damage might result from it. As for enlisting the help of Mr. Conway, nothing could be so likely to prove harmful. At the best, it would set a further strain on the daughter's difficult relations with her father; at the worst, Constance might be provoked to some course still more reckless than the one she had in mind. No, to have the matter out alone with Vittorio was the imperative need.

It was time to act. She must take advantage of the uncertain number of seconds Constance would spend before the looking-glass. Once determined she moved swiftly. With her sense of treachery leavened by a little glow of triumph in her presence of mind, she opened the door and, as Constance glanced round in surprise, retired with an air of injured pride. Outside, with quivering fingers, she slipped the key into the lock and turned it as gently, yet as rapidly, as she could.

It was an exciting moment. Though dexterous she could not at once fit the ward into its grooves, and her fumbling made a noise which brought Constance in three strides to the door. It was locked just in the nick of time, but the sound of the handle being rattled and shaken on the other side gave Lucy an acute spasm of discomfort. She could taste all the bitterness of her imprisoned victim, constrained even from raising her voice to protest or call for assistance; and full of compunction she sought for some way of making her feelings known.

In her bag were the pencil and tiny pad she kept handy for theatre memoranda. She drew them out and, moving to the nearest light, wrote hastily: 'Dearest Con, Tm going down to talk to Vittorio. Do stop rattling the door-handle because if anyone notices they may call your father. You can't imagine how I hate treating you like this, but soon you'll see things clearly and forgive me. I could only do it for someone I loved.'

She thrust the note under the door, and took the precaution at the same time of removing the key. A voice behind whispered, 'Damn you! Damn you! Damn you!' in a paroxysm of loathing; and her eyes travelled nervously towards Mr. Conway's apartment, but his door remained closed and the gleam of light beneath it had reassuringly vanished. Feeling more like a trapper than a rescuer, she went downstairs.

Vittorio, in tussore-silk pyjamas, was spraying his hair with a scented lotion. It was obvious enough that he was expecting some visitor other than herself, but by a quick adjustment of his features he managed to conceal annoyance and display only surprise, greeting her affably in his sonorous French. She cut him short, resolved not to waste an instant in politenesses.

'Vittorio, I have locked Constance up in her bedroom. You can guess why.'

He turned away to put on his dressing-gown. 'Really? What has she been doing—naughty girl?'

'You know quite well what she has been doing—that's to say, what she intended to do.'

'I? No! How can I know? I was just going to bed.'

'I don't doubt it. Come, Vittorio, there's no need for pretence. I have had a talk with Constance. Why did you break your good resolutions?'

He flung off his untenable innocence lightly and without apology.

'My good resolutions were broken for me. Do you think a man can go on for ever resisting a temptation that is offered to him almost every day? Oh, Miss Lucy, it doesn't sound very gallant to say that, I know, but if she gives you the impression that it is I who have been the tempter—'

'Not at all. She gives no such impression. You should know her better than that, Vittorio. Nothing would induce her to lay the blame on your shoulders; but I do all the same. You could have stopped this romantic foolishness if you had wanted to.'

'I could have stopped it? I, above all people! Ah, no, Miss Lucy, I didn't expect you to be so unjust. Surely you must see that she allows me no peace!'

'You amused yourself with her,' she replied sternly. 'You embraced her, you awakened ideas she had never had before. She came straight from a convent—'

'The girls from convents are generally the most passionate,' he murmured with his rakish smile.

Lucy would not pay him the compliment of a rebuke. 'Naturally, she fell in love with you, a schoolgirl's infatuation for the first man she had met on intimate terms. And when you found that all this emotion and devotion was a nuisance, what did you do? Did you make a really sincere, really sensible effort to discourage her? No, you were weak, you went on doing what you knew was wrong because you hadn't the strength of mind to tell her the truth.'

Painful though the moment was, she could not but smile inwardly to hear herself saying lines so reminiscent of the theatre, but she believed it was the kind of talk Vittorio understood and approved, and she was not mistaken. Conventional sentiments in dramatic language always appealed to him, and he could be depended upon to make a response in kind.

'Weak!' he returned with a gusty sigh which could not, however, disguise his enjoyment of the situation. 'Yes, perhaps I have been weak but I am a human being, not a saint or a statue. What sort of man is it who refuses to kiss a girl when she invites him? Not an Italian, I promise you. Besides, mademoiselle'—he tapped himself feelingly on the breast—'I have a heart and she is sensitive, this poor child.'

'If you really had a heart your whole behaviour would have been different. You could never have considered letting her come down here tonight.'

'It was what she wanted.'

'Only because she thinks it would make you love her. In any case, we don't give children everything they want. Good God!' she cried in a sudden flare of exasperation, 'think of the harm that would have come of it! To be seduced at the age of seventeen by a man she'll never see again! Anything might happen to her afterwards.'

'Seduced is truly not the right word,' he assured her with a faint laugh.

'You told her that to go on merely kissing was childish—a pendulum without a clock. That made her think she ought to give you more.'

'Miss Lucy, I swear—I swear on my sacred word of honour I told her that in the hope of ending the whole affair in an agreeable way. Positively you must believe that.'

Lucy did believe it, but with the irritation one is prone to feel on being reminded that one's opponent may have a point in his favour, she answered crossly: 'A pity, isn't it, you weren't more honest and not quite so agreeable?'

He shrugged his shoulders at this and made a leisurely gesture of lighting a cigarette to show he would attempt no further defence, and Lucy perceived she must be less truculent if her night's work were to be usefully completed.

'But it's not too late,' she began again in a somewhat more conciliatory tone. 'She's safe enough for the moment at any rate.'

'Do you propose to keep her locked up till morning?'

She turned upon him in dismay. 'Vittorio, after all I've said you wouldn't—'

'I tell you, I count myself the seduced, not the seducer.'

She was able to master her temper and even to be jocular. 'Well, you mustn't be exposed to the risk of losing your virtue, my friend. We must save you from that, even if we have to explain the position to her father.'

It was a pleasure to see his provoking smirk become an uncertain grin: Mr. Conway might neglect his daughter, but it was probable that he would be an uncomfortable person to encounter if he were forced to take notice of a misdemeanour.

'Ah, no!' Vittorio's nonchalance was not very well feigned. 'You wouldn't treat our poor Constance as unkindly as all that. Your heart is too good. Besides, you may trust me now. I was only teasing you.'

Lucy stood meditative, fingering the key inside her coat pocket. 'If I can't trust you,' she said at last with a smile, 'at least I can keep a good eye on you. But what about Constance? That's the question.'

His eyes sought hers in a glance full of unseemly amusement. 'Without me, I think her sins will not be too dangerous. . . . Tomorrow morning I shall be gone.'

'That's just it. I have an idea she may follow you.'

'Follow me! For what purpose?' The look of horror which overspread his face dispelled all Lucy's doubts as to whether she was doing right to lay her cards on the table.

'Partly out of bravado, to revenge herself on me for interfering tonight, and partly because it would be a grand sentimental adventure for her.'

'Impossible!'

'No, in her present mood she's capable of every kind of silliness. She's already mentioned some notion of running away to Assuan.'

'But she has no money.'

'She might concoct some excuse for getting a little money from her father. Or she could even sell clothes and things.'

'And when she arrives?' he inquired balefully.

'At her age one doesn't meet such difficulties in advance. She might have some scheme of going to work, or she might imagine you'd marry her—'

'Marry her? My God!'

'She has thought of it,' said Lucy with all the inward reproaches of a double-dyed traitor.

'Oh, but you can't be serious, mademoiselle!' In his agitation he spoke coldly and formally as if Lucy herself had devised this menace to his comfort. 'To be chased about the country—not able to escape even in Assuan! It would be fatal—absolutely fatal. Why, it might come to the ears of my manager!'

'You can accuse no one but yourself, Vittorio. If you hadn't allowed the poor child to deceive herself—but I won't repeat what I've said. Since you've let the wretched business get so far, there's only one thing you can do to make an end of it.'

'Something unpleasant, I suppose?'

'Unpleasant for you, but twenty times more unpleasant for her—and I wish it were the other way round. Vittorio, you must go and talk to her frankly at last. Forget she's sensitive and forget how much you like to appear charming. Tell her what a hopeless mistake it was to think she could win your love by this madness tonight. Explain that it will be no use writing to you or expecting you to write to her. Finish it—finish it once and for all with your own words.'

He listened, earnest and attentive, no longer able either to view the matter with ironical detachment or, at the moment, to extract dramatic satisfaction from it.

'Do you really think,' he asked after a pause for consideration, 'that I could persuade her to leave me alone?'

'Of course, if you honestly want her to.'

'I've tried before, you know.'

'You've fooled about with her, being cold one day and kind the next when your mood changed. Tonight you must leave not a ray of hope. Otherwise—well, I've warned you.'

'But it's dreadful to inflict such a blow. Have you thought?' He lowered his voice with slightly unctuous emotion. 'She might do something desperate.'

'No, no, don't flatter yourself,' said Lucy coolly. 'She will be very unhappy, but she's young and healthy; she'll recover. We've all suffered miseries in our youth through things like this, and come to our senses afterwards. And I shall be here for the next few weeks to do what I can for her.'

He sighed deeply and effectively. The sense of drama was enfolding him again. It was, after all, an interesting scene he was being called upon to play: he braced himself for it.

'Where shall I speak to her?' he demanded suddenly.

'In her room. I'll give you the key. Her father's gone to bed, and you needn't be there long.'

He tightened the cord of his dressing-gown as though he were girding himself for a physical struggle and, assuming a noble and self-sacrificing look, announced: 'I am doing it for her own good. It will be as painful to me as to her, but since you advise it as her well-wisher—' He spread out his hands in a gesture of benevolent resignation.

'You'd better get it into your head,' said Lucy, handing him the key, 'that you're doing it to save Vittorio Guglielmi from having a certain amount of trouble in the future. Perhaps that will help you to stick to the point. Now I'll go up with you as far as her door so as to make it look all right if you should be seen by anyone.'

'You think of everything, Miss Lucy,' he declared admiringly, and added on a note of mockery as she escorted him towards the staircase: 'Since you organize so well, wouldn't you like to be present at the interview?'

She looked at him with distaste and distrust. His volatility, the quick shiftings of his humour, were always uncongenial to her, and never more so than now. One could not rely upon him to hold the same attitude for two minutes together. She stopped at the foot of the stairs and gazed squarely at him. 'Look here, Vittorio, you'd better not play any tricks, do you understand? I shall allow you twenty minutes and if you're not in your room by then I'll come and fetch you.'

His raffish smile returned as gay and shameless as ever.

'Twenty minutes, Miss Lucy? One could manage quite a lot in twenty minutes.'

She started angrily to mount the stairs but he caught her by the arm, exclaiming, 'Miss Lucy, I was teasing. Don't be cross with me! I shall be a good boy and do just as you ask, I promise on my honour as a gentleman.'

'Very well,' she rejoined severely, and tried to proceed, but he caught her arm again.

'The little English Constance, the innocent convent girl, she shall remain a virgin, thanks to you.' He leaned his head towards her and whispered laughingly, 'My one virgin, Miss Lucy. What a triumph of good morals! Thanks to you, I shall always be able to remember her as that—my one dear little virgin!' His laughter broke out loud, and in a kind of sportiveness which could only be expressed in his native tongue he chanted exultantly: *'La mia verginina! La mia verginella! Trionfo della moralità Inglese!'*

Lucy was glad that tomorrow would remove him from her sight for ever.

Chapter 17

Lucy did not believe that any good purpose could be served by her speaking to Constance again that night. She waited only to be assured that Vittorio had faithfully done what she required of him, and then, tired and agitated by all the unpleasant experiences of the last few hours, retired to a bed which offered only desiccated rest. The next morning she rose earlier than usual, intending to seek a reconciliation with Constance before she went to her work, but there was a note lying on her doormat which made her decide to postpone her overtures indefinitely. The envelope was addressed severely to 'Miss Kendon' and the communication began without a greeting:

> Please don't come near me or attempt to speak to me. If you come to my room you will be locked out. If you speak to me, I won't answer you. I hate you more than I've ever hated anyone in my whole life. I could not have imagined that anyone was capable of such a treacherous and degraded act, but I suppose you want to go round smashing up other people's love affairs because you haven't any of your own. You betrayed my confidence and turned the only man I shall ever love against me. I don't know what I am going to do, but one thing I do know—I wouldn't speak to you again for all the money in the world. I am writing this at six in the morning after the most horrible night I've ever spent, and I shall never be happy again as long as I live. That's what I owe to you, the person who called herself my friend.
>
> Constance Conway

Lucy was suffering from the indigestion and depression which follow a bad night. She felt indignant at the girl's wilful misunderstanding of the situation, and hurt beyond measure by the contemptuous reflection upon her own motives. She was not in the mood to discern that Constance was too young to suffer without a scapegoat, and too sentimental about Vittorio to cast the blame where it was due. She had by no means supposed that she would be forgiven without argument, but these galling aspersions were more than she could meekly bear. It was Constance now who must apologize. She stared at herself woefully in the dressing-table glass, and saw her reflection blurred by angry tears. No love affairs of her own! Those were undoubtedly the words that rankled; Constance had not lost the schoolgirl's faculty for cruelty. Incapable of having love affairs—she who had once enthralled the good-looking, delightful Henry Felix, compared with whom Vittorio was as dross! But it was true, that was the bitterness of it; a bitterness unexpected, for lately she had been almost content to regard herself as a sexless being. Since attraction was lacking, it had seemed as well not to miss it actively. But now she recoiled, picturing herself as she must have appeared to others—a dreary creature with no power to awaken warmth. In this gloomy light, trifles took on a miserable significance. Vittorio had always punctiliously called her 'Miss Lucy'; he had treated her with respect and gentle mockery and a tendency to be deliberately shocking as if she were a maiden aunt. Eugene had not found it embarrassing to be with her at a disgraceful entertainment. Surely he would have reacted differently to her presence in the days when she had been pretty and graciously feminine?

Her mind wandered down a cindery track and returned again to the offensive phrase. No love affairs and certainly, until she had shaken off the blight which had fallen upon her, no prospect of any! Her illness and its aftermath had deprived her not only of physical beauty and the graces that go with it, but even of inducements to remedy the want. In her present sphere of activity there were no such opportunities as she had taken for granted during her career on the stage. Her clothes had become tired; her strenuous work and equally strenuous economies left her without energy for being well groomed. And since Egypt was for her only an artificial background, a stage upon which she was playing a role soon to be discarded, she had made a point of not wasting time in regrets for vanished elegance. It had seemed a merit to have accepted this part of her misfortune with resignation.

But Constance's mortifying words shattered her complacency. It had been based, she realized, upon an assumption that, however far she might let herself go in Egypt, once at home all could be made right. This morning that seemed horribly improbable. She had got out of the habit of being an attractive woman, and it might be more difficult to recapture than she had supposed. In the stress and strain of the last seven months some virtue had gone out of her.

It was with spirits at the lowest ebb they had reached for some time that she paid her afternoon visit to Lotus Building. The burden of her quarrel with Constance lay heavy on her mind, and, still smarting from a sense of injury, she decided to tell Daisy what she had done for the foolish girl and how ill she had been repaid. Daisy had never seen Lucy's protégée and had taken very little interest in what she had heard about her, but Lucy was in so despondent a humour that even the thin shadow of sympathy would be gratifying. She was therefore particularly exasperated to discover Mr. Mosenthal in Daisy's sitting-room.

A waiter was clearing the table at which they had been lunching, but although his presence had evidently imposed a silence on them, it was clear from the tension of the atmosphere that they were in the midst of some sort of scene. Accustomed, whenever she happened to come upon them together, to being treated as an intruder, she immediately suggested returning to the theatre; but to her surprise Mosenthal, with an almost hospitable gesture, beckoned her to a chair.

His general habit was to greet her with about the same degree of civility as one might show to an obliging chambermaid, for he found it a little awkward that one of his minor employees should have the run, so to speak, of his private life, and his naturally bad manners were rendered worse by an impression that, if he were polite, she might be encouraged to take liberties.

Today, however, his fears were in abeyance. For the second time he needed Lucy's help, as he conceived, to tide him over a situation fraught with dangerous possibilities. So, although he did not rise at her entrance or utter any form of salutation, he indicated by offering her a chair that her arrival was acceptable.

'Now, here's your friend,' he said affably to Daisy. 'She'll give you some good advice. I wonder how long this fellow intends to take before he gets out.'

The waiter, to whom this remark was perfectly audible, speeded neatly through his task and retired with a dignified pretence of being deaf. Lucy meanwhile, annoyed but distracted from her melancholy, endeavoured to guess from Daisy's air of patient suffering what problem was about to be opened to her.

'Well, Miss Kendon,' Mosenthal observed in something better than his usual casually condescending manner—though his policy of keeping her at a distance never permitted him to use her Christian name—'you seem to be a fairly intelligent woman. Perhaps you'll be able to talk Daisy into a reasonable frame of mind. We've been having a little discussion about a plan of mine, and she's taking up an entirely wrong attitude.'

Daisy's eye remained fixed dejectedly upon a remote point in space.

'As you know,' he went on, 'my parents live in South Africa, and I haven't seen them for nearly fifteen years. What with one thing and another I've never been able to go back there. But now I have a chance of paying them a visit and doing some business in Johannesburg at the same time, and it just happens that for once in my life I have things arranged here so that I can get away. I shall only be gone two or three months at the outside. Now can you imagine Daisy would be such a fool as to expect to come with me?'

Lucy could not think of any answer that would be pleasing to both, so she only said lamely: 'I suppose she'll be very disappointed if she's left behind.'

'Disappointed? Why should she be? She never heard about it till this morning.'

'That's just it,' Daisy broke in, subduing a voice charged with trembling emotion. 'I've had no time to get used to the idea. Not that I ever *could* get used to it!'

'I told you as soon as I came to a decision.' He spoke quite kindly, for her grief flattered him and he had become very fond of her. 'There was no point in bothering you while it was all up in the air.'

'You could take me with you if you really wanted to.' She seemed to be stating a sorrowful case without hope of winning any victory.

'My dear girl, you're crazy! Have I got to go into it all over again? How the hell can I turn up in Johannesburg with a girl on my hands that I'm not married to? What would my father and mother think? How could I introduce you to my sisters?'

Daisy's stricken face informed him that he had been cruel, and he continued with a conciliatory gesture: 'It would be a rotten position for you. I'd be living at home and you'd be stuck in a hotel wondering what to do with yourself. Now here the season's coming on, and there'll be lots of things you and Miss Kendon can do together—as long as you keep out of mischief.'

Lucy, seeing that a plain statement of her own plans was unavoidable, gathered her strength to make it, but he cut across her tentative beginning:

'Remember, you won't be living alone. Your friend is going to have a room in the building.'

'Do you mean me?' cried Lucy. 'But I can't, Mr. Mosenthal. I couldn't think of it. I—'

Again he cut her short. 'That's all right. You won't have to pay for it. It'll be nice for Daisy to have you on the spot.'

'Mr. Mosenthal, I can't *be* on the spot. I'm sailing to England on December the third.' Now that the moment had come, she spoke firmly and without apology. The project he had opened to her was too disagreeable for hesitant methods. She must make it clear that no compromise was possible.

'Sailing to England?' Mosenthal was nonplussed. He had had some vague idea that she was saving up to get home, but he had not expected to be told, abruptly like this, that she was sailing on a definite date. Coming so soon after the enormous condescension he had shown her, he found her disclosure not only inconvenient but almost an affront. Yet, to make his irritation still more profound, instead of being able to shrug his shoulders and indifferently dismiss the matter, he was obliged to demean himself by pleas and persuasions. He could not let her go. To leave Daisy in Cairo without some reliable companion was unthinkable.

'Is there any reason,' he inquired with ill-concealed annoyance, 'why you've got to go on that particular date?'

'Yes, Mr. Mosenthal, I've booked my passage.'

'That can be rearranged.'

'I'm afraid that's utterly out of the question,' said Lucy with a sharpness born of fear. 'I've been preparing to leave for some time, and everything's cut and dried now.'

'It's the first I've heard of it. Have you given notice at the theatre?'

'There's still ample time to give a month's notice, and I think only a week is required.'

'Did your voice come back then?'

'No, not yet. But when I get home I shall take some lessons to bring it back gradually if I can.'

'Have you got some job waiting for you?'

'No, Mr. Mosenthal.' She looked at him squarely. 'But I'm quite a capable woman and thanks to you I've had some valuable experience. I shall get work all right.' Seeing him rapping on the table with a fretful hand, she added in an effort to propitiate: 'Daisy knows I've been saving my fare ever since you were kind enough to give me the job at the Adelphi.'

If the moment thrust upon her for breaking her news was unfortunate as far as Mosenthal was concerned, it happened to be an auspicious one with Daisy. At any ordinary time she too might have found cause for vexation in having been so little consulted, but now she saw in Lucy's departure some prospect of gaining her way with Siegfried, and she struck in eagerly: 'Oh, yes, Lucy's been set on getting home for ages. I thought you knew.'

Very carefully he extracted a cigar from his case and lit it with deliberate slowness. He was tempted to remind these foolish women that Lucy had obligations which should make her place his wishes before her own, but it was beneath his dignity. He did not seriously consider her as his debtor in anything but a technical sense, and he was rather ashamed when, as if she had guessed something of his fleeting thought, she proceeded: 'I've not forgotten that I still owe you four thousand piastres, but it seems to me I can pay them back just as well from England as out here.'

'Did I ask to be paid back?' He was glad to have an excuse for rebuking her. 'I called it off long ago. For God's sake, don't harp on it!'

He walked up and down the room, waving his cigar as an angry cat might wave its tail, while Daisy, with friendly and even grateful interest, asked questions about Lucy's ship and berth and the details of her preparations. He did not speak again until he had got his too flattering impatience under control and could assume the right degree of benevolent contempt for his audience.

'Well, Miss Kendon, it isn't my place to give you advice'—his manner implied that he stooped from a considerable height to do so—'but I must say I think you may come to regret being in such a hurry to get away. You leave Egypt just when the best time of the year is beginning and arrive in London for the worst part of the winter—and you won't find it an easy winter after living in hot countries so long. You give up a good job to go back to a lot of doubtful prospects. The boats are crowded and you'll have a thoroughly uncomfortable journey. Now if I go to South Africa in a fortnight, I'll be back by February. Wouldn't it be more sensible to wait till then? You'll have a nice room in this building while I'm away and a first-class passage home when my trip's over. What do you say?'

Lucy was not a person of flexible character and desires, and she had fixed her hopes too long on being in England by Christmas to find herself capable of deferring them now. She knew that Mosenthal's offer would sound a reasonable one to anybody not acquainted with her strong feelings, and she knew that to refuse it would occasion lasting displeasure, but the difficulty of her position only served to make her more determined.

'I'm sorry, Mr. Mosenthal,' she replied stolidly; 'I wish I could do what you want, but you don't know what it would mean to me. I love England. All my friends are there—except Daisy, of course—and all the things I care about. I don't like Egypt and I've never been happy here. I want to see my sister again and the people I'm fond of. I'm a fish out of water here.'

At another time Mosenthal might have been disposed to lend a moderately sympathetic ear to this statement: in his Jewish respect for family ties he would at least have approved of her longing for her sister. But today he could see only that his plans were being thwarted and his greatness insulted. He could not bring himself to utter any more explicit pleading. A resentful challenge was the last card his pride would let him play.

'So you're going just at the one time Daisy will be needing you?'

'Daisy can't need me as much as all that,' said Lucy, and in her growing alarm she continued tactlessly, 'Don't press me, Mr. Mosenthal! I should have to refuse you. I know you've done me some great favours, but I've tried to repay them in every way I could, both in the theatre and out of it. I couldn't do any more. Daisy wouldn't expect it.'

There was nothing in the reception of this answer to indicate that it was to have lifelong consequences for her. No significant pause or gesture made the words memorable. Mosenthal only responded, 'It's your own business,' took a languid puff at his cigar, and blew out smoke as if he blew the whole subject away. Daisy, seeing Lucy's fixity of purpose as a godsend, said pleasantly, 'Oh, no, my dear, I wouldn't stand in your light for anything. It's natural that you should want to get home.'

Mosenthal rose and, with a casual word of farewell thrown over his shoulder, flicked some ash on the carpet and retired. He could not allow himself to lose his temper with a person so beneath his notice, but inwardly he burned with sullen hostility. To think of the wretched woman haughtily requesting him not to press his appeals upon her, warning him that she would reject them! To think of her daring to show, by her reference to serving him, 'both in the theatre and out', that she was conscious of her private usefulness! There had been a moment when he was tempted to inform her that her services either in the theatre or anywhere else were no longer required, but his defensive vanity forbade him to pay her the compliment of open vindictiveness. Let her work out her notice and fling herself to the miserable fate which unquestionably awaited her in England!

Daisy, on the other hand, who knew Mosenthal too well by now to suppose that he would go to South Africa without her if she had no chaperon in Cairo, was oblivious to everything that would normally have offended her. She wanted only to be kind and responsive.

'I don't blame you a bit,' she whispered to Lucy when the door had closed on him. 'People always want to get away from a country where they've been unlucky,' And by a magnanimous effort of recollection she concluded: 'I felt the same when I was in Australia.'

Chapter 18

One morning a few days later Lucy was returning to the theatre from an outside errand when she had an encounter which both embarrassed her and amused her. Chappie Paulos, whom she had never met since the unhappy day in Alexandria when she had vainly tried to borrow money from him, came face to face with her suddenly on emerging from a shop. At such close quarters neither could pretend not to have seen the other, though both revealed by the awkwardness of their manner how clearly they remembered their last interview.

'I didn't expect to see you over in Cairo, Mr. Paulos,' said Lucy, to account for the slight hesitation in her greeting. 'Do you come here often?'

'Oh, every now and then. Sometimes for business, sometimes for the races. What about you? You settled down here after all, eh? I thought you would. I heard Mosenthal lets you have a job in the theatre till your voice comes back. Is it still—still—?'

'Still missing. Yes, I'm afraid so, but I'm not trying it, not even thinking about it till I get home.'

'That's right. That's sensible.' They were walking in the same direction, and he felt it incumbent upon him to persist in his civil inquiries. 'And how do you like this work you do now? Not so much fun as being on the stage, is it?'

'No, but it's an interesting way of marking time.'

The idiom puzzled him, but he nodded sagely and went on, 'I suppose you're crazy to get back to the footlights? I don't blame you. A gay life, eh?—with plenty of admirers. That's the thing.'

She answered with a smile: 'We always worked pretty hard in the companies I was in. Music to learn, costume fittings, hours of hanging about at rehearsals—the public doesn't see all that.'

'Oh, but you had some gay times, all the same, I'll bet! Nice little supper parties after the show, nice little presents from the boys. Yes, yes, you had some gay times!' he insisted expansively.

'I suppose I did.' Lucy found that by some unreasonable evocative power Chappie's foolish words had conjured up for her a picture of Henry so vivid that the enchantment of it outweighed her sense of loss.

The joy of that great conquest flooded back upon her as lavishly as if she still retained the fruits of it. Henry, so affectionate, so handsome, so glamorous with famous ancestors and fashionable occupations—what prestige his attentions had given her at the theatre! How surprising and delightful had been his first courtship! The flowers, the extravagant luncheons and suppers, the lamp-lit tables . . . the delicious awareness of new clothes bought to beguile him . . . the tantalizing motor rides when each had wondered if the time was ripe for them to kiss, to declare themselves. . . . Ah, those tentative movements of one towards the other, those brushing caresses of finger-tips, those quick turns of the head that brought their eyes into a smiling duel—one would have thought nothing could ever equal that for pleasure. And yet the warm glow of an established intimacy had surpassed it.

She might remember, if she put her mind to it, the crossing of each little Rubicon. The first time they had been able to yawn in front of each other without apology; the first time they had compared notes about family difficulties and spoken freely about money . . . the morning when they had argued and chatted in forgetfulness, at last, of their effect upon each other, and then suddenly noticed that they had become friends in becoming lovers.

That stage too had passed. The war, which until now had seemed merely an evanescent background for timeless embraces, broke over and engulfed them. Their love had become feverish. His visits on leave from France, so short, so full of suspense, so inevitably encroached upon by the superior claims of his family, were a sweet agony that shook the nerves more than his danger. She had been quarrelsome, he defensive; and in that year of cruel uncertainties, 1917, it was easier to make a breach than to heal one.

But this last bewildering phase had not for long obscured her gratitude for their happiness, which opened out before her now in such a radiant vista that the dusty boulevard and the silly tiresome person at her side passed for a moment into oblivion.

When she came back Chappie was speaking commiserating words: 'Well, never mind, it isn't all over yet. There will be gay times also in the future. You just have to fatten up a little bit and get some more colour into your face. Then you'll be ready for anything.'

Sustained by her past glory, she stood incapable of being humiliated.

'What is this job of yours?' he asked. 'I hear you're head bottle-cleaner and cook or whatever the saying goes.'

'No, I'm *under*-cook and bottle-washer. I do anything and everything—chiefly anything.'

'Do you see much of Mosenthal?'

'Very little.'

'But you hear quite a lot about business, I dare say.'

'What business? The theatre?'

'The theatre—and other things as well. Mosenthal's got many fingers in the pie.'

'He doesn't tell me about them.'

'Still, it's a sure thing you pick up a bit of news here and there, especially being so friendly with that little pal of his.'

'We don't talk business,' said Lucy flatly.

'What, two clever girls like you! Don't she want to know how he's getting so rich when he started with nothing? Maybe you heard how he came to Egypt with two pounds in his pocket?'

'I seem to have heard,' Lucy returned ironically. It was a piece of information which grew more and more weariful.

'I tell you that man can make money out of air. He'll be a millionaire before he's finished, you can take it from me. Everything he touches makes money and he always gets out at the right time, as if an angel whispered to him.'

'Perhaps one does.'

'I wish I had an angel whispering to me,' Chappie ventured with a side-long glance. 'It would be worth while sometimes to know what a man like Mosenthal is up to.'

Lucy took enough of his meaning to remain silent.

'It couldn't do no harm to him, and I might get a lot of benefit out of it. I have a little flutter occasionally, you know, apart from the cotton market. And if anybody puts me on to a good thing, well—they don't get left out in the cold.'

'I'm afraid I've never understood these matters at all,' Lucy rejoined tonelessly. 'Finance of every kind is a mystery to me.'

He would have said more, but another look at her unresponsive face convinced him that she was either too stupid or too priggish to be of service, and he was glad that he had not committed himself any further.

'Finance is a mystery to everyone.' He tossed the subject aside. 'But a few people, like Mosenthal, seem to know a bit more than others; that's the difference. Hallo! Here we are nearly at your theatre. You going straight in?'

He looked at his watch, and working his mouth to a strange and unprepossessing line seemed to engage in inward debate. 'Twelve o'clock. Do you think the manager will be inside?'

'Mr. Prince-Carter? Why, yes, probably. I left him in his office.'

'I was wondering if you'd do me the little favour to take me in and introduce me. I suppose he knows who I am?'

'I'm sure he does,' she said with flattering gravity.

'You see, when I'm at a loose end I like to go to the theatre here just the same as I do in Alex. I must be the most regular theatre-goer in Egypt, because, with all my languages, I can understand everything. French, English, Italian, Greek—it makes no difference to me what company I see. Now in Alex they know me and they make me feel at home in the theatre. You saw the way they treat me there. Altoni at the Lyrico says if I wasn't in the house on a first night they wouldn't open the show; at the Opera House it's the same thing. But here poor old Chappie is no better than anybody else. I just pay for my seat—my box, I should say—and walk in when the show begins and walk out when it's over.'

'But you know most of the artistes?' Lucy suggested sympathetically.

'No, how can I? They nearly always play Cairo first, and until they've been to Alexandria I don't meet them. When they arrive in Alex, I arrange a nice little lunch and all that, and they come and see my perfumes, and we grow friendly in no time. But here it's a different matter. Poor old Chappie is quite out of things here.'

Lucy murmured polite incredulousness.

'So I been thinking I ought to get acquainted with one or two of the managers, and then when I happen to be in Cairo there'll be someone who can take me round and give me a few opportunities of meeting people.'

'Yes, by all means. Come in! I'm sure Mr. Prince-Carter will be glad to see you.'

'Of course,' he continued, suddenly grudging the extent to which he had belittled himself, 'I could have arranged it long ago if I'd given some thought to it. I could have got one of my artiste friends to fix it up for me, but I suppose one introduction's as good as another, eh?'

'Kind of you to say so.' The mischief in her voice escaped him.

'I wonder if this Prince-Carter is free to come out to lunch. Should I ask him, do you think?'

'Do! He likes good lunches.'

Chappie questioned himself as to whether etiquette required, in the circumstances, that he invite this stolid and unentertaining young woman to join them, but he decided against it. She was anything but well dressed, and there might be somebody at Shepheard's Hotel who knew him.

Yet when she had presented him to the manager with such a description as was due to him, mentioning his perfumes and his wonderful hospitality, he felt he must make up to her for any slight she might be feeling and, as she retreated, he called affably after her: 'By the way, Miss Kendon, if you like to send me a postcard, telling me what size and colour you want, I'll let you have a couple of pairs of stockings.' He turned to Prince-Carter with his usual facetious explanation: 'All the ladies get silk stockings from Chappie. That's what he's there for, isn't it so, Miss Kendon?'

'You're certainly very generous with them, Mr. Paulos.'

'Now then, no compliments! I know the girls are after something when they pay me compliments.' He winked gaily at the manager, in high good humour at his satisfactory reception, for his invitation had been cordially accepted.

Lucy pleaded a number of tasks that must be attended to without delay, and left him basking in the rays of Prince-Carter's somewhat specious geniality.

No one knew better than Lucy how specious that geniality could be, for she worked on difficult terms with her superior—terms which might have proved unbearable if she had not borne the day of her deliverance perpetually in mind. Arthur Prince-Carter was a weary and angry man whose nerves were strained to breaking-point by the necessity of having to play the role of a cheerful and debonair one. Gossip said he had a ne'er-do-well son whom Mosenthal's money had retrieved from an exceedingly unpleasant scrape, and if that were true it might lend a pardonable colour to the obsequiousness, quite embarrassing to witness, with which he flattered every opinion, deferred to every caprice, and bore with every insolence from his master. Either in gratitude or to make himself valuable, he habitually undertook an inordinate amount of work, much of which would normally have been outside his province, and in consequence he was always tired and on edge.

But the manager of a theatre is not supposed to give the impression of being a harassed drudge. He is a host to the public and must appear obliging, alert, yet at ease; and Prince-Carter, who had been connected with the stage all his life, was as much a showman as most actors. Wearing his evening clothes with conscious distinction, handsome in a rather actorish way, his hair going picturesquely grey at the temples, the deep lines on his face serving only to give it 'character', speaking in a sympathetic, murmuring voice, but always ready to throw back his head in that rich, full-throated laugh whose essential artificiality could only be detected by a very fine ear, he masqueraded as a convivial figure. But when he retired to his private office to spend himself resentfully in toil brought upon him by his own servility, his face seemed all troubled creases, his broad straight shoulders bent forward as if under a physical burden, and he became a bundle of nervous irritabilities.

To Lucy his attitude was disturbingly unsteady, for although her assistance was useful and she had relieved him of many paltry duties, he could not help suspecting, when he thought of her friendship with Daisy Joy and Daisy Joy's relations with Mosenthal, that her real purpose in the theatre was espionage. Whenever anything went wrong for which he might be held to blame, or whenever, being momentarily off his guard, he let himself go and said what he felt on some matter of policy, he would be worried afterwards by a gnawing fear that she was taking a report to her private 'head-quarters'. Reassured at last by the absence of any retribution from the high place, he would lapse into incautiousness once more, and once more become a prey to anxiety.

Lucy, having very little subtlety and no skill at all in the politics of business, could not guess at the reasons for his confused and vacillating manner, nor did she perceive that her known intimacy with Daisy set a strain on her relations not alone with him but with several other employees of Polyglot Amusements, whose behaviour towards her was a mixture of effusive amiability and disconcerting watchfulness. She had occasionally noticed how, when someone began to voice a grievance, someone else by a frown or a slight movement of the head would convey a warning reminder of her presence; but she put this guardedness down to sheer unpopularity on her part, and never realized she was in a position to be feared.

It was tiresome to be unpopular, but the effort of winning confidence seemed scarcely worth while. Diplomacy did not come naturally to her, and, after all, her connection with these people was temporary.

Prince-Carter had a wife who would have been an even greater trial to Lucy than himself, only that she was not compelled to see so much of her. She was an ex-actress, perhaps ten years older than her husband, whose chief characteristic was a sweeping imperiousness, an overwhelmingly aggressive dignity of carriage, adopted to compensate her for the failure of her career and the eclipse of personal attractions which had once been considerable. She was proud of her fine diction and always spoke in a loud elocutionary voice that made even the most trivial utterance sound as if it were being delivered from the centre of a stage; she was proud also of an extremely stately figure, and displayed it whenever possible in striking and majestic postures. In her stock-company days many years ago she had frequently been cast for empresses, Roman matrons, and other such statuesque and noble women, and by some rather pathetic process of the mind she had come to identify herself with these and to regard herself as entitled to an extraordinary show of deference.

The one triumph her now vanished beauty had brought her was the subjugation of the good-looking youth whom she had married, and in this she continued to exult, publicly ordering him about, commending and rebuking him with an arrogance few other men would have endured for an instant: but he was as pliable with her as with Mosenthal, never having shaken off the awe he had felt on finding himself her husband at the age of twenty. Of late years she had taken to calling him Prince instead of Arthur, because a name sounding like a title helped to serve her passion for grandeur. She invariably pronounced it with an unctuous emphasis which made strangers look round, expecting to see royalty.

Prince-Carter himself had grown so accustomed to this and other eccentricities that he was almost unconscious of them, and seldom became aware of the ridicule they provoked. His colleagues humoured her—for her delusions were transparent—by an attitude of extravagant respect, but there was a good deal of subterranean mockery and grumbling. She came to the theatre much oftener than was reasonable, interrupting her husband during momentous interviews and offering suggestions with an air of regal authority. Mosenthal alone could subdue her lofty demeanour; she had just enough common sense left to know that her living depended on him; and perhaps she had not quite forgotten that disgrace from which, it was said, he had rescued her only son, now banished to some obscure part of Europe. But even with him, she was capable of tactlessnesses which made the onlookers cringe. Fortunately, Prince-Carter's efficiency outweighed his wife's power to irritate: in any case Mosenthal encountered her seldom.

Lucy, on the other hand, saw her two or three times a week and found it hard to bring her sense of humour to bear upon the annoyances she suffered. As a fellow artiste now exiled from the stage, Mrs. Prince-Carter considered her an ideal audience for lengthy reminiscences; while as one of Prince's subordinates she was a suitable object for queenly patronage which was sometimes very irksome to endure. Lucy had grown to dread the sight of that tall, commanding form and the sound of that resonant voice.

Today her arrival was particularly untimely, for she appeared just as Lucy, who had been on her feet all morning and wanted her lunch, was in the ladies' cloakroom preparing to leave the theatre.

'Ah, Miss Kendon,' she cried, flinging the door wide open to make her usual imposing entrance; 'at last I find a human being! The building seems empty—empty.' By a remarkable hollowness of tone she conveyed the idea of an emptiness disastrous, insupportable. 'Where is my husband? Where can he be?'

'Good morning,' said Lucy. 'Mr. Prince-Carter had gone out to lunch.'

'Gone? Gone already? How very trying! Now I shall have to have my luncheon alone.'

Lucy dried her hands with great concentration. She was determined to avoid being honoured with Mrs. Prince-Carter's company during her lunch-time respite.

'While I am here, I'd better make one or two telephone calls. Would you oblige me by getting the numbers, Miss Kendon?'

Really, thought Lucy, the woman's insolence was beyond a joke! As if she didn't know perfectly well how to use the telephone!

'You can ring up from Mr. Prince-Carter's room,' she said with detached politeness. 'That 'phone's quite free at present.'

'Oh, but I shall be lost without you, Miss Kendon. I am a perfect child when confronted with a telephone. In fact, my husband says I'm a child in all the practical details of life. What I should have done if I'd been faced with your difficulties I *do* not know.'

Lucy, covering her exasperation with small talk, led the way to the manager's office. She found the required numbers in the directory, telephoned a message to a grocer and another to a dressmaker, and undertook to carry various greetings and admonitions to members of the company. Mrs. Prince-Carter had seen the show the night before, and as usual she felt it incumbent on her to point out where errors had been made. She had hoped to catch the producer before the morning rehearsal ended to let him know where the pace was too fast and which players were inaudible.

'This modem passion for speeding-up is going to be the ruin of the stage,' she intoned as if she were speaking from a pulpit. 'In my young days it was a very different thing, I assure you. We were taught to enunciate clearly, beautifully, to round off every word.' She herself rounded off every word with maddening perfection. 'But nowadays, what do we hear? Muttering! Mumbling! Half the lines are thrown away. And they won't learn, the young ones today. Give them the merest hint and they take umbrage at once.'

Lucy was craving to get away to her little French restaurant, but in her fear that Mrs. Prince-Carter would accompany her, she was obliged to linger, with the air of waiting for somebody, while the inflated voice, so ostentatiously rich, so full of modulations, poured out anecdotes revealing the wilful incompetence of the younger generation of actresses, more especially the leading lady of the company at present in possession.

'In my opinion, Miss Kendon,' she said severely, fixing Lucy with a flashing eye, 'there is nothing that betrays ignorance so completely, so shockingly, as refusing to accept advice from someone more experienced than oneself. And when I say more experienced, I mean more experienced. I was an accomplished artiste, Miss Kendon, an accomplished artiste when that flat-chested little person was in her cradle.'

Lucy replied somewhat equivocally that she had no doubt of it.

'I should hardly like to tell you how many years it is since I had my first part,' the voice went on implacably. 'It was not a speaking part. I merely had to be asleep on a cloud wearing draperies. I was supposed to be a goddess. They chose me, Miss Kendon, because in my youth I was picturesque; I could carry myself well. It's an art very few girls have today. I shall always recall one unfortunate experience I had during the run of that show.' Lucy repressed a sigh and resigned herself. 'This cloud that I lay on was suspended from the flies on wires. I had to take my position before the curtain went up; then the cloud was lowered and, of course, I had to stay where I was until the scene changed. I was in full view of the audience for a whole act, fifteen feet above the stage, cut off from everything, with no possibility of making an exit.'

She paused for Lucy to ask: 'What happened? Did you faint or fall off?'

'No, my dear, to faint would have been comparatively pleasant. What I did was to contract a chill, a very bad chill, internally.' She laid a dramatic hand on her abdomen. 'No sooner had the curtain gone up than I wanted to retire *urgently*. Can you imagine, Miss Kendon? There was no possibility, simply no possibility. I couldn't move, I couldn't budge, until they were ready to raise me by a pulley. Hundreds of pairs of eyes were fixed on me—we had a splendid house that night—and there I was in anguish. Can you picture a more frightful situation?'

'No,' said Lucy fervently, 'I can't. Did you manage to get through the act?'

'Miss Kendon, I couldn't. I could not.' The voice was tragically vibrant. 'It was a long act. It seemed to go on and on. I became more and more desperate. The effort of trying to look like a goddess while in such a state! I shall never forget it.'

'What on earth did you do?'

'I signalled until I managed to attract the attention of one of the stage-hands in the flies. He bent down to listen to me, and I hissed up at him: "Get me out of this! Get me out! I'm not well." And at last I made him understand that it was serious, and they hoisted up the cloud and let me go.'

'So it was all right,' said Lucy with relief.

'Yes, and now, looking back, I can see the funny side of it. The faces of the people on the stage as they saw the cloud gradually disappear from sight! It nearly dried them up, but I must say they glossed it over amazingly well. I watched the last part of the act from the wings, and the audience hardly noticed anything. Of course it's wonderful what an audience *will* fail to notice. Now I remember one occasion at the Royal Court Theatre in Liverpool—"

Lucy had been casting about for some way of escape, and had decided there was nothing for it but to be unscrupulous. 'Excuse my interrupting you,' she said with only the slightest twinge of conscience, 'but it's just occurred to me where your husband is likely to be lunching, Mrs. Prince-Carter, if you still want to get hold of him.

He's almost certain to be at Shepheard's with a man called Chappie Paulos. Have you heard of him?'

'Paulos! The perfume collector from Alexandria who gives away silk stockings? What on earth can Prince be doing with him?'

Lucy explained. 'I was sorry you weren't here to meet him too,' she added with an airy untruthfulness rarely achieved by her. 'You would have been amused at him, and I'm sure he would have been awfully pleased. He adores everything and everyone connected with the theatre. What a pity you missed him! He's such a character!'

'A tuft-hunter, I understand, but wonderfully generous. I always enjoy meeting a character, don't you, Miss Kendon? I can forgive a man a great many faults if he has a real character of his own. Did you say they had gone to Shepheard's?'

'That's what I gathered.'

'Well, I think I'll stroll along there. I shall probably catch them having an appetizer before they go in to lunch, so I shall be able to get a word with my husband. It's rather important. As a general rule I make a point, as you know, Miss Kendon, of not interrupting my husband's business engagements.'

Lucy led her at once out of the office and through the foyer. She could not but smile to see the statuesque figure moving off at a pace which was very rapid and yet affected to be a saunter. In a few minutes she would be lunching with Chappie and Prince-Carter, that was certain. And Chappie would not be very pleased, for although his passion for theatrical people was great, it did not quite extend to seeking the company of an extremely overwhelming lady who had left the stage fifteen years ago.

Setting off to her restaurant as soon as Mrs. Prince-Carter was out of sight, Lucy acknowledged that she had played a not very admirable trick. 'But oh!' she said to herself with relish, 'how he deserves it! I hope she tells him anecdotes all afternoon!'

Chapter 19

Lucy had eaten her meal at leisure and was about to pay her afternoon visit to Daisy when a bulky frame interposed itself between the table and the doorway, and she saw with surprise Eugene's wide, tanned face, so much too large for its features, and ebony eyes, more sombre with shadows than ever.

'Why, Eugene!' she cried, half rising. 'How did you know I was here?'

'I called at the theatre. The man in the box-office told me where I'd probably find you.'

He sat down rather heavily, staring straight before him in a way that made her feel a little apprehensive, and his thick yet supple brown fingers lay absolutely still upon the tablecloth.

'You got my note?' she asked. She had written a day or two before to remind him that she still considered herself indebted for half his loss on the night of their unfortunate outing.

'Yes, Lucy, I got your note.'

'Well, how much do I owe you?'

'You owe me nothing, Lucy.'

There was something peculiar about his tone. It was quite lifeless, yet charged with significance.

'Nonsense!' said Lucy with a cheerfulness that scarcely rang true. 'I really must insist on settling up. By the way, have you had something to eat?'

'Thank you, I don't need anything to eat.' He moved his gaze effortfully from nothingness to her face. 'If I could have some—some burgundy . . . half a bottle of burgundy, we could talk.'

She signalled to the *patron*. 'If you haven't had your lunch, don't you think you ought to eat something as well?'

'I've had what lunch I want, my dear Lucy.'

He spoke mildly, abstractedly, studying her face with a sort of rueful intensity.

'I thought you played at your restaurant during the lunch hour.'

'I do. The lunch hour is over.' He held up his watch to her.

The wine was ordered, and she sat back waiting for him to speak. He had something of importance to say, she was sure of it, and in the gloomy silence of the next few moments she speculated with increasing fear upon the nature of his communication. It seemed evident that their visit to that infamous house had produced some repercussion.

At last, lowering his head and once again reposing his hands quietly before him, he remarked in a level and dispassionate voice, 'I think you're about to see the last of me, you lucky woman.'

'Eugene, what on earth is the matter?'

'Merely that I must abscond or else be arrested. In either case, I don't imagine I'll see much of you in the future.'

'But, Eugene!' Her exclamation was cut short by the arrival of the burgundy. She waited, every emotion held in suspense, until the ritual of service was over. 'Eugene! What are you talking about? What have you been doing?'

'Well, it looks as if I've been embezzling my employer's money. Actually, it was completely unintentional, but I should have no hope of proving that in a court of law. I've just got to decide whether to face the music or try and run for it, that's all.'

'You'd better tell me about it.' She clasped her nervous hands together, and resolved to listen calmly. 'What is it that has happened?'

He raised his head once more and fixed her with a full, clear glance. His eyes looked more liquid than usual, less hard and bright, but they were as steady as ever. Indeed, the lids with their thick black lashes seemed to perform the feat of remaining motionless while he talked. The stillness of his whole person was remarkable.

'I hoped you'd never have to be told,' he said. 'I thought somehow I'd be able to make it all right, but it's useless. You wanted to know how much was in the pocket-book they stole—I pretended to make light of it; I didn't want to worry you, and I was so afraid you'd insist on going to the police. Actually, the pocket-book had three thousand piastres in it, and it wasn't my money.'

'My dear, is this—? Oh, it's a joke! It couldn't be true!'

'I wish you were right. It was given to me for the salaries of the orchestra, and this is pay-day.'

Stunned as she was, Lucy roused herself to inquire: 'Why were you carrying it about?'

'Misfortune, Lucy, sheer misfortune! There are times when circumstances conspire against us.' Over his glass of burgundy his small white teeth showed in an unutterably mournful smile. 'I should have given it to the manager to put in the safe, but it happened that I hadn't any cash of my own on me that day, and as you and I were going out on our jaunt, I thought, "I can draw on this for tonight and replace what I take before I hand it over tomorrow."'

'Is that what you meant when you said, "I put money in my purse"?'

'Quite right, my dear, worse luck! Your memory is good!'

Lucy faintly shook her head. How could anyone be so foolish as to entrust money to Eugene! But, of course, she told herself dismally, his present employer knew nothing of weaknesses revealed in India and Australia.

'I should have thought,' she said quietly, 'that if it was your job to pay the orchestra, they'd give you what was necessary on pay-day and not before.'

'Part of the conspiracy of circumstances, my dear, part of the conspiracy.' And rather to Lucy's surprise, for he was not usually a repetitive speaker, he muttered the phrase over again before replying: 'Normally it isn't my job to pay the orchestra, but our proprietor went to Port Said a week ago—he has another restaurant there, you know—and seeing that he wasn't going to be back by today, he doled out enough cash to tide us over till his return. You'd think,' he went on after a brief pause, 'that the manager would be entitled to draw on the firm's banking account, wouldn't you? But no, old Palmetti likes to keep everything in his own hands. That's typical of the man.' His eyes and his voice dropped with a sudden lassitude.

'And what exactly is the situation?' It took all her courage to ask. She would have been so glad at that moment to leave him, to get rid of him, while she possessed only this knowledge too vague to demand action from her.

'The situation, Lucy? I should have thought that would hardly require description. I've gone about for nearly a week in an appalling state of mind, as you can imagine. Every night I've made plans to decamp, and every morning I've resolved to stick it out another day, hoping against hope that some miracle would happen to make things all right without anyone being the wiser. But today puts an end to all that nonsense. The salaries should have been paid this morning. I got out of it by telling them I'd forgotten it was treasury day and left my pocket-book at home. We have a tea-time performance at five, and I said I'd bring it with me then. They were quite unsuspecting. I passed it off so casually. I'm a good liar,' he added with a slight apologetic laugh.

'An exceptionally good liar,' she agreed, remembering how convincingly he had made her believe that his loss was trifling. 'I only wish we'd gone to the police that night.'

'Perhaps we should have done, but I rather lost my head when I thought of confessing I'd been using my employer's money in a den like that. No, Lucy, it wouldn't have done any good. The police wink at most of what goes on in that underworld, and, in any case, what an unsavoury business it would have been for both of us!'

'So is this!' she wanted to retort, but she suppressed the desire, thinking, 'I won't pour more water on a drowning rat.' Then, as the realization of her own plight closed in upon her, she reflected, 'I might spare my pity. It's I who am drowning.'

He waited for her to speak, but she was mute. His gaze, which had been abstracted, resumed its still watchfulness and he continued: 'I can't turn up this afternoon without that money, and, frankly, I'm not too anxious to turn up at all. I've everything in readiness to make my exit. If I can get out of Cairo by one of the afternoon trains before I'm seriously missed, I dare say I can find somewhere to lie low until there's a chance of clearing off altogether.'

'You'll be getting yourself into very serious trouble if you're traced.' She spoke only to gain a little time—to postpone for a few minutes the dreadful sacrifice which, from the beginning, she had known to be inevitable.

'I shall be getting into serious trouble if I stay.'

'Not as bad as if you try to run away, Eugene. Oh, my dear, couldn't you go and make a clean breast of the whole affair? I'll come with you if my support will be of the slightest use.'

'Impossible, Lucy! If Palmetti were back I might risk it, but being an underling the manager's bound to act officiously. Well, for that matter, he has no choice. The band can't live without salaries, and if salaries aren't forthcoming it's his place to get something done about it. I'm the first to acknowledge that.'

There was something in the tone of the last words, a barely perceptible slurring, a slightly painstaking reasonableness, that inspired Lucy to say sharply, with a sudden obscure and desperate hope: 'Eugene, you haven't by any chance been drinking, have you?'

Oh, if it should only turn out that he was drunk—that this was all an alcoholic fantasy like that tale of a needy mother by which he had once obtained money from her to spend on his favourite barmaid!

But no—there was no prospect of reprieve. Her sanguine impulse vanished as he answered clearly, concisely, and with perfect steadiness of voice and glance. 'My dear girl, I have drunk some wine—some of the *vin ordinaire* they supply with our meals at the café. I have also had one glass of this burgundy. You surely can't suppose, knowing what you do about me, that I could be affected by that?'

'No, not by that. I only thought if you *had* been drinking . . . you don't show it outwardly, and yet you become so different—capable of different acts—' She broke off, unable to endure his reproachful eyes.

'No, no, Lucy,' he said gently. 'In the position I've been in since last Sunday, I've had to take more care than ever not to risk losing command of myself. I'm in a tight corner.'

Lucy was ashamed of her suspicion, but she could not help wishing it had been justified. To discover that Eugene had relapsed back into his old courses would be a painful business but nothing compared with the excruciating misery he heaped upon her by being unfortunate and in need of aid. She sank back in her chair, too oppressed to question further, while he returned to his project:

'Well, if I'm going to do my bolt, I shall have to manage it before five o'clock. The only thing that stands in my way is—what you've guessed, I dare say—money. You owe me nothing, Lucy, but I'm afraid I'll have to owe you something, if you can bear to help me out. I've hardly a sou. Five or six hundred piastres would see me through, for a few days at any rate, and after that I must live on my wits. I've done it before and I suppose I can do it again.'

She braced herself for the irrevocable step. Delay was dangerous to her morale: already she was beset with temptations. Why not give him the means to run away and let him take the consequences? Why not desert him—slink out of his presence now with any excuse she could muster, and collect her money and escape before she was engulfed? For a delirious moment she seemed about to plunge into treachery. Then she clasped her hands together until she had the illusion of drawing strength from their pressure, and said vigorously: 'I will not lend you money to do anything reckless and dishonest, Eugene. I understand how you must feel, but you know in your heart it would be disgraceful to go off, and foolish too, because you're such a very noticeable person that you'd soon be tracked down, wherever you went. That would mean—something pretty frightful.' (She could not bring herself to the indelicacy of saying 'prison'. In her father's vicarage, where she had learned the principles on which she was about to act, people who were in danger of going to prison appeared to live only in a remote and barely credible world: and for all the vicissitudes of the last few years she had never quite flung off the Market Rookestone attitude.)

'You must turn up this afternoon,' she went on, 'and take three thousand piastres with you, and that will be the end of the matter as far as your restaurant is concerned. I have the money in travellers' cheques, and if we go along to my room to fetch them right away, and then cash them at Thomas Cook's, you'll be in ample time to settle with your orchestra before the tea-time performance.'

She paused and turned away to conceal the embarrassing fact that she was breathing as fast as if she had been running, and when she looked at him again, she saw an expression upon his face—a mingling of relief and admiration with shame and distress—which moved her to pity. He had been so cool that she had lost sight of his unhappiness in her own, but now she could perceive how much he was suffering. She wished she could set him at ease by representing her sacrifice as a light one; but it was too enormous for that pretence.

'Lucy, my dear, dear friend!' He laid his hand affectionately over hers. 'How will you get back to England if you give me the money you've been saving?'

'I shall begin saving again—and you'll repay what you can, won't you, Eugene? A little every week?'

'Every penny I can squeeze out, Lucy. My good angel! Oh, but I can't accept so much from you. I can't. Let me go—let me make a mess of things in my own way! I won't have that money!'

'There's no alternative. Our visit to that house was a mutual piece of bad luck, and it's only just that I should take my share of it. Come, finish your wine, and let's get it over. If we argue about it I may change my mind'—she gave a feeble laugh—'and then you'll be in the soup.'

'My God!' he exclaimed and his diction was suddenly uncertain, his intent gaze clouded. 'You're a wonderful person—the best I ever met in my life! I wish I were in a position to ask you to marry me.' Lucy found herself gratified and even to some degree comforted by this assurance, though Eugene was one of the last men she would have chosen for a husband. On their rattling tram journey to Karnak House and afterwards to Thomas Cook's he talked a good deal about her noble qualities and the pride a man would feel in being united to them. It was the first time in many months that anyone had addressed her as a woman eligible for marriage, and it served to divert a few of her afflicted thoughts.

Chapter 20

Lucy parted with her savings at Thomas Cook's: all but what had been paid as a deposit on the fare to England. Then she went into the public gardens and sat on a bench as motionless as if she had been stunned. The effort of giving up what meant so much to her had been such a wrench as numbs the faculties. She could not think, could hardly even feel.

At last, as one who has been stupefied by a physical impact reluctantly pulls himself together to see where his blood flows and what bones are broken, she summoned up enough energy to take stock of her new disaster. There were many sources of pain, but none worse than the irony of her having so rashly, only a few days ago, rejected Mosenthal's offer to send her home in comfort at his own expense if she would wait in Egypt but two extra months. Two months! Even if she were allowed to keep her job and Eugene were scrupulous in paying back whatever he could spare, it would take her twice as long as that to amass the whole sum necessary for getting to England now that she was thrust back almost to the beginning again. With what an aching, grinding regret she went over that interview with Mosenthal and imagined a different ending for it!

Was it too late? A feeble gleam shot through the blackness. She had displeased him, it was true, but if she humbled herself, if she explained, entreated . . . Oh, she would do anything. Pride should be trampled underfoot. She would be Daisy's creature.

Or perhaps, even if he no longer needed her, he would take pity, seeing her wretchedness. If he offered to refund her loss she would accept his charity. Her little hope took strength. Daisy might be in a kindly mood and inspire him to generosity. If Mosenthal were to make her happy by taking her to South Africa with him, she might wish Lucy to be happy too.

Yet to have to tell the story . . . Merely to anticipate it set her nerves on edge. Her limbs grew as restless as before they had been inert, and she got up and began to walk about, first in the gardens, then the streets, too engrossed with her disturbing train of thought to be more than half conscious either of her own movements or the passage of time. Sheer fatigue eventually compelled her to take refuge in a café.

The tea-time music of a little under-rehearsed, impersonal, and listless orchestra brought Eugene's circumstances vividly to her mind, and she hoped that at this moment he was safely giving his afternoon performance with all the anxieties of the last six days unsuspected by his colleagues. Great as her fortitude had so far proved—and she could not but consider it with pride—it would be more than she could endure if her costly effort to save him from disgrace should turn out to be a waste. Had she been a fool to make that effort? She was oppressed by a sudden dolorous foreboding. After all, he had been in disgrace before, and had survived, but she depended on the caprice of Mosenthal and Daisy to deliver her from what might be the total wreckage of every plan she had cherished.

The foreboding became a fear. Now that Eugene was no longer with her, looking at her so unswervingly, compelling her belief with his steady voice and his air of probity, she began to perceive that the affair had features which required more investigation than she had given them. The description of his employer's financial arrangements did not seem, in retrospect, to be quite convincing. And, remembering with a special concentration exactly how he had behaved after the theft of his pocket-book, she found it more and more incredible that he had really been concealing the loss of a formidable sum which was not his property. Indeed, whatever aspect of the case she now examined, something to distrust appeared in it. By what mesmerism could she have been persuaded while he spoke?

And yet . . . and yet why should he have deceived her? Where was his motive? What temptation could have arisen to make him stoop to a piece of villainy so heinous and so easy of detection? Had he, for all his protestations, been drinking and bereft of conscience? His manner had undoubtedly been queer, but that she had put down to the stress and danger of his situation: he was trying, she had thought, to remain calm under difficulty, and this had imposed a certain awkwardness upon him. But looking back . . . oh, no, she could not have been so abjectly befooled throughout the whole encounter! It was a morbid fancy. She must shake it off. She must reassure herself.

He had promised to let her know tomorrow whether all was well, but what was there to prevent her from calling at his restaurant in the meantime to find out for herself? She might not have the chance of speaking to him, but merely to see him safe at work again would restore her confidence. She consulted her watch. It was six o'clock; the tea hour would be quite ended and the orchestra retired by the time she reached Palmetti's, and in any case she should have been at the Adelphi by half-past five to relieve the box-office clerk. She must try to visit Eugene during the later session, and in the meantime, even on so desperate an occasion as this, duty could not thrown wholly into abeyance.

It was only by the exercise of most rigorous self-control that she was able to give as much attention as was needful to her evening's work. Towards midnight she arrived at the restaurant. The orchestra had evidently just finished its performance. One or two of the musicians lingered on the platform, disposing of band-parts and instruments. Three others were settling themselves in the obscure corner where it was their custom to take supper. Lucy's heart began to beat dreadfully; Eugene was nowhere to be seen.

She stood irresolute, wondering how she should couch her inquiry for him, and found herself gazing straight into the harassed face of a waiter who was trying without enthusiasm to show her to a table. For a moment her mind became almost blank; her only thought was that no man on earth could look so tired as a tired waiter, and that this one might be a fitting representative of all the fatigues of the human race. She saw him with extraordinary clarity: his pallid features that seemed to be moulded out of lard, his puffy eyelids and the circles under his eyes, his drooping mouth, his drooping clothes—all revealed themselves with an awful distinctness, mutely declaring that they would be remembered for ever. She averted her eyes, unable any longer to hold the depressing picture, and explained in a humble and uncertain tone: 'I'm looking for Mr. Pryor—Mr. Eugene Pryor. He's in the band.'

There was a pause. Then, with an inflexion of such pitying contempt as only Latins know, the waiter answered her:

''E play 'ere before. 'E don't play 'ere now.'

'Oh, but surely,' she gasped, 'surely that's a mistake? He told me this afternoon that he was playing here. He *told* me so,' she repeated wildly, as if by her insistence she could make the false words true.

'Then, lady, 'e told you a lie,' said the waiter with a disdainful shrug. ''E don't play 'ere since before yesterday.'

'But didn't he come today? Didn't he arrive here at all?'

'No, lady. 'E don't belong 'ere now—not since before yesterday.' His languid voice revealed no desire to be more communicative: he was too tired even to find dramatic value in the situation.

Her apprehensions had not been sufficiently clear-cut to prepare her for the blow. She could only stare bewildered into the unhealthy face, trying in vain to find some link that would connect what she had just heard with Eugene's tale of difficulties.

The waiter returned her stare, at first with weariness, then with a faint dawning of compassion, and jerking his thumb towards the musicians at their supper-table, he suggested not unkindly: 'It's better you speak to somebody 'oo know about 'im. I call the leader, Mr. Solomon.'

He shambled off, and like one in a trance she followed him, and waited near at hand. She saw him bending over a little stocky, genial-looking man whom she recognized as the violinist; she saw the group at the table glance curiously towards her, and realized without emotion that they were probably classifying her as a drearily unattractive female in pursuit of an absconding lover. It did not matter what they supposed. Pride was gone.

The violinist rose and approached her. The expression on his face was one of amused concern. As he spoke his companions in the background watched the little scene with varying degrees of interest, and the waiter hovered within earshot, showing no sign of any feeling but his consummate fatigue.

'I hear you're looking for Eugene Pryor. I'm afraid you won't find him here any more. In fact, I don't think you'll find him in Cairo.' His conciliatory Jewish voice seemed to be suppressing a tendency to mirth; it was evident that Eugene was being regarded as something of a joke.

'Not in Cairo? Are you certain? I was with him today, only this afternoon.' The words fell soberly. She had gathered strength by now to learn with calmness how she had been tricked.

'Well, somewhere round five o'clock he was catching the train to Alexandria. One of our boys went with him to the station.'

'What happened exactly? Was he in any trouble here?'

'Oh, no, his troubles here came to an end on Thursday when we got someone else to replace him. He doesn't seem to have told you he'd stopped working here.'

'But why? I want to know why! I *must* know.' She intercepted a humorous lift of the eyebrows flung at large in the direction of the musicians, and erased it by saying carefully: 'You see it's a very serious matter for me. I'm an old friend of his, and I've been trying to help him. I was on tour with *The Prince of Palermo* when he was the conductor.'

'Is that so?' The change in his attitude was instantaneous. His air of idly taking part in a comedy situation dissolved. 'Look here, you come and sit down and let's get things cleared up. I can see you're quite upset. Come along, there's one of the boys who can tell you more about him than I can.'

She suffered herself to be steered gently to the table. Her normal reserve, her instinct to conceal humiliation and the bitterness of grief, no longer asserted itself. It was nothing to her that she was about to discuss her private affairs in a company of strange men. They were ciphers; she scarcely distinguished one from another.

The violinist repeated what she had told him, and with murmurs of concern, they shuffled their chairs about to make room for her. Once again the waiter placed himself within hearing distance and followed their talk with impassive attention, and soon another waiter joined him, for it was nearly closing time and few patrons remained to demand service. Heedless of their presence, Lucy spoke and listened like an automaton.

'You'll pardon us if we get on with our supper,' said Mr. Solomon, sitting down before a plate of cold meat and a flaccid-looking salad. 'They can't close up until we've finished. This is Mr. Gavronsky, our 'cellist.' He indicated a thin, sensitive-faced young man, Jewish like himself, but of a much finer grain, with high cheekbones, delicately cast features, and downy wisps of red hair clinging to a head prematurely bald. 'He can put you wise about our friend Pryor. They shared the same digs, you know.'

Lucy turned inquiringly towards him, and to banish the air of constraint that hung over him, and indeed over the whole party, with the exception of their spokesman, she said firmly: 'I suppose he must have been drinking. I should have realized it when he came to see me today. I wonder now that I didn't. But his manner was so absolutely sober—he seemed so sure of himself—I was completely taken in.'

'I don't blame you,' the violinist rejoined with vigour. 'My word, what a gift of the gab he has! It would take anybody in. If he'd depended on *talk* there's nothing he couldn't have got out of us; but here he had to do something else besides talking. He had to play—and that was the end of him.'

Staring blankly at the tablecloth, Lucy nodded. 'I remember now. I'd almost forgotten. He never could play when he was drunk. That was the test; that was how he used to give himself away at singing rehearsals.'

'Yes, he could talk but he couldn't work. It was pretty queer the way liquor affected him, one of the queerest things I ever struck. It gave us a big shock, didn't it, boys?'

'When did he start drinking again? It must have been within the last few days? I could swear he was all right up till last Monday.'

'Ah, yes, dat is true,' exclaimed Gavronsky, in eager stumbling speech with a strong foreign accent. 'He vas all right till Monday certainly. It vas Tuesday ven his friends came. Before dat, ve did not even know he has had drinking trouble before.'

'What happened? What friends came?'

'A bad lot. Two men he has known in Singapore, and vun more who has come over vid dem on der same ship—all noisy, silly people like fishes, isn't it so, Mr. Solomon?'

'That's right. Of course, you saw more of them than I did as they came round to your digs. The only time I set eyes on them was when they dropped in here on Tuesday for lunch and spotted Pryor. I think they were motor salesmen,' he explained, 'the ones he'd met in Singapore anyhow. They'd known him when he was on the batter out there, and they thought it would be funny to get him on the batter again. I don't admire their sense of humour.'

'They got him to drink port,' put in the drummer. 'After that he went on to whisky. And after *that* there was no holding him.'

'Yes,' said Solomon, 'by Tuesday evening already he was a bit different. Naturally we didn't know what was wrong at first. He was talking as sensibly as ever; it was just his playing that seemed off colour. By Wednesday lunch-time he really began to worry us, and in the evening he didn't turn up at all. Gavronsky and a boy went and found him lying on his bed as screwed as he could be. They managed to get him round here, but he couldn't play a note. What a night! I don't think any of us would care to live through another performance like that! That was the finish as far as the management was concerned.'

'I tink if I could have made him go back to his bed,' Gavronsky speculated regretfully, 'he still could have been all right der next day. But just ven I was taking him home quiet like a lamb, his friends have come for him again, and he vas out nearly all night—and in der morning ill like death.'

'Not too ill to come round here and try to touch us for the shirts off our backs,' said Solomon. 'However, we were wise. I was anyway. I believe the cashier and one or two of the waiters fell for his story and lent him a bit. Marvellous, considering everyone knew he'd just got the sack for drunkenness! But he was plausible—my God, how plausible he was!'

'Then all the situation he described to me was pure imagination! Did you, if I may ask, get your salaries paid today?'

'Of course.' They looked at one another with wry amusement.

'I see. He told me he had been given money to pay your salaries and that it had been stolen from him. I replaced it.'

She spoke in a cool and matter-of-fact tone; nevertheless her listeners at the table were compelled to express their dismay, and even the waiters exchanged lugubrious glances.

'But how could he make you swallow a tale like that?' Solomon gazed at her reproachfully over his well-laden fork. 'It wasn't his business to deal with our salaries.'

'He told me a rigmarole'—her voice faltered, but she managed to collect herself—'only it all seemed quite reasonable at the time—he told me the proprietor had gone to Port Said and left money to cover expenses in his absence. Eugene had to pay the orchestra—'

'Why should he?' said Solomon a little impatiently. 'I am the leader of the orchestra. It would be my place to take charge. Besides, Mr. Palmetti is not in Port Said—never thought of going, as far as I know.'

'I understand that he'd gone to attend to his other restaurant there.'

'He hasn't got another restaurant there or anywhere else.'

'Really?' She was still cool, but beneath the deadness of her outward senses a fierce anger began to blaze, against Providence, against Eugene, against herself for having been his dupe. 'Then that was just a touch of local colour. No wonder he called himself a good liar! It was probably the only word of truth he uttered today.'

'I hope he hasn't got too much from you,' said Gavronsky with real solicitude, 'because by dis time he is not any more in Egypt. He has gone vid his friends to catch a ship vich sails from Alexandria at midnight—a tramp boat. I don't even know der name.'

'Are you sure? That might have been an invention too.'

'No, dis vas true. I heard his tipsy friends say many times dey vill not leave him behind, and ven he lost his vork here, he has decided it's no good to stay longer. Yesterday he told his friends if he can get enough money for his ticket, he will go vid dem. He vas explaining how he knows a rich lady who vill lend him some money.'

'A rich lady!' Lucy's body shook with a gust of soundless laughter.

'If they were so keen on having him with them, these friends of his,' said Solomon, 'why didn't they pay for his ticket? It was the least they could do after getting him sacked.'

The 'cellist dismissed the idea with a politely deprecating gesture. 'Dey had no money demselves, Mr. Solomon. You have to remember dey have been drinking and being crazy like madmen all over Cairo.' He turned again to Lucy. 'If I had vunce realized der rich lady vas a pack of lies, I vould not have helped him to get away, doing his luggage and all. But like a fool, I believed every word. So many details he gives—how she looks, vere she lives, how he comes to know her, everything! And I vas sorry he is going away vid such bad friends, but he is finished in Cairo anyhow, so it vasn't much use to argue. I packed up his trunk for him, and I took him to der station.'

Lucy's anger broke in a thin stream through the shell of her indifference. 'Oh, just to think how cleverly he worked it! Pretending he'd committed an offence he might go to prison for! Threatening to do a bolt so that I'd give him money to get him out of the mess! Oh, what a cat-and-mouse game it must have been for him! How he must have enjoyed it, knowing in advance everything I was going to say and do!'

Once again there was a general movement of sympathy among the listeners, and everyone had some word of censure for Eugene's conduct. There was even a suggestion that, on the off-chance of a delay in the sailing-time of the boat, they might ring up the police at Alexandria, or at any rate inform the police in Cairo. But Lucy had begun to shiver with an inward coldness, and she could only whisper: 'No good, no good! It's hopeless. There's a sort of hopelessness about everything I do. . . .'

Pride was gone. Courage and control were going. She must get away while still some vestige remained. She rose unsteadily and groped for her handbag.

'You look pretty bad,' said Gavronsky, laying down his knife and fork to study her face with troubled eyes. 'Vould you like I should take you home?'

'How much did he get from you?' Solomon demanded with candid inquisitiveness.

She looked at her shabby handbag and thought fleetingly how many times she had resisted the temptation to buy a new one. Then, turning on her heel, she said harshly: 'All I had.' Tears sprang to her eyes and, before she had reached the door, were streaming down her cheeks. She let them fall unhidden and unchecked. All the scrupulous restraint of a lifetime was broken down and she did not care who saw her suffer.

With steps at once urgent and aimless she came into the street and crossed the road oblivious of traffic, oblivious of eyes swiftly glancing, swiftly averted, aware of nothing but her intolerable anguish of rage and hatred. A hand closed on her elbow; mechanically she jerked her arm away and turned to see who had accosted her.

'I am sorry from der bottom of my heart,' said Gavronsky timidly. 'Don't be cross, please, if I insist to take you home. Such a shock you had—it's not right you should walk in der streets alone.'

She shook her head, not trusting herself to speak.

'Please, vere do you live?' he persisted gently. 'Can we go by foot or is it better I call a cab?'

The furious impulse to resist his kindness—to resist all kindness as long as she should live and walk by herself friendless and despairing—evaporated under his mild gaze. Sobbing she told him her address and allowed him to bundle her into a cab. And there, so far was reticence overthrown, she sketched out unasked, in barely coherent phrases, a fuller outline of her calamity.

Gavronsky listened with quick understanding, and when she bent her head into her hands to taste, in a fresh throb of agony, the full reality of her desolation, he took her arm again and said earnestly: 'Today I have seen vun oder person veeping, and I believe his tears are still more sad dan yours. You can guess who it is? No? Vell, it is dis criminal idiot, Eugene, and at der time I imagined it vas just drunken tears, but now I see it is der first sign, perhaps, he is becoming sober. He sat dere in der train ven I told him good-bye, and he vas crying like a child, and der last I saw of him, his friends vas giving him a drink to cheer him up.'

Lucy paused on the verge of proclaiming her contempt for Eugene's maudlin hypocrisy. The curtain of her own woe was suddenly pulled aside, and she remembered, with an intensity the keener for her overwrought condition, exactly how he had looked when she had offered him her money—that peculiar mixed expression of relief and shame which had shown her the depth of his unhappiness. She perceived that although, through most of their interview, he had taken a pride in lying with artistic skill, his victory had yielded him no triumph; and as moral sensibility revived in him, his mouth, she knew, would be full of dust and ashes.

'He was mad,' she cried with a new kind of anger. 'He was mad and weak and wicked and treacherous—to himself as well as me. If he could only have kept his promise to himself, and saved up and got to England . . . But perhaps he *has* gone to England?' And she thought how ironical it would be if Eugene's vices were to be rewarded by bringing him to his goal at the cost of ruining her.

'No,' said Gavronsky mournfully. 'It is very bad. It is vorse even dan you tink. He has gone back to India—India vere already he admits, vid his own lips, he has been in so much trouble.'

'Gone back to India? Then I'm afraid that's the end of him!'

Lucy found that her heavy sigh concealed no trace of exultation.

CHAPTER 21

THE NEXT MORNING Lucy carried her tale of misfortune, honest and complete, to Lotus Building, and was heard with something less than graciousness. On the previous afternoon she had broken her appointment without sending word, and Daisy had waited for hours to tell her a prodigious piece of news. She had even put herself to the trouble of ringing up Karnak House and the Adelphi and, having discovered there was no question of either illness or exceptional pressure of work, she had taken umbrage so profoundly that the most self-evident excuses could not altogether soothe her ruffled feelings.

Besides, it went very much against the grain that Lucy should be entirely taken up with her own sordid affairs—this drab and disgusting story of a brothel, this ridiculous business of letting herself be gulled by a man whom she knew to be a thoroughly bad lot—when she, Daisy, had matters of the first importance to think and talk about.

At lunch-time yesterday a dignity had been conferred on her which, ever since, had steadily gathered greatness in the privacy of her meditations; and the tidings which would have been communicated in undisguised excitement if Lucy had come at the appointed time were now only to be imparted with an air of kindly condescension. For Daisy was no longer quite the same person as she had been twenty-four hours ago: she was more high-toned, more fashionable, and more exclusive. The social neglect from which she suffered, and sometimes suffered acutely, as Siegfried's obscure mistress was about to come to an end. Within a fortnight she would appear before the world as an elegant and expensive young lady travelling in delicious respectability with a chaperon. And no ordinary chaperon either, but a lady of impressive name, a lady of position and culture, in fact, a more or less titled lady—the Hon. Mrs. Calderon-Chauncey. It was hardly possible therefore for her to regard Lucy, that foolish friend whose difficulties grew more and more squalid, with quite the same tolerance as she would have felt before this noble prospect was opened to her.

Mosenthal, annoyed and inconvenienced by Lucy's refusal to stay in Egypt, had not let the grass grow under his feet. Indeed, grass never did grow under his feet; the energy with which they trod whatever path he set them on laid waste every trace of unnecessary herbage. Daisy could not be taken to South Africa, that was certain: his sense of filial and family duty would never permit it. Equally, he eliminated all possibility of leaving her alone in Cairo; the mere thought of it bred jealous fancies in multitudes. Besides, now that he regarded her with affection, he could enter into her feelings far enough to see how dull and bored and uncomfortable she would be without him. It was a picture that flattered him, but he did not want to turn it into reality. So he made haste to design a compromise. Daisy should have a sea voyage too, but not with him. He would find some impeccable companion for her and send them off together, and when he had accomplished his business in South Africa, instead of coming straight home, he would meet her over in London or Paris. Once having fixed things up so that he could get away from Egypt at all, he might as well make the most of the opportunity.

It was a good workable plan, and it had the incidental merit of being a slap in the face for Lucy Kendon. He set the wheels in motion without delay, giving no inkling to Daisy, however, until he had made sure of the first essential—a suitable person to keep her company. It was a matter that offered certain difficulties, since ladies whose virtue was of that irreproachable standard he required in a duenna might be inclined to look askance at their charge. But numerous private sources of information were open to him, and without having exposed himself or Daisy to the risk of any mortification, he was able, before two or three days had passed, to interview a highly eligible candidate.

Mrs. Calderon-Chauncey, while not quite elderly, was reassuringly *passée*. Her manner was perfectly decorous, and yet, without obtrusiveness, she made it clear in a few moments that Mosenthal's relationship to her prospective ward would be no concern of hers. She had an air of being alert and capable, and Mosenthal, who was the shrewdest of judges, decided that, though she would do herself proud, he might rely upon her not to stoop to actual cheating in money matters. Altogether he felt justified in announcing, with a considerable toning down of his usual arrogance, that, subject to Daisy's approval, she might count upon the engagement.

To say that Daisy approved would be a reckless understatement. She was rapturous. In such entrancing circumstances she could even bear a few weeks of separation from Siegfried. And then, to be reunited with him under conditions so wonderful! To be taken about Paris—the theatres, the shops, the far-famed gaieties—by a man with money! To be in London yet free from the necessity of earning one's living, revisiting the old familiar scenes as a changed person, improved, glorified out of recognition! Except it were to become Siegfried's lawful wife with all the attendant privileges, the future could not disclose any vista more exquisite. And first there would be the quiet yet eventful weeks with her distinguished travelling companion, who would surely provide some contact with that world of polished breeding and refined splendour to which, in secret, she aspired. She was determined to watch her, imitate her, pick up everything she could from her; and although it was not a part of their bargain that Mrs. Calderon-Chauncey should introduce her to the circles she might be presumed to frequent in London, Daisy intended so to ingratiate herself that she was not likely to be excluded.

It was no marvel then that, when the first fever of excitement had abated, a somewhat lofty sense of her own consequence took possession of her, and that in this frame of mind she could not regard Lucy as anything but a tiresome and unworthy friend.

Most particularly did Lucy show herself unworthy in her reception of the glorious news. Wholly concentrated upon her self-created woes, she scarcely attempted to muster a word of congratulation. Indeed, her jealousy and envy were palpable, and for a dreadfully disconcerting minute or two she actually seemed to be hinting that she might be allowed to take the place of Mrs. Calderon-Chauncey; but Daisy effectually prevented the request from being made in plain terms. It was too absurd, painfully absurd, to imagine oneself exchanging the stately widow who would help to launch one into society for dreary Lucy—Lucy whom one had seen every day for months, who could reflect no prestige upon anybody, and who was really beginning to look quite out at elbows.

No, there was nothing to be done for Lucy beyond promising to lay the matter before Siegfried as soon as he was at leisure to hear of it. It was hard to refrain from saying, 'I told you so,' considering how often she had tried to warn the idiotic girl against being friendly with

Eugene, and she could not help reminding her once or twice—very gently, of course—that she had been simply asking for trouble: but on the whole her attitude was carefully aloof. It would not do to hold out any hopes, for Siegfried, as she privately knew, was far from well disposed towards Lucy at the moment. Lucy must not be encouraged to believe that she had any claim on Siegfried. He had assisted her in the past, thanks to Daisy's good offices, but she had no right to think of him as a tireless philanthropist constantly in readiness to foot the bills for her catastrophes.

And honestly, it was a bit thick the way she had got his back up and then came along expecting him to help her as soon as she landed herself in a scrape! Daisy's memory seldom functioned if its workings were likely to give her any discomfort, and already she had more than half forgotten how Lucy had come to antagonize Mosenthal—how, in fact, if she had done what he required of her, Daisy herself would not now be looking forward to months of radiant delight. The gratitude and sympathy of less than a week ago had quite dissolved, and it was not with a desire to play the advocate that she repeated the story to her lover.

On the contrary, she took a somewhat deprecatory tone, anticipated his disgust at Lucy's reckless stupidity, and showed clearly that she considered any further benevolent interference on her behalf would be little better than a waste.

Mosenthal listened with sardonic satisfaction. He would have liked to say 'Serve her right!' She had been disobliging to him and had inflicted a wound on his dignity: it was a just visitation of Providence that, after having so high-handedly rejected what he had offered, she should be left with nothing. Perhaps if Daisy had proved a more zealous apologist he would have been content to enjoy her friend's discomfiture with a fleeting relish, and would even have felt sufficiently appeased by it to make the grand gesture of coming to her rescue. But Daisy's attitude allowed him to remain implacable.

He expressed himself as surprised and shocked at Lucy's behaviour. It was most improper of her to have associated with such a reprobate as Eugene and disgraceful that she had permitted him to take her into one of the notorious houses of the Arab quarter. He would not believe—and Daisy only faintly attempted to persuade him—that she had misunderstood the nature of the entertainment to be found in such a haunt. The *danse du ventre* was not, in any case, the sort of spectacle a nice young woman would consent to witness.

The whole escapade, he declared, was so utterly unseemly that to refund the stolen money would be to put a premium on loose conduct in his employees. He acknowledged that it must be a hard thing for her to lose the savings of so many weeks, but she had brought the blow upon her own head, and the best he felt inclined to do for her was to let her hold her job at the Adelphi. Even that was a concession, because she had talked of giving notice and he did not as a rule like to keep unsettled employees in his business.

A slight qualm disturbed him when Daisy, thanking him warmly for his indulgence, had promised to communicate this decision. After all, the wretched girl had served her turn and the sum involved was insignificant. Wouldn't it be as well to give her the amount she needed and have done with her? But when he remembered the unyielding and insolent pride with which she had so recently opposed him, it became easy to suppress the impulse of generosity. She had ridden a high horse, and it was fitting that she should take a toss.

Chapter 22

Lucy, in her laborious game of Snakes and Ladders, had made a great many moves to climb a very small ladder, and had now been swallowed by the snake which takes the player back to the beginning. The dice, moreover, seemed to be loaded. Her assets were fewer, her position was worse, than when she had first recovered from the fever. Illness, adversity, and unaccustomed work through the blazing months of summer had done nothing to restore her voice or her good looks. Her wardrobe badly needed renewing. The tonic effect of being successful and desired was something she had not enjoyed since her arrival in Egypt. She felt reduced, embittered, and—such had been the futility of all her efforts—degraded.

And now even the solace of friendship was denied to her. Constance had averted angry eyes at their two or three chance meetings in the entrance hall of Karnak House, and Daisy, ecstatically busy with arrangements for her voyage, preferred the company of Mrs. Calderon-Chauncey. The situation was delicate, for Lucy could not repress her strong conviction that Daisy owed her something better than the treatment now being meted out; while Daisy, knowing that more had been expected of her, was guarded and uneasy. There was no open rupture between them—Lucy dared not risk her job; Daisy could hardly break off so close an intimacy without more tangible grievances—but there was a perceptible change in their relations.

Nevertheless, when Daisy had sailed, luxuriating blissfully in new clothes, new luggage, and almost a new personality (she was living up to her chaperon with all the histrionic ability she possessed), Lucy was obliged to concede that she left a gap. There was no one now with whom to spend the lonely afternoons, no one she could talk to on familiar terms, not a single acquaintance who might help her to recall the years of her prosperity. Daisy had never been an entirely satisfactory comrade, but Lucy was bound to her by many ties of shared experience; they had grown used to each other, and the parting was, at least on one side, keenly felt.

The loss of Constance was still worse; she had inspired an affection based on some firmer ground than mere propinquity, and it was hard to be so ill-rewarded for an act of pure self-sacrificing kindness. She had hoped that the girl's insulting and cruel letter would be followed by an apology; not perhaps within the first few days—she was unlikely to come to her senses as rapidly as that—but after a fortnight, say, or three weeks. At the latest a month? She felt so certain that Con must be only a few degrees less forlorn than she was herself that as the days extended into weeks, resentment became increasingly difficult to maintain, and when the month of grace had quite run out and there was still no penitent gesture from Constance, she abandoned policy and surrendered.

She wrote a note appealing for a truce and put it under Constance's door. In it she reminded her almost with eloquence that it needed love to spur one to the thankless task of interfering between people bent on folly; and emphasized her conviction that the memory of Vittorio would soon be reduced to its true proportions of insignificance. Then, assuming pardon, she went on to describe how her own plans had been thwarted and she herself left desolate.

She came back that night from the theatre with her depression a little lifted, for she never doubted that she would have a visit or, at any rate, a message of reconciliation. But she was vexed and disappointed to find that she had been mistaken. There was no letter, no contrite tap on her door, no outpouring of eager, impetuous regret such as she had all along been counting on. She was apparently contending with a nature more sullen and obdurate than she had imagined. It was not worth while to strive against it; the friendship of Constance must be written off as one more bad debt.

The next morning, however, when she was preparing the tea and toast on which she breakfasted before going to the theatre, her hopes were raised by a light yet deliberate knock and, hurrying to open the door, she discovered to her astonishment Mr. Conway standing stiffly with the envelope addressed to Constance in his hand.

'Good morning! I'm afraid I must be disturbing you,' He spoke with the barest perceptible softening of his usual austerity. 'I believe you wrote this letter to my daughter. It was handed to me last night by the present occupant of her room.'

'What! Is she no longer there?'

'She went to Palestine a week ago. Since you were evidently expecting an early reply, I thought I had better return your letter instead of forwarding it.'

'Thank you so much,' said Lucy, and her embarrassment was submerged in relief. It was almost happiness to know that the silence which had wounded her was not a proof of callous indifference to her misfortune. 'Do come in, Mr. Conway, if you'll excuse the state of my room, I'm very anxious to hear about Constance. I dare say you can tell that from what I wrote—'

'It was necessary to look at it—' his manner repudiated any suspicion of personal curiosity—'because I had to find out from whom it came. I read it—' He paused as if he had intended to produce some reason which evaded him, and ended by repeating as a simple statement: 'I read it.'

Lucy wondered with a twinge how much her remarks would have conveyed about the affair with Vittorio, but she managed to answer collectedly enough. 'Then you'll know I haven't seen her for weeks—not to talk to, anyhow. I should be so glad to have news of her, Mr. Conway.'

He gazed abstractedly at her unmade bed and a disorder of garments she was hastily endeavouring to conceal, and, with the slightly laboured air which the necessity of bestowing attention upon Constance always inspired in him, responded: 'I was aware that there was some estrangement between you because she was moping round in a very tiresome fashion, altogether at a loose end. You used to keep her occupied.' He allowed his distaste to be tempered by a faint inflexion of gratitude. 'Fortunately, one of my colleagues in Palestine turned out to have a couple of daughters more or less the same age, and by a lucky accident they got together, and Mrs. Mansard, my colleague's wife, rather took the girl under her wing. As you had done.'

'How long ago was that.'

'Two or three weeks, I fancy.'

'Ah, that was why she was able to hold out against me all that time,' thought Lucy wistfully, but she felt a genuine pleasure, too, in knowing that her protégée had fallen into safe hands.

'It struck me as a good idea,' he continued in his detached way, 'to ask the Mansards to take her on with them to Palestine as a sort of paying guest. Better than having her hanging round Cairo all alone. They're nice people, I believe, and she was very eager to go with them.'

'It sounds just the sort of thing she needed. Will it last long?'

'Until I'm ready to leave. Five or six months perhaps.'

'Then I don't know when we shall meet again,' said Lucy. 'Of course, I'm delighted that she's made new friends, and I hope she'll settle down and be happy with them; but I can't help being hurt to think she could go off without a word of goodbye when, for all she knew, it would be the last she'd see of me. We'd quarrelled, it's true, but she'd had ample time to get over it. I never dreamed she'd bear a grudge so long.'

'She's a silly creature,' he observed in mild contempt. 'I'm very much indebted to you for having looked after her—as I gather you did—when she was playing the fool over that young Italian. If you hadn't stepped in, there would have probably been a most awkward situation.'

'Well, as long as she's being properly taken care of *now* . . .' said Lucy pointedly, and she was tempted to offer him a more explicit piece of her mind, but his remote face, frigidly handsome, giving out nothing, contracted in a frown of entire self-absorption, warned her to save her breath. He was perturbed not because his daughter had been in danger, but because the consequences of an indiscretion might have been a nuisance to himself. Constance would have become a well-poised woman long before he could be turned into an affectionate and prudent father.

'Would you like her address?' he demanded with patient politeness.

She shook her head. 'No, thank you, Mr. Conway. I don't think I'd better have it. Somehow, since she disappeared like that without bothering about me, I'd rather not make the first approaches, and if I had her address I dare say I'd give in.'

He hardly seemed to listen to her reply; his gaze had lost its abstractedness and was fixed with some interest on her electric kettle and tray of breakfast china.

'The water,' he said firmly, 'is boiling.'

'Yes, I've just noticed. I must make my tea.'

'But where is your teapot? Have you heated it?'

'Not yet. I'm afraid I've got to wash it first.'

'While your kettle goes on boiling. Well, you won't have very good tea this morning, Miss Kendon.' He looked almost distressed. 'There's more finesse in brewing tea than some people imagine. It isn't only a matter of warming the pot. The water should be fresh and freshly boiled. Stewed water is a lamentable mistake—lamentable.'

'I didn't think two or three minutes could make much of a difference,' said Lucy, somewhat humbled.

'Two or three minutes may make less difference to a pot of tea than to a soufflé or an omelet, I agree, but there is *some* difference, certainly. As for the habit which so many housewives persist in, of keeping a kettle perpetually simmering on the stove, nothing could be more deplorable. But, then, those are the same women who give you salad-dressing out of a bottle and omelets like slabs of scrambled egg. They ought never to be allowed in a kitchen. They fry everything that requires to be grilled. They use damnable bottled sauces that conceal the flavour of the food. Their method of boiling rice is horrible. They put sugar and dry mustard in their mayonnaise. Their cooking is a national tragedy.'

His sorrow and anger compelled her to express fellow-feeling. He glanced at her for the first time as if he saw her and might remember what she looked like, and when she had filled the teapot he took the caddy from her hand, and asked quite affably: 'What tea do you use?'

'Oh, just some kind of Indian.'

'Some kind of Indian!' The dawning benevolence faded from his eyes. 'Is that a loose way of designating Ceylon, or do you mean tea from an unspecified district of India?'

'I suppose I mean Ceylon.' In spite of herself she was ashamed, apologetic.

'Very well, you should say so. "Some kind of Indian" is a nonsensical description, I assure you.' He extracted a spoonful of the tea-leaves from the caddy and crumpled them between his fingers. 'This is not much good,' he told her dispassionately. 'At least, I shouldn't find it so. Myself, I use Darjeeling—Wright and Woodbury's special blend of Darjeeling. Do you know it?'

Lucy acknowledged her ignorance.

'I should be surprised if you did,' he conceded. 'It's unprocurable in Egypt through the ordinary channels. I get mine from Wright and Woodbury direct. Something under a pound a month—that's all I need for I only drink it in the mornings. It's really most kind of them to supply such a small quantity.' His enthusiasm was more marked than when he had thanked her for protecting his daughter. 'Would you care to sample it? I could let you have a few ounces.'

'I'd like to try it very much.' Honesty obliged her to add: 'But I'm sure it would be too dear for me to get as a regular thing.'

'It *is* dear—very dear, but it's exquisite. Quite a remarkable tea, so subtle and delicate, yet so full and clear. And it suits the water here to perfection. Is your palate clean?'

'How do you mean?' Lucy faltered.

'Have you still got a good sharp sense of taste? Or have you dulled it with incessant smoking and pungent, over-flavoured food and drink?' He regarded her with a solemn yet distant contemplation, like a priest awaiting the answer to a question in the confessional.

'I think my palate's all right. Not that it's had much practice lately.'

'Then the least you can do for it is to see that the things it has to encounter every day are the best obtainable. It's a very poor economy to stint your palate in the matter of necessities. Economize about luxuries if you like—or if you must—but let your necessities be absolutely first-rate always.'

Lucy considered this advice too impracticable, so far as her own case was concerned, to be seriously disputed, and turning it aside with a conciliatory smile, she suggested: 'It would only be insulting your palate, I'm afraid, to offer you a cup of this.'

He rejoined with gravity, 'I should try it gladly, Miss Kendon; I have no prejudice at all against teas of—er—moderate quality except for daily drinking. But I'm on my way to keep a business appointment and I must hurry off. Forgive me for having interrupted your breakfast. (Very sensible, I see!—nothing but tea and toast. You don't spoil your appetite for lunch.) I'll send the sample of Darjeeling, and if you want more I've no doubt Wright and Woodbury would supply you.'

He was gone, leaving her, for the first few minutes, devoid of any other emotion than surprise. Apart from the exchange of superficial greetings, she had never spoken to him before, and though she was familiar with his shortcomings as a parent, she still found it wonderful that, instead of making the smallest inquiry into his daughter's perilous behaviour, he had reserved the whole stock of his interest for this ludicrous discussion of tea.

The packet of Darjeeling was duly presented, Lucy's thanks and diffident comments were graciously received, and for the future, on the rare occasions when they met, Mr. Conway's civilities were warmer than they had been; but that is not to say that they became actually warm. Constance's father remained, in fact, a very ineffectual substitute for Constance, and Lucy often grieved for her faithless friend, remembering even her rashness and her adolescent extravagances with longing affection.

During the next few months Lucy's progress in saving money was decidedly slower than it had been before the disaster of Eugene. There were many impediments and she had lost the spirit to contend with them. Whilst she had believed her goal lay almost within sight, she had felt equal to the innumerable acts of self-denial, great and little, imposed upon her by stringent economy; but now that she had seen her hard-won substance all laid waste she was utterly disheartened and sometimes it seemed hardly possible to continue the struggle.

Although in her early days on the stage she had known some adversities, her life on the whole had been decidedly comfortable, and it went against the grain to have only one room for a home and to be compelled to do without a hundred and one amenities she had formerly taken for granted. She had moods nowadays in which it no longer appeared expedient to refuse herself every indulgence. At these times, with a sense of guilty luxury, she would, gratify her hankering for a bottle of scent, some flowers to vary the monotonous aspect of her bedroom, a luncheon or dinner more expensive than she usually permitted herself. Such lapses made unaccountably large inroads upon the week's earnings, but having once fallen it was hard to pull herself up.

Then it became imperatively necessary to buy some clothes. She could not maintain a decent standard of appearance for her work without them. A year had now passed since her first arrival in Egypt; of the wardrobe she had brought with her everything not unsuited to the climate had been worn to the last degree compatible with neatness, and it was months since she had seen herself dressed in garments acceptable to a critical eye.

Daisy, making a grand clearance before launching on her voyage, had offered her various discarded things of her own, but she was of a much shorter and slighter build, and her taste inclined to a confectionery style quite out of keeping with the requirements of a business woman. Her frilly muslins and diaphanous georgettes would have been of no service to Lucy, and she could avail herself only of a few accessories and one or two evening dresses that lent themselves to alteration and would come in useful at the theatre. Even these it was hard to take with a good grace. Daisy's manner had been so maddeningly bountiful; yet in the old days at Adelaide her more accommodating figure had been clad in Lucy's most cherished *toilettes*, and money had been freely lent her to buy what else she needed. She could not help remembering such matters when Daisy herself had so far forgotten them.

Yet, disappointing as that friendship had proved, there were nevertheless many days during the long, unprofitable stretches of time she now travelled through when she regretted Daisy's absence and looked forward to her return. While she had been able to enjoy the more endearing society of Constance, she had often begrudged the hours her unwritten treaty forced her to spend at Lotus Building; but in her present loneliness, those tranquil afternoons, those drowsy, desultory, intensely feminine conversations, could not but be missed.

She was not, of course, entirely without other more or less intimate acquaintances. Gavronsky, the Polish 'cellist from Eugene's café, was on cordial terms with her, and from time to time they had a pleasant meeting; but there was not much in common between them, apart from a mutual kindliness, and when he became engaged to a somewhat overwhelming young musician of his own nationality their intercourse gradually lapsed.

Occasionally there were visiting artistes who turned out to be congenial. The theatre, however, provided fewer openings than might have been expected. English performers seldom appeared there, and in any case she was not quite at ease nowadays with people on the stage, even her compatriots. She felt among them like a sort of theatrical charwoman with a tale of having seen better days.

Sometimes she would try to get in touch with associates of long ago, doubtful though the chances were of renewing contacts broken since the middle years of the war. A few of her letters were returned by the dead-letter office, and the fate of others remained unknown.

Others again were answered and resulted in a further correspondence, but the satisfaction to be got from it was never really worthy of the effort. When she let herself go, she produced gloomy outpourings which had to be torn up; and when she restrained herself, the effect was merely one of dim plaintiveness. Even her sister, to whom she wrote constantly, had probably failed to take the full measure of her distress, and it seemed unkind to be for ever inflicting lamentations upon her. As time went on, Lucy suppressed more and more her desire to be pitied for her woes and began to single out for description only the brightest aspects of her scene. This exercise of courage served to restore a little of the self-respect damaged by her prolonged experience of failure.

Meanwhile Daisy communicated with her fairly frequently by means of postcards and notes scrawled hastily on the writing-paper of various internationally known hotels; but Lucy could not resist the conviction that these attentions were paid less from kindness than the need of an audience.

The route selected by Mrs. Calderon-Chauncey for their European travels was from Alexandria to Sicily, with a brief visit to Malta, then from Messina to Naples, and from Naples on to Rome, Florence, Milan, and Venice, pausing a few days in each city while Daisy conscientiously imbibed culture. From Italy they went to Switzerland and relaxed while they studied a segment of the postwar world preparing to make winter sports a more serious matter than they had ever been before. Then they proceeded to Belgium and examined, not too assiduously, the devastations of war, finding it a great consolation that the occupants of an army of graves had all died nobly for King and Country. After this—it being now the end of January—they went to London, and Daisy's chaperon handed her back, safe and undefiled, into the keeping of Mr. Mosenthal.

Lucy was apprised of these various movements in bulletins which assured her reiterantly that everything was very, very interesting, and that they were having a wonderful time. Postcards from Italy called her to witness that Daisy had inspected the Forum and the Colosseum, the Vatican, the Pitti and Uffizi Galleries, the cathedral of Milan and the Doge's Palace. From Switzerland came pictures of icy mountains and luxurious hotels, and from Brussels a photograph of the little bronze boy who makes a fountain by performing an action which English boys scarcely care to mention, much less accomplish, in public. ('It's really most interesting to see what a different way the Latins look on things,' was Daisy's broad-minded comment. She was frequently obliged to bring a gracious tolerance to bear upon the conduct of Latins.)

But though enthusiasm was monotonously unflagging, Lucy seldom felt that it rang true. Even among the pleasure-seekers of the Swiss Alps, even, in fact, at the Ritz in London, and the Ritz in Paris, with Siegfried lavishly doing the honours, the note of spontaneous joy seemed to be lacking. Lucy could not believe it was entirely envy and disappointment that made her suspect the tour was falling a little below expectations.

CHAPTER 23

SUBMITTING herself unreproachfully once again to the rigours of Egypt's out-of-season climate, Daisy was brought back in March, a time of the year when any man less spartan in the cause of money-making than Siegfried would certainly have found excuses to remain in Europe. He, however, perceiving the great advantage he had over his rivals by being accessible and alert just when they were sure to be in retreat, achieved an almost superhuman disregard of comfort, both on his own behalf and that of his employees. Yet his enemies, far from admiring, compared him with the petty Greek merchants who, afraid of losing the smallest sale, kept their shops open through the noonday hours when all other trade was suspended.

Daisy returned with her feelings in a confusion which no one in the world was less able to disentangle than herself. Her life in Cairo was not a very brilliant one at best and would be duller still during the long stretch of impossible weather that loomed ahead. On the other hand, though nothing could have induced her to admit it, the tour abroad had not been very brilliant either and she was tired of the incessant moving about and having to be appreciative. Cairo had become her home, and it was pleasant in some ways to be able to relax again, especially now that she could look back, through a haze that would rapidly become rose-coloured, upon these months of cultural progress. Nevertheless, even Daisy's high talent for self-deception would require a little time to blind her to the fact that she had hoped for more from her travels than they had actually given her.

Of course she was glad, immensely glad, to have made such a voyage; her prestige in her own eyes was very much enhanced by it; but though she had tried so hard to be charmed with everything, there had been disillusioning features. Mrs. Calderon-Chauncey, after all, had not provided many keys to unlock the doors of the fashionable world, and she had proved rather a dreary companion in spite of Daisy's really patient and persistent efforts to be on agreeable terms with her. Her prefix of 'Honourable' turned out to be a mere shadow-title having no currency at all except in writing, and Daisy had often been hard put to it to let casual acquaintances know that her friend was thus distinguished. (She always referred to her as 'my friend', and implied, wherever possible, something in the nature of a family connection.)

As a matter of fact, in engaging the services of this expensive lady, Mosenthal had for once got the worst of the bargain. Mrs. Calderon-Chauncey came of no very exalted family and had married the scion of a moderately noble house, chiefly on the strength of an ability to make herself useful in his declining years. He had lingered on, against all the odds, to be seventy-six, leaving her to discover that she had bartered the whole stock of her assets for position and security, which were never attained. With her husband in a state of decrepitude she had lived an obscure life, and on his death he had left her only modest resources, which had diminished to meagre proportions during the war. She had been eking them out ever since by trading upon snobbery of a kind which is now old-fashioned but which was then sufficiently widespread and active to provide her with a comfortable livelihood.

Such work as she did was done conscientiously. The programmes of sightseeing arranged to keep Daisy decorously occupied were adhered to even when both parties would have been grateful for a respite, and in Switzerland she accompanied her protégée to ice carnivals and ski-jumping contests in weather which made it infinitely tempting to remain in the well-heated drawing-rooms of the hotel. But she performed these tasks with such a palpable lack of zest, such an air of long-suffering, politely yet not quite adequately concealed, that Daisy felt obliged to be perpetually apologetic.

Mrs. Calderon-Chauncey's sole consolation for the fact that her husband had lived at least a dozen years too long was to represent herself as one who had sacrificed her all on the altar of duty and was destined to go on for the rest of her days in a state of mild martyrdom. Her smiles were sweet and sad and expressive of kindly indulgence towards those who might be capable of mirth, her conversation was either abstracted or audibly painstaking, and her whole manner signified a condescension achieved with effort. It was an imposing manner, and Daisy continued to stand in awe of it long after she had realized that it was not what she had at first supposed, a blend of hauteur and graciousness typically aristocratic.

One took no liberties with Mrs. Calderon-Chauncey, not even the liberty of secretly admitting that she bored one stiff. One went on playing up to her, giving her the deference she so plainly expected, and telling oneself how wonderful it was to be travelling under such auspices. Perhaps no one could have helped placing a high value on a privilege that cost so much, but in Daisy's case there was an additional reason for making great efforts to be pleased. It would have been dreadfully uncomfortable to confess to oneself that, after all, it might have proved a better plan to do the tour with Lucy and just as easy to arrange if one had really wanted it. No, no, no, Lucy could not compare. . . . Mrs. Calderon-Chauncey was delightful, so quiet, so refined, so good at finding her way about old churches and ruins and picture galleries. One never would have seen such multitudes of old churches with Lucy.

Of course it had been a disappointment to meet so very few people who could be described as 'worth while'. They had begun promisingly enough in Malta by looking up a naval officer named Calderon, who had given them tea on a battleship and lunch at a fort, but their progress through Sicily and Italy had been barren of any contact that she could treasure in memory or regard as an investment for the future, and in Switzerland, where she had gone in especially high hope, they had remained quite outside the only circles that attracted her.

In truth, she had not enjoyed herself in Switzerland and at moments felt almost actively unhappy there. The exclusiveness of the winter-sporting fraternity had been so utterly inexorable, and yet some of them were the very sort of people she hankered after. She had actually gone to the trouble of taking skating and ski-ing lessons, supporting a perfect welter of discomforts, but they had availed her nothing. Everyone seemed able to penetrate her disguise, to realize that she was not a genuine devotee, and the beginners were, if anything, more sceptical of her good faith than the experts. How she feared them and wanted them and strove to be like them, those fresh-complexioned, well-bred, ill-mannered young men and women, so hearty with each other, so cool with her, who formed half the population of every hotel! How she detested and envied their hardihood and the silly pride with which they made light of their physical injuries! How she struggled to infuse into her speech the easy, careless arrogance of theirs!

It was all in vain. Clever though she was at believing what it was pleasant to believe, she could not persuade herself that they ever imagined her to be one of themselves. On the contrary, she was afflicted with a tormenting notion that they saw through and through her, saw through to her humble family and her ramshackle childhood, and divined—though she was always known as Miss Joy—her squalid marriage and the shifts she had been driven to by poverty.

It is highly improbable that the young people in question had anything like the acute penetration she gave them credit for, but she was right in thinking she could make no headway with them.

She was obliged to console herself as best she could with the undeniably tedious knitting and bridge-playing ladies who were only too glad to cultivate her chaperon.

Her optimism, overcast but by no means extinguished, now fixed itself tenaciously on London, where there would be Siegfried's masterful presence to support her, and where Mrs. Calderon-Chauncey (how wearisome it grew to pronounce that once fascinating name!) must surely belong to some set, however limited, to which it would be creditable to have *entrée*. Her engagement officially terminated on the day of Siegfried's arrival, but after the many friendly attentions she had received, it seemed unlikely that she would part from her clients as impersonally as a shop assistant who had finished serving. A little show of hospitality was the least one could expect of her.

And it turned out truly that in London Daisy tasted more genuine pleasure than anywhere else on the tour; though her aureate dreams were only dimly fulfilled. It was lovely to be reunited with Siegfried, it was lovely to stay at the Ritz and to patronize shops and places of entertainment whose names were legends to her; she never grew tired of these luxuries. But Siegfried was conspicuously less of a personage in London than in Cairo, and Mrs. Calderon-Chauncey's hospitality consisted merely of two tea-parties at which no one was present whom she could identify from the evidence of *Vogue* or *The Tatler*. She made a few efforts to seek out the friends of old times, chiefly, it must be admitted, so that she could show them what a splendid metamorphosis she had undergone; but seven years had passed since her elopement from England, and pre-war members of Daly's chorus were not to be traced by casual methods. There was one she had known who was easy enough to find, having recently become a star, and she ventured to pay her a dressing-room visit—only to wish at once that she had kept away; for her reception was very off-hand and the other's metamorphosis still more splendid than her own.

No further prospect of social intercourse was open to her, except by getting into touch with her long-neglected family, and this was a temptation she felt compelled to resist. They were not likely to do her credit with Siegfried or anybody else.

So, as Lucy had surmised, throughout the whole trip she was in want of an audience and everything fell a little flat. Yet her aspirations after a life of elegant gentility were stimulated rather than diminished by all these frustrating experiences, and she came back to Egypt longing more fervently than ever to attain a position in which all should envy, none despise her. To do this, she had perceived very clearly from the first, it was essential that her attachment to Mosenthal should be legitimized, and she was filled with an almost painful eagerness to learn the progress of certain negotiations which were now on foot in Australia.

Her husband had been tracked down three or four months ago, and the solicitors acting for her were empowered to take any step not visibly outside the boundaries of the law to make sure that he would not oppose divorce proceedings. She was still in the dark, however, as to how far these arrangements had been carried; and while there remained any doubt in this matter Siegfried seemed determined not to discuss the future with her. After long and vigilant observation, she was now convinced that he had not yet determined whether he would marry her or not, and never would make up his mind until her freedom was plainly in view before him.

It was with the keenest impatience, therefore, that she waited for him to see their lawyer in Cairo, who might be relied upon by the time of their return to have some news from his Australian ally. And Siegfried had undertaken to speak to him the very day after their arrival.

Unluckily, she would not know the issue until he got back from his office that evening. He had taken no notice of her hints that he might ring her up and tell her briefly how things stood, and, fearing to appear too avid, she had refrained from open entreaty and was resolved to busy herself as calmly as possible with unpacking and settling down once more in her old quarters.

She had refrained also from summoning Lucy, much as she would have liked an ear to receive her traveller's tales and the avowal of her present anxiety; but her attitude towards her old friend, after passing through a variety of phases, was now finally established as one of amiable and abstracted condescension—closely resembling, in fact, her late travelling companion's attitude towards herself—and it did not seem fitting that she should make the first approaches. Besides, she was by no means certain that their programme of daily meetings and close confidence ought to be revived. If she became Mosenthal's wife and embarked upon a brilliant social career, it might be far from good policy to be so familiar with one of his humbler employees.

Not that she proposed to *drop* Lucy exactly. That would be rather uncharitable after the wretched girl's long run of misfortunes—most of them, alas, brought on by her own folly! No, she would not drop her; she would simply alter the tone of their relations while remaining very, very kind, very affable in every way.

Yet, although she had no intention of letting their friendship be restored to its pre-Calderon-Chauncey basis, it somehow annoyed her that Lucy had not so far made any overtures of welcome. Was it possible that she too desired to keep her distance? Such ingratitude was not quite beyond her, perhaps, for her character had sadly degenerated in recent months. Yes, Lucy was not the same person. One would, of course, go on seeing a little of her, but she was not the same person at all.

Thus she reflected as her first afternoon wore on and there was no sign of Lucy, and the lover who held her entire destiny in his hands continued absent. If only he could have telephoned! She did not criticize him even in the privacy of her thoughts, but she was on tenterhooks and it was a solace to be able to criticize someone else instead.

About half an hour after his usual time for coming home there was a telephone call from his secretary: Mr. Mosenthal was detained at the office and would not be with her for dinner. He had found a great deal of business urgently requiring attention and was having some sandwiches brought to his desk. He might not be in till late that night.

For once Daisy's submissiveness could scarcely endure the burden put upon it. This was too bad, too inconsiderate—it really was! She could not reproach him for being kept at his office; but to send her a message by his secretary when, with a few words from his own lips, he could have put her out of her suspense . . . oh! it was enough to drive a person wild. If it had not been after normal office hours she might actually have been impelled to ring up the solicitor herself and venture direct inquiries, a step which Siegfried would regard as a most unwarrantable interference with matters in which she should have only a lay figure's concern.

This bold measure being unfeasible, she cast about for some other way of shortening the slow interval that must pass before he brought enlightenment to her, and decided to go to the theatre. It was a plan which had several small advantages, and as she got into a charming Paquin dress—her very pleasantest souvenir of Paris—she began to feel her spirits brighten perceptibly. By a happy coincidence it turned out that it was a first night at the Adelphi, and therefore a better opportunity than usual for making an effective appearance. Then Lucy would be there and she could meet her without having gone out of her way to do so, thus satisfying her present desire without jeopardizing her future purpose.

Daisy did not bother to reserve any seat for the performance because Siegfried's box was always kept free for him on opening nights, whether he chose to occupy it or not: the management knew that he might stroll in during a second or third act even if he missed the first. It was here she loved to sit, although, being nearest the stage, it had an exceedingly poor view: but to be in possession of it carried a certain prestige, at least among the employees of the Polyglot Amusement Company. When a show was not doing first-rate business, other boxes might be freely given over to the holders of complimentary tickets, who helped to 'dress the house', but Siegfried's remained a place of honour to which none but the specially privileged were admitted. It was from this high station that he had first gazed on her with approval when she had sung and smiled and jested in *The Prince of Palermo*.

She was sorry he would not be with her tonight; she could have achieved a much more impressive entrance with his support. Still, after all these months, even alone she could not fail to create some little stir. The management would surely be on the *qui vive*, the artistes would notice her, the lovely yet solitary creature in the stage-box, and would ask questions about her and be told that she was the Power behind the Throne. Respectability was out of her reach in surroundings where so much was known about her, but to be suspected of wielding influence over a rising potentate was the next best thing.

And the audience, the general public, to which she was a stranger, they too would be wondering as to the identity of the beautifully dressed young woman seated alone watching the stage with gracious attention.

So she pictured it, her journey abroad having already assumed a retrospective glamour that rendered her in her own eyes a more romantic figure than she had been before. But as it often happens to those who have counted on achieving a particular effect oy the manner of their entrance, she found the stage laid, so to speak, with a perfect disregard of dramatic requirements.

The foyer, when she arrived, was crowded with violently unfamiliar people, all of whom appeared to be absorbed in laughing and chattering and hailing one another. It was obvious at a glance than in this assembly she was altogether an outsider, and an outsider who excited no curiosity whatever. As a matter of fact, Daisy, having been cut off from Egyptian affairs for five months, had no notion when she set out for the theatre what entertainment she was to see. The waiter serving her lonely dinner had mentioned something about a first night but at the time she had been too engrossed in her private chagrin to pursue the subject; so she was unaware that the company now making its debut had just been imported from Athens and that the Greek community, headed by all its leaders, was turning up in patriotic strength. They took no more notice of Daisy than the British community would have taken of some unknown Greek upon a similar occasion.

What was worse, Prince-Carter, so far from hurrying forward to do her honour after his customary fashion, happened to be heavily engaged in receiving the Greek Minister and several dignitaries. Daisy had to stand aside and wait for him exactly as if she had been an ordinary member of the public.

While she was doing so, she caught sight of Lucy threading her way through the loquacious groups with a parchment scroll in her hand, and greeted her a little more enthusiastically than she had intended because she was pleased at that instant to recognize someone who was bound to behave cordially towards her. But Lucy was evidently busy, and though she made a show of cheerful surprise, it was clear that the encounter had been awkwardly timed.

'I'm frightfully sorry, Daisy,' she said after they had exchanged rather constrained embraces. 'What a nuisance to be in such a rush after not having seen you for ages! I would have got in touch today, but we've been up to the ears, as we always are on first nights. And now I have to dash round to the back. This scroll thing is from the

Greek Minister to Mme Karavia, the leading lady, and it's got to be delivered at once. The curtain can't go up till she's had it. I'll be back in half a minute. Don't go!'

She disappeared, leaving Daisy with a quite irrational sense of having been slighted. A nice thing to be thrust aside in favour of a lot of Greeks!

Prince-Carter now returned from escorting the ministerial party to the boxes reserved for them and, fully alive to the delicacy of his position, began to apologize with fawning gallantry. 'Dear lady, do—please *do* forgive me! You cannot—you positively cannot imagine my dilemma, seeing you come in just when I was up to the eyes in diplomatic duties. How delightful to have you back in Cairo again! Why didn't you send word that you were going to look in on us, dear lady? Then we could have killed the fatted calf!'

He laughed nervously, and Daisy, soothed by his deference, responded with suavity: 'It was just a last-minute idea, Mr. Prince-Carter—a sort of sudden impulse. I knew Mr. Mosenthal's box would be empty in any case, so I thought I might as well use it,' The manager laughed again, very nervously indeed.

'My dear, dear Miss Joy, you shouldn't keep us in the dark about these angel's visits, you really shouldn't. If I'd had the slightest inkling that you were likely to honour us, you may be sure nobody should have come anywhere near Mr. Mosenthal's box except over my dead body. Unhappily, my wife has been using it during all these months, and she's in there now with a friend.' He paused; but Daisy's icy gaze forced him to proceed rapidly. 'Of course, you must let me find you another box if—er—if you wouldn't care to join them there.' Then, as she remained ominously mute: 'The ones farther back are much better for seeing from. I fancy there are one or two left.'

Perhaps if Daisy had been in her normal state of composure she would have realized that nothing could look more unbecoming in her than to raise any dispute about a question so trivial, that the only attitude she could fittingly take was one of graceful surrender. But she was, for the reasons which have been given, sensitive and defensive, and to be asked either to resign her rightful place or to share it with Mrs. Prince-Carter, whom she had always looked upon as a most tiresome and ridiculous person, seemed an affront not to be borne.

'I thought,' she said with a pained smile, 'that it was always understood Mr. Mosenthal might be using his box even if he didn't arrive in time for the beginning.'

'Oh, quite, Miss Joy, quite! It was only because I knew *for certain* he wasn't coming that I installed my wife there. I was with him today, you see—had to present my report and all that sort of thing—and he told me he expected to work till midnight. It never occurred to me that you might drop in alone. Stupid of me!'

He had played a trump card, but that only made Daisy angrier and more determined to win the next trick. She assumed a tone of saccharine sweetness: 'Well, no harm's done, Mr. Prince-Carter, so please don't bother about it. I'm sure your wife won't mind moving, will she? I'd *rather* sit in our usual box, if it's all the same to you. I should feel quite a stranger if I went anywhere else.'

Prince-Carter would have liked very much to explain that it was not all the same to him, that he had seldom been required to do anything more shockingly uncongenial than informing his wife that she must make way for another. Daisy, however, represented Mosenthal, an even greater power than the one which governed his private life, and he had no alternative but to fall in with her wishes. The theatre is yours, dear lady,' he rejoined with a courtly sweep of the hand. 'Box A shall be delivered up to you immediately. Oh, first I must find out where I can put my wife instead. Excuse me!'

Smoothing back a lock of his thick greying hair in a movement which gave him an entirely fictitious air of assurance, he turned to the booking-office to inquire what accommodation was free. The answer was dispiriting. It was an exceptional house that night, and the only box left in the first tier had been sold even while he was talking to Daisy. The upper tiers were far less esteemed by those who enjoyed cutting a figure on such occasions, and as that was his wife's chief purpose in coming to see a play of which she would understand not one word, he faced his task with peculiar disrelish. It was a comfort to him that Lucy returned from her errand at that moment and Daisy stayed behind to speak to her, so at least he was not obliged to have her with him while he dealt with Blanche.

The overture was being played as he beckoned his wife from her seat and hurriedly explained what had happened, and he was glad that the music prevented her friend from hearing their conversation. For the friend was her dressmaker, with whom she was always ineffably majestic (and to whom, moreover, she perpetually owed money), and he guessed that it would be a cruel humiliation for her to have to strike her flag in front of anyone whom she so loved to patronize.

In truth, what for most women would have been a minor inconvenience, to be passed off with a laughing apology and a few confidential strictures upon Daisy's vulgarity, was for her an appalling insult, a disgrace hardly to be lived down. She was perhaps the only other European in Cairo who had as strong a sense of the importance of petty distinctions as Daisy herself.

She stood at the back of the box clasping her sculpturesque draperies about her with quivering hands like one who has been stricken. 'It's impossible,' she cried in a tragic whisper. 'I can't believe it! No, no! You've made some mistake, I'm sure of it. No woman—not even that woman—could seriously wish to turn me out of this box in full view of the whole audience. Why didn't you suggest that she should come and sit with us?'

'I did,' he answered with a propitiatory shake of the head.

'And do you mean to say'—no words could convey the vibrant amazement of her tone—'do you mean to say that she refused?'

'I put it to her indirectly and she took no notice. After that I didn't like to mention it again.'

'Oh, this is insufferable! This is more than human nature can bear.' She flung an anguished glance towards her companion, who leaned back luxuriously, fanning herself with her programme and surveying the occupants of neighbouring boxes in happy unconsciousness of the impending blow. 'How can I tell her we're being chased away like—like beggars at the gates? Oh, I can never look her in the face again.'

Prince-Carter, who knew that his indebted wife kept the dressmaker in a good humour by sharing with her from time to time such mild treats as her connection with the Polyglot Amusement Company put in her way, could not help feeling some sympathy with her agitation, but it was his business to get them both into some other seats as speedily as possible, and instead of offering commiserations he only said rather sharply: 'Come along, Blanche, the curtain will be going up presently. You can explain afterwards. Don't let's have a scene about it.'

Nothing, as he recalled the moment he had spoken, is more egregiously tactless than to warn an angry woman not to make a scene. Mrs. Prince-Carter's control, before maintained with difficulty, now came near to breaking. 'This is too much!' she muttered in broken, despairing accents. 'To be treated like a dog in a theatre where my husband is supposed to be manager—to be publicly degraded with his full consent. . . .'

'My dear,' he protested imploringly, 'you can't believe I wanted to let you in for this.'

Her hands moved as if to thrust him aside, and her voice, rising in a trembling crescendo, cut across the interruption with a fierceness that alarmed him. 'Publicly degraded—and by whom! By Mosenthal's harlot, a glorified chorus-girl! . . . No, that's too flattering—a glorified street-walker!' She wheeled round upon the dressmaker, who had heard snatches of the altercation and left her chair to find out what was the matter. 'We're not good enough,' she exclaimed in a revulsion of bitterness, 'to sit with Mosenthal's fancy woman. Get your things, my dear! We must move out. We must make way for the blonde guttersnipe.'

They began to collect their handbags and their gloves and cloaks, Mrs. Prince-Carter snatching hers together with the vigour of an avenging goddess, her friend fumbling and groping in a fever of bewilderment. Prince-Carter ran a very hot palm across his brow, and even in his misery found time to thank heaven that an especially fine outburst of music had prevented the disturbance from reaching the adjoining boxes. When they came out into the passage, they saw Daisy and Lucy earnestly conversing some distance away—far enough to be quite out of earshot—and again the manager congratulated himself. But the escape was so narrow that he was shaken in every nerve, and he could hardly believe his good fortune when his wife walked with a haughty and impetuous stride to the nearest staircase, announcing in a serpent-like hiss that nothing would induce her to spend another instant in the theatre. The dressmaker followed in confusion, and he saw them down safely to the first exit door before going back to where he thought he should find Daisy.

Only Lucy, however, now remained in the passage, and she had stayed to tell him that Daisy had already gone into the box, the curtain being up. He went after her directly and murmured courtesies in the most self-abasing terms, but she appeared extremely intent upon the play, and he was soon glad to retreat. She was evidently still resentful, like the little upstart she was, at finding her chosen place taken by someone else. Well, it was consoling to reflect that Mosenthal, exacting and inconsiderate though he might be, would probably have common sense enough to see the affair in its real proportions.

Had he carried with him any idea of the seething rage and consuming mortification which possessed her, he might have guessed that his days at the Adelphi were numbered. As it was, he resumed his ordinary occupations in a state of ignorance which, if not precisely blissful, at least gave him some chance of recovering, little by little, from the tremors he had undergone.

But the eyes which Daisy fixed on the stage were glassy and her limbs were rigid. Every word of Mrs. Prince-Carter's fearful, incredible diatribe against her seemed to be beating about in her head with the malignant clamour of a trapped hornet. She would have liked to writhe, to cry, to tear the velvet-cushioned ledge on which her fingers rested, and instead she sat, for perhaps the first time in her life, looking as cool and stately as a queen. The same process which burned and seared her within had frozen her body to the semblance of a statue. The Greek play was no more unmeaning to her than any other language would have been while the sound of that desolating invective filled her whole brain.

She had lingered in the foyer only a minute or two after the manager had departed to perform his distasteful mission, and then had strolled upstairs with Lucy to be in time for the rising of the curtain. The door of the box stood half open, and assuming that it was already vacated, they had approached and been on the verge of entering. The discussion within had reached that exact juncture when Prince-Carter had so misguidedly hinted his dread of a scene, and Lucy had at once retreated and tried to draw Daisy with her. But Daisy had been unable to resist the temptation to overhear. The music which submerged the speakers' voices within the auditorium had no such power in the passage at the back of the boxes. Mrs. Prince-Carters diction was remarkable for its clarity, and Daisy spared herself nothing.

At the word 'guttersnipe' she shrank away, crestfallen to a degree which made her unwilling even to seek the relief of imparting what she had heard. So great, in fact, were her astonishment and dismay that they released some fund of nervous stamina in her, enabling her to talk to Lucy with well-affected unconcern, and at the same time to turn over swiftly in her mind the question of how she should behave towards the Prince-Carters.

Her first desire had been to slap Mrs. Prince-Carter's face, her second to leave the theatre immediately in such a manner as would give her enemy the maximum of discomfort. But the months spent in studying the lofty bearing of Mrs. Calderon-Chauncey had not been unavailing, and the briefest deliberation convinced her that her only dignified course was to feign ignorance of an attack so degrading. The problem of punishment could be dealt with afterwards.

As for Lucy, on her part no pretence was necessary: having moved out of hearing rapidly, she had gathered nothing except that her superior was having an uncomfortable discussion with his wife. Indeed, she had only the vaguest idea as to what the cause of the awkwardness might be, not being aware that Daisy had actually demanded the ejection of Mrs. Prince-Carter from her box. The whole affair had occupied so short a time that one could not imagine anything serious had been happening. Nor would she have guessed, even if Daisy had confided in her, that the foolish little drama was destined to affect the lives of everyone involved in it, herself not less than the others.

It took all the pride Daisy could summon to render her capable of sitting steadily through the first act. Her inward fury grew perpetually more turbulent, her wretchedness more onerous to bear alone, until the theatre seemed a visible cage from which she must break out or go mad. The figures on the stage, declaiming gibberish to an accompaniment of cryptic gestures, became an active provocation; the aloofness of the audience was in some way sinister. She managed to hold herself in restraint until the curtain began to descend and then, before the house lights went on, she fled from the place by the most obscure exit.

Her wrath had given her courage, and looking neither to right nor left, she bent swift steps towards the building, only a hundred yards away, where Mosenthal had his office. Every window showed dark except the row of four belonging to his suite. She ran upstairs and arrived panting at the door which bore, upon a white glass pane, the inscription 'Managing Director'. Under the names of various companies was written in small but firm letters one terse instruction, PLEASE KEEP OUT. But Daisy did not even knock. She burst into the room as if she had been pursued, and would have delivered herself of heaven knows what melodramatic utterance if she had not been checked by the sight of Siegfried's private secretary standing wearily beside the great man's chair with books under his arm and papers in his hands.

Siegfried looked up and saw with quietly regardful eyes her splendid dress, her woebegone countenance, and the quick rising and falling of her breast under its fashionable swathe of tulle. His face betrayed no surprise, but he turned to his secretary and said briskly: 'All right, Feinstein. Leave the books. I'll go through them later. You'd better get me out a clear estimate for that Murdock scheme. No one could be expected to understand that muddle you've just shown me.'

'Is that all tonight, Mr. Mosenthal?' asked the secretary, haggard with fatigue.

'No, stand by. I may want you again.' Then he took another look at Daisy's face and corrected himself: 'Well, perhaps we could knock off. After all, I've been at it since nine this morning.'

The secretary, who had been at it since seven, wished them both good night with gratitude he was at pains to conceal and departed, praising God for his unforeseen release. Mosenthal sent a slow, drooping gaze after him. 'That fellow's an intelligent worker,' he murmured reflectively, 'but a bit of a clock-watcher. Well, what's the trouble? Can't you wait till I come home to find out about that beautiful husband of yours?'

'It isn't that.' She sank into a leather armchair, redolent of cigar smoke and strikingly incongruous as a setting for her pastel-coloured flounces and cascades of ostrich-feather trimming. 'It isn't that, Sieg. It's something else.'

'Get it off your chest!' he enjoined her harshly. The confusion and shame of her expression, coupled with the elaborateness of her *toilette*, had suggested the intolerable thought that she might be about to confess some attempt at infidelity. He waited in a stern suspense while she struggled against her rising tears for words. When they came they were the strangest he had ever heard her speak.

'Oh, Sieg, Sieg, do you know what I am? I'm your harlot. I'm your fancy woman. I'm your guttersnipe. That's what I am—your guttersnipe—your street-walker.' For the second time in the year he had lived with her, she began to cry. Tears of the purest self-pity rained down her cheeks and dripped upon her tulle fichu, until it seemed to be hung with bright glass drops.

'Now, what the hell's the matter with you?' The tone he used was not unkind, for his suspicion had already been dispelled, and once again her abject childish manner of weeping moved him. He even went so far as to hand her the spotless silk handkerchief from his breast-pocket.

Thus encouraged, Daisy poured forth, in a voice shaken with sobs, the whole story of her dreadful experience, her outraged sensibilities, her loathing for the vile woman who had traduced her; and her longing for early and sudden death. Soon, feeling the ease of unburdening herself, she grew calm enough to watch the effect she was having upon her audience, and it was everything she could have wished. Siegfried was angry, angrier than he cared to admit; she knew him by now and could divine the bitter displeasure that lay beneath his pose of apathy. Verbally he offered little consolation to her wounded self-esteem, but he walked up and down the room frowning and pressing his fingers against his pursed-up lips in a fashion which boded ill to the Prince-Carters.

'I'm glad,' he remarked when the last detail had been told, 'that you had sense enough not to show you'd heard anything. It could only have made you look cheap. The best thing is to tell nobody, not even Lucy Kendon. We don't want any gossip about the matter at all. The moment an affair like this gets talked about, it'll be turned into a joke, and then there'll be all sorts of rubbishing exaggerations and, believe me, they won't do *you* any good. Now, remember, I want no talk.'

Daisy assured him she was of the same mind.

'As for Prince-Carter's wife,' he continued soberly in response to her unspoken question, 'she's always been a silly bitch, and I'd better get her out of your way. Naturally you can't be expected to risk meeting a creature like that all over the place.' He was not strong-minded enough to repress a sigh. 'I'm sorry about Prince-Carter. It won't be easy to find as good a man for the job.'

'Will it really be necessary to sack him?' Daisy inquired, thrilled but a little frightened to see what powers she had set in train.

'Looks like it. We can't very well order him to do away with his wife.' He took another turn about the room, and then asked with the shadow of a smile: 'Don't you want to hear about your husband—that precious Hugh MacLowrie of yours?'

'Of course, Sieg. Oh, of course I do.' The eagerness of two hours ago flooded excitingly back upon her.

'He's a scoundrel if ever there was one. Our man in Sydney tells us he's never dealt with such a shady customer, and that's saying a good deal, because he's probably a rather shady customer himself. MacLowrie's willing, it seems, to lie low and say nothing while you go ahead with the divorce, but—as we expected—at a price. And, my God, what a price!'

'Oh, Siegfried!' She fixed her tear-stained eyes upon his face in an agony of apprehension.

'You may well say, "Oh, Siegfried!"' By way of humorous comment he jingled the money in his trousers pockets. 'We realized all along he'd try to blackmail us, seeing that under these crazy English laws you're in no position to divorce anyone; and a certain amount of blackmail we were prepared to stand for. But, God's truth, not that much! I decided today to let the whole thing rip—to cable to the solicitors telling them that our dear MacLowrie may go to hell.'

Her heart sank. She could not speak, could not do anything but stare helplessly at her lover's face.

'That's what I decided today,' he went on smoothly, 'but tonight I'm not so sure. I don't like the idea of people calling you "Mosenthal's fancy woman". As a matter of fact, it makes me sick. So I've half a mind to pay that blackguard what he wants and let you get rid of him.'

He strolled over to the window and looked intently down into the street while Daisy held her breath listening for his next pronouncement.

'Yes,' he said musingly after a very long silence. 'That sort of talk must be stopped. You'd better begin taking some Hebrew lessons, my dear. It'll be something to keep you busy during the next few months, because we shall have to live apart while this divorce business goes on.'

'Hebrew?' cried Daisy. 'But, Sieg, what for?'

'I shall be wanting you to become a Jewess.'

Daisy hailed the prospect of her conversion with a rapture almost saintly.

CHAPTER 24

MOSENTHAL waited what he considered a discreet interval and then, on a pretext which he scarcely troubled to make convincing, he informed Prince-Carter that his services would no longer be required. He was sorry to allow a personal matter to interfere, even covertly, with business; but the more he thought of it, the more heinous did Mrs. Prince-Carter's offence appear, and the man was notoriously under her thumb and probably shared her opinions. Now that he had resolved to marry Daisy, it was more than ever desirable to uproot from his employment someone who had heard her referred to—perhaps habitually—as a glorified street-walker.

If he had found that his whole staff was in the same position, his whole staff would have had to go, for not only was his affection for Daisy very great but his views on the dignity and sanctity of marriage were strictly in the Jewish tradition. Though he was willing to infringe custom by an unconventional choice, yet, once he had chosen, his future wife assumed in his eyes a character he was as ready to protect as if it had been immaculate. Indeed, now his intentions were no longer uncertain, the very quality of his love seemed to undergo a refining change, so much did the decision raise her in his own esteem.

Daisy was gracious enough to plead Prince-Carter's cause in sweet and womanly but rather feeble terms, but when it was proved to her—as she had half expected it must be—that her appeal came too late, she conceded that possibly she had been foolish to try and set things right. She was too forgiving; she knew it to be one of her weaknesses but she had never been able to cure it. Meanwhile, what with divorce arrangements and her impending conversion to the Jewish faith, she had something better to think about than the unpleasant fate which had overtaken her enemies.

Prince-Carter's dismissal came as a shock even to those who disliked him. He was known to have been exceptionally hard-working and a valuable man at his job, and a number of rumours went rapidly into circulation. Some were concerned with his ne'er-do-well son, and others facetiously suggested that his wife's habit of giving gratuitous advice to the artistes had driven the Greek company to threaten a strike unless they were relieved of her. But the explanation that found most credence was naturally that given by Prince-Carter himself. He offered it only to a few with whom he was on confidential terms; they, however, confidentially passed it on to others, so that by degrees it crept almost into general currency.

Prince-Carter's story, told in perfectly good faith, was that Lucy Kendon, the bosom friend of Mosenthal's mistress, had wantonly repeated some incautious utterances of his own. What other treacheries she had committed he could not be certain, but as to this one there seemed no room for doubt.

The actual circumstances were these. Having suffered a most disagreeable night at home as a sequel to his most disagreeable evening at the theatre, he had fallen next day into the usual temptation to discuss his trials with his nearest colleague, Lucy. Of late he had tended to feel less insecure with her. After all, he had often let slip unguarded comments in the past and no harm had ever come of it. So in describing the ridiculous fuss Daisy had made about the box, he had criticized her conduct with a good deal of frankness. And Lucy, though she had not said very much, had certainly conveyed an idea that she agreed with him.

He had grown a little nervous on learning that, within an hour or two of listening to these complaints, she had paid a visit to the subject of them, and when, about ten days later, he had been dismissed on obviously fabricated grounds, he could only come to the conclusion that she had betrayed him. He himself had done nothing, said nothing, which could otherwise account for his being cast off after years of servitude, and those rash words spoken by his wife had been heard only by the dressmaker, who swore that she had mentioned them to nobody.

The case against Lucy looked so clear that soon he began to talk of her mischief-making propensities to his friends as if he had had downright proof of them. And these reports were whispered about, with all the embellishments his sympathizers chose to add, until her reputation as a go-between and spy became familiar to almost every member of the Polyglot staff except herself.

If he had been a man of any moral courage he would, no doubt, have taxed her angrily with her double-dealing, and together they might have pieced out what had really happened; but, fearing further injury, he preferred to avoid open quarrels, and during his fortnight under notice he treated Lucy with exemplary politeness.

Lucy herself, little as she had esteemed him personally, was sincerely distressed to hear he had been deprived of his job. No suspicion that she was being held to blame for his downfall ever crossed her mind, for there was nothing in her conscience to give rise to one. Prince-Carter's reticence on the topic of his impending departure seemed quite natural to one who was herself reticent, while that 'strict confidence' in which the tales of her duplicity were passed about was always respected as far as her own ears were concerned. She did now and then wonder whether Daisy's silly insistence on the occupation of the stage-box could be somewhere—somehow or other—at the root of the trouble, but that seemed a rather far-fetched theory.

Six months ago she might have questioned Daisy with some freedom; a year ago she would have been ready to cross-examine her; but such simple courses were no longer possible because there was now hardly any intimacy existing between them. Their friendship was reduced to a thin façade, maintained, on Daisy's side, for the sake of charity and temporary convenience: on Lucy's, out of respect for some sentiment which made it hard to fall away completely from an attachment once important to both of them. They had been on an unsatisfactory footing before Daisy's journey to Europe; yet Lucy, driven by sheer loneliness to suppress old grievances, had anticipated her return with pleasure, and was prepared to make the best of her. There was no one else linked to her by so many associations.

But Daisy was not in the mood to let anyone make the best of her. Since she was now assured that she was to achieve the greatest of her ambitions, wealthy and honourable domesticity, her whole being was concentrated upon preparing for aggrandizement, and it seemed more than ever regrettable that, apart from Siegfried, the only familiar company within reach was that of a shabby young woman hopelessly out of touch with high life, whom later it would be necessary to get rid of. Not that she would break her good-natured resolution to spend a certain amount of time with her—at any rate until there was someone to take her place—but she could not begin too soon to let her gather that their ways must ultimately lie asunder. Any other attitude would be misleading and unkind.

Lucy, however, though she was willing to bear many of Daisy's self-flattering little airs with resignation, could not so entirely pocket her pride as to tolerate friendship on the terms now offered to her. A lifelong habit of independence asserted itself. Daisy's condescensions became an exasperating burden, and she looked forward with relief to the time when she might cast off even the pretence of bearing it. It was better to be lonely than to live at the beck and call of one who had grown so painfully out of sympathy with her.

And in the days which followed Prince-Carter's dismissal, the same days which were so rapidly and visibly widening the gulf between herself and Daisy, she had cause to feel very lonely indeed. Not only, unknown to herself, was she held responsible for Prince-Carter's ill-fortune, but every piece of mischief which had been carried, or was thought to have been carried, to Mosenthal or his deputies during the last year was resuscitated in order that it might be laid at her door. The result of all this subterranean gossip was that, although nobody dared to show open disapproval of one whose enmity was thought to be so dangerous, she was met on every hand with a most decided lack of cordiality.

It was dreary working under these conditions. More and more she tended to lose confidence in herself, to believe that her illness had ruined not only her voice but had caused her personality to become, in some incalculable way, unpleasing. And with all the ambition that was left to her fixed solely on escape from Egypt, she still postponed the effort of trying to rehabilitate herself. To go on saving money was labour enough, much heavier labour than it had been at first; for the strong momentum, the vivid, fortifying hope, were gone. They could not survive the crushing set-backs of the last half-year.

But with the increasing uncongeniality of her work, she was given a new impetus towards escape, and once again began to economize resolutely. The Ministry of Shipping had just revised passenger rates: in 1920 the lowest second-class fare on a P. & O. liner was nearly half as much again as it had been in 1919. All the incidental expenses would be advanced proportionately and a larger sum must be amassed than she had originally aimed at.

Fortunately for those who stood to gain by it, there was enough political strife to keep Cairo animated all through the summer. The Adelphi was not closed and, as in the preceding year, Lucy deputized for anyone, behind the scenes or in front, who happened to be missing from the depleted staff. But now nothing was allowed to be interesting or enjoyable to her. The new manager seemed to take a positive pleasure in giving her all the duties she most evidently disliked and then hindering her in the performance of them. No sooner did she tackle a piece of work with efficiency and goodwill than she was compelled to switch off and do something disagreeable to her. Messages and instructions arrived at the last minute and she was blamed for the resulting unpunctuality. Details she was accustomed to entrust to others were neglected and the subsequent apologies still seemed to leave her in the wrong. She resisted various temptations to complain to Mosenthal—any such measure would be constructed as an attempt to abuse a privileged position—but she could not repress her sharp anger in the face of so many provocations, and the antagonism that had taken root in misunderstanding thus received daily nourishment.

Impeded at every turn, she began at last to slacken and to lapse into moods of indifference. Her work had lost its zest for her, and her leisure afforded her very little in the way of recreation. She seldom got an evening away from the theatre, and now, instead of spending the broiling afternoons in Daisy's apartment, luxuriously extended on a chaise-longue while she chatted and sewed, she had nothing to do but read in one of the ill-ventilated dressing-rooms, or else take a hot and noisy tram-ride to Karnak House for the purpose of lying down.

Daisy, to be on the safe side of the divorce law, had left Cairo and was living in a villa on the coast. Here she was frequently attended by a Rabbi who had undertaken to teach her Jewish lore. She was an earnest student, being extremely anxious to do the thing in style, and, besides, the lessons were a way of killing time. Her teacher found her very weak in committing Hebrew to memory and was glad that he had only to impart a smattering of it; but on the other hand he had never before had a pupil, even amongst the most orthodox Jews, to whom the doctrine appeared so simple and acceptable. Every tenet of the faith was equally delightful to her; she was never known to question anything.

The Rabbi, less pleased by this ready acquiescence than might have been expected, several times thought it his duty to remind her that the Jews wanted no converts drawn to their creed by motives of self-interest. She replied with perfect sincerity that she was absolutely convinced of the superiority of the Jewish religion over all others. Although, as she frankly admitted, she had only become interested through being engaged to a Jew (the Rabbi knew nothing of the husband against whom she had recently filed her suit), once having begun these studies, she had recognized that here was truth. So she said and so she thought—and would have thought of any religion ever professed if marriage with her lover had been the prize for piety.

It was while she was being thus initiated that Siegfried, on one of his discreet visits, told her a piece of news which, her mind being intent on higher things, she could listen to with composure. Her tiresome friend, Lucy Kendon, was no longer giving satisfaction in her work. It was strange: no one could deny that she had shown promise at the start, but he had recently been having some very bad accounts of her. The man who had come to replace Prince-Carter at the Adelphi said she was erratic, often incompetent, and always rubbing one or other of her associates up the wrong way. Damaging reports had also been coming in from other sources, and since smoke could hardly exist in such quantities without fire, it must be assumed that she had ceased to be an asset to the firm and ought, on principle, to be weeded out.

How was it to be done? It was a distasteful business, having to sack someone whom Daisy had once been fond of, but Mosenthal could not let it be whispered that inefficient employees were tolerated when Daisy happened to favour them. What a fool the woman had been to refuse the chance he had offered her of going to England last year! He did not remember the details of the matter very clearly, but he knew she had behaved stupidly and sacrificed all claims to his indulgence. Still, he would be reluctant to leave her absolutely stranded. Could Daisy put forward any suggestion as to how she should be dealt with?

Now although, from the surface of her mind, Daisy regarded herself as Lucy's good Samaritan, who had looked after her in illness, befriended her in poverty, and stood by her when she was deserted on every hand, yet down among the sundry items of knowledge she chose to hide from herself, the fact remained that nothing she had done for the aggravating girl had been of the least benefit to her; that Lucy, in short, so far from being grateful, probably considered herself as an injured party. And this was something that Daisy found very galling. She was obliged to take refuge from such an uncomfortable conviction by telling herself again and again that she had squandered her benevolence on a *most* undeserving case.

So that, hearing of the disintegration of her protégée's character, she could only shake her head apologetically and murmur that it was all the doing of that odious drunkard, Eugene Pryor. Poor, poor Lucy, he had demoralized her completely! She had never been the same since he had turned up last autumn. Look at that escapade in the house of ill-fame, for instance! (Daisy could not bring herself nowadays to call a brothel by its name.) What could she make of that except that Lucy had started to deteriorate very soon after coming into contact with him?

Yes, poor Lucy, she could not help feeling sorry for her. Nevertheless, she quite understood that Siegfried must not put up with behaviour from one member of the staff which would not be permitted in another. It was an affair in which she (Daisy) ought definitely to take no part. It was a business affair and should not be left to the judgment of a woman, especially a woman so foolishly soft-hearted as she was.

Siegfried was not without some vague sense of responsibility towards Lucy, and to wash his hands of her as uncompromisingly as if she had been Prince-Carter seemed over-harsh in view of what he recollected of her history. Once again for a brief moment he entertained the idea of paying her fare to England and getting her out of his way. But no! he was displeased with her—exceedingly displeased—and it would be madness to reward her for having grown quarrelsome and unreliable. Her slackness annoyed him the more by contrast with her former diligence, and he felt that she had probably taken to trading on her known intimacy with Daisy—persuading herself that nobody would complain because she was Daisy's friend.

Well, in that case, she would have a rude awakening. No, he was damned if he would present her with a handsome cash bonus because she had turned out a failure! She was lucky, very lucky, that he did not intend to give her two weeks' notice and let her go to the devil.

He pondered the matter with as much attention as it seemed to deserve among the more important subjects which engaged his mind, and in due course arranged that Lucy should be transferred to Alexandria. He had a brand-new cinema there which wanted a box-office clerk. The salary would be four hundred piastres a week, half what she was getting now; but so that the reduction should not be too drastic he had worked out that she could make it up to five hundred by translating film sub-titles into or out of French. This was the only concession he would make to the fact that Daisy had once enjoyed her society. He had already been excessively good to her. What would have happened, he asked himself, if her career had been wrecked by illness in any country where he and Daisy were not!

Lucy received an impersonal letter from the firm announcing that the staff of the Adelphi was about to be reorganized. Another post would be available in Alexandria. Its terms were stated. She might take it or leave it.

She did not surrender without an energetic struggle. She taxed the new manager with having treated her unfairly; he argued suavely that the smooth running of the theatre had been his sole concern and suggested that she should take her grievances to the managing director. She requested an interview with Mosenthal, and was met with a cool, official denial; he was heavily engaged and the question of her employment at the Adelphi could not be reopened.

She wrote to Daisy, hotly, vehemently, but her letter was a protest, rather than an appeal, and was therefore little calculated to have the desired effect.

Daisy wrote back, sweetly, patiently, and very, very sensibly. She was sorry, she explained, to learn what had happened; no one could be sorrier; all the same, she could not possibly break her one unswerving rule—to let Mr. Mosenthal conduct his business in his own way.

It was a pity that Lucy had recently lost interest in her work—no doubt she was out of sorts, and Daisy sympathized with her—but Mr. Mosenthal would never put up with feminine interference, and it would be wrong for her to attempt it. Finally, after more in the same vein, she produced, by means of various oblique allusions, a trenchant summary of all the kindnesses Lucy had received from him in the past, and hinted that it would be inadvisable to look for more. After all, she had not been thrown out of work. A lot of trouble had been taken to provide her with another job, and five hundred piastres a week was exceptionally good money for a box-office clerk. It was a piece of luck, too, that she might look forward to spending the rest of the summer on the coast.

When Lucy saw how Daisy's Siegfried had become 'Mr. Mosenthal', she knew that every thread that bound them was irrevocably broken. Nothing now could be expected from her sometime friend, and to address any further petition to Mosenthal himself would be futile unless it had Daisy's blessing. She turned from them both and concentrated her last efforts upon an earnest search for some other sort of employment. It was completely unsuccessful. Armies of recently demobilized men were reducing women to their former low status in the labour market. There was no work of any kind within her province that could possibly yield her an income of five hundred piastres a week, and much as she would have liked to free herself once and for all from the firm controlled by Mosenthal, she perceived that it would be a childish gesture, impressive to nobody, only destructive and humiliating to herself, to accept a worse position elsewhere.

Lucy's departure from Cairo was a matter of self-congratulation for at least two persons. Prince-Carter's substitute at the Adelphi felt glad that he had mustered the courage to rid the theatre of one whom he had been led to think was an inveterate mischief-maker. Daisy, on her part, could not fail, on reflection, to see how undesirable it would have been for Lucy to go on living in the same city as herself. With things as they were, their threadbare comradeship could just be allowed to peter gently out, whereas if she had remained in Cairo, Daisy would have had to meet her on every visit to the Adelphi, if not oftener.

If Daisy had been cunning, if Lucy had been unscrupulous, their affairs must have followed a very different course. Daisy would then have exerted herself to the utmost to clear a potential enemy out of Egypt altogether. But in truth, she was no schemer. She fell into the much more dangerous category of people who, instead of shaping circumstances to fit their needs, intuitively adjust themselves to circumstances, easily forgetting whatever it is uncomfortable to remember.

As for Lucy, it no more occurred to her that she could release herself from bondage by making her presence actively vexatious than that she might get to England by flying over the sea.

England! How far, how incalculably far now, had that glorious goal receded! No matter how often she assured herself that this new affliction could not last, that it was too bad to last—no matter what extravagant patterns of hope she tried to weave—she could not render herself insensible to the miserable fact. To save five or six thousand piastres out of an income so diminished would be like rolling the stone of Sisyphus.

Egypt had become reality. It was no longer an odd and unaccommodating stage-setting which she would presently quit for ever, having played her part—a prison with lath and canvas walls destined for certain to be overthrown. It was the real world, sordid, substantial, and permanent.

Chapter 25

THE PASSAGES of time which move slowest in real life are precisely those which most require to be hurried on in a novel. The record of uneventful years is necessarily dull and must be condensed to make it acceptable. Lucy's story, which now in actuality began to creep along at a snail's pace, must here be given its swiftest impetus. Years are to be disposed of with fewer words than weeks or even hours of the preceding time, and the developments of a decade reported with less minuteness than the incidents of one afternoon in the earlier chapters. With her removal to Alexandria she settled down to an existence seldom varied except by occurrences too slight in their effects to be chronicled.

She worked at a monotonous job, she was constrained by lack of means to suffer a monotonous style of living, and she made monotonous attempts to save money which were unfailingly frustrated by small setbacks. Now there was a dentist's bill to be settled, and now she had to pay a premium to ensure herself a good lodging. Prices were high and mass production was not as yet catering for refined tastes. A new pair of shoes might demolish the savings of a month.

In her second year at Alexandria she all but relinquished the hope of ever being able to escape by her own endeavours.

From this time forward she grew less rigorous in the practice of self-denial. She joined a library, bought herself a gramophone, and spent a little on furbishing up her appearance. Her voice she regarded as irrevocably gone, but her looks had improved with the gradual amelioration of her health—though she would never again be effortlessly pretty. The bloom, the freshness, she had brought with her to Egypt were entirely vanished, but still, she had regained something of that attractiveness which was just beginning to be known as sex appeal.

Yet what a difference there was between being a presentable box-office clerk at a picture-house and being a successful artiste in a good company! It was not the more desirable among the patrons of the Forum who managed to make the transaction of buying tickets an occasion for overtures, yet the day came when she found herself unable to treat such gallantries with disdain. Unless she were prepared to submit to a lowering of her standards, she must do without companionship altogether.

Her furnished room was in an apartment house compared with which the place where she had lived in Cairo was luxurious and fashionable. She had no channel of approach either to the kind of people she had been brought up with, or those whom she had been accustomed to meet during her theatrical years. Therefore she was obliged to choose between two evils—to be solitary or to grow less fastidious.

She took herself in hand and in the course of time was able to apply something of her old gaiety to her new circumstances. Superficially she was less reserved. She no longer kept the men who tried to flirt with her completely at arm's length. With a few of them she made friends, and with one of them she had a love affair.

It was not an affair she could feel very proud of, but it was the best within her reach, and after her long abstinence she took pleasure in being courted, even though the lover fell far short of her ideals. She likened her reaction to the mingled enjoyment and exasperation of acquiring a flatteringly lavish gift which happens to be quite out of keeping with one's taste. A gift is an agreeable tribute, but it may also be a continual reminder that one has not got the thing one wants.

Lucy's suitor was in a regiment stationed at Aboukir. He held a captain's rank, but was not of the circles from which officers are drawn except in war-time. The new class prudery which has replaced the prudery of sex had not yet come into being in the nineteen-twenties. No one then tried to pretend that class distinctions did not exist, or that if they existed, they did not matter. To Lucy it was—as it would have been to any other woman of her training—a painful come-down to accept an admirer who was not a gentleman, whose accent was tainted with cockney, whose manners were ostentatiously refined yet full of saddening little blunders. She did not like to ask what he had been before the war. He was good-natured, cheerful, and appreciative, his looks were prepossessing, and his high spirits gave his society a certain charm that compensated for many of his defects.

Many but not all. She could not pretend to herself that she was more than mildly fond of him nor deny in her heart that he was capable of both shaming and boring her. Daisy, if driven by adversity to tolerate a lover so apparently second-rate, would soon have produced reasons for believing him to be one of the most remarkable of men. Lucy was not so ingenious at transforming her geese into swans. She could only tell herself philosophically that Gordon might have been worse; and since the love she gave him was of a somewhat feeble quality she tried to make up for what he was unconsciously missing by treating him with the utmost kindness.

But after a few months the exasperation began to outweigh the pleasure. His cheerfulness palled: it rang false like the breezy bedside manner of a doctor who prides himself on carrying about a sunny atmosphere. She lost the knack of being amused at his high spirits, and found it a nerve-strain to be constantly playing the role of 'understanding pal' and 'real good sort'. It became clear that they could not go on much longer. Fortunately, she was able to break away from him gradually. At various times he had asked her to marry him, but with nothing but his army pay he could not afford to be pressing. As his first ardour waned he had let that desire fall into abeyance. No promise bound them, nor were there any strong links of intimacy to be severed: the discipline of his camp, the hours of her work, had never allowed them to form a close comradeship.

Chance favoured her efforts to part without emotional disturbance. Gordon's regiment was drafted back to England. Her cooling off had just reached the stage when he could no longer doubt the drift of her feelings, and his enforced withdrawal spared him all the outward appearances of humiliation. They said goodbye in a friendly fashion, and kept up correspondence for nearly a year.

The experience had served to restore her confidence, and perhaps the ease with which she had handled it set her a little off her guard. The next affair was a good deal more troublesome. The lover now—if that term can be applied to anyone whose affections were so little moved—was a young journalist who came to the Forum to write notices for one of the local papers. Their work brought them into contact, and they discovered, with mutual sympathy, that they had belonged originally to the same world and were the victims of not dissimilar fates. Leslie too was the product of a country vicarage, had been brought up in a tradition of comfort, order, and well-being, and was thrust by calamity into an inappropriate framework.

He was one of that great legion of expensively educated young Britons whom four years of war had uprooted and whose lives were hopelessly deflected from their normal courses. Under ordinary conditions they would have become business men, professional men, or members of the leisured classes, but the war had reduced their capital, disturbed their training, or broken up their estates. Many were not old enough to have seen service, and these were, if anything, still more unlucky than those who could claim favour through their military records. Leslie was in this category. He had been a boy of eighteen, still in a training camp, at the time of the Armistice; now he was getting on for twenty-three, an orthodox representative of the post-war generation—restless, sceptical, introspective, improvident, sensation-loving, an admirable butt for the generation that had done its best to ruin him.

At the time when Lucy met him he was writing a novel which he confidently expected to place him beyond the necessity of ever working in an office again. Being badly in want of someone to display it to, he offered to read it aloud to her, and she supposed she might be performing a useful work by encouraging him. She had done a considerable amount of reading since leaving Cairo, and now rather prided herself on knowing a good novel when she saw one.

But she was too unskilled to assess the value of so youthful a production as this, and she over-estimated its merits. She could see that it was a callow piece of autobiography, naïvely sophisticated, self-consciously shocking; she guessed that it had little hope of publication; but she could not tell how nearly it was the counterpart of tens of thousands of similar essays in self-expression, generally unfinished, which round off a certain phase for those who are destined never to write seriously again. She thought he was promising, was pleased to be his consultant, and grew a little sentimental about his future, imagining that he might remember her gratefully when he trod the summits of renown. Stimulated by her interest, he soon discovered that she was a charming woman and for a time he tried to make her happy, but he was an egoist in a most volatile and experimental stage of immaturity. His fancy roved, his attention evaporated unless hers was wholly focused upon himself, and while he thought it perfectly natural to impose demands upon her, he retreated at once if she showed any sign of believing herself to have a claim on him. From Lucy's point of view it was never a satisfactory attachment, yet in spite of herself, she found her emotions not a little involved in it.

She was eight years older than he, and of those eight years the last four had taken more than their fair share of her youth. Leslie scarcely troubled to conceal his impression that a wide gulf of time separated them. He did not profess to be in love with her: she was only too thoroughly aware from the first that she would not be able to hold him an hour against a prettier face or a more eligible listener, and it was this perpetual realization of her disadvantage that entangled her feelings.

In shallow liaisons insecurity may be a substitute for love. She knew in her heart that, if she had been better situated, Leslie would have had small appeal for her; that the possessiveness he inspired was based, not upon his worth, but upon her need and loneliness. She remembered sorrowfully how, years ago, she had warned Constance against just such an error of over-valuation as she had fallen into now. Yet, though her reason angrily rebelled, for months he kept her on the *qui vive*.

Little by little her dreams of helping to nurture a brilliant talent collapsed absurdly. Spurred on by her eagerness in the days when it still had the merit of novelty, he had managed to finish his book, but it was doing the round of the publishers in London without much prospect of ever finding its way into print, and his literary impulse was exhausted. She recognized that his ambition to write had been an ill-founded one and that he had no other purpose strong enough to save him from his tendency to dissipation.

Their final parting was exceedingly unpleasant and would have been agonizing if she had really loved him. There were angry scenes, recriminations on her side, repudiations on his, and at last they agreed that, since they grated so upon each other's nerves, he had better keep out of her way. He took up soon after with a good-looking French girl who served in a tobacconist's shop, and when she occasionally encountered them together in the street or in some café, he would greet her so sheepishly that she decided at last it might be kinder to pretend not to have noticed him. By then another film critic was writing up the shows at the Forum, and she suspected that this part of Leslie's work had been rearranged at his own request. Altogether it was the most mortifying relationship of her whole life.

When she considered how she had placed it in the power of this shoddy being to humble her, she was bitterly ashamed, and it gave her a sharper pang than ever to recollect the happiness of the past. Her love for Henry stood out against the background of her retrospections like some great headland on a coast that slowly recedes from view, and she fixed her eyes upon it, committing its features to memory as anxiously as a traveller who knows that he may never see so beautiful a shore again.

At about the time when her sense of abasement was most depressing, a circumstance arose which brought her comfort. It took the shape of a letter forwarded from the head office of the Polyglot Amusement Company—a letter from England, very voluminous, and in an unfamiliar handwriting. It was something unusual to hear from anyone in England nowadays. She looked at the signature first, then at the paragraph immediately above it; then she glanced tangentwise from page to page until she came to the beginning and steadied herself to take in every word from the first to the last, reading with a sensation more nearly akin to happy excitement than any she had felt in a great while:

6 Willow Studios,
Chelsea,
London, S.W. 3.
15th Oct., 1924.

My dear Lucy,

I have only the very faintest hope that this is ever going to fall into your hands, but all the same I've been quite certain for at least a couple of years that I ought to write it. Even if you never see it, I still think it *must* be written, and now I have a peaceful afternoon before me and am sitting quietly at my desk determined not to put my conscience off another moment. Of course, it would be nicer if I could believe you were really likely to get this letter, but I'm afraid that's almost too much to expect after being completely out of touch all these years. There's just an off-chance that someone in that firm you used to work for will have your present address, and that's why I intend to post this instead of dropping it into the waste-paper basket.

I came across an Egyptian newspaper this morning, and it brought things back to me with such vividness! When I saw the announcement of the show at the Adelphi and remembered how often I went there with you and how you taught me to use a sewing-machine in the wardrobe, the whole atmosphere of that time came back to me just as if it had been yesterday—and then I thought how miserably I had repaid all your kindness.

It has weighed on my mind ever since like a crime. Do you know, it's five years this month since you saved me from making a total idiot of myself over that Italian bank clerk, and for about four I've been wanting to apologize for the way I behaved to you. The older I grow, the bigger the remorse grows, because I can see more and more clearly what an appalling young man he was, and it seems unbelievable that I could have given up an absolutely first-rate friend on account of *him*.

That night when you locked me in my room—have you forgotten?—stands out in my remembrance quite plainly. From the first, after writing you that frightful letter, I knew I'd gone too far, but I was so wretched I couldn't climb down. Oh, my utterly crushed and pulverized pride! How it ached!

A few weeks afterwards I went to Palestine, and the change of scene and the experience of living an ordinary family life did a tremendous lot for me, but it took me a long time to forgive you for scotching my so-called love affair, and even when I started getting over that a bit, it was awful to think you knew how my pride had been trampled on.

Of course I was under the impression that you were practically on your way to England. I had no idea that any misfortune had befallen you, otherwise I might have behaved better. I like to think so.

It wasn't till a year or so afterwards when we were back in Europe that my father told me you'd written me a letter that I never got, and how he'd read it. He said that your money had been stolen and that you hadn't been able to get to England after all. I'm still in the dark about how such a thing came to happen, but I can guess what a dreadful blow it must have been for you after all your planning and saving. If I'd dreamed what troubles you had to cope with at the time, I shouldn't have added to them.

Poor Lucy, I suppose you had to begin saving up all over again. My father said you were still in Egypt when he left and that was months afterwards.

Anyhow, by now it must be a long while since you got away, and I hope this reminder of your old troubles will just be a sort of amusement to you. Whenever I go to a theatre I look for your name on the programme, thinking that you're probably back on the stage. Or perhaps you've been married for years and little children are tottering round your feet? If by any miraculous chance you should ever come to read these words and have forgiven me, do please write, if only a few lines. I should love to find you again.

I won't go into details about myself, seeing that the purpose of this letter is simply to get my repentance off my chest, but just in case it should be destined to reach you, I may as well say this much.

First and foremost, you may be pleased to know that, when you started me off with dress-making, you were setting my feet on exactly the right path for them. I've been enormously interested ever since, both in making clothes and designing them, and now I'm very nearly earning my own living by working for someone who has just opened a small shop. Before that I studied at the Chelsea Polytechnic so as to get some training, and if I can possibly manage it I intend later on to have six months in Paris. One of these days I am going to be a great couturier. *I really am.* That's something I've made up my mind about. It'll be very hard for you to believe in my career because, when you first came to my rescue, I had taste I shudder to think of. I've changed beyond recognition. You'd like the look of me better now.

You'll be surprised to hear that I've reached quite a good understanding with my father. As soon as I grew up and stopped being a bother to him, he became much more reconciled to my existence. He lets me have a small allowance, and I live among a group of friends in Chelsea—mostly art students. I don't see him often, but when we do meet, he teaches me all about the right things to eat and drink (which I couldn't possibly afford) and seems only faintly embarrassed by my presence. He does well as an architect and has a little house at Campden Hill, where he lives with great elegance and precision like one of those clocks with beautiful works that tick very quietly under a glass shade. Two men servants look after him and everything is comfortable and well ordered, though he never shows much sign of enjoying it. Meanwhile I inhabit a studio-bed-sitting-room and my meals consist chiefly of fish and chips from the shop round the corner. I'm much happier this way than I should be in the atmosphere of his house.

Well, it's no use saying any more until I hear whether this ever finds its way to you. It's a funny business writing a huge letter to someone who may be a thousand miles off or may be living in the next street! Heaven knows how long it will take to track you down—if ever it does. At any rate it ought to be in time to bring my Christmas greetings!

Dear Lucy, when I count up all the benefits you conferred on me—from listening to my confidences when I never stopped talking for one moment about my own ridiculous affairs to saving me from being seduced by an awful young man who didn't even want me—I wonder what in the world I could ever do to repay you. I should feel so much better if I could be sure that you would hear of my contrition.

Your still affectionate
Constance
(and in case you've forgotten)
Conway

Lucy could hardly wait to begin answering this most welcome communication. Never was forgiveness more readily accorded, for her disappointment over Constance whom she had sincerely loved had exceeded even that induced by the defection of Daisy. She spent long hours eagerly engrossed in the composition of her reply, using all the art she could muster to convey a fair picture of her plight without letting it appear that she had utterly lost heart.

Though she felt entitled to commiseration, she was firmly resolved not to be depressing. She made a joke of her drastic attempts at economy and her innumerable failures; she contrasted her former aspirations ironically yet airily with the indignities she had managed to survive; and indicated how low she had sunk in the social scale by a graphic account of Chappie Paulos's dilemma whenever he was faced with the painful alternative of recognizing her or cutting her dead. He had compromised at last by recognizing her when he was alone and averting his eyes when in company; and so inspired was Lucy's pen that she succeeded in depicting both the man and her situation in a quite lively caricature. The affairs of Mrs. Siegfried Mosenthal also had their place in the news (for Constance had known something of her) and although the memory of that misplaced friendship could still rankle, she chose to use gentle malice rather than heavy disparagement, and turned it into a jest. When she read over her finished letter, she could not refrain from mocking herself in a sardonic postscript: 'Well, thank goodness I can see the funny side!'

To drop her bulky envelope into the letter-box was a gesture so satisfactory that for days she drew courage and patience from it. She no longer felt cut off, forgotten, and an outcast from her own kind. She was in touch now with the one person in England who had actually seen her in exile and was certain to understand her predicament and realize what it must mean to her.

Constance wrote back immediately recording a vow that the first substantial sum of money she ever obtained by her work should be at Lucy's service. It was a delightful letter, impetuous, affectionate, heart-warming in its responsiveness; but Lucy, pleased and grateful as she was, could not forbear to smile at the sanguine hopes of her would-be deliverer, a girl of twenty-two whose earnings at that time, as it transpired, had only just reached £2 10s. a week.

CHAPTER 26

TO SAY that the receipt of her first letter from Constance marked the turning-point of Lucy's destiny would be a dramatic overstatement, but it was true that, from that time forward, nothing ever seemed quite so flatly dreary again. Her correspondence with most of her friends in England had gradually petered out, having little live news to sustain it. Constance was, in any case, the only one of them who had been to Egypt and who could therefore form an accurate idea of her circumstances. It was extraordinarily encouraging to know that someone youthful, vital, and enthusiastic was following one's fortunes with interest and had pledged herself to one's rescue. Not that she could ever count upon a promise so romantic, but it offered good material for day-dreams, like having a ticket in a lottery.

They wrote to each other once a fortnight with perfect regularity, and Lucy found in those letters a soothing outlet for all the pent-up self-discoveries of years. She threw off her reticence to an extent that surprised herself, and returned almost the equivalent of the ardent confidences she had once received. She even told Constance about her abortive love affairs and—greater freedom still—about her quietly pervasive sentiment for Henry and her feeling that, though he was lost to her, she had betrayed him in stooping to what was unworthy.

Greatest freedom of all, she gave her a full description of an incident which would have been the most painful in her whole experience if it were not for the saving grace of a single beauty that made her glad to have endured it—an incident she could never think of afterwards without a fusion of exultation and despair.

It happened in January 1927 when she had been in Egypt nearly eight years. Skimming through the local English paper, while she boiled the kettle for her morning tea, Lucy's eye was caught by a familiar name in the social column. The Marquess and Marchioness of Redfarrow, she read, had arrived in Alexandria from Malta, and would stay a day or two at the Hotel de Paris et New-York on their way to Cairo, where they would embark on a journey up the Nile.

Lucy was sufficiently interested to think about this item of information a number of times during that day and the next. The Marquess of Redfarrow must be Henry's elder brother, his father, who had formerly held that title, having succeeded to the dukedom a few years ago; and although she had never met him, he was endowed, like everyone who belonged in any sense to Henry, with special significance for her. She had been accustomed once to hear a good deal about him and knew from photographs what he looked like. Each time she went past the Hotel de Paris et New-York on her way to and from the cinema she let her eyes stray across the wide veranda, hoping to get a glimpse of this important member of Henry's kith and kin. But although on one occasion she recognized no fewer than three faces, his was not among them.

The three faces were grouped about the same table and belonged to Chappie Paulos, Mosenthal, and Mosenthal's beautifully dressed wife, delicately pink-skinned in despite of several Oriental summers, golden-haired, still girlish in figure, still, thought Lucy wistfully, every man's idea of a pretty woman. Against her knee leaned a child three or four years old, a little girl whose amber-coloured hair contrasted attractively with the fine dark eyes inherited from her father. Lucy would have been glad to pass on with a feint of being intent upon something at the other side of the street, for she was well aware how much it embarrassed Daisy on her rare visits to Alexandria to be obliged to exchange politenesses with her, and she had often gone out of her way to avoid a meeting. Today, however, there was no escape. The child had captured her gaze an instant too long, and in that instant Mosenthal had seen her.

Mosenthal always greeted her rather kindly these days. His attitude was not the same as Daisy's because, as Lucy had never been his most intimate confidante, he did not feel under any necessity for keeping her at arm's length. Obscure and isolated as she was, he no longer supposed—as in the far-off times at Lotus Building—that she might take liberties. He was a great financier, a name to conjure with not only in Egypt but much farther afield: the Polyglot Amusement Company was now of only minor importance to him, and Lucy, as a cinema box-office clerk, was so manifestly beneath his notice that he could afford to be affable. His sense of grievance against her had been assuaged years ago, and he remembered very little of the events which had caused her to be reduced to her present status.

At the moment when he caught sight of her walking by the veranda of the hotel, only one thought came into his head—namely, that here was someone who was glancing admiringly at his beloved second child, incomparable throughout the world except for his first. So he nodded to her with a sort of supercilious amiability, and Daisy, her attention being thus caught, was compelled to offer a sweet smile. Chappie followed the magnate's lead, a little ill at ease; on the occasion of their last encounter he had stared glassily in the opposite direction.

Lucy decided that it would be uncivil not to pause and show some interest in Daisy's offspring, so she drew near and Siegfried called her on to the veranda.

'What do you think of Miss Selma Mosenthal?' He took up one of the baby's little hands and presented it to Lucy. 'Shake hands with the lady, Selma. Shake hands, there's a good girl!'

Lucy observed that, although his features still from habit wore a sneering expression, it was greatly softened, and he seemed now to be good-humouredly deriding himself, his own weakness in so blatantly filling the role of proud father, rather than indulging his general tendency to be scornful. She strove to make the appropriate comments while Selma, firmly gripping her hand, shook it up and down as if she would never stop. Luckily, it was not difficult to be complimentary, for the child was very engaging.

'How are you getting on, Lucy?' Daisy was gracious. 'You're looking well.'

'I'm feeling well too. How are you? You're looking lovely.'

'Do you really think so? To tell you the truth, I'm a bit washed out. I find life pretty exhausting during the season.'

'I hear you've just moved into your new house, Daisy.'

'Yes, such a job! I thought it would never be finished. First the building, then the decorating, then the furnishing—it's taken two years at least. Mr. Mosenthal would have everything just so.'

'We had to build some sort of shack for ourselves,' he explained with lordly modesty. 'We never could find a rented house that was satisfactory.'

'They say you've done it all on a very magnificent scale.' Lucy was wondering how she could bring the conversation to an end. They had not asked her to sit down, and the men had only half-risen from their chairs and then lazily sunk back into them. She felt very awkward and out of place, standing there in her homemade clothes with every imperfection shown up by Daisy's expensive elegance; yet it was hard to light upon words that would form a pivot for leave-taking.

'Well, I wouldn't call it magnificent,' Mosenthal declared with his characteristic shrug, 'but it's moderately comfortable. What do *you* think, Paulos?'

Chappie cleared his throat before answering deferentially: 'It's no use to deny you got a glorious house there, Mr. Mosenthal. It's the best house in Heliopolis, I bet you anything . . . and it should be too. My word, that's one way of spending a fortune!' With an unctuous shake of the head he implied his respectful envy of wealth and lavishness much greater than his own.

'It'll be a nice home for Selma and Maurice, that's the important thing,' said Mosenthal, gently pulling a lock of his daughter's hair. 'You want a decent garden and room to expand when you have children to bring up.'

'There you can have an army of children.' Chappie swelled with vicarious pride. 'By Jove, yes! Children in regiments.'

'I'm quite willing, if only my wife will oblige.'

Daisy did not much relish this kind of coarse allusion, and Lucy took advantage of the momentary silence which followed to say that she must be getting along to her work.

'Still at that picture-house—what's its name—the Forum?' Daisy inquired with the air of a benevolent patroness, res.'

'I must look you up the next time I come to Alex. I'm afraid I've been terribly booked up this time.'

Daisy said something to this effect at every meeting. It was years since she had charitably treated her old comrade to a luncheon or an afternoon tea—though she did make a point of remembering her at Christmas. Only recently she had sent an expensive felt doll dressed as a pierrot, which had worn the label 'Charming Boudoir Ornament'. Daisy knew, of course, that Lucy had no boudoir, but it would be pretty in her bedroom, and she had a theory that luxury gifts of this kind mean a lot to women living alone and are more welcome than necessities.

As when one puts one's fingers into water of extreme temperature, one cannot tell for a fraction of time whether it is cold or hot, so Lucy, hastening away from the smart hotel, did not at first know whether she was laughing or raging. After a moment she perceived that she was laughing. Daisy was a joke. That simpering affectedness, those transparent attempts to dissolve the past by pretending it was not there—was it possible that she had ever found such absurdities hurtful? Why, they were a rich comedy, and henceforward she would never think of them without amusement.

She repeated to herself the terms of Daisy's condescending question: 'Still at that picture-house; the what's-its-name indeed! As if it was altogether beneath her dignity to know for certain where I am! Pretty ridiculous when she sent a frightful present to the Forum for me this Christmas, and I wrote and thanked her for it! Or perhaps she means to suggest that if I'm still at the same place it must be because I like it. I dare say by this time she's convinced herself that I do.' Lucy's inward laughter became a little acrid.

'And there's that incredible Chappie Paulos fawning on them for all he's worth. He's a joke too, but rather a stupid one. I wonder how long it is since they took him up—or let him take *them* up? He didn't seem very sure of his footing. Perhaps he never would be, he's such a natural-born toady. How he'll love it, being introduced to the theatre people straight from the horse's mouth, as it were! It's going to cost him a lot in stockings.'

Continuing thus to divert herself, she took her place in the box-office and proceeded to dispense tickets. This was an exceptionally busy week. Charlie Chaplin was appearing in a picture called *The Gold Rush* which attracted audiences from all the various races of foreigners in Alexandria as well as a higher percentage than usual of the Egyptians themselves. Lucy was kept occupied at her pigeonhole.

By the time the last house had well begun, however, the pressure had slackened. She could look up from her rolls of tickets and her drawer full of money, and talk to her companion at the adjoining pigeon-hole or contemplate the people going by in the street, picking out the faces she had seen before. Some she had an opportunity of knowing well and studying closely; she could often hear snatches of conversation, since it happened that only a few feet from her desk there was a panel upon which were displayed photographs from the film, and many of the passers-by stopped to examine them.

The box-office, shaped like a triangle with a flattened apex, stood in the middle of the entrance. On the other side of it was a second panel with another set of 'stills', and from where she sat Lucy could get an imperfect view of anyone who looked at them. Tonight, staring vacantly past the head of her fellow-clerk, while they beguiled an empty moment with a discussion of the merits and demerits of artificial silk, her eyes lighted on two well-dressed ladies accompanied by men in dinner-jackets. They had the air of strangers to the town out for an after-dinner stroll, and she registered them vaguely in her mind as a party that might have come off an English cruising steamer. They had paused to inspect the photographs, and someone was apparently proposing that they should go in and see the picture.

Suddenly the abstractedness was dispelled from Lucy's gaze. One of those men bore a most startling resemblance to Henry! That slender back, that quizzical attitude of the head, that shiny nut-brown hair—it was a likeness to bring the heart leaping to the throat. Her complaint about a night-dress that had not washed well tailed off abruptly as the party began to cross over to her side of the entrance hall. The man who reminded her of Henry was obscured for an instant from her line of vision, but as he passed in front of the box-office she was able to survey him from head to foot.

Her hand went up to her lips in an involuntary gesture. It was Henry! It must be Henry! The tall, thin figure, the graceful carriage, the fine-edged profile with the lock of hair that tended to fall forward—all those were Henry's as she remembered him . . . and yet there was a difference. She could not have sworn that it was he until her glance fell upon his long fingers holding a cigarette. There was no doubt about those hands, and no doubt about that peculiarly deliberate way of drawing in a puff of smoke and then rapidly exhaling it as if it were not what he had wanted after all.

'It *is*—it's Henry!' she whispered soundlessly, and sat petrified. Her companion's voice, extolling the durability of a knitted silk jumper, dropped through the air and pattered against her senses no more heeded than falling leaves on a deserted road. All the attention her faculties were capable of bestowing was fixed upon a single object; and so intense was her watchfulness, so swiftly did her eyes move after him and her thoughts follow her eyes, that it seemed for long seconds as if everything else had slowed up and was in a state of suspended animation.

The ladies were scrutinizing the photographs on the panel nearest her, and Henry was standing beside them awaiting their pleasure. She could see his face plainly, though it was not turned directly towards her, and she knew now why at first she had not been sure of him: he had been twenty-seven when they parted in 1917, and now he must have turned thirty-six. Nine and a half years had deepened the lines about his mouth and eyes and made his thin face look a little smaller. His lips were more compressed, and there were ruts in his cheeks where before they had been smooth.

At first it came as a shock to her that he could have changed at all; the Henry she had enshrined in her memory had been perennially boyish. Then she recalled what the same stretch of time had done to her and was astonished that he had not changed much more. He might, she reflected, have lost that youthful slenderness and that ease of motion which showed how closely his mind and body were in harmony; but no! there he was leaning against the framework of the panel poised as beautifully as if time belonged to him. There he was—his hair still thick and bright, his eyes clear, alert, ready to be interested, his whole expression as sensitive, as eager as ever.

While she watched, she listened, every word of the brief, casual discussion taking on a vivid clarity, for her very sense of hearing seemed rarefied.

'Well, let's go in and see it,' was the first remark she caught. 'Why not? It's bound to be a good picture!' His own voice, very complaisant, yet full and firm—she could hardly believe that nearly a decade had passed without a sound of it.

'Pity to spend the evening sitting in a stuffy cinema,' said the other man. Lucy did not spare so much as a glance for him.

'How much air can you breathe, Ralph?' It was his old familiar strain of jocose reasonableness. 'Anyhow, we shall be getting plenty of it between Cairo and Assuan.'

'I like Charlie Chaplin,' said one of the women. 'He's different from the ordinary run. I think he's a very good actor really. Henry loves him.'

'He doesn't amuse me at all,' the second man asserted flatly.

'He amuses me a lot,' said Henry.

'I'm not certain whether I've ever seen him,' the other woman put in with a touch of mild contempt, 'but I know the children have. I'm quite willing to go in if you others feel like it.'

'We've probably missed half of it by now,' the man called Ralph suggested hopefully.

'I don't think so. It isn't very late'—this was the woman who had first spoken. 'Ask at the box-office, Henry.'

For a portentous particle of a moment, Lucy thought he was about to address her, but instead he pointed at a time schedule exhibited on another placard. 'It began about five minutes ago. Now what are we going to do? *Faites vos jeux, messieurs et dames! Rien ne va plus!*'

'All right, let's go in since you're so keen, Esme,' said the less enthusiastic of the ladies.

The others acquiesced, and Henry, crying 'Good, I wanted to see it!', smiled.

That smile—she could have wept, could have laughed, to be so poignantly reminded of all she had most loved in him. Oh, that cordial, grateful smile of his, signifying his delight at having got his own way without pressing for it! How many, many times she had subjugated her will to his merely for the joy of bringing it to his face! That it should be there, as luminous and lively as ever! She could not see it, caged in as she was, without warming to the reassurance that some things were right with the world.

She pulled herself together to take the decisive step which she had realized for several seconds was inevitable. Henry must not recognize her. She could never survive the humiliation of being discovered by him in her present situation on an occasion when he was accompanied by friends and wife. With his smile still in her eyes, she turned away in time to miss his approach to her pigeon-hole. 'Take over for a few minutes, Miss Danieli—would you mind?' she whispered, and retired without pausing for an answer.

There was nowhere to go but the ladies' cloakroom, a sordid little vestibule. She shut the door urgently behind her and started to walk up and down, unaware that her hands were clenched dramatically.

Henry—Henry himself out there! This was the primary fact that she repeated again and again. Henry, who had once been her cherished darling, her soul's love! And he remained delightful; time had done nothing worse than trace a few interesting lines upon his face. She gloried in his immunity. She gloried in the pang his smile could still inflict! To love him still and yet to be precluded from his friendship was as nothing to what it would have been to confront him despoiled, deteriorated.

Despoiled! Deteriorated! She paused before the starkly lighted glass of the dressing-table, and took stock of herself. She was thirty-five, and tonight, after several tiring hours at her post, all those years were in evidence. That phase in which her figure had been too thin was long past; since somewhere about her thirtieth birthday she had been coping with a tendency to gain more weight than was desirable, and although her efforts to keep it in check had been fairly successful, there was no doubt that she had lost the contours of youth. She had avoided growing fat, but her waist and hips had thickened and the fashion for short skirts and straight lines was by no means flattering. She glanced down at her feet. The artificial silk stockings which had given rise to her interrupted argument were slightly wrinkled round her ankles, and her shoes were worn and out of shape. It had been obvious for weeks that she ought to discard them, but her feet did not take kindly nowadays to new shoes. This dingy detail seemed the last straw. With bowed head she began to cry. Her tears splashed on the dusty dressing-table.

She thought of those women out there with Henry. Though she had only perceived them obliquely, she retained a very sharp impression of what sort of women they were. She had noticed their well-groomed hair, their slim legs set off with fine silk, the fur stoles slung over their shoulders. She could guess how easy and agreeable were the processes by which they were able to appear *soignées*—how pleasurable it must be for them to choose what they would wear, to try first one jewel then another, to turn this way and that in front of ample and relucent mirrors. What would she look like compared with them? What would Henry feel, seeing her tonight, after perhaps having treasured a gracious picture of her?

On no account must they meet, either tonight or tomorrow or any other day. They were severed even more completely than she had understood. She could be nothing to him now but an object of embarrassed pity, and the sight of his distress as he beheld her so ravaged was an agony she was resolved to spare herself.

She dried her eyes, removed the traces of tears with her powder-puff, and went back to the box-office. Miss Danieli was preparing to close up for the night, the hour being so late that there was not likely to be any further demand for seats. She broke off her occupation of pouring money into a bag to ask in her groping, careful accent—for she was a Greek employed chiefly for her knowledge of languages: 'Are you all right, Miss Kendon? I think you have felt a little bit funny, isn't it so?'

Lucy took possession of her desk, saying: 'The worst is over.'

'It's a pity you went away so quickly. Did you notice those people who were in evening dress? The two men were English lords; very high ones.'

'Were they?' Lucy stared into her cash drawer. 'How did you find out?'

'Well, they are staying at the Hotel de Paris. The manager from there—the one with the hair *en brosse* and the tall collars—came just at the very minute when I sold them their tickets, and afterwards he explained to me who they are. Look, he gave me his journal. I thought you would like to read it.'

She presented Lucy with a newspaper folded so as to give prominence to some topical comments.

Under the heading 'A Gardening Marquess', Lucy found the enlightenment it had not yet occurred to her to seek.

> The Marquess and Marchioness of Redfarrow, who arrived in Alexandria on the S.S. *Osiris*, lunched yesterday with M. Paul Boucard and spent part of the afternoon in the Botanical Museum. Lord Redfarrow is extremely interested in the cultivation of tropical plants in England, and under his direction the greenhouses at Nunsbourne, his father's famous country seat near Dorking, have been much enlarged. Lord Redfarrow is the only surviving son of the Duke of Surrey, his elder brother having been a member of the ill-fated Fryer-Heyford Expedition to Brazil in 1924. It will be remembered that four of the party were lost when a canoe capsized in the Amazon.
>
> After a brief stay in Cairo, Lord and Lady Redfarrow are to travel up the Nile in the newly finished dahabeah *Princess Zubaydah*. They have joined forces with the Earl and Countess of Blanchess, whose last visit to Egypt took place two years ago when they were guests of H.E. the High Commissioner. The voyage will be as much a novelty to the *Princess Zubaydah* as to her passengers, for she was only launched last week.

So that was it! Henry's brother had been killed and it was Henry instead who had adopted the title previously borne by his father. Henry would be a duke, a rich one too, for his family had retained its great possessions almost inviolate. The old duke, Henry's grandfather, had been notoriously mean with money, and his dependants had never received very liberal provision during his lifetime; but at any rate his economies had held the estate together, and the constantly increasing value of property in London had made it possible to pay immense death duties without dispersing treasures.

It was really rather an odd affair. Henry, the heir to a dukedom—and here she sat in this queer little prison of a box-office, the woman who had once known him better than anyone in the world! For all her sadness she could not help smiling to find herself in a situation with such vast potentialities for melodrama.

'It is surprising, eh?' said Miss Danieli, pleased with the earnest interest accorded to her small titbit of information. 'We don't get such noble people here every night. Let us go in and look at them. They must be near the side because they came so late.'

'It will be dark,' said Lucy, not very persuasively.

'Still, we will see a little—better than nothing.'

Lucy nodded. It would be her last glimpse of Henry; she might never set eyes on him again as long as she lived. She could not resist the opportunity. To be with a companion unconscious of the magnitude of the experience was a safeguard.

They hurried through the business of checking up and disposing of their takings for the night as rapidly as they could, and in their outdoor things sought admittance at the most likely entrance to the circle. Their party was not difficult to find. The white shirtfronts of the men were identifiable almost immediately, and as Miss Danieli had conjectured they were at the side. Their seats were so near the doorway that it was unnecessary to advance more than a step or two up the aisle to see them as distinctly as the feeble light would allow. Lord Blanchess was on the outside: a grudging smile flickered upon his lips. Next to him sat the woman who had not been able to remember whether she had seen Chaplin: she seemed amused, but puzzled, and Lucy heard her exclaim: 'How ridiculous!' as if this were an accidental effect. She must be Lady Blanchess, because the other woman had been called Esme, and Esme was undoubtedly the name of Henry's wife. Then there was Henry with his wife beside him, both laughing audibly. Her head was in deep shadow, and even Henry's, which was nearer, could be only dimly discerned, lit by the greyish phosphorescence reflected from the screen. In such obscurity the ageing of his face was not apparent. He might have been the same young man who had laughed at Charlie Chaplin with her in the days when going to the pictures had been a rather Bohemian adventure.

She fixed her eyes on him with a devouring intentness, and saw that his arm was flung across the back of his wife's chair, touching her shoulders. A tremor of jealousy ran through her, but she steadied herself. She was determined to keep herself in hand and, since this must be her parting reconnaissance, she would disregard everything but the essential quality of her vision, the redeeming beauty of the ordeal—that Henry was all but unchanged, that she had watched him and heard his voice and been confirmed in her love.

But when she was walking with her colleague towards the tram-stop at which they always parted company, the jealousy corroded her feelings again and she thought it cruel that a woman should at this moment be leaning on Henry's encircling arm, cosseted and protected, while she tramped through the streets in shabby shoes. She had an impulse to assert herself, to claim at least her honest share on his past. Miss Danieli was asking her which she thought was the finer of the two noblemen, the one with the little moustache or the other.

'The other,' she replied promptly, and then discovered with astonishment that she was saying succinctly: 'I once knew him very well.'

Miss Danieli looked as if she supposed herself not to have heard aright, and Lucy went doggedly on with her affirmation. 'He was a great friend of mine. It was in England, years and years ago, when I was on the stage.'

'Really? Which one was your friend?' She sounded like a nurse humouring the delusion of a feverish patient. 'The *marquis* or the count? I don't know who is which. It was the one with no moustache who bought the tickets. Is that the *marquis*?'

'Yes, but at the time I'm talking about he wasn't a marquess.'

'Perhaps you have made a mistake and it is a different person,' Miss Danieli suggested dispassionately.

'It certainly isn't a different person!' Lucy's protest was not as cool and rational as she could have wished. 'I knew him the minute I saw his hands. I'd know him anywhere in the world.'

'Why didn't you speak to him?'

'Because, among other things, he was with three people I've never met.'

She was beginning to regret her indiscretion. The wind had been taken out of her sails, and she could guess what small conviction her story must carry to one who had only seen her during the last year or two. Her brief career as a musical-comedy actress was a dim legend to the casual fellow employees of these latter days: she was not in the habit of communicating much about the past. So she did not take offence at Miss Danieli's thinly veiled incredulity. She only wished her foolish words unsaid.

'He is at the Hotel de Paris. You will see him there, perhaps, or send him a note?'

'No, I—' Lucy paused on the threshold of an explanation, and decided that she would rather be disbelieved. 'No,' she said flatly, 'I shall not try to see him.'

'A pity, if you are such old friends.'

'I am changed,' she acknowledged, 'and he has stayed the same—except of course that his position has improved.'

Miss Danieli shrugged her shoulders, sustaining the air of one who holds aloof as the reluctant witness of some folly too inane to arouse emotion, and intimated that she must catch her tram. Lucy walked on alone.

She came up to the building where Chappie Paulos had his flat—now furnished anew, it was said, in the very latest style of austere waxed oak, rough-woven curtains, and large pottery vases—and at the same moment he advanced from the opposite direction with a somewhat highly coloured young woman at his side. Lucy's preoccupied eyes stared at him unseeingly.

Chappie felt uncomfortable. He thought he was being cut, and this was an indignity he could ill endure from one whom he himself had been tempted to cut so often. He was very sensitive about Lucy because he could not forget that he had once refused her the means of deliverance; and the sight of her going steadily down, as he conceived, had exasperated him for years. Still, he had been willing to be gracious, after observing the gracious behaviour of Mosenthal, and he found it disconcerting not to have the option.

Lucy's eyes awakened and recognized him too late. He was on the other side of the glass doors when her lagging perceptions conveyed their message. She smiled, well pleased with her lapse. Henry's image, so elegant and so debonair, seemed to shed contempt on that unshapely figure with its graceless motion. It shocked her to realize she had once invoked his charity. For pleasure or for pain, her thoughts were marvellously lucid tonight, and the scene that had been played between Paulos and herself on that stifling, broiling morning at the end of her illness opened to her remembrance in all its squalor. For years it had lain in the mistiest recesses of her brain, a souvenir too harrowing to be deliberately brought forth; but tonight she permitted herself to recall the whole interview and every feeling that had animated her.

That burning desire to escape which had nerved her up for the most reckless efforts-—thank heaven time had softened such a passion as that! She was homesick still, but not with the same insistent, desolate repining. She had been obliged to adjust herself to the inevitable, and although England had never ceased to be the ultimate bourne of her hopes, her longing had become a jogtrot affair, only dully disturbing. The quality of urgency was gone.

Gone, and she could not but be glad it was gone. Oh, how she had struggled and suffered in her heavy fetters! Oh, the blank unbelievable misery of that day which had revealed the ruin of her voice! May 1919, and now it was January 1927—Egyptian January, mild, delightful, flowery month! It was a folly to hanker after England in such weather as this.

But the sight of Henry had had an unsettling influence upon her, and she did hanker. 'In London now it's cold winter,' she said to herself reprovingly, and the words lit up a little diorama that only heightened her zest. The brilliantly illuminated shops glowing with luxury through the dark air of frosty afternoons; herself driving through busy streets in a snugly closed vehicle from which she would emerge to drink tea among the anglicized palms of an hotel lounge where neither heat nor cold ever penetrated—a temperate zone in which everything was smooth, flattering, designed for enjoyment, so that even when the skill of the creators failed one might still be soothed by their intention; the richness of artificial light falling on the green leaves and scarlet geraniums of window-boxes; the flower sellers in the streets with their stiff rosebuds, their lilies of the valley, their dazzlingly white camellias, their violets the colour of cloudy amethysts . . . it was thus that her nostalgia portrayed a wintry London. She tried to think of fog and icy slush, but found they could not quench the beauty of the fantasy. Fog diffused a strangeness, a mystical privacy, that positively lent attraction, and as for the weather underfoot, it could only make the temperate zone more delectably inviting.

Such was the effect of her revivified love. It had shattered that atmosphere of stagnant calm in which she had lately enveloped herself and had restored, at least momentarily, her power to see the objects of her longing with enchanted eyes.

She walked for a long time with her mind like a stormy night, black and bright by turns as Henry's destiny came into contrast with her own; lightning that shimmered over her prospect to leave it in greater darkness than before. Reaching home at last, she began a letter to Constance. She was not strong-minded enough to conceal herself and her broken fortunes from Henry without the solace of letting someone know of it.

Although his visit to Egypt passed off without any relaxing of Lucy's determination not to approach him, it was nevertheless the occasion of a profound change even in the outward aspect of her life. Some days later she read among the social items of the *Egyptian Gazette* an announcement which sent her blood tingling angrily through every pulse. The Marquess and Marchioness of Redfarrow—so it ran—were in Cairo and were about to proceed on their journey up the Nile; their activities before embarking had included a dinner party given by Mr. and Mrs. Siegfried Mosenthal who had recently taken possession of their newly built residence at Heliopolis; the Earl and Countess of Blanchess had also been of the company.

Lucy throbbed with a spasm of jealousy which made every former sensation of the kind fade to insignificance. The thought of Henry sitting as a guest at Daisy's table, basking in her sugary smiles, taken in perhaps by her meretricious sweetness . . . the thought of Daisy preening herself upon her capture, vaunting her friendship with one who had every attribute that could appeal to her snobbery . . . the thought, the mere unsubstantiated thought, excited such rancour as she had not thought herself to be capable of harbouring. Compared with this, to have beheld him lightly embracing his wife was a pleasure.

After a few days her resentment subsided to less intolerable proportions, its deflation being helped by a piece of gossip which indicated that Daisy had done a considerable amount of string pulling to get the Redfarrows to her party. It was decidedly a consolation to know that their acquaintance was new and would have little chance of ripening into intimacy, since Henry was not expected to return to Cairo.

But the bitterness of her heart-burning was not without an important sequel. It filled her with an active and pungent dislike of the situation she had hitherto schooled herself to dislike passively. She shook off that attitude of submission which prudence had managed to impose on her, and resolved rather to accept a worse job with a lower wage than go on working in the firm presided over by Daisy's husband.

As it happened prudence was not compelled to support any outrage. Lucy had a stroke of luck. She was inspired to seek advice from M. Toudouze, the manager of the Hotel de Paris et New-York, who, as a regular patron of the cinema, was in the habit of passing the time of day with her; and by creating a favourable impression at a favourable moment, she obtained a clerkship in his hotel which turned out to be actually an improvement on the position she resigned.

Chapter 27

If Lucy had understood precisely what it meant to Daisy to entertain the lords of Redfarrow and Blanchess to dinner, together with their ladies; if she had been given a glimpse of Henry as the Mosenthals' guest, polite, bewildered, striving gallantly not to find his host and hostess distasteful; if she could have witnessed Daisy's vain toiling to draw him out of his courteous and baffling remoteness, she might perhaps have felt that kind of amused compassion which banishes anger. She had abundant reason, of course, to know that Daisy had grown to be a snob of the most incorrigible order, and she had been aware at once—very hurtfully aware—that the occasion represented a palpable step forward in a career devoted to the conquest of society. What had not been demonstrated to her was the fact that this career was costing an effort out of all proportion to its extremely moderate success; that the struggle to entice the Redfarrows to her party had left Daisy virtually panting; and that, as usual, the party had somehow failed to get her anywhere. It was a step forward, but when she had achieved it her feet trod on ground no firmer than before.

She might here and there with much exertion manage to gain what seemed to be a foothold, but still, for all her travail, security of standing was denied her. A nature much more vindictive than Lucy's might have thought it adequate revenge to behold hope so perpetually thwarted.

Not that the frustration was acknowledged. That was medicine too shockingly unpleasant ever to be taken. Indeed there was something almost admirable in the way the ambitious woman laboured on, smiling in the face of obstacles, bearing rebuffs as if they gave no pain, repressing her dismay when the ground suddenly crumbled;

going through so much to get so very little, and for ever assuring herself that she was having a marvellous time.

When she told Lucy that she found life exhausting during the season, the languor of her tone might be a trifle overdone, but she spoke in good faith. Her share in seasonal activities that were not of her own making or seeking was pathetically small; still, to be exhausted was the proper attitude, and she strove after exhaustion as others strive after repose, and let a little of it go a long way. No woman in Egypt said more frequently, or believed more persistently that she had scarcely time to think, that she was worn out with parties and race-meetings and visitings, that it was as much as she could do to keep pace with the demands that were pressed upon her. And when it was no longer admissible to speak or believe thus in Cairo, then she broke off so that she might resume the plaintive boast on the Riviera, or in Paris, or in London; for she devoted fully six months of the year to Europe now and hung on the skirts of the fashionable world as tenaciously as if it were running from her. And so, unconsciously, it was.

If we compare the fashionable world to a skating rink where only advanced performers are encouraged to disport themselves, we may say that money will purchase a spectator's seat but will not give you the ability to skate. Supposing you have thoroughly mastered the accomplishment in some other arena, you are welcome to step out of your seat and take the floor, and the skaters already there will accept you as one of themselves and even clear a space for you to cut figures; but unless you are proficient—or can at any rate flounder very amusingly—you had better keep your place, or you will suffer peculiar humiliations. Mosenthal never tried to skate. He preferred to sit in a good ringside position making fun of the people on the ice. Daisy, on the other hand, was constantly impelled to try her skill, but she was so afraid of falling that she had a stilted, mincing style which soon gave her uncertainty away.

Mosenthal was very indulgent to his wife, providing her with whatever means she required for her social pursuits even when he himself held aloof from them. Married, she had much more freedom than she had been permitted as his mistress. His habitual distrust of women had been so far allayed that he actually gave her a munificent allowance. He remained very fond of her, even when her affectations excited his ridicule. Her endearing submissiveness could still excuse a multitude of faults; and she had borne him two superb children, producing them in quite the most satisfactory order, first a son, then a year or so later a daughter.

On the whole he was not displeased with her for choosing to cultivate so diligently the people who were almost universally regarded as best worth cultivating. He had a self-made man's natural wish to see his children established easily and by right in a sphere where he himself required a courtesy passport. When she needed his support for some project he was inclined to frown upon, Daisy was generally able to get her way by indicating the potential advantages for the children.

She herself believed that her desire to lay a foundation for the children's future was the first incentive of all her manoeuvrings, and although this was a sublimation, it had its elements of something nearer truth than Daisy often attained. She was a devoted mother, a very pattern of maternal sentimentality. She and Siegfried between them, in fact, were unwittingly doing all in their power to ensure that the children should develop into pampered and useless beings.

Siegfried had a taste for magnificence and it gratified him to equip the nursery wing at Heliopolis with every costly device procurable, to furnish the playroom with such vast glass cupboards of elaborate toys that it resembled nothing so much as a shop, to have a redundance of highly skilled nurses and governesses, and a perfect posse of servants in waiting. He did that sort of thing for its own sake, feeding his deep-rooted Oriental appetite for showy luxury. Daisy had another motive that was stronger. Such splendours were to create an impression on mothers and fathers in select circles, and thus she might have the chance of forming intimacies which would be of value to her. For if she toiled to advance her children in the world, she was not without some quiet hope of using them as a means for her own advancement.

But the impression created was the very reverse of her intention. The ostentation which surrounded the little Mosenthals was severely criticized. Though Daisy never missed an opportunity of writing a good name in her address book, she was hard put to it to get the sort of guests she wanted for the children's parties which she gave, on such a princely scale, two or three times a year.

When forced to admit the existence of difficulties, she attributed them to the misfortune of her having had to travel a rather long illicit road before reaching lawful wedlock. She could prove conclusively to herself that she had been justified by extenuating circumstances of the most irresistible nature, but it was nevertheless a skeleton in the cupboard.

Yet, if it was a skeleton, it was also a scapegoat. Things did sometimes go so manifestly wrong that even Daisy was obliged to recognize failure, and then, instead of having to lay the disconcerting blame upon herself, the Daisy of the present, she was able to accuse the past. She was seldom right. Among those who already objected to the Mosenthals, the past was one additional objection, nothing more.

Guiltily, in the secret cavities of her heart, Daisy kept a second scapegoat—Siegfried himself. Dearly as she loved him, reverently as she looked up to him for his wonderful adroitness in amassing money, grateful as she was to him for the sumptuous background he had provided, she could not but suppose him to be in some respects a drag upon her progress. It distressed her to make this avowal because she was a passionate enthusiast for the sanctity of the married state and for perfect mutual loyalty between husband and wife (the more so since she had an unhallowed earlier marriage to live down), but Siegfried's manners really were inclined to be crude, and he did make such a song about being a Jew—a Jew who had come to Egypt with two pounds in his pocket. Surely it was time to drop that belittling reminiscence into oblivion! It embarrassed her beyond words to hear him telling great personages about his humble beginnings and his early struggles. After all, there were some decidedly cultured and respected Jews. Why—if he *must* be so Jewish—why couldn't he convey the idea that he sprang from one of the clever families or the famous rich ones? It would be so much kinder to the children later on. But no! He seemed to take a positive delight in flaunting his low, illiterate antecedents and nothing would ever change him. It was extremely mortifying, and accounted, she thought, for not a few defeats.

Once again she was mistaken. Mosenthal was not by any means popular; he inspired a good deal of dislike; but he had at least the virtue of being true to himself, a character formed of definite and real substance rather than of plastic composition. He was accepted more readily than Daisy, had she but realized it, because he was easy to 'place'. Daisy was a doubtful type and consequently aroused mistrustfulness. She spoke in the right accent and had no small share of plausible charm; yet she trod so warily and was so evidently in fear of going wrong, one could never quite believe her to be natural.

Siegfried himself only dimly apprehended that she was being something less than a success. He was too busy shaping and solidifying the sumptuous background to notice how scantily the foreground was filled out. And Daisy kept up appearances with him as with everyone and made the most of each small victory.

There *were* victories, of course, though none so brilliant as her fancy had once conceived them. Notabilities, both in Egypt and elsewhere, were sometimes inveigled by curiosity, by flattery, or by a half-amused enjoyment of sheer lavishness, to Daisy's select entertainments; and perhaps they would return her hospitality, thus enabling her to meet other notabilities. Then again, there were distinguished people who wanted some favour of Siegfried—a donation to charity possibly, or a post in one of his companies for a young son or nephew. These, however, rarely followed up their friendly overtures after getting or not getting what they asked for. Many and many were the fond illusions they had raised and blighted!

There were also numbers of people, less distinguished, who courted Daisy as sedulously as she courted others. These could contribute little to her aggrandizement, but she turned to them, often gladly enough, when there was nobody 'worth while' to occupy her. Men of business with an eye on potential capital, wives of Siegfried's senior employees, place-seekers and intriguers of every species, as well as some sycophants, like Chappie, who had nothing to gain but the glory of proximity to riches and influence—such were the only companions who freely offered themselves. It was a comfort to have them there, waiting in the backstairs regions of her life for what attention she chose to bestow.

Chappie, for instance, who had spent years fawning his way into Siegfried's good graces—he was not the sort of friend one would care to produce at the Residency, but he had his uses. His obsequiousness was soothing. One could take him up when one liked and drop him when one liked, and, since he was not worth the making of an effort, one could be at ease with him—or as nearly at ease as it was in Daisy's power to be. She scarcely even counted it against him that he had met her first when she was a soubrette who had been glad to accept a few pairs of silk stockings. Indeed, his very insignificance in comparison with what she aspired to—coupled, necessarily, with his earnest perseverance—gave him a certain lowly footing in the Mosenthal household.

Daisy was not sorry now that her circle of acquaintance had been so very small in the days when that dreadful Mrs. Prince-Carter had called her 'Mosenthal's fancy woman'. Lucy was the only person in

Egypt who had known her well during that time, and in so far as she could permit herself to think at all of that mutilated friendship, she was thankful that matters were so arranged as to keep Lucy at a distance. Sometimes a slight qualm of conscience would assail her, and then she would promise herself that on her next visit to Alexandria she would really take the poor thing out to lunch, but when the opportunity came her reluctance always got the better of her good nature.

None the less, it quite shocked her sense of fitness when she heard that Lucy had given notice at the picture-house. In some vague way she felt that it was reprehensible going off like that without so much as a word, not consulting anyone, not showing the faintest remembrance of her obligations. Siegfried had provided her with employment all these years, and then she just handed in her notice as if no such thing as gratitude existed.

'I admit she's been growing more and more impossible for ages'—this was her sorrowful comment to Siegfried—'but all the same, it shakes one's faith in human nature when people behave like that.'

'Come off your perch!' he adjured her derisively. 'A woman who has to earn her own living must take what chances she gets. If she's climbing a step up, I can only say I'm glad to hear it—though I'm afraid it's more likely to be a step down.'

'She seems to have forgotten what she owes you,' said Daisy.

'She owes me nothing at all. I think there was some trifle of a money debt when she had that illness, but either she paid it back or I cancelled it. Or she paid back some of it and I cancelled the rest. And anyhow, my God! I haven't got as long a memory as that!'

'But you found work for her. I don't know how she would have managed without you.'

'I found work for her and she's done it and been paid for it—a fair bargain on both sides. She owes me nothing and she's free to make any other bargain she likes. Better yourself when you can, that's the only rule in business. You followed it, didn't you, my dear? And, judging by looks, you've come off pretty well by it.'

Daisy could only turn away in silent disapproval, and Siegfried went after her and playfully tweaked one of her diamond ear-rings. Children and the family life he loved had produced a sort of uncouth vivacity in his manners.

It was highly unpleasing to Daisy, the next time she went with her husband to stay at the Hotel de Paris et New-York—their invariable sojourn on his business trips to Alexandria—to find Lucy established there as one of the reception clerks. This was positively too much! After all, one couldn't, one absolutely couldn't, occupy the principal suite in an hotel where one of the women in the office called one by one's Christian name and had been privy to forgotten episodes in one's past. It was all she could do to be civil on the occasions, fortunately rare, when she could not avoid speaking to her.

She expressed herself about it to Siegfried with unaccustomed emphasis. She had never, she said inaccurately, been more annoyed or uncomfortable. How Lucy could have done such a mean and tactless thing as to take a job in that hotel was beyond comprehension! To be called by her Christian name at the reception office! Every waiter, every chambermaid, every page-boy in the building, must be talking about it. And who could tell, since Lucy had become so shamefully inconsiderate, what else they might be talking about—what disparaging nonsense might be in circulation? Anger and fear had made her ruthless. It only needed a guest as important as Siegfried to say one word to the management and they might rest assured Lucy would not be there when they happened to come to Alexandria again.

But this was a point at which Siegfried drew the line. There were other hotels in Alexandria, he informed her coldly, where they could stay in future since this one no longer proved suitable; if it came to that, they might take a service flat, and he had often thought it would be pleasanter to do so; but one thing was certain. Lucy Kendon had left his employment, and he could not have her back, and that being so, he did not intend to do anything that would jeopardize her livelihood. She had gone down in the world, she was no longer young, and she and Daisy had once been thick as thieves. He made it clear in one terse utterance, repelling argument, that Lucy's post was to be inviolate now and always as far as they were concerned. Daisy was wise enough to submit, and Siegfried's private secretary received instructions to look for an apartment.

Chapter 28

In 1928 Constance began working in Paris for the celebrated couturier Jasky. In 1929 she married a poor but clever young French artist, Roger Leloir, who had been supplying the firm with designs. She wrote to Lucy to assure her that marriage would make no difference to her scheme of applying the first sufficient sum she ever acquired to her friend's redemption from the land of bondage. It was a thing she had sworn to accomplish and she would not fail. To this assurance Lucy, with much labour of composition, replied thus:

You know what it means to me, my dearest girl, to be so sure of your affection, and I've been proud to think of your planning such a sacrifice on my account. But you mustn't dream of sending any money to me, especially now that you're preparing to go into a working partnership with your husband, which is going to cost you all the capital you can get together, you may be sure. I couldn't and I wouldn't accept a penny, so put the idea right out of your head. There are other reasons besides the fact that you're married and your plans are changed. First and foremost, I've been saving something steadily for the last two years, which means that I've got my fare put away and a little bit over.

I didn't tell you before, dear Con, because I've enjoyed keeping it up my sleeve, thinking how marvellous it would be if ever you did send the money—and I knew that one of these days you would—for me to pretend I'd used it and then hand it back to you in England, like William Cobbett's sweetheart and the bag of guineas. You see, it's been much easier for me to save in this place than it was when I worked at the cinema even though I get paid less. Living in and getting three meals a day makes a tremendous difference. Then when I was in digs I used to get so lonely that I went out as often as I could, and that cost money, however parsimonious I tried to be. Here, having a decent little room where I'm quite content to read and sew in my spare time, and one or two very nice people on the staff who drop in for a chat, I only go out when I want fresh air. My work being in the same building is also very handy.

You've heard some of this before, but I'm just trying to give you an idea of my ways and means. There's another reason why it would be wrong for me to accept my travelling expenses from you, which is not so cheerful.

Dear soul, I'm no longer young enough any more to leave a safe job without having something definite to go to. Between ourselves, I'm thirty-seven, past the age when I can compete with young girls in the search for jobs. I ought to have a fair little nest-egg in the background before I tackle a new life in England. I still believe I'm adaptable enough for anything—more adaptable than I used to be in my youth, as a matter of fact, because I've been trained in a hard school—but, naturally, I want to improve my position, not to slide back. So my scheme is to stay here till I have either a post in England to go to or enough extra money to live on for four or five months while I look for one. This seems pretty stodgy to you, I dare say, with all your vitality and hopefulness, but there's ten or eleven years between us, and Fate has brow-beaten me a bit, you know.

Now, Con, if you want to do something for me, something just as good as you could possibly do with money, will you try to get me a job? If there were a job with a living wage waiting for me, I could sail tomorrow. You say that you and Roger are leaving Paris as soon as you see any opening in London. When you get there will you keep a sharp look-out wherever you go for anything that might seem like a prospect for me?

You know my qualifications, so use your own discretion. After all this while in Alexandria, my French and Italian are very fluent, though I says it, etc. I've learned to type quite accurately as you'll judge from my letters (I paid the last instalment on the portable yesterday, thank God!). Shorthand, I'm afraid, is no go. I'm thoroughly accustomed to handling money (other people's) and I've picked up everything I could about the routine jobs in theatres, cinemas, and hotels—so you can't complain of the range of choice. I really and truly am a capable woman, and if you can land me a job, I won't let you down.

She drew the long letter to a close with a flourish of reiterated good wishes, congratulations, and compliments. Then she rose and stood at the window of her attic room, staring out to where the sea appeared beyond and between the roof-tops. She felt easy and happy and could even believe that she had laid her hand at last on the key of her release.

After a few moments of symbolic contemplation, she returned to the typewriter, put her last sheet back, and added a postscript:

I have read in the paper that Henry has lost his wife. I suppose you will have seen it too. I'm very sorry, because I've always thought of her as a nice woman. I envied her, but not with any malice. I've been tempted to write a letter of condolence, but perhaps it wouldn't be in the best of taste. On second and third thoughts I'm sure it wouldn't.

Constance's answer left nothing to be desired except fruition.

Your future job [she wrote] shall become my Holy Grail. I shall make it my quest. It will be engraved on my heart like 'Calais'. Now that you've deprived me of laying my wealth-to-be at your feet I shall develop such a nose for jobs that I'll probably end up running a registry office. How exactly like you to save up huge sums of money in secret so as to give me a surprise! Dear Lucy, I'm only glad for your sake, not mine. Since I married my beautiful, peerless Roger I realize more than ever what an act of mercy you performed when you locked that door. And don't think your noble deeds in Cairo are the only things I'm grateful for! Our systematic correspondence has done more than you may have guessed to keep my nose to the grindstone throughout the last few years. Writing a résumé of one's progress or non-progress regularly once a fortnight, and knowing that somebody else is going to see it and judge one by it, is a most effective way of warding off fits of idleness and dissipation. After having boasted to you so often that I was going to be a great couturier, I couldn't very well let myself begin to drift. I've always striven to be able to report a little headway, if only an inch.

Since my last letter quite a lot has happened—well, I mean quite a lot has not happened. Roger and I tried to get backing for the start we want to make in London and didn't manage it; and after vast amounts of discussion, we decided to be glad. The time isn't really ripe, and there's still plenty to be learned by staying with Jasky. Roger is drawing for a new French fashion paper too (I'll send you a copy of it) and that may come to something.

Oh, I mustn't on any account forget to tell you a thing that may interest you. The other day I happened to be in the *salon* at Jasky's when a woman was trying to explain some alterations to an assistant whose English is poor and a fitter whose English is nil. So I sidled along to the rescue. She, the client, had brought back a model I designed myself—called 'Cornelia', on account of its superb Roman matron lines. She was an elderly woman, sixtyish or more, very commanding. With her was a man like the remains of a matinée idol—though there was a cowed sort of look in his eyes. She kept addressing him as 'Prince' in a most frightfully regal tone, so I thought he must be one of those stray European royalties who often wander into the *salon* for one reason or another. I was a trifle puzzled because his accent was so perfectly English and the lady seemed to bully him so much. For that matter she was a little overwhelming with all of us.

Of course, you're on? You've guessed it long ago. When we came to take down the name and address it was Mrs. Prince-Carter, that woman you used to find so maddening when you worked at the Adelphi. I'd kept the name somewhere in the back of my mind all these years, and I couldn't resist inquiring as we walked to the door whether they were the Prince-Carters who'd once lived in Egypt. They asked me where and how I'd heard about them, and when I mentioned you—well, the effect was *rather* peculiar, dear, if you know what I mean.

Mrs. Prince-Carter drew herself up to her full height, which is very high indeed, and said icily: 'That person!' So I also drew myself up. I think I said: 'May I ask why it shouldn't be that person?' At this she got more high-horsy than ever and boomed back at me: 'I don't—I do not—care to express my opinion of that person. A number of years have passed since I heard anything of her but I am a woman of fixed opinions and I have had no inducement to change that one.'

(I give her mode of speech as best I can. You used to imitate it beautifully.)

Her husband tried to tone her down but she wouldn't be toned, so I shook off the others who were standing by ready to bow her out, and we stopped on the landing.

I said, 'Miss Kendon is a friend of mine. Why do you speak of her like that?'

'Friend or no friend, I call her a person.' At this point she began to get quite carried away. Her eyes flashed fire and she went on in the most awe-inspiring style—'Furthermore, if you have the misfortune to be in communication with her, you may tell her this: Her machinations against us have failed, abjectly failed. So far from being ruined, we have thrived and prospered.'

While she was talking in this strain, which made me afraid for a moment that she was a raving lunatic, Mr. P.-C. kept saying: 'My dear, my dear!' in a mild, nervous kind of way which only goaded her on.

At last I extracted from her some incredible farrago about your having carried tales about her husband to that wretched Daisy Joy woman, whose very name I hate because of the way she treated you. She said that after Mr. P.-C. had toiled and slaved and turned himself into a mere beast of burden—which made him look none too comfortable—he had been suddenly dismissed, and that you were known to be the cause of it. I defended you as best I could, being completely in the dark, but even P.-C. himself, who is apparently quite sane if somewhat intimidated, seemed to hold the same opinion.

I'm not passing this on out of a sheer love of circulating unpleasantness, but because there appears to be something here which sheds a little more light on the character of Daisy the Detestable and which it might give you some satisfaction to clear up. Obviously you didn't and couldn't make mischief in the wanton way these people believe, but Daisy might have done so and let the blame fall on you. A woman who could behave as she has done towards you is capable of anything.

We finally wound up with speeches on these lines: *Mrs. P.-C.*: 'If my husband had had *my* spirit he would have thrashed the matter out then and there with Mosenthal and everyone else, but, the moral cowardice of some men being what it is'—here she gave him a dirty look—'he preferred to take it lying down.' *Mr. P.-C.*: 'My dear, my dear, there were reasons. Don't let's rake over these old ashes. In the long run the whole business turned out to be a godsend, and whoever caused the trouble ought to have our gratitude.' *Me*: 'I'm positive you've been misled. Miss Kendon could never have done it, knowingly at least. I'll write to her about it and you shall hear the result, because it's a pity to bear a grudge against anyone who doesn't deserve it even if you're never likely to see them again.'

We parted quite friendly. Mrs. P.-C. had passed through a wonderful gamut of moods in the course of twenty minutes' talk and ended by being ceremoniously gracious. As they went downstairs two or three other people were coming up and I saw them glance back, much impressed, I dare say, when they heard her calling the poor man 'Prince' in rich, ringing tones.

I made an inquiry about them, thinking you might like to know how it comes about that your old *bête noire* has gone so grand. Her husband is publicity manager for the Asturias Hotel in London which is run in conjunction with the Asturias in Paris. It's an excellent position, probably not very lavishly paid, but he gets about a lot and has some good perquisites, I fancy, and he can afford—or perhaps he can *not* afford—to provide his wife with an occasional dress from Jasky's. I gathered from our conversation that Prince-Carter couldn't get any other work in Egypt after leaving the Adelphi, and they came to England with the last money they had. Their luck began to change on the boat, where Mr. P.-C. ran the sweepstakes in such a striking style that he got a job from one of his fellow passengers on the strength of it. What job I didn't ask, but evidently it was something that leads one to become publicity manager to a vast luxurious hotel, so all's well.

If you have any message for them I'll gladly transmit it. I hope you don't think I'm a busybody but—here re-peruse justification given above.

There was another half-page or so of closely typed matter, but Lucy paused before going on with her reading, trying to let her intelligence play clearly over the episode that Constance's story recalled. She had been aware for years of the real reason for Prince-Carter's dismissal, but this was the first inkling she had ever had of being herself held to blame for it. Was it possible that here at last was unearthed the source of all that mysterious hostility which had done her so much damage in Cairo, had been, in fact, the undoubted cause of her removal to an inferior post? She struggled to synthesize her random memories of a period nine years gone, and recaptured enough to show her that she was probably not wide of the mark.

Her peace of mind, though shaken, was now too secure to be overthrown, and the discovery that she had been held accountable for a long past injustice, even one for which she had been so penalized, was stoically borne. She was shocked, aggrieved, but she could not withhold gratitude for having been spared the worry and annoyance of learning about the mistake at a time when she might have found it difficult to vindicate herself. As it was, she could rebut the charge completely.

That English dressmaker in Cairo who had been a shrinking witness of Mrs. Prince-Carter's fury on the occasion of her banishment from the stage-box had seen no need to preserve secrecy after her client had left the country. She had described her harrowing experience to several friends. The tale had reached Lucy's ears at second-hand, but still sufficiently free from distortion to enable her to piece a few circumstances together which had not seemed before to have any connection. It was plain that Daisy had heard nothing to her credit while she had stood listening outside the half-open door of the box. And with this realization it had flashed upon her mind that those unlucky moments might well have cost Prince-Carter his livelihood. Being ignorant, however, that the guilt had been fixed upon herself, she had merely added it in silence to her stock of reasons for being very glad to do without Daisy's friendship. And now she counted it a blessing that the same letter which told her she had been accused brought her the opportunity of declaring her innocence.

It gladdened her heart too to know that the Prince-Carters had met a better fate than she had feared for them. Their startling rise to prosperity, at a time of their lives when failure must have been especially hard to live down, strengthened her increasing faith in her own future. It was a portent, a prophecy. She began to glow, caught up on a wave of optimism which lifted her towards a glittering shore. She felt thrillingly, tremblingly certain of rich happiness to come. Not alone that smiling tranquillity which the young never envy their seniors, but *rich* happiness!

She steadied herself and went back to Constance's letter, where she read what restored gravity:

Yes, I saw the announcement of Lady Redfarrow's death and intended to tell you in case you'd happened to miss it. You were wise, I think, to refrain from writing to him, even if only to express your sympathy. Not that he *ought* to expect ulterior motives after your having left him unmolested all these years. Still, I suppose incipient dukes are run after a good deal and become pretty guarded. I must say I should never have had the fortitude to let him become so entirely lost to me without making a sign. I mean—assuming I had gone on caring for him. (You are too reasonable to take offence if I suggest that your sentiment would probably have worn away much faster if your life had taken its normal course.)

You little knew what a narrow escape you had from having the choice taken out of your hands. At the time when you first told me about your attachment to him, I was terribly tempted to get in touch with him and explain what a plight you were in so that he could help you. I only desisted at the thought of the ghastly humiliation it would be for you if it went wrong.

Having as you say a sanguine temperament, I stick at nothing in my day-dreams for you. But alas! dukes, present or to come, are a little beyond me. I must pull up. This isn't a line of talk that will please you so soon after his bereavement. By the way, it's nice to see that his wife left him two sons. There was an attractive photograph of them recently in *The Tatler*. I wonder if you came across it?

Well, Lucy, this is enough for the time being. I won't repeat all my felicitations at the improvement in your outlook. I put my most radiant aspirations for your prospects and mine into a neat little nutshell by simply remarking that I confidently expect to be

Your future dressmaker,
Constance Leloir

Lucy folded up the letter and unfolded it, and folded it again with restless fingers. She gazed out of the window, she turned back into the room, she walked up and down, happy but curiously agitated, hardly understanding what moved her most—Constance's goodness, her high infectious hopes, or the idea of Henry with his two attractive sons.

She had known of their existence for a year or two. Picking out references to Henry and his relations in the English magazines had been a wistful hobby of hers ever since coming to live in the hotel. The staff had access to a considerable range of periodicals after the visitors were done with them, and no one made more use of the privilege than Lucy. But evidently there was a back number of *The Tatler* that she had missed, for the photograph mentioned by Constance had never come her way. She put down her letter and went in search of it.

Chapter 29

Time, throughout the greater part of this story, has made a toilsome journey, but now, at least, he runs downhill. He moves so fast that the reader must keep a sharp look-out to perceive him at all, and even Lucy, for whom a year is not a word in a book but a period of twelve laborious months, complains rather of the rate at which he hurries her onward than of any sluggishness in his progress.

It is near the end of 1930, and Constance has not as yet contrived to find her a job. Two or three times she has discovered hopeful openings, but she has never succeeded in keeping up the interest of potential employers after letting them know that the woman who would so perfectly fulfil their requirements must be fetched all the way from Egypt. Constance dares not take the responsibility of urging her friend to risk the journey to England without any sure prospect before her, but she is almost in despair of ever being able to carry out her undertaking while she contends with the disadvantage of trying to sell goods she cannot display.

Her efforts are the more laudable in that she is prodigiously busy laying tangible foundations at last for the achievement of her life's ambition. She and her husband are about to inaugurate the firm registered under the Companies Act as 'Constance Leloir Ltd.'. They are making a start in a small way but the address will be in a good Mayfair street, and though they can only have some upper rooms to begin with, later on they confidently expect to take over the whole house. Roger's principal responsibility is the *decor* and furnishings, which are to be extremely distinguished: she, with his assistance, is designing a collection and supervising its evolution in the workroom. It is a subtle travail, an immense tax upon the ingenuity, for the clothes must be discreet yet striking, individual enough to give people something to talk about, yet not so individual that only the eccentrics will buy. Besides such occupations as these, both of them are battling with less creative but even more troublesome tasks, which spring up before them freshly each day in unnumbered multitudes. The engagement of the staff, the initiation of trade contacts, the working out of schemes for publicity, the preliminaries directed towards acquiring a clientele—these are but the most conspicuous of the cares engrossing them.

Their capital leaves not the smallest margin for extravagance. To save expense they are giving their personal attention to a hundred little details that swallow up time and energy. Yet, though tired and sometimes irritable, they are very happy. Roger's talent as an artist does not preclude him from having that French aptitude for economy—that positive enjoyment of economy—which his wife can only faintly emulate. He makes an adventure of reducing their outlay, yet never stints where lavishness may serve a useful purpose.

How she could ever have pictured herself—thus she addresses her correspondent in Egypt—running such a concern alone she cannot now imagine! It would have been impossible; she must have failed at once. Roger is masterly.

She goes on, very apologetically, to explain why it is that she is not inviting Lucy to throw in her lot with them. Their resources are so limited that, for the time being at any rate, the staff must consist strictly of those who are experienced either in making clothes or in selling them. When the firm is sure of itself, when it can safely expand, then it would be delightful to shape out a place for Lucy.

Lucy smiles affectionately. She can detect in this the restraining hand of the wise Roger. He has appeared from the first to be a young man of sense, and she believes strongly what she guiltily admits it was difficult to believe when Constance was quite her own mistress, that the great ambitions will bear fruit.

Roger, in fact, has proved an excellent match, and it is chiefly through the very favourable impression he has made on Mr. Conway that the necessary capital has been raised for Constance's project. By good luck and the virtue of being a Frenchman he has an educated palate for wine, and his wife has given him some coaching in the congenial attitudes. The epicure, a man of principle, puts taste before wealth in one whose affiliation to himself he cannot wholly ignore.

He is glad his son-in-law has been chosen from a race which, unlike his own, is gastronomically civilized, and glad too that Constance's well-being is now clearly and finally, even in the eyes of the world, someone else's affair—for while she was at large without a protector he could never feel perfectly secure against disturbance. He waits a year to see if the marriage is going to work, and then he yields to his daughter's importunities and allows her to demonstrate that a man who is sound on the topic of clarets could not possibly lack the capacities desirable in the partner of a successful couturier.

Lucy is grateful that the problem of accepting or rejecting a position in Constance's firm does not arise. She would much prefer to avoid entering into a direct business relationship with her friend. She has considered often what pitfalls might lie in wait for those whose sympathy is founded only upon written communications and some memories of an earlier time, and she is certain it would be a mistake to let Constance commit herself to any intimacy with her that could not be easily revoked.

She has no fear of being disappointed—she knows a hundred reasons for regarding that as the unlikeliest eventuality in the world—but she is diffident and dreads lest she herself should prove a disappointment. She keeps a strict check upon all such habits and tendencies as she supposes might be tiresome to a lively and advanced young woman; she reads to gain enlightenment on current trends of thought and the fashions Constance takes such pleasure in; and when she finds herself resenting any change, she questions herself sternly as to the logic of her reasons, and grows quite adept at separating genuine distaste from that mere irrational clinging to the standard of one's own heyday which is at the root of so much friction between the young and their elders. In short, without specifically attempting it, she preserves—or rather seems actually to gain—youthfulness of outlook.

Something even of her old impatience possesses her. It exasperates her acutely to count the days and weeks and months as they rush on not carrying her, perceptibly, any nearer to her goal. Every month when she takes her little savings to the bank she debates the question of whether it really is good sense to go on waiting. The P. & O. Line this year offers a new mode of travel, the Tourist class, which is cheaper than second class and an improvement on third. She might pay the entire cost of the journey with all its extras and still have fifty pounds left for the future. Why not be in England for Christmas?

She is several times tempted, but prudence again asserts itself. After all, English winter, whatever its beauties, will be a strain on a constitution so long inured to a hot, dry climate; warm clothes will be indispensable and must eat a good way into fifty pounds. If she had a job to go to it would be worth while to bear any trial, but otherwise it is clear that she ought to wait till the spring. She takes herself in hand and resolves to do so.

She will continue to prepare herself, meanwhile, with all possible physical and mental diligence, for making a creditable entrance into whatever life may be destined to open out to her. She will use every moment of freedom to enrich her mind and cultivate her looks. Maturity suits her. She would be a handsome woman now, she thinks, if only she had time and means for making the most of herself. Her skin is good, her hair has recovered its lustre if not its colour; she has nice teeth and a smile that has gathered charm with the ripening of her character. Her face being fuller, the sharpness of her features is no longer apparent. Indeed her face has profited very much from the thickening of her figure.

Nevertheless, this *embonpoint* distresses her. She is constantly essaying new ways to cope with it, but most of them are either ineffectual or else too arduous to be persisted in. She explains her difficulty to Constance, assured that one who goes among so many smart women must be in a position to advise her expertly, and she receives back an admirable book of exercises, chief of which is the *danse du ventre*.

She does the *danse du ventre* every morning before dressing, but she can never feel quite right about it. No one, she believes, could call it a suitable series of movements for a dignified woman approaching forty, and to her it brings back unhallowed memories. However, to please Constance, she is tenacious and derives undoubted benefit. She is able to stand before her mirror, and say proudly: 'At any rate I'm *firm*.'

But firmness alone does not satisfy. She wants to be slender, or if slenderness is too much to hope, she wants to be svelte enough to wear what she pleases—assuming she may one day have money enough to look on clothes as something better than a regrettable necessity. She decides to go on a rigid diet. She has been dieting mildly for years, but this time she will be drastic. She will live only on salads until she has lost seven pounds of weight.

She keeps it up for five days, her mood ranging from depression and irascibility to pure exhilaration, and then has the misfortune to go shopping in a cheap department store where there is a chocolate counter. With the rich, heavy, sugary smell she is suddenly overwhelmed by a ravenous longing for chocolates. She has resisted a dozen more plausible allurements every day in the shape of sober and savoury nourishment, but for some reason incalculable, the chocolates move her appetite as nothing has ever done before. As she breathes that thickly impregnated air, she is seized with such a craving as shows her for the first time what must be endured by morphine addicts. She lingers, her eyes wandering greedily over the pyramids of glossy brown and the ingenious patterns made with tinfoil. Her fancy plays with their persuasive fillings—the nuts, the caramel, the liqueurs, and oh, heaven! the creams! The sensation of biting through that yielding texture, the agreeable glimpse of white or mauve or rosy pink, the delicate inquiry of the palate into the question of flavour—could there be any seduction to compare with this?

She struggles, knowing she is lost. Arguing and pleading with herself, shocked at her own folly, reminding herself how sorry she will be afterwards, she reaches the door of the shop; then she goes back and buys half a pound of assorted chocolates. She begins to eat them there and then, wandering about the various departments; she finishes them in the street and in the tram, her morbid hunger compelling her to devour them one after another, though from the first taste she has known them to be Dead Sea fruit. It is not so much that she had over-estimated their charm as that she had forgotten their defects—the cloying lusciousness, the thirst-creating sweetness that lingers in the mouth. She arrives home feeling even more foolish, more sick and sorry, than she had anticipated.

This unhappy lapse has taken place during the two-hour interlude in her long day's work. She is thankful that she still has nearly an hour in hand because she is suffering from a reaction of disgust which must be given time to wear off before she can go on duty again. She returns to her room with a heavy tread. It is on the attic floor, higher than the lift ascends, and on the way up there is a place she loves or hates to pass, according to the state of her spirits. By a trick of light on the staircase one's shadow on the wall is fined down to very much less than its normal width though the rest of the proportions remain the same. So that, as Lucy mounts the last few steps, she sees rising before her not her present silhouette but the lissom and elegant figure she brought with her to Egypt.

Sometimes she is amused by this shadow, and pauses to enjoy the sight of it. It is a visible reminiscence and a flattering one. But when she is dejected or out of temper, it seems to taunt her ironically. Today nothing can exceed the mockery of its response to her approach. Looking as slender as it possibly can, it mimics her deliberately stolid movements with a satirical air as if to remind her of the difference between those who gormandize chocolates and those who are in decent control of themselves. Lucy has an impulse of anger that makes her want to push the thing away. She raises her hand in a gesture of repelling it, and the shadow answers with a mincing parody.

She sees that she is being absurd and gives a petulant laugh. Then she laughs again rather more mirthfully, for really she has been strangely ridiculous and deserves an even worse dyspepsia than she has. She reaches sanctuary and, flinging her hat and bag upon a chair, hastily pours herself a glass of water. While she is drinking it, her eye is caught by a strange object on the mantelpiece—an envelope propped up against the clock, the sort of envelope they use for cablegrams. She puts down the glass very nonchalantly, she opens the envelope very nonchalantly, as if she received cablegrams every day. She reads:

> CAN YOU SAIL IN ABOUT A FORTNIGHT MOST PROMISING PLACE FOUND FOR YOU STOP REGRET NO TIME FOR CORRESPONDENCE BUT CAN ALMOST GUARANTEE YOUR SATISFACTION STOP PLEASE CABLE REPLY LOVE CONSTANCE

Lucy stands quite still with the message in her hand, feeling nothing. After a long minute of total paralysis she moves slowly to the window and stares into the faint silver haze which she knows to be the sea. Her eyes are full of tears, overflowing with tears, which drip unheeded down her cheeks, but she feels nothing.

Chapter 30

It has been said often and in a variety of ways that to get what we have long wanted is a sort of tragedy, so inevitably are our highest hopes ordained to be defeated in fulfilment; and many readers will be convinced in advance that, if this tale is true to life, Lucy's return to England is bound to be attended by some circumstance or other that will take the satisfaction out of it. But a person of resolute character, who has attained to the consummation of a desire after an arduous struggle, is not so ready to be disappointed as pessimistic philosophers imagine, and will, on the contrary, frequently tend to find attractions and merits invisible to the eyes of others, out of a sheer determination to be pleased.

Such was the case with Lucy. When the first numbness had worn off, she entered upon a period of happiness at once exciting and profound, and so eagerly did she grasp at every occasion for enjoyment, that she turned inconveniences into amusing adventures and shortcomings too plain to be ignored into foils by which her next delights would seem more vivid.

To describe the realization of wishes is generally a sort of anticlimax. It will suffice to explain the material facts—that Lucy exchanged cables with Constance to certify herself of her good fortune; that she gave a fortnight's notice to her employer, and booked a Tourist berth on the first liner bound for England from Port Said in January 1931, and was able, owing to the season, to get a cabin to herself.

It was not until the ship had sailed that she noticed on the passenger list the name of Mrs. Siegfried Mosenthal. The discovery left her perfectly unmoved except for a little mild wonderment as to the cause of Daisy's journeying to England at such an unlikely time. Had she thought herself in any danger of meeting her, she would have been displeased, but Daisy had ignored her existence for years, and it was not to be supposed that she would cover the vast distance between her first-class state-room and the Tourist cabins, even, or especially, if she deigned to learn the names of the inferior beings who occupied them. So Lucy did not perplex herself by trying to decide what attitude she would adopt if they should be thrown together. She was not quite allowed, however, to forget Daisy's presence on board.

Daisy, though she was serenely unaware of it, was the chosen object of gossip wherever she appeared. Her clothes and jewels, the wealth which enveloped her in an almost palpable aura, her husband's ever-growing notoriety as a financial genius, all served to draw attention upon her; and partly because her luxury aroused jealousy, partly because her affectations gave offence, this attention was very often disposed to be unfavourable. She was accompanied by a personal maid, a governess, and a nurse, who were not as discreet nor as impeccable in their loyalty as might have been desired, and since tittle-tattle is a means of passing time at sea, Lucy could scarcely avoid being made acquainted with a number of particulars concerning her former friend's standing and mode of life. She knew, for instance, that Daisy's social progress was slow but by no means sure; she knew her days were so empty and her aims so obvious that her servants cruelly described her, after the title of a once popular song, as 'All dressed up and no place to go'; she knew that the occasion of her present voyage was to take her little son to a fashionable preparatory school, and that he was guarded carefully meanwhile from playing with children who were deemed to be upon a lower plane. On the whole, the impression she derived was rather pathetic, and out of her own happiness she could almost have found charity to absolve Daisy of all her sins against her.

But absolution was not required, as she was effectually shown in the one unlucky moment when they came face to face. It was the night of the Tourists' fancy-dress ball. Two or three distinguished people from the First Class had been invited to judge the costumes, and a number of others trailed over with them. Among these was Daisy, leaning on the arm of an old military gentleman, who was evidently finding her very agreeable. Her face, still pretty, though its lines were becoming rather hard, was gaily animated, her sweetly feminine laugh sounded full of enjoyment. She looked benevolently about her. She could afford to smile upon this humbler breed of travellers.

All of a sudden her eye fell on Lucy, who, hemmed about by a group in fancy dress, had been unable to rise from her deck-chair in time to make an escape. Her smile stiffened and froze, her laugh hung in the air unfinished, and, for a painful instant, Lucy could read upon her face the conflict of her uncertainty—whether to risk a greeting or to cut her dead, since it was too late to pretend not to have seen her. Lucy spared her the trouble of decision by giving her a bright but vague nod—a nod so very vague that it would leave the recipient uncompromised—and moved away to the far comer of the deck. She did not go below because a faint irrational hope stirred in her that Daisy would feel compunction, would seek her out to inquire how matters stood with her; and in the mood engendered by sea and sky and music, and the atmosphere of freedom, and her own inward tranquillity, she was very willing to be a little sentimental. But when she looked back, Daisy's brigadier-general was talking to someone else, and Daisy herself had vanished, not to reappear. It was the only incident throughout the whole voyage that left any shadow of distress behind it, and her concern was not altogether for her own pride. Daisy drunk with prosperity was a sad spectacle.

With what relief she conjured up the thought of that dear friend to whose quixotic notions of gratitude she owed so much of her present well-being!

And within a few days there was Constance herself waiting for her at Tilbury. Constance had wonderfully and beautifully changed! That graceful figure, that polished and reposeful elegance! If she had not been prepared by photographs, Lucy would never have recognized her. Indeed it seemed scarcely credible that here was the plump, untidy girl whose taste she had once been in the habit of correcting: she was abashed at the remembrance. While they waited for the gang-plank to be lowered, she hung over the rail of the deck rejoicing in the sight of her, childishly hugging the certainty that Daisy, though she should be clad in the finest sables that ever came out of Russia and adorned with the purest and largest diamonds Cartier could supply, would never, as long as she lived, attain to a distinction so immediately convincing as this.

In the meantime, like nearly everyone about them, they were exchanging those hearty yet constrained utterances which are the highest flight conversation reaches when carried on in public with a distance of about fifteen yards between the speakers.

'How are you?'

'Was the voyage all right?'

'How nice of you to meet me!'

'You'll find this weather a change after what you've come from.'

'I'm yearning to get to London.'

Scraps of dialogue in this mode were being flung heavily to and fro along the whole length of the ship, and Lucy did not make a better thing of it than anyone else. At last the people waiting below were allowed to come on board and then began that sort of impeded bustling, that haste without speed, that progression from delay to delay, which is the usual mode of getting from a ship to a boat-train. Farewells to fellow-passengers, preoccupation with luggage, and the observance of passport and customs regulations, prevented Lucy from making any attempt either to speak coherently to Constance or to appreciate the glorious fact that her feet once more trod upon the soil of England.

It was as well for her that this was so. England gives no very alluring welcome in customs sheds, and as for Constance, if they had been thrust at once into the intimacy of peaceful seclusion, each must have put up a barrier of shyness which might not have been easily overturned! As it was, embarrassment gradually fell away in a casual running commentary on immediate topics, and by the time they were settled in the train, neither dreaded the ordeal of being obliged to reveal emotion.

Constance had bought two first-class tickets and, the ship having been sparsely filled, they were able to get a compartment to themselves. For a few moments after the train had started they sat opposite one another in silence, beaming, then Constance held out her cigarette case. Lucy shook her head.

'I still don't smoke. I used to count that as a saving of three piastres a day. Oh dear, I mustn't begin with reminiscences of that kind, must I? Where *shall* we begin?'

'Wouldn't you like to know what's going to happen to you?'

'Yes, very much, in a way. But it's been rather pleasant not knowing all this while—just drifting along and leaving everything to you.'

'It was brave of you to come while you were so completely in the dark. I was afraid you wouldn't.'

'What, after all our plans?'

'It must have been a plunge for you.'

'Well, I saw it as a case of "now or never". And I liked being in your hands. It was a luxury.'

Constance's glowingly frank yet diffident smile gave her altered face a sudden familiarity. 'Yes, I thought it would be fun if you could once bring yourself to it. Not that I held back any information on purpose, but there was only time to get one letter to you before you sailed, and that wouldn't have been much help, since your arrangements all had to be made and done with beforehand.'

'I understood that,' said Lucy. Her eyes were drawn to the scene outside the window and Constance let the discussion hang in suspense while she gazed.

'I'm afraid it's not much of a landscape,' she suggested apologetically after a longer interval than Lucy realized.

'Ah, but I know what's behind it.'

'Darling, you'll have some disillusionments! How long since you were here?'

'I left for Australia at the end of 1917—just over thirteen years ago.'

'Well, you must prepare for shocks.'

'I am prepared. I know that the countryside is being spoiled and that cheap-and-nasty building is going on all over the place, and in London the noise and traffic are getting worse every day. I know that Regent Street's been rebuilt and that Park Lane's in a state of upheaval, and that some of my favourite landmarks will have gone. I suppose I'm in for a few hard knocks about things like that, but I've braced myself up for them, Con.'

'Good! Then you may not find it so bad after all.'

'So bad! Oh, my dear, I wonder if you can possibly imagine what it feels like to be here at last?' She laid her gloved hand on the window-pane. 'This peculiar greyish-green colour and the look of the trees—so different from Egypt—and the quiet homely light about everything.'

'Quiet homely darkness, you mean! Oh, Lucy, Lucy, you sentimentalist, you may miss that Egyptian sunshine.'

'No, I've prepared for that too. When I have any hankering after Egyptian sunshine, I'll remember it at its worst—only an electric fan between oneself and suffocation. I shall remember all the pests that flourished through it. . . .'

'Cockroaches, for instance. I don't think you ought to forget the cockroaches, Lucy.'

'I couldn't, bless their souls, for a lot of reasons! Every time I have the smallest temptation to grouse about my life here, I've promised—I've faithfully promised myself to think of cockroaches. There are plenty of other things I shall think of too. I'm not a sentimentalist. I'm a realist.'

'I do believe you are,' Constance replied with a serious, penetrating glance. 'It's only people with good truthful memories who can afford to get what they've set their hearts on.'

'You mean they won't forget how badly they wanted it and how dreary things were without it? True. But sometimes to forget absolutely must also be a help. Do you know, Daisy came over on this boat. Wasn't it a coincidence? We didn't speak. She was travelling "first", of course.'

'Did she see you?'

'Yes and no. I might say that she saw without looking and then looked without seeing.'

'What a mean little animal she must be! Is she on this train?' Constance's expression was so fiercely contemptuous that Lucy was quite glad to be able to answer: 'I believe a car was expected to fetch her. Her doings were pretty fully reported on board.'

'She's a monster, and I only hope I may have the pleasure of telling her so. Perhaps I shall one day.'

There was something in this of the old impulsive and hot-headed Constance. It was a folly that banished the last vestige of the awe inspired by her poise and beauty. Lucy leaned back, perfectly at ease. 'Tell me what's going to happen to me, Con.'

'Aha, now we're getting down to business. To begin at the beginning, you're coming to spend a few days with me and Roger.'

'Good; I was wishing for that.'

'You mustn't expect *grand luxe* because, at the moment, we're in a frenzy of preparations for our opening. How nice that you're home in time for it! We're going to open at the end of February with such a party, my dear—such a party!'

'And I'm invited? Well, I'm sure all this *will* be a change!'

'But in the meantime every day produces some new upheaval! Did I explain to you how we live? The *salon*'s on the first floor, the workrooms are in a mews at the back of the house, and our flat is above the *salon*. We're running alive with workmen. You must be ready for anything—painters and decorators peering in through your bedroom window, electricians suddenly putting their heads through your floor-boards, plumbers strewing your way with bits of piping—'

'Oh, Con, I ought to go to an hotel. I shall be frightfully in the way.'

'Nonsense—if you'll permit me to say so. If you can put up with it, I guarantee we can. I just thought you'd better be warned, that's all. I dare say you were picturing us quite settled in by this time.' She drew a deep but not uncheerful sigh. 'It all takes so much longer than anyone would believe possible. Now, where was I? With such millions of things to talk about, I keep getting side-tracked.'

'My job?'

'Ah, yes, of course. After you've stayed your stay with us, you'll have a few days for pottering round—visiting your sister and all that—and then you start work. You must be mystified as to what sort of job it is, and it's going to be fiendishly difficult to describe. If I just say you're going to be secretary-housekeeper-companion-help to a man with a daughter, that sounds fearful, so I've got to use artistic methods of approach. Do you like the Royal Botanical Gardens?'

Lucy's smile was bewildered.

'They're commonly known as Kew Gardens.'

'I adore Kew Gardens.'

'Very well. You're going to live practically at the front gate, and in the most enticing house you can think of. Have you ever heard of John Churchfield?'

'I seem to know the name,' said Lucy with about as much truth as such a statement usually calls for.

'He's a lecturer at London University; his subject is French literature. He also does translations and criticisms. He translates French novels and poetry, and I believe he's "discovered" one or two important modern writers. Desherbes, for instance, was more or less unknown both in France and England before John Churchfield took him up.'

Lucy succeeded in looking as impressed as anyone could to whom the name of Desherbes conveyed nothing, and Constance reassuringly added: 'I'll lend you one or two of his books before you go there. Now, as to the work, first and foremost you're to be his secretary. For that, of course, your French will come in useful. He was pleased about the Italian too, though he says he doesn't often get a use for it. In the second place, he wants someone who is trustworthy with money and able to keep orderly accounts of the housekeeping and all that. In the third place, he has a daughter of about fifteen. (He's a widower, you see.) She's at a boarding-school, but when she comes home for the holidays you'll be a companion for her. She's inclined to be lonely, I suppose. I've never seen her, but I'm told she's clever and bookish. She won't be much trouble. In the fourth place . . . am I making it sound like rank slavery?'

'Not at all,' said Lucy, who had been following every word with the utmost intentness. 'It probably isn't a whole-time job to do his accounts and his typing, and it certainly couldn't be a whole-time job to keep an eye on a girl of fifteen—unless she were a second Constance. What's worrying me a little is the housekeeping. I can pick it up, I'm sure of that—my mother was a wonderful housekeeper—but after thirteen years of living abroad in lodgings and hotels—'

'My soul, that's exactly where this job seems to have been designed for you by a just and loving God. Dr. Churchfield has a sublime French cook who does all the catering. She can't or won't learn English and she won't stand interference. The consequence is that there has to be some French-speaking person about who can do the ordering for her and pass on instructions and who's willing to be a sort of liaison officer rather than a housekeeper. It's a situation that has resulted in a certain amount of friction. Superior young women with fluent French and every modern convenience have a knack of rubbing her up the wrong way.'

Lucy nodded like a mandarin to show how keenly she was listening, and Constance went on: 'The difficulty, Dr. Churchfield says, is to find a secretary who won't consider it a come-down to share housekeeping duties with the cook and not try to usurp her authority. You get the idea? Tact is more important than domestic knowledge. You can learn what's necessary as you go along. Last, my dear, but positively not least, Dr. Churchfield is an impassioned collector, and his house is a miniature museum and art gallery. The servants are not allowed to touch any of his treasures, so the dusting has to be done either by himself or his secretary. You won't mind that, will you?'

'I'll like it, so long as he doesn't collect mummies or specimens of repulsive insects.'

'On the contrary, you'll find him surrounded with musical boxes: those and multitudes of other nice things—most of them beautiful as well. He's a true virtuoso. Oh, Lucy, it's a lovely house, and Dr. Churchfield is such a dear. You'll be delighted, I'm certain you will.'

'I'm certain I will,' Lucy repeated with conviction.

She sank into a reverie, the scene of which was a charming composite picture made out of her memories of Kew Gardens . . . the verdant expanses, the avenues of noble trees, the neat little wildernesses, the well-fed happy birds fluttering about the tea-tables, the strange pagoda—best surveyed from the distance, for she could recall that it was dullish when one came close to it—the vast glasshouses full of luscious tropical plants that harboured no tropical pests, and the quiet, secluded museums into whose pleasantly desiccated atmosphere no violent emotion seemed capable of penetrating. . . .

'You don't ask about money,' Constance was saying.

'No, I don't ask about money.'

'You may be disappointed. It's thirty shillings a week "all found". But you'll have more leisure—you'll be much more your own mistress.'

She paused on an appealing note, and Lucy cried eagerly: 'My dear, my dear, it's exactly the kind of place I was wanting! I wish I were a demonstrative person—it's hard for me to express myself on big occasions—but I do assure you, Con, I didn't expect anything nearly so good. To live in a home, a comfortable decently run home, after hardly having seen the inside of one for years and years, and to do work that's varied and personal. . . why, it's just the very thing I was longing for! The best office job wouldn't have suited me half so well, honestly, Con!'

'I shall feel terribly guilty if it lets you down.'

'No, no, no, I won't have that! It was grand of you to take the responsibility, but here it ends. You've got work for me and that's enough. If you went on feeling responsible it would only worry me.'

Constance frowned thoughtfully, blew a delicate arabesque of smoke, traced out its line with an ornamental flourish of her cigarette, and at last remarked: 'You're absolutely right. If I felt responsible, *you* couldn't feel free. Lucy,' she added solemnly, 'when you've once taken up this post, what happens to you is your own business.'

'Agreed!' said Lucy with equal earnestness.

For a few minutes all the contemplative powers of her whole being were fixed once more upon the shifting prospect framed by the window. They were passing an apparently unending vista of shabby houses and mean back-yards, but in her present contentment she could not find them either ugly or squalid. She had no aesthetic training making it easy for her to perceive that the groupings of slate roofs and crowded chimney-pots, the subtle gradation of drab colours under a pallid sky, might have qualities gratifying to the eyes of an artist, but her love enabled her to see beauty where her untaught reason would have rejected it. As for the sordidness of these dwellings, their grime, their poverty, their discomfort, she was aware of them only remotely, for they were a picture, a painted scene, a sliding panorama that would go on unfolding and unfolding until it unfolded London. It seemed scarcely possible that substantial human beings, thinking, sentient, endowed with vitality as obtrusive as her own, ate and slept and talked and planned and toiled in houses that were mere dissolving views along a railway line. The sooty washing hung out in back gardens had no more reality than properties in a pantomime. The window-boxes and stunted trees and hen-coops and dust-bins were mere touches of verisimilitude supplied by a designer whose mood wavered between cynicism and sentiment. However conscientiously she assured herself that all these houses were very dreary, very shocking, and regrettable, she could not repress the exultation they awakened by the simple fact of their belonging to London.

She turned back into their compartment, which she could imagine, as in childhood, to be a flying chariot capable of taking them to any destination they might set their fancy on, and realized she had lost the thread of what Constance had been saying.

'So the moral is, there's no knowing where a good deed may lead you. It isn't often my father puts himself out to oblige anybody, but, incredible as it seems, he did—in a sort of way—exert himself for you.'

'Your father!' Lucy made a swift lunge to catch the gist of the matter. 'I—I thought it must be Roger,' she stammered.

'Roger? How Roger?'

'Well, Dr. Churchfield's French associations—'

'No, my dear, Dr. Churchfield's cook is the only French association with any bearing on this case. My father is very fond of Mme Villard, and she likes him, because when he dines there, he always makes a point of seeing her afterwards and discussing every detail of the meal; and, believe it or not, he's a very captivating man with cooks: he loves them so—the good ones. You have a valuable ally in my father.'

'But hadn't he forgotten my existence?'

'It was recalled to him. He was reminded that you were the person who forcibly prevented me from having a welter of illegitimate babies (I piled on the agony a little) by an Italian bank clerk.'

'And do you mean to say he actually got me this job on the strength of it?'

'It wasn't quite as plain sailing as that, but he did remember that Dr. Churchfield's rather unsuitable secretary was going to be married, and he did invite the doctor to a little dinner so that I could do my stuff. That was going a long way for him, but it was very soon after he'd given me the first thousand pounds for setting up in business and—have you ever noticed?—when people once start being magnanimous, they find it quite hard to stop.'

'It's a most wonderful piece of luck for me. How *did* you manage to convince Dr. Churchfield I was worth sending to Egypt for?'

'I aroused his sympathy by telling him your whole story. Forgive the liberty! It was too good a card not to be played. Also I dishonestly but diplomatically let him understand you were coming over in any case at just the time when he'd be needing you. He would have grown chary at once if he'd known you were going to give up your other job and take the journey specially for him.'

'That was very wise of you,' said Lucy.

'Of course if I hadn't been able to make practically certain about it all beforehand, I wouldn't have cabled you.'

Lucy was reiterating her thanks, her hopes, and her enthusiasm, when Constance laid a finger against her lips and whispered, 'Hush, my dear! Reverent silence! We're approaching recognizable parts of London,' thus setting her friend at liberty to apply herself solely to the occupation of window-gazing.

No sustained conversation passed between them again until they were driving away from St. Pancras Station in a taxi. Then Lucy asked anxiously: 'Do we go through Piccadilly?'

'We could!'

'Let's!'

'You'll be disappointed. They've built a new tube station and the Circus is still all upset. The Eros hasn't been put back yet.'

'I know. It doesn't matter. I shall make allowances. Let's go down Shaftesbury Avenue.'

'Very well, darling. "All zat my lady want, she shall 'ave." Constance crouched forward and tapped on the window to give instructions to the driver.

When she resumed her place, Lucy was sitting rather tensely with her hands clasped against her chin. 'It is queer,' she said, 'to think this is actually you—this beautiful lady actually that wild girl who sometimes used to deserve a good slap. Con,' she went on with an abruptness which showed the subject had been in waiting on her lips, 'what about me? Do you find me much changed? Oh, naturally you do after ten years! I mean, do you find me quite—quite spoiled—hopeless?' The question tapered nervously into inarticulateness.

Constance surveyed her candidly with eyes well practised in the art of inspection. 'You've changed for the better,' she responded slowly, 'when I last saw you, your appearance was nothing like so good as it is now. You were painfully thin and your face was sallow and strained—'

'Ah, I'd been ill then, but now I'm so much older. Be frank with me: I can stand up to the truth.'

'I am frank. I was watching you pretty closely on the train; I had to stare at you a lot to get used to the fact that you're good-looking. You see, when we parted, you were by way of being plain.'

'Oh, Con, good-looking! Am I? Am I really? With this figure? With these nondescript clothes?'

Constance went on inspecting as dispassionately, one might suppose, as if her companion were a wax model. 'If you dress to your type, your figure will be an asset. Your type is "the fine woman", very gracious, rather Edwardian. I should enjoy dressing you, your carriage is so good. I'll tell you what! We must make you a *toilette*, a dinner dress and a coat—something simple but *grand*—to wear at my opening! Lucy, you shall be my first client and bring me luck! The clothes will be a payment for the dressmaking lessons I had from you in Cairo. What a lovely idea!'

'A lovely idea for me, but what will Roger say to it?'

'He'll like it, because it'll give me so much pleasure.' She paused, then added with less certainty: 'Or if he insists on being the hard-headed man of business, he can put a nominal sum down in the books just to salve his conscience. It'll be my affair anyhow. Roger's very much indebted to you, you know; even more than my father if you come to think of it.' She threw out her elegant hands in a movement that seemed to evoke the outline of the projected *toilette*. 'My dear, it's going to be entrancing—and you must treat your face and hair exactly as I tell you. You'll look like a very unostentatious duchess. Now, you attend to London while I work it all out in my head. It must be superb but useful, definitely useful.'

She was still sunk in real or pretended deliberation when they came to Shaftesbury Avenue, where Lucy peered from side to side checking off the names of the theatres. When they drew near the Pavilion, she knocked on the glass and told the driver to pull up and wait.

'What are you going to do?' cried Constance.

'Buy some flowers. Look, there they are, the flower women, just the same as ever; with gardenias and violets and those ravishing lilies of the valley. Let me get out, darling!' She was visibly excited. Her voice shook.

'Darling, we have flowers, masses of flowers. The flat is full of them.'

Lucy paused, holding the door ajar. 'But you could do with some more? You haven't got any like these, have you?'

'My angel, don't. I got quantities of flowers this morning. There aren't enough vases for any more. And the extravagance! Consider the extravagance!' She spoke coaxingly, rallyingly, but a little apprehensively too. It was almost alarming to see Lucy so divested of her sobriety.

'It doesn't matter.' Lucy alighted swiftly from the taxi. 'If they'll be in the way we needn't take them home. We can leave them in the cab.'

'Lucy—'

'I just want to *buy* them; I just want to *hold* them.'

She made off with the air of one who is resolved not to listen to reason, and when she emerged again from the moving throng on the pavement, clasping in one hand an immense posy of violets, in the other lilies of the valley so closely pressed together that their trembling delicacy was almost lost to sight, there was something in her face which silenced laughter.

Chapter 31

Dr. Churchfield turned out to be a much younger and gayer person than Lucy had expected. She had taken it for granted from his academic position and his distinction as a connoisseur and a man of letters, as well as from his being a widower, that he must be elderly and very staid. Indeed she had formed a mental picture of him, small and gentle, with greying hair and feminine hands, and, after the donnish tradition, a tendency to absent-mindedness. But instead she found a tall, robust, athletic man of about forty whose prevailing characteristics were his vivacity, his shrewdness, and the ardour of his enthusiasms.

Her first view of him was very engaging. He had considerately suggested that, before moving in, she should come to tea accompanied by Constance so that they might have some talk about her work. They were received in a spacious room which the maid described as 'the office' but which looked more like an informal sort of museum in the process of arrangement. Every part of the wall that was not hidden by glass-fronted cabinets was closely covered with small pictures, while, stacked against the wainscoting, were a number of frames for which it appeared that no space had been found. Scattered about the room were tables, on each of which stood at least one oblong ornamental box inlaid with pearl, ivory, or a pattern of coloured wood. Even the typewriter contended for place with mysterious boxes, and three or four exceptionally large specimens were accommodated on the floor. Every nook and cranny disclosed some object or assortment of objects which set snares for curiosity. The figure of the doctor himself, impressive and surprising though it was, could hardly fix Lucy's whole attention when there was so much to distract it.

He was standing in the middle of the room, intent on what appeared to be an elaborate Buhl desk, and it cost him, visibly, a slight effort of will to detach himself from it and give them both a cheerful greeting. 'Good afternoon, Constance! How d'you do?' His peculiarly brisk and incisive voice indicated a temperament impatient of all loitering methods of approach. 'Is this Miss Kendon? How d'you do? Sit down, won't you?

'So this is your office?' said Constance as he cleared a chaise-longue by lifting two inlaid caskets down to the floor. 'I've never seen it before. It's very unofficial.'

'You mean it's very untidy. As a matter of fact, I'm obliged to use it as an overflow room for items I haven't quite decided about. But it's getting cleared up by degrees. I shall have it cleared up eventually, never fear! That'll be something for Miss Kendon to help with.'

'I can't sit down until I've looked around a little here,' said Constance. 'This is a most bewildering house. You seem to collect so many different kinds of things.'

'But never more than two or three kinds at a time. It isn't that I lose interest: I really seem to arrive at a saturation point.'

'You discover you've got all the good specimens anyone could wish for?'

It was evidently his habit to give every question a reasoned reply. 'Yes, I should sound boastful if I put it so myself—but yes. I don't collect from inexhaustible sources or with inexhaustible resources. I don't collect old masters or old manuscripts, for instance, which might keep me on the go for a lifetime. I'm a small-scale virtuoso, as a man with a moderate income is compelled to be. All the same,' he added, suddenly beaming, 'my small scale covers a very choice gamut.' He waved his big hand affectionately towards the walls, the cabinets, and the scattered tables.

'The last time I was here you were just getting to saturation point with these.' Constance directed Lucy's attention to a little regiment of glass obelisks on the mantelpiece.

'True.' His sigh mingled pride and regret. 'There may be a better collection than this, but I doubt it—I doubt it very much. To add to it would be only to achieve boring repetitions. Miss Kendon, I think I may safely tell you that you are now looking at a portion of the finest collection of glass obelisks in England.' He picked one out and put it in her hand.

'Are they paper-weights?' she asked, admiring the exquisite urn full of leaves and flowers which appeared, so unaccountably, inside the prism-shaped glass.

'Yes and no. They're not what is generally understood by paper-weights. People think of those smooth round lumps of glass with coloured pictures or patterns embedded in them; very pretty, but they're much commoner and lend themselves to fake. Now here, you notice, the picture appears three-dimensional and is formed by the actual shape of the glass, with perhaps a little embellishment of paint. An ingenious trick, isn't it? You look behind and see merely some pieces nicked out of the prism. You look in front and have the illusion that there's a tiny urn inside the crystal.' He took the obelisk from her, ran his silk handkerchief over it with a light and loving touch, and returned it to its position. 'I'll tell you more about them,' he said simply, 'as you get more familiar with the place.'

'These are the things that captivate me,' said Constance, examining one of the uniform rows of odd little pictures.

'Ah, the men's fashion plates. You care for those?'

'Yes, I find them even more attractive than women's plates. They're rarer, I suppose?'

'Much rarer. I began that collection when the demand was almost nil, but even then it was hard to get decent runs of them.'

Lucy's eyes wandered incredulously over the clear, meticulous drawings of men in sumptuous opera cloaks, men with high cravats and curled hair, romantically bearded men with low-waisted coats, dazzling waistcoats, and peg-topped trousers, whiskered men in unconvincing sports clothes . . . exotic, fascinating, manifestly fictitious beings.

'Have you reached saturation point with these too?' Constance inquired.

'Yes, I'm afraid so. Would you like some? I have a few duplicates.'

'I should be entranced.'

'Nothing could gratify me more than to find such a good use for them. Miss Kendon must remind me to sort them out and send them.'

Constance thanked him with befitting gladness, and asked whether he had yet exhausted musical boxes.

'Musical boxes!' His face lit up with unaffected joy. 'My dear Constance, I am in the very height and frenzy of my passion for musical boxes. Since you were last here my devotion has grown by leaps and bounds. You might as well ask a lover in his most doting throes whether he has discarded his mistress yet!'

'Have you ever heard a good musical box, Lucy?' Constance was artfully playing the role of interlocutor.

'I've never heard any sort of musical box since my childhood.'

'Then your visit is well timed,' said the doctor. 'I have a new Nicole, a beauty—oh, a most exceptional thing! You shall listen to it! Talk of being entranced—this will entrance you if anything could!'

He returned to the Buhl piece of furniture which Lucy had taken to be a desk and, opening the lid of a kind of superstructure, revealed a complex and beautiful piece of machinery under glass. He pulled a lever and released a catch. There was a faint whirring, the softest preliminary whisper, then a tune began. It was truly a ravishing sound, delicate, pure, precise; rich yet light, intricate yet lucid; a sound unique, imitating no other, incapable of being imitated, a music so set apart from all the accustomed noises of the world that time itself seemed to stand still and listen with them.

'The notes drop into the ear like jewels,' he murmured in a pause between two airs and Lucy answered: 'How exactly right,' for in its high artifice, its clarity of outline, its polished brilliance, this music more resembled finely wrought jewellery than anything else imaginable.

The doctor allowed a second and a third air to come to an end, then pressed back the catch and silenced the mechanism. 'Well,' he demanded, rubbing his hands in blissful self-congratulation.

They both assured him of their pleasure.

'This box,' he said, 'has more than a hundred tunes. Miss Kendon shall play them to me while I work.'

Lucy, acquiescing, could not but smile to think of the contrast between the occupations of the future and those of the past. To produce jewel-like melodies for a cultured gentleman writing a lecture or translating a poem would be a wonderfully far cry from selling cinema tickets or showing hotel visitors to their bedrooms.

'I never knew,' said Constance, 'that any box had such a repertoire.'

'After the invention of the movable cylinder there was nothing but the expense to prevent one from having as many tunes as one liked. This box must have belonged to some extremely rich amateur. You see, it's mounted on a writing-table specially made to match, with a dozen extra cylinders.' He pulled out a drawer so that they might examine the rolls of shining brass studded over with innumerable minute projections.

'Surely it's hard to come by such a thing, especially in this condition?'

'It needs a certain strain of cunning, I admit. This one I got from a country clergyman and gave him a wireless instrument in exchange. I had to fire him with a craving for wireless which will probably result in a dangerous addiction.'

'Is this,' Lucy ventured to ask, 'your favourite?'

'Not musically, though it's very good. But I have several that are even finer. This, for instance. It's a Paillard.' He laid caressing fingers on one of the inlaid caskets. 'You shall hear them all when you come here.'

Lucy was touched and flattered at his unquestioning assumption that she would share his interest in the treasures of the house. And, in fact, his immense gusto was so infectious that it would not have been easy to withstand it even if unresponsiveness had been a merit. 'I look forward very much to it,' she returned sincerely.

'There are some pretty specimens in the drawing-room. We'd better go up there in any case. Ivy will be wanting to serve our tea, and after that I must introduce you ceremoniously to Mme Villard.'

They followed him out into the hall, where, after a moment's irresolution at the foot of the stairs, he paused by a console table. On it, between two tall vases of flowers, stood an extremely ornate coffer which Lucy now recognized as a musical box.

'This,' he said, 'is the one we use as a dinner gong.' He raised the lid, disclosing a mechanism more complex but less chastely workmanlike than the one they had seen. 'It's a degenerate affair,' he explained in a tone of fond indulgence. 'It has drums, bells, all sorts of nonsense. These later contrivances are very decadent. The more they strove after realistic orchestral effects, the more they lost the illusion.'

'It's nice to look at, all the same,' said Constance. 'I should like those little silver birds to put on a dress.'

'They strike the bells with their beaks.' He pulled the lever and the cylinder began to revolve. The noise fell out in a thick shower, resonant, luxuriant, flooding the house with sweet polychromatic janglings; the bells chimed, the drums, at erratic intervals, achieved an inappropriate tattoo, and a humming-bird in full plumage, which inhabited a little glass-enclosed bower at the front of the cabinet, performed excitable gyrations on its perch.

'It's amusing but certainly regrettable,' he acknowledged, as they made their way upstairs, pursued by mellifluous arpeggios and the rather macabre rattlings of the drum. 'Still, it's loud and lively, and more entertaining than dinner gongs in general. Now *this* one'—he stopped before them on the landing—'is of quite a different quality. Ivy wakes us up in the morning with this one.'

The landing was dark and at first appeared to be furnished only with pictures and bookshelves, but after a second or two Lucy discerned a structure like an overgrown grandfather's clock, which she supposed must be a musical box because it could be nothing else.

'The Polyphon!' announced the doctor, so much in the manner of one formally presenting a friend that Constance replied with an urbane, 'How d'you do?'

'Here,' he proceeded, not seeming to notice anything unnatural in this courtesy, 'we have the very last of its line—the ultimate development of the musical box before it gave way to the gramophone. This one used to stand in a public house and was worked by putting a penny in the slot.'

'That's rather a come-down, isn't it?'

'Yes, Constance, I'm afraid it is. There's no doubt this is something of a poor relation, but it's much simpler and more robust than the others. It has an enormous number of tunes too—popular music coming right up to 1905, or thereabouts. You observe'—he tapped on the glass pane of its door—'large steel disks have taken the place of the cylinders. The sound is less fragile, less elegant, than we expect from the early boxes, but it's very agreeable, nevertheless—gay and sparkling, you know, with an excellent bass. Just the thing for rousing one in the morning.' He patted it gently as if to assure it of his approval, then turned and flung open a door, and they entered the drawing-room.

It was a large and handsome apartment, stretching across the full width of the house, with four symmetrically placed windows looking out upon Kew Green. It had the aspect of a museum turned voluptuous. Lucy stared about her, spellbound. She had never seen an extensive private collection before and had not expected that taste could be so nonchalantly combined with comfort, and that variety apparently unrestrained could convey an impression of the most admirable unity. She did not know what all these enchanting objects might be—it was months before she could identify with certainty every different kind of glass and porcelain, of peep-show and panorama, of water-colour and engraving and aquatint, of hair picture, tinsel picture, silhouette, and miniature—but even to her untaught eyes the assembled effect was profoundly satisfying. She was looking, she thought, into a little world where beauty was permanent and craftsmanship worth while, where profusion was no squandering, and covetousness no vice, a little world where the severest conflict was the rivalry of treasures, and the greatest change the removal of something from its familiar place. She felt an impulse of pure happiness that swept away reserve.

'Oh, Con,' she exclaimed, 'this is nicer than anything I was picturing!'

Dr. Churchfield nodded benevolently in time to the beat of a tune he was playing on a very small, neat, and dulcet-toned musical box.

'The Stephanie Gavotte!' she declared, and would have been glad to get up and dance to it.

Dr. Churchfield went on nodding, but his gaze had become abstracted. He was lost in contemplation of the melting silver notes, and one might believe from his face that he saw them dripping before him in a palpable rain.

As Lucy came to know her employer better she grew surprised that anyone who was at once so genial and so domesticated should be content to live a celibate life, but Constance set her curiosity at rest by explaining that he was reputed to have been attached for years to a lady who was not free to marry him.

He managed, nevertheless, to make his bachelor existence highly enjoyable. He kept an excellent house and took some pride in the ordering of it, he entertained casually but very hospitably two or three days a week, and was much visited by immensely diverse kinds of people. Scholars and critics, hearty young athletes with whom he was in the habit of playing squash, bons-vivants allured by the well-known skill of his cook, penurious undergraduates, French novelists and English publishers, rival collectors, astute dealers and craftsmen of numerous species—Lucy wondered whether there was another man in England who could boast such a range of acquaintance, all on the most cordial terms with him.

Never anywhere, she believed, did conversation prove more absorbing than in that house. The sequel to every dinner party was that one or other of the guests would be beguiled into talking until the small hours and then persuaded to stay the night. Two spare beds were invariably kept made up and aired and the spare-room vases filled with flowers, whether anyone was known to be invited or not. With all these associates Dr. Churchfield was perfectly himself, kind, appreciative, didactic, vigorous in his dislikes, fervent in his enthusiasms, full of quiet jokes and caprices, never modifying his strong individuality in the smallest degree, never wasting a moment in conventional gambits when there was any chance of getting by a direct route at what he conceived to be essential, either in a subject or in a person.

His naturalness had set her at ease in the first hour of their intercourse. It spared her the least necessity of adopting an attitude, or groping towards a suitable system of decorum. Dr. Churchfield favoured no decorum that was not intrinsic. Artificial courtesies as a means of preserving a becoming distance between employer and employee would have been intensely tiresome to him: he neither offered them nor wanted them.

From the beginning he treated her without aloofness as an agreeable human being who had undertaken the performance of certain tasks for which she must get what she deserved, whether praise or blame. He was solicitous for her well-being, and his manner towards her was friendly to the point of intimacy. What method of keeping her at arm's length he would have used if she had so misjudged as to make her presence in his household obtrusive, she could not guess, but there was little doubt that it would be firm and unmistakable.

Fortunately the faculty of self-containment, which she had developed to an uncommon degree during her many years of exile, made it an extremely simple matter for her to live with others at close quarters and yet not to encroach upon their privacy. She had no tendency to take offence at imagined slights, and no touchy concern for her dignity, and since both her working hours and her leisure were very fully occupied, she knew nothing of that vacancy of mind which must be filled up by magnifying tiny causes of dissatisfaction. She was, in fact, a very contented woman, and by being contented she was likeable and easy to get on with.

Even the temperamental Mme Villard, though she had her dour humours, was on the whole kindly disposed to one who showed such intense respect for her proficiency and such willingness to learn from her; one moreover who understood the prestige of a gifted cook and did not put on any airs and graces when she came into the kitchen. Lucy had not embarked on her duties without feeling some trepidation as to her effect upon Mme Villard, whose disfavour would certainly have been an embarrassment, but having once entered into pleasant relations with a colleague so valuable she settled down comfortably to the full enjoyment of all the privileges that now fell to her lot.

After the arid wastes through which she had travelled so long, to walk and talk with Dr. Churchfield, to handle lovely and rare possessions, to savour the amenities and refinements of well-ordered home life, to be in contact, if only obliquely, with distinguished personalities—such an existence was only to be described in the time-worn imagery of the green oasis, where every cool refreshing pleasure is heightened by comparison with what has been endured.

At first it had the strangeness of a dream. She could not get used to the idea that this free and happy being, whose days slipped away in so many congenial employments, was really herself; that it was no longer her destiny to be always cast among aliens, or to be severed from everything that was most dear to her. When she closed her eyes in her snug little bedroom with its patchwork quilt, its glazed chintz curtains, its embroidered pictures, and the Bristol vases which were never empty of flowers, she was sometimes assailed by a wild temptation to rise quickly and turn on the light lest, taken unawares, she should find herself back in one of her Alexandrian lodging-houses.

And indeed this life would have had a dream-like quality even for one who had not known solitude and privation. The beauty of the house, the richness of its contents, its proximity to the magical gardens, the odd way in which it combined an atmosphere of peaceful seclusion with an atmosphere of sociability—here was an environment which must have been wonderful to anyone. It produced a curious sense of unreality, heightened—perhaps in part created—by the remote, fantastic music with which the doctor played as with a toy, and which came to seem like some soothing familiar spirit whose voice had influence upon his mood. Forgotten drawing-room ballads preserved in melodious tinklings, polkas and German waltzes scintillating brightly as fireworks, concert pieces thinned down to a ghostly echo of what they must have been, operatic arias distilled and crystallized—he used these pellucid airs as an accompaniment to thought, and there was scarcely a room in the house without its selection of musical boxes.

In this rarefied world time flowed gently for Lucy. The cold of February and March was so intense after the almost perpetual summer of Africa, that she put off her rediscovery of London until spring, seldom going out except for a brisk walk to one of the hothouses of Kew Gardens. It is easy to wait for what we know to be within reach, and with London only a few miles from her door she could well curb the nostalgia which had made her ache in Egypt. Not that she was altogether segregated. Dr. Churchfield would give her a lift to Constance's flat whenever he happened to be driving to town in the evening; and on her free days, muffled up like a member of some polar expedition, she would occasionally venture the journey by bus. So she was at least able to be fitted for her new clothes, and to wear them with satisfaction at Constance's spectacular 'opening', which came off, all the better for two postponements, towards the end of March.

At Easter, Dr. Churchfield's daughter, Laura, returned home for the holidays. She proved to be much as Lucy had imagined her on learning that she excelled at school in all intellectual activities and had spent about a third of her childhood in her father's house without ever breaking or damaging any article belonging to it: a quiet, self-possessed, and highly rational creature, not the intractable stuff from which geniuses are made, but pretty certain, one might guess, of following some academic pathway with sedate glory. She was so well read, so well informed, so free from anything known as schoolgirl nonsense, that Lucy was inclined to be a little afraid of her; but after a few days she began to reveal, besides an uncommon aptitude for cerebration, a great sweetness and simplicity of character.

Owing to her mother's death she had been sent to a boarding-school at the early age of six, and her holidays, with very few exceptions, having been spent in the house her father himself had christened 'Dr. Churchfield's Repository of Learned and Polite Amusements', her contact with the world had been so slight that she had retained a child's freshness of outlook. Her precocity of knowledge masked a most endearing *naïvete*, and as she had inherited her father's directness and unpretendingness, Lucy soon found herself on a very friendly footing with her.

Laura enjoyed Lucy's specially garnered reminiscences of far travels and unusual experiences, while Lucy, to be companionable, revived some kinds of reading and even study abandoned for ever, she had supposed, on leaving the vicarage of Market Rookestone: and so far from being oppressed by these acts of good nature, discovered that she was enriched by them. The weather growing more clement, they walked frequently in the Gardens, which Laura knew extremely well; and soon Lucy was taking an interest in the growth and flowering of individual plants, was conversant with the arrangement and principal features of every greenhouse, and had learned the graces of that pleasure-ground as they can never be known except to the familiar visitor. It was a pastime that continued to give her delight long after Laura's holiday was over: and this delight was not in any way abated by her stealthy recognition of an ulterior motive.

Chapter 32

It was no coincidence that brought about that meeting between Lucy and her long-lost Henry which, unless the author's plan has failed, the reader has long foreseen, and should be awaiting with some slight impatience. If the drama of a coincidence has been expected, there will be disappointment, for all that happened was that, when Lucy felt sufficiently 'set up', when she was assured that the last trace of her bondage had been quite effaced from her, she wrote Henry a letter.

It was May. She had been with Dr. Churchfield four months, living well, happy in her surroundings, interested in her work, pleased with her associates. She had been gathering pleasant kinds of knowledge, such as give one a sense of luxury to possess; through her intimacy with Constance she had seen something of a number of ornamental women whose deportment had an inspiring influence on her own; and, feeling safe in her job, she had used up for clothes a substantial part of the money still in hand. On Constance's dashing advice she had also taken long sessions with a hairdresser and was undergoing a course of beauty treatment which, if it wrought no very striking physical changes, was exceedingly valuable in its psychological effect. In short, she had reached a state of well-being in which it did not seem as if she would be at a disadvantage even beside Lord Redfarrow.

She therefore wrote to him in these long-meditated terms:

My dear Henry,

I wonder if the name at the end of this letter will still convey anything to you? If it doesn't, then cast your mind back to September 1917, when you were home on leave from France. That was the last time I saw you—to speak to. It was at the Trocadero, a dinner that ended in a quarrel. Do you begin to remember? I sailed for Australia.

Well, Henry, now I think you know who I am. And the *next* thing you'll want to know is—why am I suddenly writing to you after having been out of touch for fourteen years? It's quite simple. I've always had rather a hankering to see you again. I was very fond of you; I had a great friendship for you. But I couldn't have made any approach years ago, even if I'd had the chance, because it would have looked then as if I were trying to win you back and all that sort of thing. Now, after such a lapse of time, I think you may feel safe!

I've had the queerest life since we last met, you'll hardly believe it. I know everybody says their life story would make a book, but mine really would. Just imagine, for instance, that I was once so near to you I could almost have reached out my hand and touched you, and instead I went away and hid myself. That was in Alexandria in 1927. You were seeing *The Gold Rush*. It was one of the strangest moments of my life.

What about you? I'd like to hear all about you too if it wouldn't bore you to tell me. I've hesitated a lot about writing because you must be unutterably grand and lordly these days, and I'm still a wage-earning woman, but if I go on putting it off much longer, we shall never meet at all, and I do think that would be a pity. My suggestion is this: I understand you're living with your father at Nunsbourne (yes, I always read up the bits about our gardening marquess in the papers), and if so, you probably come to London quite often by car. Well, as the above address will tell you, I'm at Kew, and that's not much out of your way from Dorking. So, if you agree that it would be nice to meet, will you telephone me here the next time you're going to town, and we could take a walk in the gardens and do some chatting.

Thinking out a letter like this does bring back such a swarm of memories! Do you recollect the first time you sent me a basket of flowers (when I was playing in *The Lady with the Scarf*) and how the florist miscopied the name and it got handed up to the wrong person? I'd never had a bouquet at the theatre before, and I nearly wept—perhaps I did weep—after seeing it given among half a dozen others to the leading lady, with your card on it too! But mostly we were laughing. Do you remember those ridiculous notices we had printed and used to pin up surreptitiously in hotel bathrooms—please do not stand up in the bath—and how we used to picture the bewildered faces of people who didn't realize it was bogus? We did play some silly jokes.

I hope you'll want to answer this. It would be rather a sell if you didn't, but somehow I think you will.

Your always well-wishing

Lucy (Kendon)

P.S. Don't forget to expect me to be fourteen years older.

It was an artfully artless letter, and Lucy had few misgivings as to the results; for she knew that Henry had loved her dearly, and that only his numerous family complications and his dependence on his father and grandfather had prevented him from marrying her, and she did not really suppose for a moment that he would have any difficulty in recalling her to mind or would be otherwise than pleased with the prospect of seeing her again.

Not that she was so naïve as to presume he had treasured her memory with anything like such warmth and persistence of sentiment as she his. She was perfectly aware that his marriage, his children, the many duties imposed on him by his high social position, and all the other activities and interests of an exceptionally crowded life, must long ago have dimmed her image, and she had not ignored the strong likelihood of his having at this very time some other attachment. But when she considered what emotions and experiences they had shared, she could not but believe her letter would arouse at least his kindly curiosity. Their love affair had not been one of those which are ended through the satiety or sudden recoil of one of the parties, leaving behind a residue of distaste. It had come, owing to adverse circumstances, to an untimely close, and she was sure that Henry, for a little while at least, had regretted his stubbornness not less than she had regretted her anger. It was thus reasonable to take his good will for granted.

As to her motive in writing, it went only a little further than she had avowed. Her desire to see him again was naturally coupled with a desire to make the occasion of their meeting so successful that she might go on enjoying his friendship; and it was not without some intention of being able to appreciate a congenial subject that she had so eagerly found entertainment in Kew Gardens. But she cherished no fanciful ambitions. The idea of this approach had been slowly germinating for many weeks, during which she had not wasted one opportunity of reminding herself that he was busy, sought after, and certain to be bound by many ties closer than she could now ever hope to achieve. She asked for nothing better than that he might draw some pleasure from her company which would make it worth his while to seek it again. If any more romantic notion ever crossed her thoughts, she coldly and firmly discouraged it.

She felt convinced that he would answer her, and she was not mistaken. Three or four days passed, which she filled out with as many engrossing occupations as she could induce Dr. Churchfield to supply (for even without romantic notions the situation had its element of excitement); then she received, in a very large envelope with a very small coronet, a typical Henryish note, punctuated chiefly with dashes, and running aslant the page in spidery strokes that gave his most studied correspondence an air of reckless haste:

My dear Lucy,

How nice of you to write! Of course I'd like to see you again—I've often thought of you and wondered what had happened to you—When I didn't find your name in any of the programmes I pictured you married with heaps of offspring, etc. If not, why not? You'll have to explain all—Let's take a look at each other next Thursday. I'll go to Kew and wander round the Temperate House, the central part, between half-past three and four. I ought to call for you but the Temperate House is such an irresistible setting for a rendezvous. Can you find your way to it?

Yes, we had some good times. It'll be fun to meet.

Love,

Henry

N.B. Ring up Nunsbourne if Thursday won't do.

Nota Molto Bene. By the way, I must be about fourteen years older too.

Before keeping her engagement Lucy made a point of spending an evening with Constance, who had helped to inspire her with audacity; and together they investigated the errors most tempting to fall into at such a reunion and most diligently to be avoided. It was agreed in a cosy discussion over numerous cups of tea that she should not be too obviously sentimental lest, with his more casual outlook, he should feel embarrassed for her; that she should not indulge overmuch in reminiscence (it would be very easy, Constance suggested, for a long series of reminiscences to sound like a claim upon the present through the past), and that she should only enlighten him by degrees as to the hardships and misfortunes she had borne, the effect of the whole story conveyed at one hearing being likely to create depression and to obscure the air of cheerfulness and serenity which was now one of her greatest attractions. Lucy was glad that she had taken her clever and understanding friend into her confidence. There was great comfort in talking such a matter over, and she was sure she had benefited from Con's warning against too much reminiscence. It would have been a pitfall. There was so much to remember.

Yet when Thursday afternoon came and she walked between the brilliant flower-beds, past the miniature temples, and along the stately avenue of acacia trees, timing herself to reach the Temperate House at precisely a quarter to four, she felt almost unpleasantly cool. There is a wretched instability in the human nervous system which makes it difficult ever to achieve a correct balance of emotion except through retrospect; and after having been seriously disturbed by excitement all day, she had suddenly discovered while dressing that she was not excited in the least—that she was, in fact, slightly sickened by the whole business and could not imagine what all the fuss was about. It seemed to be someone else's fuss. Some other woman, of singularly fatuous disposition, was forcing upon her this exasperating ordeal. Yes, ordeal! How in the world she could ever have regarded it as something to be anticipated with delight, she could not now conceive. Henry, indeed! Who was Henry more than another man? He was a stranger about whom she knew nothing. The whole affair was nonsensical.

Nevertheless she had dressed and made up with meticulous care, and at the sight of herself wearing extremely well-chosen clothes, clothes rather bolder perhaps than she would have bought without Constance's urgings, and not to be worn negligently, but therefore so much the more tonic in their effect—at the sight of herself looking truly handsome and elegant, her faint revulsion was ameliorated to the extent that it became a mere dead calm, and it was in this condition that she stepped out of pale sunshine and chilly breezes into the warm, protective, exotically-laden air of the vast greenhouse.

Still maintaining the same becalmed demeanour, she wandered into the groves of luxuriant foliage, and saw without tasting either relief or regret that there was no one in sight who could by any possibility be Henry. She had already decided that in the event of being there first, she would go up to the gallery and watch for his approach, thus enabling herself to catch a steadying glimpse of him beforehand—for she had supposed she would be nervous. And because, without feeling any of yesterday's sensations, she was under a kind of numb compulsion to carry out yesterday's plans, she began to mount the embowered staircase.

She had hardly got beyond the first turn of the spiral when a very peculiar agitation took possession of her. Quite without any preliminary disquiet, she noticed that she was trembling. It occurred to her that some dreadful change would have taken place in Henry. That evening in Alexandria when she had rejoiced to see how benignly time had dealt with him had made so fortifying a memory that she had given little thought to what might have happened in the intervening four years. Now all her calm was overthrown by a nightmarish fancy. Henry coarsened beyond recognition, Henry with everything she had loved about him gone. . . .

Breathless, shaken, she emerged from the festooned windings of the stairway, and stood on a long, narrow platform hung with trading green, looking out upon the amazing vista of a thousand forms of sub-tropical plant-life mingled in apparently boundless exuberance. She paused with her hand on the rail, assailed by a momentary giddiness. Then she peered apprehensively down to what was discernible of the aisles.

'Well, my dear?' She wheeled round to face a tall, thin, distinguished-looking man whom she could not, in the complete vacuity of judgment imposed on her by shock, have described as either familiar or unfamiliar.

'Oh!' she gasped, 'how you startled me!'

'Did I? I'm so sorry! How idiotic of me!'

'You seemed to spring from nowhere.'

'Why, I thought you knew I was here. I thought that was why you'd come up.'

She forced herself to survey him with composure and saw that his smile was as timorous and uncertain as her own. It was a useful perception, for it put her on her mettle, and she was able to answer in a lighter and more animated tone: 'I came up to steal a march on you. I wanted to have a look at you without being looked at.'

'And I came up for precisely the same reason.'

She could have sworn, when she heard his not very spontaneous laugh, that he too was inwardly quivering, and she was moved by such a contrition for persuading him to undergo this trial that she had no other desire in the world than to put him at his ease. All her former care for the impression she would make on him, all her much-deliberated schemes for launching conversation, went out of her head. She turned away from him, staring over the tops of the fantastic trees, and heard herself saying: 'Oh, Henry, I'm so overcome with shyness . . . I find this absolutely nerve-racking, don't you?'

'Absolutely!' His voice sprang to life with the word.

'Well, don't let's speak for a few minutes. Let's just gaze at the view.'

They stood side by side, both grasping the rail and conscientiously inspecting the wonderful profusion of verdure displayed beneath them—the multitudes of flowering shrubs, the tree ferns like gigantic baskets of green feathers, the boldly sweeping fans and lances of the palms, the delicately fronded boughs of the mimosa, the sinister angularities of the monkey puzzle—and at last, from letting her eyes ramble over plants that crept, plants that drooped, plants that clung, and plants that reared themselves superbly to the roof, she stole a glance at Henry, and this time he was really smiling.

'An admirable spot this,' he said pleasantly. 'I ought to come much oftener. I suppose you never come at all. People always ignore the show-places that lie just outside their own front doors, don't they?'

'As a matter of fact, I come here nearly every day of my life.'

'Do you honestly? Why?'

'I like it here. I like the gardens—and I especially like the greenhouses,' she added cunningly.

He too assumed a certain slyness. 'Ah, now I begin to see why you got in touch with me.'

'You mean because you've become a greenhouse expert?'

'Yes, you're thinking of building one or something. It's greenhouses, not me, you're interested in?'

She could not help laughing to hear him so innocently putting the cart before the horse. 'So you imagine I've lured you into Kew Gardens for the sake of cribbing some valuable information about hot-house plants?'

'I shouldn't be at all surprised. You admit you've been reading about my exploits in the papers.'

'Your Nunsbourne triumphs? Yes, Henry, I couldn't refrain from writing to you when I heard you were the only man in England who had succeeded in growing the—what's it called?—the—'

'The Camellia Formosa. No, my dear, others have succeeded in *growing* it, but mine's the only plant that has flowered. So *that's* what you wanted to see?'

'You've hit the nail bang on the head,' she returned, and they looked at each other gaily and without constraint.

'It's nice up here among the tree-tops,' he said, 'but I think it'll improve matters if we go and have some tea, don't you?'

They traversed the platform and descended again to the conservatory. On their way Henry pointed with his stick to various rare ferns which he could duplicate at Nunsbourne, and seemed gratified when she responded with a knowledgeable interest.

'This place is full of my favourite smell,' he told her, pausing to breathe it in before they crossed the threshold. 'Do you know what it is?'

'I know what it used to be—fresh lavender. You used to carry little broken bits of it in your overcoat pockets and crush them in your fingers.'

'Did I?' He had the air of being pleased with the recollection, and lingered over it before going on: 'Well, my favourite smell now is wet moss. Isn't it good? Do you like it?'

'Yes, but it's not as nice as new-mown hay, Henry.'

'On the contrary, it's nicer—less hackneyed at any rate.'

They strolled towards the tea pavilion arguing the merits of their preferences—the scent of warm earth after a shower, or of pink hawthorn on the bough, the poignant fragrance of early jonquils, the aromatic breath of rose geranium—and while they talked, Lucy now took courage to consider Henry as Henry and not merely as an embarrassed gentleman whom she must humour and propitiate. She was glad she had had that brief opportunity of studying him in Alexandria. It bridged the gap of fourteen years so smoothly that the deepening ruddiness of his cheeks, the crows-feet round his eyes, and the tiny shadows of sunken contours about his nose and chin were changes she already began to take for granted: and the sadness of having to acknowledge that Henry had grown distinctly older was quite lost in the pleasure of observing that he was as attractive a man of forty-odd as it would be possible to desire. She wished indeed he could have been as suitably prepared for the alteration in her own person. Still, on this score she would not allow herself to be unduly concerned. She was confident by now that she was a good-looking and graceful woman, and she relied upon it that, after he had got used to the idea of her being no longer the girl of twenty-five he had parted with in his youth, he would judge her appearance on its merits and not find it wanting. So it was chiefly towards agreeableness of manner that she directed her efforts.

But by the time they were debating whether it was warm enough to sit out of doors for tea, she was not conscious even of her manner. Henry's own was so unchanged and after those few awkward moments in the gallery he had slipped so naturally into a kind of detached intimacy, that artifice would only have been tiresome. It was charming to discover how much he had remained himself. That peculiar inconsistency, for example, between what he said and how he said it—how he laid down the law with the utmost possible diffidence of address; and that alertness of interest which made him attend so carefully to one's smallest communications; and again, a certain searching literal-mindedness, partly exercised in fun, with which he caught up one's insincerities and exaggerations—there was so much of the old Henry, well known, thoroughly understood, in all these qualities, that by degrees she ceased to tell herself, 'How strange! He is just what he was!' and would have been surprised to find him different.

They were some time in arranging themselves at the tea-table. At first it seemed too cold for the open air, and they went into the kiosk. Then the sun shone out more brightly and they moved back into the garden, where the breeze instantly compelled them to change their table. But at last they had agreed upon a spot exposed to the sun, yet sheltered from the breeze; and Henry had assured her, with the most scrupulous politeness, that white bread and butter was the worst thing she could eat, and had prevailed upon her to try brown toast, and they settled down comfortably to talk.

'What's all this about your seeing me at the movies in Alexandria? Why on earth didn't you speak to me?'

'You were in a party.'

'What difference does that make? You ought to have spoken to me, whomever I was with. You know I'd have liked to see you.'

'I didn't think you would—that night.' It was very curious to discover that she was almost enjoying the remembrance of her humiliation, so delightful was the present contrast.

'You were sensitive about my wife,' he suggested gravely. 'That was very sweet of you, but really unnecessary. Esme was—oh, not the sort of wife one would conceal one's old friends from. She was awfully nice, Lucy.'

'I always felt she was. I liked the way she laughed at the picture.' Lucy's voice swerved away as she recalled that envying moment.

'Were you as near as that?'

'For a few seconds. I went into the circle specially to look at you. Not to spin it out, Henry, I was a clerk in the box-office. What's more, I was such a very shoddy specimen of a box-office clerk that, if I'd really hailed you as my old friend, I believe you'd have fallen into a swoon.'

'My poor Lucy!' Bewilderment and distress drew heavier lines upon his face, and she ran on swiftly to get the painful explanation over.

'I had typhoid fever in Egypt and lost my voice, and got stranded. I was there years and years—through no fault of my own. I only came home at the beginning of this year.'

'Lucy! This is—this is—My dear! Why didn't you let me know?'

It was worth a good deal of suffering to hear him say that—to be told in these few casual words that he had always counted himself her friend.

'Well, you see,' she answered at a much sedater pace, 'it was very soon after you got married, Henry. It would have looked rather squalid, I thought, after that quarrel of ours and—oh, you know what I mean . . . sort of badgering you for money. You'd have felt you were never going to get rid of me.'

'I never wanted to get rid of you,' he said gently.

'I knew you didn't at the time of our quarrel'—it was astonishing how easy it was to speak freely even about matters which had once profoundly affected their emotions—'but later, when we'd actually drifted apart—'

'I never wanted to be rid of you,' he repeated.

She made a close examination of her teaspoon. 'I mean—when you were married, quite newly married, it would have been tactless—'

He interrupted a little irritably. 'I wasn't always newly married, and you say you were stranded for years.'

'Yes, but—well, it's a long tale. I'll tell it some other day when you're in the mood to be harrowed.' She. looked back over all the times she had rehearsed this interview in her mind, and reflected that never once had she foreseen how, within the first half-hour, she would be thus coolly premising another meeting. Yet now it seemed the most natural prospect in the world, and she was sure that Henry accepted it not less readily.

'I'd like to hear about *you*,' she said. 'Things have changed a lot for you since we last met. I didn't know till that night in Alex that you'd lost your brother.'

'Didn't you? His death was very widely reported.'

'Yes, but I wasn't reading the English news much at that time. It made me homesick.'

'He died in South America. It was all a most tragic business. My father has never really recovered from the blow. It was so *unlike* Dicky to go off on a madcap adventure of that kind.' He sighed and fidgeted, then said rather fretfully: 'I always feel so guilty, Lucy, having improved my position at the expense of my brother's death. Isn't it a wretched state of affairs?'

She took time for thought and answered seriously: 'I don't see that it would make it any better if it had been just a plain evil without a redeeming feature. Your family must have been glad that you and your sons were there to carry on. And you should be glad too, Henry. It would have been hard if the title had had to die out.'

'No, it would have gone to my Uncle Geoffrey.'

'And a nice thing that would have been.'

He laughed. 'So you remember my Uncle Geoffrey, do you?'

'Certainly.'

'He's quietened down considerably in the last few years. I suppose you used to be pretty well-informed about my family, Lucy. I made a practice of running to you with all my difficulties.'

'I made a practice of running to you with mine.'

'How we loved each other!' he said musingly.

'You haven't forgotten?'

'No, it was not the kind of love one forgets. Of course,' he added with his usual accuracy, 'one forgets a certain amount. We've both forgotten a lot, I dare say. But speaking for myself, I've always kept just enough to be sure it was my best experience of that—well, you know what I mean—magic.'

'So have I,' said Lucy in the same carefully matter-of-fact voice. Constance's warning against sentimentalizing rang in her ears, and she dared not show him how much her heart was moved.

'It was good to hear from you again. Mind you, I was very nervous about the meeting beforehand. I knew it would be worth while once we'd broken the ice, but I thought that was going to be a long job.'

'Funny how quickly it broke up there on that queer balcony,' she rejoined. 'I'd been working out all sorts of things to say—lines of talk that would help us over the bad patch—'

'So had I! But my great problem was how I was going to greet you—whether to be distant or intimate, and I was so afraid you'd be visibly disappointed in me.'

'But how? How could I be?'

'Well, the way I've aged.'

'Why, my dear, you must be crazy—you must be positively crazy, Henry! I think you're looking wonderful!'

'My hair's beginning to get thin. Thank goodness, though, it's going on the temples, not on the crown. I'd hate that! There's a popular fiction that women worry about growing older and men don't. It's utterly untrue nowadays. The boot's on the other foot. Women are up to all kinds of dodges to keep young, and men are still obliged to rely on nature.'

'Nature hasn't done so badly by you, Henry.'

'If it comes to that, you've got something to be grateful for too. Let me look at you. Take off your hat so that I can see your hair.'

'I'd rather do that when I've got a comb and a glass.'

'It's still the same lovely colour judging from what shows under your hat.'

Lucy accepted the compliment a trifle uneasily, though she was grateful for the skill of her hairdresser.

'I was hoping,' she said, 'that you'd forget what I used to look like and just consider me as physically a new person.'

'That's what is happening. It happens automatically, don't you find, when one meets old friends after a lapse of years? At first the changes in them are surprising, then one simply loses one's memory of what they looked like before. You're a very nice new person, Lucy.' He smiled benevolently at her.

All was well between them. Relaxed and contented, she responded to his questions about her present mode of life. Relaxed and contented, she listened to him expounding his system of improvements on his father's estates. She described the method by which she catalogued Dr. Churchfield's collections; he speculated whether it would be a useful mode of dealing with the contents of his famous glasshouses. Then—as if they had nothing else to talk about, or rather as if they had all time in which to talk about everything—she inquired into the nature of the existing catalogues, and was amused to notice how, in exemplifying, he assumed that she was conversant with the geography of Nunsbourne.

When he asked her whether she thought he had done well in substituting orchid houses for the old vinery, she checked him: 'My dear Henry, I never was at Nunsbourne in my life,' and in response to his expression of almost incredulous astonishment she protested good-humouredly, 'You don't recollect the difficulties. You wanted to take me, but your grandfather was in residence in those days, and he wasn't at all sympathetic to your *penchant* for actresses. You had various ideas of smuggling me in or passing me off as a respectable clergyman's daughter, which I was, and denying the theatrical stigma; but I stood on my dignity and wouldn't go. I've often regretted it.'

'What a shame! I must have been a feeble sort of creature to mismanage things like that. How could you put up with me?'

'No,' she said sturdily, 'you weren't feeble. There really were enormous obstacles. Your grandfather was liable to get a seizure if anyone upset him.'

Henry chuckled ruefully. 'Oh, God, yes! Didn't the old boy play us up for years with that perpetual threat of a seizure! In the end he died of pneumonia at the age of eighty-five.'

The conversation was suspended while he paid the bill and bought some cigarettes, then they sauntered along the avenue called Pagoda Vista.

'We must definitely right this wrong about Nunsbourne,' he said earnestly. 'I should so much like to take you over the place.'

She wanted to tell him how enchanting it was to see his long fingers carrying a cigarette to his lips with precisely the same neat, deliberate gesture she had always, quite unreasonably, loved him for, but this was clearly a case for acting upon Constance's advice, and she desisted.

'You must come for a week-end,' Henry went on. 'Will your Dr. Churchfield let you do that?'

'A whole week-end wouldn't be very convenient for him, I'm afraid. We work quite hard on Saturdays. I get more spare time during the week.'

'Come during the week then and stay the night.'

'Is it permissible nowadays?'

'Most decidedly. There's a great difference nowadays, Lucy. A man of forty, you know, with two growing sons, is allowed to choose his own friends. Besides, my father isn't nearly such a martinet as my grandfather was. As a matter of fact, I've got a feeling that he'd like you very much. You must see my boys too.'

'Oh, I'd love that,' cried Lucy. 'I didn't realize they were at Nunsbourne.'

'Yes, they're too young for school yet. Ricky's going next term, though. He'll be nine.'

Lucy was beginning to put eager maternal questions when Henry cut her short. 'Look here, why can't we go down today—now? Could you get away? My car's parked on Kew Green, and while you're dropping a few things into a bag, I can ring up and say I'm bringing another visitor.'

'Another? Have you got masses of them, Henry?'

'No, no, we're very quiet except at week-ends, but there are generally two or three odd people knocking about. Not anyone you wouldn't care for, Lucy. Do come! It would be such fun.'

'I'm very, very tempted,' she exclaimed. 'It's a lovely opportunity. I wonder whether Dr. Churchfield would mind my going. Oh, Henry, if you want to do something kind for me, do come and ask him. . . . He would so appreciate the courtesy.'

Henry willingly consented, and they quickened their pace and went towards the gates. Lucy was immeasurably happy, so happy that she knew herself to be capable of imparting happiness. She was sure of enjoyment, sure of success, and her only regret was that she could not immediately make her dear friend Constance aware how perfectly everything had turned out and how tonight she would be wearing her grand *toilette* at Nunsbourne.

Chapter 33

Those who are squeamish about happy endings had better spare themselves the displeasure of continuing, which they may do without compunction since the end is certainly now as plain as daylight. But for those others who, like the author, feel an obligation to finish off what they have begun, there will have to be some delicate steering if the barque is not to perish 'overwhelmed by favouring gales'.

Navigation in such shallow waters as these is no easy science. On the one hand, disguised by a luscious exuberance of vegetation, lies a dangerous reef; on the other a barren and sandy coast. So that, if to escape a cloying profusion of beatitudes, we venture on the opposite course and hurry into a series of bald statements, it is probable that we shall run aground upon very dry land. Since, however, some risk appears to be inherent in the very nature of the voyage undertaken, and since the author does not feel sufficient confidence in her skill to promise avoidance of both the threatened perils, she has deliberately chosen the latter, holding that to run aground is at least a method—though admittedly a rather discreditable one—of bringing one's company to shore.

Turning most resolutely from all temptations to luxuriance we shall make a bold and unimpeded progress towards the last chapters, taking care to set forth only those facts that are material.

Let it then be related with austere conciseness that Henry was not involved in any other attachment at the time of Lucy's approach to him, and it was therefore so much the easier for him to become attracted again to her; and since she offered him all the peace and security of friendship with all the charm of romantic associations, it was natural that his revived devotion should soon grow possessive. He was discussing plans for marrying her a very few weeks after their reunion, but it was considerably more than a year before the wedding actually took place. There were many preparations to be made and many little Rubicons to be crossed before she could feel able to do justice to so great a match and certain of being comfortably accepted in Henry's world.

Although at forty-one, with two sons to ensure succession, Henry was no longer dependent upon the approval of his father, they were agreed that it would be desirable to let him feel his wishes were being consulted. Months were spent in gradually inuring the old duke to the idea of the marriage, and in winning for Lucy the affection of Henry's children. In the meantime she was being familiarized very thoroughly with all the splendours of Nunsbourne in the country and Felix House in London, and was learning much about domestic management on a noble scale, besides being initiated into a variety of social functions. And such diplomacy did Henry use that there was scarcely one step in her progress which failed to lead smoothly and yieldingly on to the next, nor a single vexation which was not outweighed by the attendant gain.

Until the autumn she continued to live and work with Dr. Churchfield, who treated Henry with a cordiality that removed all embarrassment from her position—indeed his house and his music provided her with as delightful a background as she could have wished for—but when their marriage had shaped itself out as a definite prospect, it became necessary for her to spend more than her leisure time in apprenticeship, and she allowed Henry to make arrangements for her to share a flat in Belgrave Square with two distant cousins of his whose means were not quite equal to their station.

They were married in the September of 1932. The wedding was a very quiet one, for the old duke's health was too precarious to justify a public ceremony; but Lucy nevertheless indulged in the enormous luxury of equipping herself with a trousseau so magnificent that the firm of Constance Leloir was quite set up by the transaction, and made a vast move forward on the strength of it. It was, in fact, such a trousseau, as not only had Lucy never dreamed of possessing, but—which says much more—as Constance and Roger in their most sanguine visions had never dreamed of supplying. They rose to the occasion, however, with a skill which made it hardly extravagant for them to prophesy that, if appearances counted for anything at all, their client was destined to be one of the most charming figures in society.

Lucy did not long keep the title of Marchioness of Redfarrow. After eight months, during which they were obliged to live a somewhat secluded life, Henry's father died, and Henry became Duke of Surrey. By this time Lucy's orientation was complete. She was, as it had always been her pride to reflect, a very capable woman, and her singular career had fitted her to be a most admirable duchess.

To begin with, her breeding had been good and her birth not such as could attract any sensation-seeking notice to Henry's alliance with her. Then, as the result of her years of work on the stage, she had acquired a poise, a freedom from nervous mannerisms, which gave her distinction in any assembly: and though she was never eloquent, she was quite effectively able to deliver a few words at a prizegiving, a sale of work, or the inauguration of a charitable committee. As for her experiences in Egypt, they had produced a degree of adaptability far greater than nature had originally bestowed on her; they had increased the range of her sympathies and strengthened her inherent firmness, and had brought her, besides, some valuable incidental advantages, from a proficiency in handling many diverse duties to a skill in languages which made her seem a woman of polished education. Finally, her sojourn with Dr. Churchfield had afforded her, more obviously, an excellent elementary training for the station and responsibility she now assumed. The miniature elegances of his house and style of living had very neatly paved the way for the grandeurs of her new domain, and she had learned, among his fashion plates and obelisks and musical boxes, an attitude which made it certain that she would be a sound custodian for the treasures of Henry's ancestral palaces.

In brief, it was doubtful if there was any duchess in England who could perform her part with a better grace, and certainly there was none happier. When she looked back, as she often did, upon the hardships of her past, she could not but marvel to think how much they had directly contributed to her present well-being. It was not merely that she had come by a wealth of practical knowledge formerly outside her scope, or even that her appreciation had a finer edge for having so long been given little to feed upon, but that Henry himself—her darling, clever, kind, congenial Henry—would never have been hers without that miserable array of circumstances which had combined, by diverting her life from any direction it might normally have been expected to follow, to keep alive and green a love it had once seemed wiser to forget. She was too much a realist to doubt that, if she had continued on the stage, other affections, passions, excitements, interests, would have overlaid her memories of him, and though a residue of sentiment must always have lingered, it would not have been strong enough to bring her back to him. As it was, in want and loneliness, her emotions had been preserved as flowers are sometimes strangely preserved in ice; and so it had come about that there was hardly an episode in all her exile too sorrowful to be contemplated now with gratitude.

Chapter 34

Mr. and Mrs. Siegfried Mosenthal, accompanied by their daughter Selma, and their close friend Mr. Jesus Paulos—accompanied also by two secretaries, a maid, and a valet, as well as their chauffeur and their favourite car—arrived in England some little time before the Coronation of King George VI, and rented, at a monstrous figure, a house in one of the streets adjoining Grosvenor Square.

Here for several weeks Daisy submitted herself to a torment resembling, in essence, that of Tantalus. Every magazine and newspaper she picked up told her that this was the most brilliant season London had ever enjoyed, every social column was a galaxy of illustrious names, and the theatres and restaurants were full of interesting-looking people some of whom might be, while others undoubtedly were, celebrities of exalted eminence. Yet these sights and glowing reports served only to remind her how much she was out of things. So far as her personal activities were concerned, there was nothing about this season to distinguish it from any other—nothing, that is to say, except the fact that she was intensely inconvenienced by traffic blocks and moved in swarming crowds through streets disfigured by half-built grandstands. The stately receptions, the splendid balls, the luncheon and dinner parties which provided the gossip writers with such a wealth of affable chit-chat were going on for the most part precisely as if she had no existence. And—here was her torment—she was under an irresistible compulsion to know all she could of what she was missing; nor, few and distant though her glimpses of bliss might be, would she have consented for any inducement to be away from London at such a time as this.

For Daisy, valiantly as ever, still pursued the fashionable world, which still beckoned her on and fled from her. Perhaps if she had been completely excluded, perhaps if she had never been allowed to taste a victory, she might have recognized the emptiness of her quest and turned her great resources and her eager energy upon some effort to lead a useful life, but it had been her misfortune always to get within her grasp just enough to make her impatient for more; and then always to find more denied to her.

And now, though she continued to take her defeats gallantly and to enjoy her little triumphs beyond their worth, there was a suggestion of tension in her struggle. The children would soon be growing up, and she had little better to offer them in the way of an assured social position than at the time of their birth. Siegfried remained a generous and indulgent husband, but he had begun to show that he had no faith in her ambitions, he had begun to make fun of her in something different from that old affectionately bantering style which had really been a mask for admiration. It was hopeless to talk to him nowadays about her great plans for the children's future: and since, with one not wholly satisfactory exception, she had no other confidant, she was often wearifully lonely.

Her circle consisted either of fashionable acquaintances or sycophants, the superior people whom she courted and the inferior people who courted her. There was no one with whom she stood upon equal terms, no one whom she trusted and revealed herself to, no one outside her children whom she loved. Indeed, such a dearth of intimacies had she unwittingly brought upon herself that she had come at last to be quite glad of the companionship of Chappie. It was if anything a point in his favour now that he had known her at a freer and easier period of her life. She had learned by this time that it was a bad policy to try to hide what she had been, and she had also, by the process that came so naturally to her, succeeded years ago in clothing that part of the past, like every other, in a roseate mist. So that

Chappie's slight association with her theatrical days was no longer a potential humiliation but a pleasant link.

Of the tribe of sycophants he was by far the most useful and reliable, and the only one who happened to be accepted readily by Siegfried. When her nerves were frayed from the realization of some blunder, his tireless flatteries were very comforting; he would put himself to unlimited trouble to oblige any member of the family, and he asked for nothing, absolutely nothing, but a few tips about the market and the glory of being in their company. Even Siegfried, scornful as he was and suspicious of the motives of all flatterers, had grown to appreciate the value of having someone about his house who combined the deference of a lackey with the zealous personal interest of a friend.

Siegfried, in fact, had taken lordly possession of Chappie, and was turning him by degrees into almost a permanent inmate of their household. And Daisy no longer felt ashamed of him and thrust him into the background when she entertained notable personages, for she had discovered that, by presenting him as a collector of perfumes and an expert with a fund of rare knowledge, she could actually make him something of an asset. In Alexandria she frequently succeeded in getting distinguished visitors to go and see his collection with her—first making it a condition, however, that he would refrain from offering them silk stockings.

Still, though Chappie had acquired a value and greatly improved his footing, he could not be regarded as an equal. He was essentially a toady, and she could only give him a very patronizing friendship and a superficial species of confidence. She could not tell him her grievances against Siegfried, for instance.

She could not, alas, tell anyone her grievances against Siegfried, least of all himself. Yet she considered him to blame, one way and another, for all her disappointments. His total want of charm of manner; his foolish insistence on living in Egypt, a country where the English colony was so disgustingly snobbish and where his wonderful financial career had always failed to bring him the respect it deserved; and those vulgar family connections which he seemed to bring more and more into evidence the richer he grew . . . how could any woman be expected to make headway in society with such appalling handicaps? And then to scoff at her for her failures—he who was the cause of them!

She was commiserating with herself in this vein one morning after he had been, as she thought, particularly derisive, when her eye was caught by two or three paragraphs in the tantalizing section of one of her journals.

The Duchess of Surrey, she read, was very sensibly holding her ball at Felix House rather earlier than most of the other great functions of the season, so as to avoid adding one more item to the congested programme of Coronation week. Extensive preparations were now on foot at the famous mansion in Surrey Gardens; the entire floral decorations would be sent from the duke's celebrated greenhouses at Nunsbourne and arranged under his personal supervision: the central stairway was to be lined with rare orchids. The writer then threw out a few adulatory details about the duke's lineage and estates and ended with a somewhat irrelevant anecdote of his two sons, the young Marquess of Redfarrow and Lord Edmund Felix, both at Eton.

Daisy gave these comments very earnest attention. In truth, she attended to little else for an hour or more. Then, thinking balefully of Siegfried and tenderly of her son Maurice, who must be just about the same age as the elder of his noble schoolfellows, she made some references to a book of etiquette and drafted the following highly disingenuous letter to the Duke of Surrey:

Dear Duke,

I really feel I am taking a very great liberty in writing to you, and I do hope you won't find it an awful nuisance at such a busy time. I had the pleasure of entertaining you several years ago in Cairo, when you were kind enough to give us some most useful advice about our garden. You came to our house with Lord and Lady Blanchess and we also saw you once or twice elsewhere. You told us then to let you know when we were in England, but I'm afraid we were never brave enough to do so.

Now we have come over for the Coronation but unfortunately, living abroad as we do, we feel rather left behind on such an occasion as this. I know it is a complete breach of etiquette to suggest it, and I have been a long time working up the necessary courage, but I wonder if, by any possible chance, you could induce the duchess to send us an invitation to your dance. I would never dream of putting such a request to you if I lived in England, but when one is mostly abroad, one loses touch with people and things over here, and then one must make the first approaches or remain out of things altogether.

I have never had the honour of meeting the duchess, otherwise of course I would write to her direct. I do sincerely trust this won't be a great bother to her.

We have with us a Mr. Paulos whom you may have heard of when in Egypt. He is a great authority on perfumes and a most interesting man. I believe he entertained a relative of yours, Lady Geoffrey Felix, when she was in Egypt many years ago. If the duchess could see her way clear to include him in the invitation, it would be so kind.

With good wishes and pleasant remembrances of your visit to Egypt,

Yours sincerely,

Daisy Mosenthal

By the way, my son, who is at school with your two boys, speaks most admiringly of them.

Lucy was having coffee and rolls in bed when Henry came into her room and, with a deliberately nonchalant movement, dropped this letter on to her breakfast tray.

'Isn't that your faithful old friend?'

She looked at the signature incredulously, then read with amazement the words above it. 'Henry,' she cried, 'it's a joke! It isn't possible!'

She stared at the paper and the handwriting, then read again, and slowly allowed herself to be convinced. 'How absolutely astonishing! It really is Daisy, and she doesn't know about me!'

'Are you sure? Isn't this some ruse of hers? It's hard to see how you could have been married to me for nearly five years without her hearing of it.'

'No, I was always quite certain, my dear, that she hadn't heard of it. If she'd found out how much I've gone up in the world, she'd have tried to make peace with me long ago.'

'Well, she might have missed the announcement of the wedding—that's quite probable since we got married so quietly—but what about your photographs in the papers?'

'My dear boy, she's not a detective. Studio portraits of the Duchess of Surrey all decked out in peeress's robes and diamond tiaras and pearl *colliers* don't look a bit like Lucy Kendon living on a small weekly wage in Egypt. Supposing she did see some resemblance, she'd never assume that it was me.'

'That it was *I*,' he corrected her softly.

'That it was I, then, you—you Henryish creature! As a matter of fact, she could even have seen the announcement in the Press without realizing that I was the person concerned. Honoria Lucy, daughter of the Rev. Jerome Kane Kendon—she might have read that in an absent sort of way and not connected it with me at all.'

'I suppose that's so. Come to think of it, if she wanted to get in touch with you, why should she adopt such a humiliating method?' He picked up the letter again and ran his long forefinger delicately round the edges of the paper. 'What do I do? Write back telling her that I regret no further invitations can be issued?'

'Oh, no, Henry, no! Let me have my fun! How could you bear to deprive me of the pleasure of seeing their faces?'

'You want your enemies delivered into your hand, do you?'

'It isn't that. You know I won't treat them discourteously, but, darling, I'd just like to see their faces. It's only natural, surely?'

'It's *far* from natural for me to have such people under my roof, Lucy. I wish you wouldn't ask me to. I bear a deep grudge against the Mosenthals as you perfectly well know.'

She set aside the tray, and pulling him down to the bed, laid her arm round his neck. 'Don't bear a grudge against them! I haven't any. I'm grateful to them. I'm grateful to Chappie Paulos. Suppose he'd lent me that money I tried to borrow from him? Suppose Mosenthal had shipped me straight back to England? Suppose Daisy had stood by me? Where and what should I be now?'

He drew himself gently away. 'Darling, I'd honestly rather you didn't receive that wretched woman.'

'Henry, you don't understand what a sacrifice you're asking of me. Have you no sense of drama?'

'None whatever.'

She sighed. 'It would have been such a gathering of the clans. The Prince-Carters are coming.'

'I can't see why on earth you invited them.'

'To give them an enjoyable evening, my dear, and for no other reason. And if they can have the pleasure of cutting the Mosenthals, that'll make it more enjoyable still.'

'And what about the Mosenthals—how will they like it?'

'Well, they'll be able to cut the Prince-Carters. Oh, darling, I swear they'll be glad to come at any price. Don't do them out of such a treat, please!'

'Treat forsooth!'

'But it will be. You're too well-bred, Henry. You don't understand how people love being able to say that they knew a duchess when she hadn't a rag to her back.'

'You're an altruist if that's the sort of pleasure you want to give them.'

She met his ruefully speculative glance with an exultant smile. 'I can afford to be an altruist. And it isn't only altruism. I want to show off.'

'I'm glad you've had the grace to admit that, anyhow.'

'Henry, don't look so gloomily at me! Listen, sweetheart, if you haven't got a sense of drama, would you mind trying to have a sense of fairness? There'll be I don't know how many hundreds of people at our ball, and nearly all of them will belong to you—your friends, your relations, your acquaintances, your world. I don't think you ought to put your foot down on my giving just a few invitations on my own account.'

Henry stared at himself lugubriously in the glass of the dressing-table. 'Well,' he said at last, 'if you put it like that . . . But there's one condition I do make. If I'm polite to the Mosenthals at our ball, it's the last time I *shall* be polite to them, so it's no use letting that woman wheedle herself into your friendship again.' He went back to the bedside and, taking her hand, continued earnestly: 'You're ridiculously good-natured, Lucy, and I believe if she tries to get round you, and grows sentimental about old times and all that sort of thing, you'll cave in before you know where you are.'

'I won't. I hated old times—*those* old times anyway.'

'Then don't lose sight of the fact, my dear, because I do warn you—and I'm quite serious—that I *will* not tolerate your having anything to do with the Mosenthals after the night of the dance.'

'Henry, I adore you when you're masterful! You do it so beautifully.'

'Do you promise to keep those Mosenthals at arm's length?'

'I promise.'

'In that case,' he rejoined in a sudden access of gaiety, 'I can kiss you.'

'By the way,' she inquired when he was combing his rumpled hair at the mirror, 'did you really ask her to let you know when she came to England?'

'Most unlikely, I should think—or perhaps it was one of those things one says to help one to get away when one's desperately short of anything to say at all.' He glanced again at the letter. 'It's an artful bit of work, isn't it, but it doesn't quite come off. I hate this touch about her son admiring ours, don't you? Have our boys ever mentioned this young Mosenthal?'

'Never.'

'Good. I'm sure the admiration is a pure invention. Nasty woman!'

Waving Daisy's writing paper in a cheerful valedictory gesture, he returned to his morning council with his secretary. Lucy sank down luxuriously into the bed, and closed her eyes. She loved it when he called his children 'our boys': that was the only make-believe she needed.

CHAPTER 35

AS DAISY walked at a stately pace up the magnificent staircase that led to the drawing-room suite at Felix House, she could not but feel extraordinarily elated. The ducal invitation was a feather in her cap, there was no doubt about that, the very finest feather she had ever been able to put there. Chappie was candidly awe-stricken, and as for Siegfried, he might scoff and pretend he didn't care whether she accepted on his behalf or not, but he had been perceptibly impressed all the same. And now that they were actually inside the house, now that they were actors upon a scene which had the splendour of an opulent film interior enriched by that inimitable quality only to be derived from time and wisdom and respect, he might wear his I-could-buy-them-and-sell-them smile as persistently as he liked, but he must be aware in his heart that it was not carrying much conviction.

She glanced round to see what sort of figure he was cutting and was not displeased. At fifty-six he had an appearance of some distinction. Baldness suited him and gave to his fine Jewish profile a suggestion of Roman antiquity; the pallor which had looked unhealthy in his younger days was now in keeping; and his black eyes had not lost their arresting keenness. He was stout, but, like many men of his build, he could wear evening dress with dignity.

Yes, he did very well. Chappie, on the other hand, was positively at his worst. Nervousness had a deplorable effect upon him. He made fussy and unnecessary little gestures, compressed his lips to hideous invisibility, and fidgeted with his few vestiges of grey hair until they stuck out round his head in ludicrous wisps. She was grateful that in such a press of people so small and insignificant a man would attract little notice.

'Smooth down your hair, Chappie,' she whispered as they came to the top of the stairs. She managed to say it almost without moving her lips and certainly without disturbing the perfect complacency of her features, which she had settled to a beautiful repose, for, though it was eighteen years since she had left the stage, she had not forgotten how to make a good entrance. She paused among the throng on the great landing, and adjusted her skirt and her scarf while a number of people who had gone up before them passed into the drawing-room. She heard their names being announced with a fine ringing flourish, but the doorway was too crowded for her to see their progress. 'Mr. and Mrs. Frank Tanbridge' . . . that would be the playwright and his wife; she had once sat next to him at dinner. 'Lord and Lady Chartley' . . . now what were they known for? Was it racehorses? 'M. and Mme Roger Leloir' . . . oh, that was surely the couple who had become so wildly fashionable as dress designers! Queer—one wouldn't exactly have expected to see people who sold clothes at a duchess's ball, but of course there was a great deal of latitude nowadays. One must not be a snob.

Now it was their turn. She stepped forward, having made sure that her convoy was properly marshalled behind her, breathed a just audible appeal to Chappie to pull down his waistcoat, and, murmuring their names into a respectfully proffered ear, sailed graciously towards the place of reception.

A hand was outstretched to her, a face was smiling blandly into hers—a face she recognized with unbelieving eyes. . . . A voice was saying, 'Hallo, Daisy! How nice you're looking!' She knew that she was turning white, that she had lost control for a moment of her expression. She heard herself say 'Lucy!' with a gasp that sounded as if she had been struck.

'Good evening, Mr. Mosenthal! How d'you do? And how are you, Mr. Paulos?' With the utmost suavity that astonishing, incredible figure was shaking hands, first with Siegfried, who had the stolidly enduring air of a man compelled to bear with fortitude some extremely oppressive practical joke, and then with Chappie, who stood plainly agape like one who has lost his senses and sees no reason to conceal the fact.

'You've all met my husband, I think. Oh, no—Mr. Paulos hasn't. Henry, this is Mr. Paulos. Of course you'll remember Mr. and Mrs. Mosenthal.'

The duke came forward and bowed with marked formality.

Though the names of the next comers had already been announced and it was time for her to go forward, Daisy remained as if transfixed. She could not find any phrase upon which to make an exit, her heart was beating painfully, and her amazed eyes seemed unable to relinquish their investigation.

'The ballroom,' said Lucy, 'is through the little ante-room at the end of this. Constance, you're deputy hostess this evening.' She turned swiftly to a strikingly elegant, graceful woman who was standing beside the duke. 'Do show Mr. and Mrs. Mosenthal their way to the ballroom. This is Mme Leloir.'

The request and the introduction were made with such rapidity and practised ease that Daisy's stupefied party were being led from the room before they had time to realize they were being dismissed.

Mme Leloir did not speak to them beyond what few words were necessary to indicate the required direction, but seemed in haste to get back to her companions. Daisy was relieved. She had sustained an overwhelming shock and could not have taken part in an exchange of small talk at that instant for any imaginable reward. She stopped near the doorway leading to the ballroom, trying to collect her violently scattered senses while one prodigious and inscrutable truth impressed itself deeper and deeper upon such intelligence as she could command. Lucy was that woman—that woman wearing a tiara and a glittering *rivière*! That woman who called a duke her husband was Lucy! Her shabby out-at-elbows friend! It was like coming upon a ghost.

'Did you see what I saw?'

Chappie's attempt at facetiousness exasperated her profoundly.

'What could have happened?' she stammered. 'Oh, where's Siegfried? What could have happened?' She felt an agitation, a pressure of curiosity, that amounted to fear.

'It seems like that ex-pal of yours must have done pretty well for herself,' Chappie went on with gathering jocosity. 'She must have had hidden charms, eh? I have to admit I wouldn't have known her if you hadn't called each other by name. My word!' He rubbed his hair distractedly. 'It was a bit of an eye-opener finding her all got up like that. Anyone could have knocked *you* down with a feather—that was easy enough to see.'

Daisy turned from him with increasing disgust. The word 'ex-pal' grated on her intensely; and it was no pleasure to be informed that her surprise had been patent to everyone. She was glad to notice Siegfried, whom for a moment or two she had lost sight of, threading his way to them from a buffet which occupied one side of the ante-room. In each hand he carried a glass of champagne.

'Here,' he said, presenting her with one, 'this is what you need. Me too, I promise you. We don't have a jolt like that every day, thank God! I suppose it's all right to drink some of their champagne before we go?'

'How d'you mean, Sieg? "Before we go"?'

'Well, she must have sent the invitation just to get a rise out of us. I can't think of any other motive—and now we'll have to slip quietly away. She's had her laugh.'

But at the threat of being ignominiously removed from this shining assemblage which was now more than ever the centre of the universe, she managed to collect her wits.

'Oh, no,' she said, 'no, I'm sure she didn't do it for that. No, really, you must be wrong there, Sieg!'

'Why, what else could she have done it for? An invitation of this kind without any why or wherefore! You haven't spoken to her for years!'

'The card came from the duke, Sieg, because we entertained him in Cairo.'

'The duke—rubbish! It came from her. Couldn't you see she was expecting us? She was as cool as a cucumber.'

Daisy had no alternative but confession, for she knew Siegfried's defensive pride and could be certain that he would not consent to remain where he suspected they were being insulted. Twisting her gauze scarf with hands that had forgotten their composure, she replied tremulously: 'The reason why we got an invitation was because I wrote to the duke and asked for one. Now you can't say she sent it to humiliate us. It would have been more humiliating if they'd refused.'

Siegfried made a grimace which indicated much in the way of distaste, contempt, and annoyance, but at any rate this new aspect of the case served for a diversion, and Chappie, who was as anxious as Daisy to be allowed to stay, added his deferential arguments.

'No, no, Mr. Mosenthal!' (For all his intimacy he had never yet ventured upon equality of address.) 'You got it wrong. She didn't mean no humiliation. If you ask me, she wanted to give you a nice surprise. She was as polite as she could be.'

'That's just what I think,' said Daisy earnestly. 'I'm sure she'd be absolutely hurt if we went off without a word of congratulation or anything. Why, we used to be the very best of friends.'

Siegfried gave her a look which, perhaps, achieved the absolute maximum of disdain expressible on the human countenance, but he did not insist on leaving, and with many *sotto voce* speculations as to the stroke of fortune which must have led to this most wonderful metamorphosis they finished their champagne and merged into the rest of the party. Chappie followed, throwing one longing look at the buffet: he had not ventured to mention that no champagne had been provided for him.

Daisy was remarkably volatile, and though she had been severely shaken, her qualms, her confusion, her trepidation, were already evaporating. With even more than her usual expertitude she was beginning to adjust herself to the evening's startling contingency and, out of all its bewilderment and strangeness, to place what she conceived to be first things first. Lucy had apparently by some miracle become a duchess, and she had once been Lucy's closest friend. She was sure that, once she got an opportunity of talking to her, they would be on the most amicable terms in no time. Indeed, she was unconscious of any reason—except perhaps the trifling matter of not having spoken to her at their last meeting—why they should not resume their old friendship immediately. The fine protective mechanism of her mind was working at the height of its ingenuity to soften or suppress every inexpedient memory, and so, far from regarding herself as one who had given Lucy grounds for animosity, she was more convinced than ever that, during those difficult first days in Egypt, she had been a comrade in a thousand. It was true there had been some little estrangement in the intervening years, but it was all readily explainable—a matter of circumstances pure and simple. Her feelings, her really deep feelings, had always been unchanged. Lucy would understand. Lucy was one of the sweetest-natured women in the world.

So, when the hostess began to wander among the company, Daisy's eyes eagerly followed her and she tried with little smiles and waves of the hand to attract her attention; but somehow, as it fell out, she invariably missed it. No sooner was Lucy about to move away from one guest, and certain, as Daisy thought, to see her and approach her, than some other would engage her, and yet another after that; or she would disappear into the adjoining room, and when Daisy, with one of her escorts, sauntered after her, the same process of frustration would start all over again. As for the duke, he was quite plainly inaccessible, for when he happened to come upon them, he merely inclined his head with distant courtesy or looked abstracted. Daisy comforted herself with the thought that he was very much occupied and probably did not quite remember them.

They were not, however, without many sources of enjoyment. The noble house, the vast and varied assortment of guests, the resplendent scale of the whole entertainment, these were engrossing in themselves; and as Mosenthal, whose sphere of influence in business was very wide, had met a number of the people present, they were often able to make interesting contacts. Daisy too had a nodding acquaintance with several exalted individuals, and extracted as much pleasure from it as nodding is ever likely to yield, while Chappie basked with almost physical gusto in reflected glories.

Still, it was tiresome that Lucy herself remained so unapproachable. The more she was thwarted, the more Daisy longed, not only to renew their old association and pave the way to some future *entente* between the duke's children and her own, but also, for immediate satisfaction, to display to all beholders her familiarity with the duchess. (She did not think of it in quite these terms; the wish was prettily veiled in affectionate sentiments, but here it scarcely requires so much clothing as Daisy herself found necessary for it.)

The hours were passing, the amusement to be got from watching and admiring was wearing thin, and unless Lucy were disentangled soon from all these invidious activities they would have to go without saying anything to her but goodbye: Siegfried had two board meetings in the morning, and he had said that no power on earth would induce him to stay later than half-past one. In the supper-room the duke, with Lucy on his arm, had visited a number of tables, but theirs had not been in the favoured orbit. Surely, surely she could not be bearing a grudge about that slight omission on board ship? Daisy had not seriously intended to cut her . . . it could all be straightened out in a moment.

She cast about for some means of catching that elusive eye, and decided to station herself somewhere near the head of the stairs, where, sooner or later, Lucy could not fail to see her at close quarters. Siegfried was talking to a co-director of one of his companies from whom he hoped to pick up a little information about the duke's second marriage, and she had deftly persuaded Chappie to go after him, thinking that it might well be his presence which discouraged Lucy's attentions. Alone, with the vague preoccupied air of one who casually keeps some rendezvous, she wandered out to the landing and took her post at the end of a long sofa placed between two doors. At the other end sat the attractive woman she recognized as Constance Leloir, and on the arm, talking enthusiastically to her, a girl of about twenty.

Daisy could not refrain from listening to a conversation shared by a celebrity, more especially as Lucy happened to be the subject of it. They were, it seemed, both singing Lucy's praises in a fervent litany:

'How well she looks! I never saw anyone who could wear jewels so beautifully. And her dress—it's ravishing, Constance. Did you design it?'

'Yes. I always think she should be faintly Edwardian. Her carriage is perfect for it.'

'How right! Much better than making her smart and up to date. Lucy's essentially a gracious person—gracious and grand but in an easy sort of way.'

'That's what's so lovely about her, the absolute unpretentiousness.' Mme Leloir appeared at this point to notice for the first time that their remarks were being overheard. She glanced round, gave Daisy a faint, blank smile, and went on without changing her inflexion: 'Most people's heads are very soon turned by getting a little power, but Lucy comes into a different category.'

'I know. She's never altered in the least since she was with us at Kew. I mean, in her behaviour towards us. Last time she came to lunch she insisted on working on the cross-references for one of my father's catalogues because his present secretary isn't very good at it.'

Daisy was suddenly inspired with a longing to take part in this dialogue. Half a dozen inducements presented themselves to her in quick succession and were rapidly resolved into one impulse. She leaned forward and said charmingly:

'Do forgive me for joining in. I can't help hearing what you're talking about and being interested. You see, I'm also a friend of Lucy's. At least I used to be.' She found that they had both fixed their eyes upon her with a somewhat glassy look, indicating she knew not what of doubt or antipathy, and being unable to retreat, she hurried on: 'I knew her when she was on the stage, years and years ago. We were on tour together and used to share digs and all that. We had some marvellous times.'

'Really?' Mme Leloir's peculiarly flat note conveyed to Daisy's ear an idea of disbelief and she rushed, unwarily, into greater explicitness: 'I was in Egypt with her. You know, of course, that she spent some years in Egypt?'

'A number of years.' The couturier and her young companion exchanged a singular stare, then both lowered their eyes to the carpet.

'She had a frightfully serious illness there, poor soul!' Daisy was beginning to grope, feeling more and more inexplicably uncomfortable. 'It was disastrous for her.'

'Yes, she was stranded.'

'Well, she would have been if my husband hadn't been able to help her.' She spoke with a full conviction of her own veracity, but still that mysterious discomfort gnawed, and Mme Leloir did not lift her gaze from the carpet.

Daisy knew for certain now that she was addressing a hostile audience, yet, though she was thrust into a defensive position, she was resolved to maintain her equanimity. 'Everything we did for her was done for the best. It wouldn't have been sensible for her to leave Egypt while things were as they were with her. We knew that it was wiser to give her a good position in Cairo.'

'And then take it away from her?'

Daisy became a little rattled. The sweetness of her tone was exaggerated to the pitch of distortion as she replied: 'I'm afraid it was a matter of efficiency. My husband's a business man pure and simple'—she offered the ghost of an apologetic titter—'and I've never been allowed to interfere in the running of his affairs, otherwise things might have been different. In any case, she refused to let him pay her fare home when he offered it; and at the time when he arranged that second job for her, she would have been unable to get work anywhere else at all.'

'Why?' a brusque masculine voice demanded. She looked up into the face of a very large and, as she thought, very overbearing man who had coolly joined their party and was standing beside the couch with his hand on the younger woman's shoulder. She had no notion of his connection with these people, nor of any right by which he considered himself entitled to share the discussion, but she heard herself answering meekly: 'She had no training—no qualifications.'

'Training! Qualifications!' He tossed the excuse upon an imaginary dust-heap. 'Why I never knew anyone with such a range of qualifications! I miss her to this day, and so does my daughter.'

He turned to another man, a portly and torpid-looking veteran, who advanced at this instant from the direction of the stairs. 'What do you say, Conway? Don't you regard Lucy Kendon—Constance's duchess—as the most all-round efficient woman you ever met in your life?'

Mr. Conway sighed pensively. 'She has an efficient kitchen,' he acknowledged. 'It takes a very efficient kitchen to put on a good supper at an affair like this, but on principle I can't approve of late suppers. However, I was persuaded to the dining-room . . .' He drifted into a speculative silence, then resumed abruptly: 'You were asking me about the duchess's cook. I can only say the table at Nunsbourne is very nearly worthy of the cellar. I'm glad they use your Mme Villard's recipe for *poulet cauchois*, Churchfield.'

Daisy apprehended that it was a suitable moment for an exit. Swiftly and mutely, but with an hauteur of deportment which she relied upon to mask the fact that she was quivering, she drew herself up and retreated through the nearest doorway.

Once again she was plunged into a pitiful confusion, but this time resentment was its chief ingredient. That wretched Leloir woman—insinuating that they had treated Lucy badly! Could anything be more unfair and more unkind? Well, she would never buy any clothes from *her*, not if she were twenty times as fashionable! And to think that she must have been misled by Lucy herself—that was what stung so bitterly! After all their friendship in the past! If only she could have talked to her and explained and put things right! But now she had begun to despair of that. Her false confidence had been shattered and she perceived that she was being designedly ignored. The whole evening—oh, that she had realized it earlier!—had been one long belittlement. That horrible busybody, Constance Leloir, had probably been told how she had asked for an invitation. Everybody in the house had been told. There was nothing to do, if she wished to retain a vestige of pride, but to go before worse slights befell her.

She searched miserably for Siegfried and came upon him at the buffet in the ante-room. He was drinking champagne on what were evidently convivial terms with an elderly man, whose rugged, heavily lined face had a very misty and remote familiarity. Judging from his bearing, he was a person of some importance, and she pulled herself heroically together to greet him with a courteous salutation.

'Good evening, Mrs. Mosenthal!' The pronounced urbanity of his bow was rather remarkable. It had something almost of bravado in it.

'I've met you before, haven't I?' she inquired, taking Siegfried's glass from his hand and sipping a little wine with elaborate gaiety.

'Yes, dear lady, quite a number of times.'

'Now let me see, where was it? Really, my memory must be going. I know you so well, and yet I can't just say where I last saw you.'

'No wonder. Seventeen years is a pretty good stretch, though no one would suspect it, dear lady, from your appearance. Much water has rolled under the bridges.'

'Seventeen years?' A nameless misgiving took possession of her. 'Then it was in Egypt.'

Siegfried, who had been watching with sardonic enjoyment, came to her rescue: 'This is Mr. Prince-Carter, my dear. Don't you remember him?'

Prince-Carter, in a spirit of mock gallantry heightened by his having been a long while at the buffet, raised his glass to signify that he drank to her.

She made a praiseworthy effort and managed to refrain from dashing it out of his hand, and even to apologize with something resembling ordinary social aplomb for not having discovered his identity sooner.

'Please,' he implored her unctuously, 'please, Miss Joy—forgive me!—I mean *"Mrs, Mosenthal"*—you were Miss Joy, you know, when I last saw you. . . . Please don't say a word about that! Why should you remember me? We meet after a long time on perfectly strange ground. Why should you?'

'I certainly didn't expect to see you here,' she retorted, stung by what she took for a reminder of her having been Siegfried's mistress.

'And I didn't expect to see you. The duchess is a very exceptional woman, giving house-room like this to people who knew her when she was—er—shall we say less fortunate than she is now? You'd think she'd be afraid of our tongues wagging, but not she! She can afford not to care what such small fry as you and I may remember.'

As if he guessed and relished her discomfiture, he waved his glass towards a vista of the ballroom where Lucy and her husband, smiling into each other's faces, whirled into sight, then vanished, in the throng of dancers.

'"Nights of Gladness"—that's what they're playing,' he said. 'Well, we had some nights of gladness at the Adelphi! My God, we had some funny times. To think I met her first when she came out in a show which was a dead flop. Let me see—you were in it too, weren't you? And then, that year when she worked as my assistant. . . .'

Daisy observed coldly that she must be going, and Mosenthal took her by the arm and steered her back to the drawing-room.

She pulled herself angrily away from him. 'What did you let me in for that for? I've never had such an awkward moment in my life! Why on earth didn't you prevent me from speaking to him? Why did you speak to him yourself? Have you forgotten what he did to me?'

'On the contrary, I've been remembering what you did to him. It was his wife who caused the trouble, and we made him pay for it. I wouldn't do as much for you today, my dear. A good man at his job too. He's a bit above himself tonight, I admit, but I wasn't sorry to hear he'd done well elsewhere.'

'If we meet that ghastly wife of his, I shall cut her dead, I warn you.'

'Never fear, my dear. She won't bother with you. She's after higher game. You've got to keep it in mind this is a duchess's house. She's too busy telling people how they used to hobnob together in Egypt to know or care whether you cut her dead, stone-dead, or half-dead. See for yourself! There she is behind those flowers. I'll bet you ten pounds she's talking about her old pal, the duchess. Come on, she won't notice you.'

Beside a tall *jardinière* in an attitude reminiscent of some antique goddess stood an old woman of majestic demeanour, addressing, or rather haranguing, a youth who gazed wildly round as if for a way of escape. Only half-reluctant, Daisy suffered herself to be drawn to the front of a lighted cabinet where, under cover of examining some china, they could plainly hear her reverberating voice:

'Say what you like, Lord Galleasse—say what you like, there's no better training for a woman who is to occupy a high station than to come in contact with the world, even if she has to do so under difficulties, and in my opinion the finest of all schools is the theatre. Where else can you learn to wear clothes, to carry yourself beautifully, to enunciate clearly and without self-consciousness, to mix with all sorts and conditions of people, to adapt yourself to any and every emergency? Tell me, Lord Galleasse, where else?'

'I don't know, I'm sure,' faltered the young man.

'I myself was an actress,' she proceeded with the air of offering a complete and irrefutable substantiation of her claims, 'and when I say an actress I mean, Lord Galleasse'—she paused ominously—'*an actress*. In those days, let me tell you, we spoke the King's English, we were taught the art of walking, sitting, standing, we were taught *manners*. Now, as for the duchess'—no one could doubt the satisfaction it gave her to pronounce that title—'she belongs to a later day, and I don't say that her theatrical training was equal to my own, but it was sound. Yes, it was very sound. I put her great success as a woman of fashion entirely down to her having been first and foremost'—she stopped dead and glared at him portentously as if she challenged contradiction—'first and foremost, Lord Galleasse, a woman of the theatre.'

The young man, still silently appealing for deliverance, muttered that he supposed they had been on the stage together.

'No,' she answered. 'There, Lord Galleasse, you are in error; you have been misled. I have seen her perform—a pleasing performance, though not, to be truthful, a brilliant one—but at the time when I knew her intimately she had left the stage. She was working for my husband. You were aware, perhaps, that he did important work in Egypt?'

'No, I—er—I don't think I caught his name,' he responded dismally.

'Arthur Prince-Carter.' It was impossible not to believe, from her mode of utterance, that the name was of less than first-rate notability. 'He was running theatres at the time in conjunction with a person called Mosenthal. The duchess, who was then Miss Kendon, was obliged to leave the stage through losing her voice, and on my recommendation other work was found for her, executive work. I realized she had executive talents.'

Mosenthal could not repress a chuckle and Daisy, who was incapable of bearing her numerous injuries any longer, turned on her heel and walked from the room with almost as sublime a dignity as Mrs. Prince-Carter could have displayed herself. 'I'm sick of this house,' she cried, coming out upon the now deserted landing, 'and I'm sick of everyone in it. It's all hateful. It's like a bad dream. I don't intend to stay another minute.'

FURROWED MIDDLEBROW

FM1. *A Footman for the Peacock* (1940) .... RACHEL FERGUSON
FM2. *Evenfield* (1942) .... RACHEL FERGUSON
FM3. *A Harp in Lowndes Square* (1936) .... RACHEL FERGUSON
FM4. *A Chelsea Concerto* (1959) .... FRANCES FAVIELL
FM5. *The Dancing Bear* (1954) .... FRANCES FAVIELL
FM6. *A House on the Rhine* (1955) .... FRANCES FAVIELL
FM7. *Thalia* (1957) .... FRANCES FAVIELL
FM8. *The Fledgeling* (1958) .... FRANCES FAVIELL
FM9. *Bewildering Cares* (1940) .... WINIFRED PECK
FM10. *Tom Tiddler's Ground* (1941) .... URSULA ORANGE
FM11. *Begin Again* (1936) .... URSULA ORANGE
FM12. *Company in the Evening* (1944) .... URSULA ORANGE
FM13. *The Late Mrs. Prioleau* (1946) .... MONICA TINDALL
FM14. *Bramton Wick* (1952) .... ELIZABETH FAIR
FM15. *Landscape in Sunlight* (1953) .... ELIZABETH FAIR
FM16. *The Native Heath* (1954) .... ELIZABETH FAIR
FM17. *Seaview House* (1955) .... ELIZABETH FAIR
FM18. *A Winter Away* (1957) .... ELIZABETH FAIR
FM19. *The Mingham Air* (1960) .... ELIZABETH FAIR
FM20. *The Lark* (1922) .... E. NESBIT
FM21. *Smouldering Fire* (1935) .... D.E. STEVENSON
FM22. *Spring Magic* (1942) .... D.E. STEVENSON
FM23. *Mrs. Tim Carries On* (1941) .... D.E. STEVENSON
FM24. *Mrs. Tim Gets a Job* (1947) .... D.E. STEVENSON
FM25. *Mrs. Tim Flies Home* (1952) .... D.E. STEVENSON
FM26. *Alice* (1949) .... ELIZABETH ELIOT
FM27. *Henry* (1950) .... ELIZABETH ELIOT
FM28. *Mrs. Martell* (1953) .... ELIZABETH ELIOT
FM29. *Cecil* (1962) .... ELIZABETH ELIOT
FM30. *Nothing to Report* (1940) .... CAROLA OMAN
FM31. *Somewhere in England* (1943) .... CAROLA OMAN
FM32. *Spam Tomorrow* (1956) .... VERILY ANDERSON
FM33. *Peace, Perfect Peace* (1947) .... JOSEPHINE KAMM

FM34. *Beneath the Visiting Moon* (1940) . . . . ROMILLY CAVAN
FM35. *Table Two* (1942) . . . . MARJORIE WILENSKI
FM36. *The House Opposite* (1943) . . . . BARBARA NOBLE
FM37. *Miss Carter and the Ifrit* (1945) . . . . SUSAN ALICE KERBY
FM38. *Wine of Honour* (1945) . . . . BARBARA BEAUCHAMP
FM39. *A Game of Snakes and Ladders* (1938, 1955) . . . . DORIS LANGLEY MOORE
FM40. *Not at Home* (1948) . . . . DORIS LANGLEY MOORE
FM41. *All Done by Kindness* (1951) . . . . DORIS LANGLEY MOORE
FM42. *My Caravaggio Style* (1959) . . . . DORIS LANGLEY MOORE
FM43. *Vittoria Cottage* (1949) . . . . D.E. STEVENSON
FM44. *Music in the Hills* (1950) . . . . D.E. STEVENSON
FM45. *Winter and Rough Weather* (1951) . . . . . . D.E. STEVENSON
FM46. *Fresh from the Country* (1960) . . . . MISS READ

Manufactured by Amazon.ca
Bolton, ON

31496949R00179